WHO IS TO BLAME?

WHO IS TO BLAME?

A Novel in Two Parts

By

ALEXANDER HERZEN

Translation,
Annotation, and
Introduction by
MICHAEL R. KATZ

CORNELL UNIVERSITY PRESS
ITHACA AND LONDON

The preparation of this translation was made possible by a
grant from the Translations Program of the National
Endowment for the Humanities, an independent federal agency.

First published 1984 by Cornell University Press.
Published in the United Kingdom by Cornell University Press Ltd., London.

International Standard Book Number 0-8014-1460-1
Library of Congress Catalog Card Number 84-7666

Printed in the United States of America

*Librarians: Library of Congress cataloging information
appears on the last page of the book.*

*The paper in this book is acid-free and meets the guidelines
for permanence and durability of the Committee on Production
Guidelines for Book Longevity of the Council on Library Resources.*

For my parents,
Alice and Louis Katz

Contents

Preface   9

Acknowledgments   11

Translator's Note   13

Introduction   15

  Intellectual Ferment   *15*
  Biographical Sketch   *18*
  Early Literary Endeavors   *21*
  Who Is to Blame?   *22*
  The Critical Reaction   *34*

List of Principal Characters   41

WHO IS TO BLAME?
A Novel in Two Parts

Author's Preface   45

Part I

CHAPTER 1
The Retired General and the Newly Appointed Tutor   49

CHAPTER 2
The Biography of Their Excellencies   57

CHAPTER 3
The Biography of Dmitry Yakovlevich   74

CHAPTER 4
Daily Humdrum   85

CHAPTER 5
Vladimir Beltov   123

CHAPTER 6   134

CHAPTER 7   160

Part II

CHAPTER 1   177

CHAPTER 2   190

CHAPTER 3   203

CHAPTER 4   221

CHAPTER 5   243

CHAPTER 6   269

Selected Bibliography   291

Preface

The impetus to translate Alexander Herzen's novel *Who Is to Blame?* was provided by the students in a course that I taught for several years at Williams College entitled "The Soul of Russia." There, as the class examined the dominant themes in nineteenth-century Russian literature and intellectual history, I found myself making frequent reference to this novel and to its extraordinary hero, Vladimir Beltov. On a number of occasions my students heard me lament the fact that *Who Is to Blame?* had never been translated into English; had it been, it would certainly have been included in the syllabus for the course. "Why don't *you* translate it?" they asked.

After several years of asking myself that same question, I decided to undertake the project. A grant from the Translations Program sponsored by the National Endowment for the Humanities supplied an additional stimulus.

Over the last few years, students, colleagues, and friends have graciously consented to read drafts of this translation. Their response has been extremely gratifying. Typically they express surprise at their discovery of a "new" nineteenth-century Russian novel; they remark on the book's wry humor and on its power as social satire. What seems to impress them most is the novel's universal themes—romantic love, social injustice, the development of a young man, the status of women, the nature of middle-age disillusionment, and the search for the meaning of life. Their comments have furthered my conviction that *Who Is to Blame?* occupies a unique place in Russian letters: it stands as a very witty and relatively brief commentary on Russian society, a delightful introduction to nineteenth-century Russian culture.

It is ironic that precisely during the years that I was working on what I assumed would be the first English version of the novel, two translations appeared—one published in the Soviet Union and the other in Canada. Although I regret any duplication of effort, I feel that my version represents a significant contribution. In particular, it is my hope that the critical apparatus that accompanies this new translation (introduction, annotations, and bibliography) will at last render Herzen's novel accessible to the general audience that it so richly deserves.

MICHAEL R. KATZ

Acknowledgments

To the Translations Program of the National Endowment
for the Humanities, to the Senior Scholar Exchange
sponsored by the International Research and Exchanges
Board, and to the Translation Center at Columbia
University

To my colleagues and former colleagues at Williams College:
Nicholas Fersen, Doris de Keyserlingk, William Wagner,
Donald Dragt, and Dorothea Hanson

To distinguished Slavists at other institutions: Sir Isaiah
Berlin, Nicholas Riasanovsky, Walter Arndt, Elena
Dryzhakova, and Alexis Klimoff

To my former students and research assistants: Sean Connolly,
Elizabeth Woods, Gregory Smith, Christopher Suits, Edward
Schmidt, Brendan Kiernan, and Jonathan Hay

To my friend Michael Mulrenin; to my wife, Mary Dodge; and to my
typist, Eileen Sahady

M. R. K.

Translator's Note

Herzen's novel was first published in 1845–46 in the journal
Notes of the Fatherland under the pseudonym Iskander. It was issued
as a separate book in 1847. A second edition was published in
London in 1859 which included the author's minor revisions. It is
this edition which is generally considered authoritative and was
included in Volume 4 of Herzen's *Sobranie sochinenii* (Collected
works), 30 vols., Moscow: Academy of Sciences, 1954–66, and in
Volume 1 of his *Sobranie sochinenii*, 8 vols., Moscow: Pravda, 1975.
It is this text which I have chosen to translate. The fate of the
original manuscript remains unknown. The system of translitera-
tion adopted is that used in the *Oxford Slavonic Papers*, with the
following exceptions:

hard signs and soft signs have been omitted in the text;
conventional spelling of names has been retained throughout;
two given names have been altered to facilitate pronunciation by
    non-Russian speakers (Aksyon and Semyon).

Introduction

Intellectual Ferment

During the decade that followed the abortive Decembrist Rebellion of 1825, Russia was a bleak and hostile place. Tsar Nicholas's official policy of repressive measures had resulted in complete political stagnation and produced, particularly among the educated gentry, a feeling of intense isolation and an atmosphere of mutual suspicion. Only a few serious journals were allowed to be published and circulated among a coterie of devoted readers. With most channels for expression virtually closed, the intellectual community was forced inward upon itself. Comradeship and companionship, sought in private encounters and intimate circles, created an environment conducive to intellectual ferment and political debate.

In the fall of 1836 the enforced official silence was abruptly shattered. In the September issue of the *Telescope*, there appeared a document entitled *First Philosophical Letter*, by Petr Chaadaev (ca. 1793–1856). Signed and dated "Necropolis, December 1, 1829," this letter contained a sweeping and passionate rejection of Russia. Chaadaev argued that his country's past was empty, its present intolerable, and that there was no hope whatever for its future. He attributed this national tragedy to Russia's geographical and historical position between East and West—thus, to its isolation from the cultural heritage of either world. As a result Russia had developed not one "single spiritual idea" that might have served as the basis for an independent national character. It was a country "untouched by the universal education of mankind"; its national tradition was "devoid of any powerful teaching"; its inhabitants were "like children who had never been made to think for themselves."[1]

Alexander Herzen (1812–70), who was to emerge as one of the most outstanding and outspoken members of the Russian intelligentsia, describes in his memoirs the public commotion occasioned by the virulence of Chaadaev's unexpected attack: "The *Letter* was in a sense the last word, the limit. It was a shot that rang out in the dark night; whether it was something foundering that proclaimed its own wreck, whether it was a signal, a cry for help, whether it was news of the dawn or news that there would not be one—it was all the same: one had to wake up."[2]

Chaadaev's accusations outraged and embarrassed the already suspicious and anxious autocracy. The author of the letter was proclaimed insane and placed under police surveillance and medical supervision. The publication of the *Telescope* was discontinued and its editor exiled to a remote village in northern Russia. Chaadaev was forbidden to publish any further philosophical letters or, for that matter, anything else.

Chaadaev's *First Letter*, which Herzen later described as "a merciless cry of pain and reproach against Petrine Russia," brought into clearer focus the intellectual unrest among the educated gentry. Herzen's memoirs, *My Past and Thoughts* (1854–66), in addition to providing a poignant portrait of the author's own intellectual development, present a detailed picture of Russian intellectual life during this period. Herzen describes in considerable detail the emergence of the circles (*kruzhki*), their ideologies and leading per-

1. Peter Yakovlevich Chaadayev, *"Philosophical Letters" and "Apology of a Madman,"* trans. M.-B. Zeldin (Knoxville, 1969), 31–51.
2. *My Past and Thoughts: The Memoirs of Alexander Herzen*, trans. Constance Garnett, translation revised by Humphrey Higgins, abridged by Dwight MacDonald (New York, 1973), 292–93.

sonalities during the 1830s, and he sheds considerable light on his own evolution as a serious thinker, a persuasive writer, and an ardent advocate of change.

These circles, which predated the Decembrist Rebellion as centers of liberal opposition to the autocratic regime, consisted of diverse groups of intellectuals united by a profound feeling of alienation from official Russia and by an overwhelming desire to alter the status quo. At the center of each group there usually stood some strong, charismatic figure. One of the most outstanding was Nikolai Stankevich (1813–40), subsequently characterized by Herzen as "a poet and a dreamer." He was actually a philosopher, a disciple and proponent of German idealism, especially that of Schelling and Hegel, and he served to popularize their ideas among young, enthusiastic Russian intellectuals. Stankevich wrote little, yet managed to breathe life into a set of ideas that inspired a generation of writers, critics, and revolutionaries. He argued that history should be seen as the development of humanity as a whole and that each nation was capable of expressing some single aspect of the life of mankind. He predicted that Russia was also destined to achieve greatness in philosophy, art, and literature.[3] In the wake of Chaadaev's gloom and despondency, Stankevich's optimistic fervor aroused, inspired, and kindled many youthful romantic dreams and ideals.

According to Herzen's testimony, the "most active, impulsive, and dialectically passionate, fighting nature" belonged to yet another major figure—the young critic Vissarion Belinsky (1811–48). Belinsky, who had considerable contact with the members of Stankevich's circle, served as translator and critic of the *Telescope* until that journal was suppressed. His political views and aesthetic criteria changed rapidly, but during the late thirties and early forties his literary criticism was firmly based on two assumptions. First, he demanded that literature should express *ideas*—that is, it should emphasize moral, social, and political values and should advocate positive ideals and progressive tendencies. Second, he

3. See Edward J. Brown, *Stankevich and His Moscow Circle, 1830–1840* (Stanford, 1966), 4–17.

argued that literature should be *natural* in its expression—it should aim to be faithful to life, "realistic."

It was on this basis that Russia's leading critic heralded the appearance of a major new talent. In 1846, from the pages of the *Contemporary*, Belinsky hailed *Who Is to Blame?* as a work of great social importance, in spite of what he perceived as its artistic shortcomings. And, in a personal letter dated April 6, 1846, Belinsky warmly welcomed its young author into the ranks of Russian men of letters: "I am completely convinced that you are a major figure in our literature, not a dilettante, not a partisan, not an amateur equestrian who has nothing better to do."[4] Clearly Belinsky viewed Herzen's novel as the embodiment of his own critical principles. *Who Is to Blame?* was first and foremost a novel of ideas, and, as a work of literature, it was completely natural in its expression.

Biographical Sketch

Alexander Herzen was born on April 6, 1812, the illegitimate son of Ivan Yakovlev, a wealthy nobleman from an ancient Russian family, and Luiza Haag, the daughter of a minor German official.[5] Herzen's mother remained a Lutheran all her life, never marrying his father according to the rites of the Orthodox church and hence never accorded the legal or social status of a wife. The child was given the invented surname Herzen [from *Herz*, "heart"] as if to stress the fact that he was the product of an unusual liaison, an affair of the heart.

His upbringing took place in a large and gloomy house on the Arbat in the center of Moscow. The boy's father loved him after a fashion, but the father's presence was always somewhat frightening and oppressive. The lad sought refuge in his mother's rooms and in the servants' quarters: Luiza was a model of uncomplaining acceptance and stoic resignation, while the servants were appropriately

4. Vissarion Belinsky, *Polnoe sobranie sochinenii* (Moscow, 1953–59), XII, 270–71.
5. This brief account of Herzen's life is summarized from Isaiah Berlin's introduction to Herzen's *My Past and Thoughts*, xix–xliii.

obsequious in the performance of their duties. Herzen's concern for the freedom and dignity of the individual may well have had its origins in the inequitable conditions that surrounded him during his childhood.

He received the normal education for a wealthy young Russian nobleman of his day. Since he was a lively and imaginative child, much care was taken to develop his intellectual gifts. Attention was lavished on him by nurses, serfs, and private tutors. He was taught Russian literature and history by a young university student who was an enthusiastic follower of the Romantic movement, especially in its German manifestation. He learned French, German, and some European history from a tutor who had escaped the aftermath of the French Revolution and who held deep convictions regarding the liberty and equality of men. The young pupil read voraciously in his father's sizable library, taking a special interest in French books of the Enlightenment.

When Herzen was only fourteen, the leaders of the Decembrist Rebellion were hanged by Nicholas I as the initial act of the reactionary policy that was to follow. Herzen was subsequently to recall the solemn "Hannibalic" oath to avenge these martyrs that he and his young friend Nikolai Ogarev (1813–77) swore as they stood on the Sparrow Hills overlooking Moscow. The memory of these aristocratic conspirators became a source of inspiration for Herzen's later revolutionary activity.

In 1829 he enrolled as a student at Moscow University, where he encountered the works of Schiller and Goethe, and later those of the French utopian socialists, including Saint-Simon and Fourier. It was during his university days that Herzen became a confirmed and passionate radical. He and Ogarev organized a circle parallel to that of Stankevich but more oriented toward French thought (politics and progress) than German metaphysics. Forbidden books were read; "dangerous ideas" were discussed. Herzen was duly arrested and condemned to imprisonment. Perhaps as a result of his father's intervention, his sentence was commuted to internal exile. In 1834 Herzen left for the town of Vyatka at the eastern edge of European Russia, where he went to work for the local administration. There, somewhat unexpectedly, he enjoyed his tasks and succeeded in exposing the corruption of the local governor. He read Dante and went through a short-lived religious phase. He also became involved with two women: he had an affair with one, a married woman, P. P. Medvedeva, after which he suffered agonies of contrition, and he began a long and passionate correspondence with the other, his first cousin Natalya Aleksandrovna Zakharina (1817–52), who, like himself, was also illegitimate, and had lived as a companion in the house of a rich, despotic relative.

In 1838 Herzen was transferred to Vladimir, not far from Moscow. There, with his friends' help, but against the wishes of both their families, he arranged to elope with Natalya Aleksandrovna. In 1840 he was allowed to return to Moscow with his wife, and soon after he was appointed to a government post in Petersburg. He remained deeply committed to the cause of radical reform and was sent into exile again, this time to Novgorod, for writing an indiscreet letter that criticized the police. By 1842, the year in which he returned from exile to Moscow, Herzen was regarded as an established member of the new radical intelligentsia and as an early martyr to its cause. He began to study German metaphysics, as well as French sociological theory and history; he published historical and philosophical essays in various progressive journals; and he composed a number of short stories on social and political themes that were widely read and discussed.

In 1847 Herzen's father died and left a substantial fortune to his widow and his son. Herzen decided to leave for Europe. Accompanied by his wife, his mother, two friends, and some servants, Herzen departed from his homeland, traveled across Germany, and finally arrived in Paris, the center of the civilized world. There he plunged into the life of exiled radicals and socialists. By the time of the revolutions of 1848, Herzen stood on the extreme left wing of revolutionary European socialism. Although ordered to return to Russia, he flatly refused. His fortune was confiscated, but with expert legal assistance he was able to recover most of it, thus ensuring his financial independence. Whether or not he intended that outcome, Herzen's departure from Russia was to be permanent.

Early Literary Endeavors

Herzen's earliest forays into literature were made during the summer of 1833.[6] In a conscious attempt to imitate the German Romantics (especially Schiller, Jean Paul, and Hoffmann), he wrote "A Tale about Myself" in an autobiographical mode, combining a romantic style with elevated literary language. Another surviving fragment that dates from 1836, "A Legend," consists of a lyrical-philosophical meditation incorporating some of Saint-Simon's ideas on "New Christianity"—that is, "practical" Christian humanism—in a somewhat obscure allegorical form. Nevertheless, this early piece reveals something of what the genuine writer would become both in its directness of expression and in its depth of feeling.

Following his stay in Vyatka (which included both his affair with Medvedeva and his romance with Natalya), Herzen began work on yet another autobiographical tale, entitled "There" (later renamed "Elena"). This piece is a remarkable literary hybrid: while the beginning is controlled, realistic, ironic, even Gogolian, the conclusion is melodramatic, sentimental, and exalted.

In 1840 Herzen tried his hand at autobiography again, this time employing a more documentary approach. He wrote *Notes of a Young Man*, an autobiography in prose, based on his own letters to Natalya Aleksandrovna. The structure of this work is clearly episodic, the style often witty, the tone detached. In the continuation, *Further Notes of a Young Man* (1841), Herzen's satire took an even sharper turn.

His works of the early 1840s bear witness to the author's gradual evolution away from Russian romanticism and toward the so-called natural school. In all of his writings dating from the middle of this decade, Herzen adopted a new, more realistic world view, searching for objective forms of expression for his own experience and that of his contemporaries. He put aside his lyrical, auto-

6. For further details, see Monica Partridge, "Herzen's Changing Concept of Reality and Its Reflection in His Literary Works," *Slavonic and East European Review*, 46 (1968), 397–421.

biographical hero and instead created a new prose genre that embraced social commentary, psychological analysis, philosophical inquiry, and publicistic oratory, all unified by the author's intelligent consciousness. It is in these years immediately preceding his departure from Russia that Herzen produced his most important contribution to Russian fiction, the novel *Who Is to Blame?* (published 1845–46) and two tales, "Dr. Krupov" (1847) and "The Thieving Magpie" (1848).

In "The Thieving Magpie," Herzen treats the same theme twice, first discursively, then allegorically. The tale consists of a dialogue between a Slavophile and a Westernizer on the subject of why Russia fails to produce women who are outstanding in the arts; this intellectual debate is then followed by a pathetic tale of the brilliant serf-actress Aneta. In "Dr. Krupov," Herzen combines both autobiography and the case study method to develop the theme of a sick society by juxtaposing a variety of human types and revealing his own differing attitudes toward them.

When Belinsky responded to the publication of *Who Is to Blame?* with the announcement that a new, "major figure" had appeared in Russian literature, he had no inkling that Herzen's first novel would also be his last. Ths author was to find his mature voice in essays, articles, letters, and in his monumental memoirs, which have aptly been called "a literary masterpiece worthy to be placed by the side of the novels of his contemporaries and countrymen, Tolstoy, Turgenev, Dostoevsky."[7]

Who Is to Blame?

In addition to the sweeping indictment of Russia, Chaadaev's *First Letter* also succeeded in conveying the predicament of the individual Russian intellectual who is at a loss to find any useful employment for his talents: "It is a trait of human nature that a man gets lost when he can find no means to bind himself to what has come before him and what will follow after him. Then all consistency, all certainty escapes him. Lacking the guiding sense of

---

7. Berlin, "Introduction," xx.

continuous duration, he finds himself lost in the world."[8] Although Chaadaev acknowledged that there were "lost souls" in every country, he sadly asserted that in Russia the condition had become "a general characteristic." It was just such a "lost soul" that Herzen attempted to depict in *Who Is to Blame?*

In a letter to Natalya Aleksandrovna dated April 1, 1836, the author recorded an idea for a new hero: "a man endowed with a noble soul" but who possesses a "weak character."[9] Several years later, after having begun serious work on the tale, Herzen noted in his diary, "I am pleased with my article on dilettantism—very pleased. But not with my tale. The [genre of the] tale is not my métier; I know this [for a fact] and should renounce tales [in general]."[10] In spite of this and similar disclaimers, chapters 1 through 4 of part I of a new "tale," appeared in A. A. Kraevsky's journal *Notes of the Fatherland* in 1845, under the signature "I." (i.e., Iskander [Alexander]. Herzen's original working title, "The Adventures of a Teacher," had been replaced by the question *Who Is to Blame?* The epigraph chosen to introduce the novel had mysteriously been omitted.

The author was extremely eager to gauge the reactions of his readers and critics. It was their enthusiasm, in particular Belinsky's favorable response, that encouraged him to continue working on the novel. In April 1846, chapters 5 through 7 of part I were published in the same journal under the title "Vladimir Beltov." The appearance of this second installment brought Herzen considerable recognition and earned Belinsky's generous pronouncement. The critic urged the young author to write more. Herzen briefly interrupted work on the novel to complete the two stories mentioned above; then he resumed work on *Who Is to Blame?* and finished part II in the autumn of 1846.

After lengthy negotiations, Belinsky managed to persuade Herzen to break with Kraevsky and to publish parts I and II of the novel together as a supplement to Belinsky's own journal the *Contemporary.* Thus in 1847 the complete text of *Who Is to Blame?*

8. Chaadayev, *Philosophical Letters*, 39.
9. G. N. Gai, *Roman i povest' A. I. Gertsena 30–40-kh godov* (Kiev, 1959), 48.
10. Ibid.

appeared; it included a dedication to Natalya Aleksandrovna, and the epigraph was restored to its rightful place.

Herzen's depiction of the hero, Vladimir Beltov, as a "lost soul" was influenced by previous efforts of Russian writers to explore those "traits of human nature" that in Chaadaev's words, had become a "general characteristic" in Russian culture.[11] Chatsky, the hero of Aleksandr Griboedov's comedy *Woe from Wit* (1822–24), who bids an angry farewell to his former beloved Sofya and to the world that produced her, stands as the progenitor of a long line of heroes from which Beltov was descended.

Herzen paid tribute to another of the sources of his own inspiration in one of a series of articles entitled "On the Development of Revolutionary Ideas in Russia" (1850): "The image of [Pushkin's] Onegin is such a national one that it is encountered in every novel and poem that receives recognition in Russia, not because [everyone] wants to imitate it, but because we constantly find it alongside us or inside us."[12] In addition, Pushkin's novel in verse, *Eugene Onegin* (1823–31), raised the fundamental issue of culpability: is it the individual or his environment that is to be held responsible for the hero's tragedy?

Herzen's debt to Gogol is evident in the colorful "biographies" that he provides throughout *Who Is to Blame?* (particularly in part I), which are influenced by the satirical portraits of landowners and bureaucrats in Gogol's comedy *The Government Inspector* (1836) and his novel *Dead Souls* (1842). Lermontov's novel, *Hero of Our Time* (1840), presented Herzen with a model of an integrated cycle of tales depicting a central character who lives out his life under the rule of very powerful passions. Finally, in an article on the works of Turgenev written subsequently and entitled "Bazarov, Once Again" (1868), Herzen locates his own protagonist in a distinguished genealogy of Russian heroes:

11. See Ellen Chances, *Conformity's Children: An Approach to the Superfluous Man in Russian Literature* (Columbus, Ohio, 1978), 53–56, for a discussion of Western influences on Herzen's fiction (esp. Hoffmann, Saint-Simon and Fourier, Balzac and Eugène Sue).

12. D. D. Blagoi, "Znachenie Gertsena v razvitii russkoi literatury," in *Problemy izucheniya Gertsena*, ed. Yu. G. Oksman (Moscow, 1963), 328.

The Onegins and the Pechorins begot the Rudins and the Beltovs; the Rudins and the Beltovs—Bazarov. The Onegins and Pechorins are past; the Rudins and Beltovs are passing; the Bazarovs will pass—even very soon.[13]

Part I of *Who Is to Blame?* contains a series of "biographies" of primary and secondary characters. Just before "digressing" on the life-history of a minor figure, the elder Beltov's eccentric uncle, the author defends his unusual artistic method:

> There is nothing on earth more individual and more diversified than the biographies of ordinary people, especially where no two people ever share the same idea, where each person develops in his own way without either looking back or worrying about where it will lead. . . . For this reason I never avoid biographical digressions. They reveal the full splendor of the universe. The reader who so wishes may skip over these episodes, but in so doing he will miss the essence of the story.

Indeed, it is through these "biographical digressions" that the author conveys the essence of his story. More than any of its predecessors in nineteenth-century Russian fiction, *Who Is to Blame?* is a novel of ideas and issues that are given artistic form through the medium of vivid and elaborate characterizations. An examination of the most important portraits that Herzen draws in the novel will therefore illustrate his principal themes and reveal his underlying intentions.

The novel begins with a portrait of a patriarchal landowner, Aleksei Abramovich Negrov, and his corpulent wife Glafira Lvovna. A retired major general, Negrov lives in the country, where he follows one golden rule: he never allows mental exertion to upset his digestion. Negrov is Herzen's principal representative of the rural aristocracy, dragging out its "overstuffed life" in an empty, boring, and useless manner. He is a vulgar and tyrannical patriarch both in his family circle and on his estate; however, Negrov is never con-

13. A. G. Rozin, *Gertsen i russkaya literatura* (Krasnodar, 1976), 163. Pechorin is the protagonist of Lermontov's *Hero of Our Time* (1840), Rudin, of Turgenev's novel of the same name (1856), and Bazarov, of Turgenev's *Fathers and Sons* (1862).

demned as an evil man. Herzen goes to great lengths to remind his readers that "life had destroyed more than one potentiality in him"; that he possessed "genuine abilities, first suppressed, then destroyed by life"; that since he had never become "accustomed to any activity," he could not possibly "imagine what to do." In fact, Negrov suffers from a strain of the very same nineteenth-century disease that afflicts Beltov, the hero of this novel—namely, "spleen" (*khandra*). Since there was no occupation for which Negrov was suited or even inclined, he did nothing at all. He lived out an endless succession of days with no activity, no purpose, no aspiration. Moreover, Herzen insists that Negrov was a "typical" representative of his class: his neighbors are described as "Negrov with a different last name"; a portrait of the household of Karp Kondratich, another local aristocrat, is included as an example of a family that, in all respects is much worse than the Negrovs.

Herzen's satiric gift is seen at its best in his detailed descriptions of the Negrov's entourage and their way of life. The master's inhuman treatment of his serfs (including, of course, his debauched affair with the lovely Avdotya Barbash); his self-assurance and vulgar "wit"; his obsession with food, drink, and carriages; his enjoyment of the pitiful "sponger" Eliza Avgustovna's scandalous accounts of aristocratic life—all serve to emphasize Negrov's complete lack of spiritual and intellectual depth.

His corpulent and soporific spouse, Glafira Lvovna, is an ideal mate for the general. She is the offspring of a debauched nobleman and a merchant's daughter. She was reared by an egotistical old maiden aunt, and her cheerless childhood and monotonous youth resulted in no development whatever of her character. She married Negrov to escape from her oppression, "adopted" his illegitimate daughter Lyubonka in a surge of romantic ecstasy, and then treated the child cruelly and callously, with no understanding whatever of her sensitive soul. In a splendid scene that culminates in pure bathos, Glafira falls in love with her son's innocent young tutor Dmitry and assumes the role of "conqueror and seducer," while the tutor plays the part of unsuspecting, chaste maiden. But just as Herzen points to Negrov's suppressed potential and destroyed abilities, so too he "explains" Glafira Lvovna's existence by the detailed account of her upbringing and steadfastly refuses to pass final judgment on her decision to adopt and rear Negrov's daughter.

While the Negrov family enables the author to present his views on the rural aristocracy, Lyubov Aleksandrovna (Lyubonka) is Herzen's contribution to the so-called woman question. The illegitimate child of a landowner father (Negrov) and a serf mother, she suffers the torments of her awkward predicament. She retreats into silence and broods over the incongruity of her ambiguous position in the Negrov household. The oppressiveness of her surroundings, the harsh treatment that she receives, her virtual isolation from meaningful human contact—all result in an extraordinary and seemingly inexplicable development of her soul and her spirit. Significantly, it is not the heroine's reading that provokes or promotes her growth; she does read, but with no great passion; she finds *even* Sir Walter Scott's romanticism boring at times! Instead, Lyubonka takes refuge in her thoughts and dreams: "she dreamed in order to relieve her spirit and thought in order to understand her dreams." Through her diary entries, recorded in both parts I and II, Herzen permits his readers to observe the intimate development of Lyubonka's character. In part I we come to appreciate her total alienation from the Negrovs, her insightful critique of their way of life, her genuine love of nature, and her empathy with the oppressed peasants. And Herzen gives a poignant account of her growing affection for the young tutor Dmitry, their mutual confessions of love, and their subsequent departure from the Negrovs' household in order to establish their own family based on mutual respect and deep devotion. In part II Herzen describes Lyubonka's married life and continues the account of her intellectual and spiritual development. With the introduction of Beltov into their happy family circle, the heroine moves beyond her kind, sweet, but limited spouse. The author reveals her strength and vigor, her wideranging intellect, her simple, natural manner, her profound understanding of the hero's plight, and her deep sympathy for him. Once again through the medium of her diary, Herzen documents Lyubonka's personal growth: the new questions that she raises and the problems that she faces, her involvement with abstract ideas and the world outside her family, her reflections on the themes of freedom and fate, and ultimately the startling recognition that she loves two men, both her husband and Beltov, but in different ways.

Lyubonka is a powerful portrait of the "new woman"—descended in part from Pushkin's Tatyana and the heroines of George Sand[14] and in part from the author's own experience and that of his beloved wife Natalya Aleksandrovna. Lyubonka is presented as an intelligent, compassionate, independent person who discovers the contradictions inherent in her position in mid-nineteenth-century Russian society. The institutions of marriage and family are called into question, the themes of upbringing and education are examined and criticized; the "trade-off" between happiness and development is presented and explored. Lyubonka emerges as a noble character, morally superior even to the hero; she aspires to knowledge and activity; she sympathizes with the victims of the system from the oppressed peasants to the repressed hero; and she is ultimately destroyed by the results of her own development. At the end of the novel Lyubonka has lost both of her loves and is sinking rapidly into a state of physical and spiritual decline. The "new woman" has emerged, but she is as yet incapable of overcoming the enormous obstacles in her path.

The young tutor with whom Lyubonka first falls in love, Dmitry Krutsifersky, is Herzen's primary representative of the new breed of intellectual called *raznochintsy*, "men of various origins and classes," those who did not belong to the nobility or to the gentry.[15] This group was to come of age during the decade of the 1860s and would engage the literary talents of Turgenev, Chernyshevsky, and Dostoevsky, among others. But in the person of Krutsifersky Herzen provides Russian literature with an early and compassionate portrait of a "commoner," emphasizing his humble origins, his modest aspirations, and his limited spiritual horizons.

The young man is introduced into the novel as a gentle, bashful soul, eager to learn, hopelessly romantic, and naively idealistic—lacking any experience whatever in the real world. The son of a

14. See Richard Stites, *The Women's Liberation Movement in Russia: Feminism, Nihilism, and Bolshevism, 1860–1930* (Princeton, 1977), 20–22.

15. See Marshall Berman, *All That Is Solid Melts into Air: The Experience of Modernity* (New York, 1982), 212–15.

district physician and a German pharmacist's daughter, his early life consisted of a humiliating struggle against poverty. He was born prematurely, grew into a weak and nervous lad, and was rescued from a conventional future only by the intervention of "fate" in the form of a philanthropic privy counsellor from Moscow who "adopted" him as a ward. Thus was Dmitry able to leave the local gymnasium and receive a decent education at Moscow University, where his love of knowledge and persistent application, rather that any unusual ability, resulted in the awarding of his degree. Fate intervened in his life once again, this time in the form of Dr. Krupov, and Dmitry gratefully accepted a tutoring post in the Negrovs' household secured for him by the doctor. There he promptly fell in love with Lyubonka, united with her at once by the common bond of their aversion to the general's tyranny; by the end of part I, Dmitry offers to marry Lyubonka and to accept a position in the civil service.

At the beginning of part II, Dmitry is shown at the peak of happiness. He and his wife have created a family founded on mutual love and are pursuing a modest life-style based on common sense. Krutsifersky's pure, gentle, loving soul is at peace with the world. As an unforseen consequence of his happy marriage and satisfying career, however, his intellect stagnates; he resides happily in a world of romantic dreams and melancholic ecstasy.

When Beltov enters the Krutsiferskys' household and gradually wins Lyubonka's heart and mind, Dmitry is almost totally destroyed. Characteristically, he admits to having come "almost to love Beltov himself"; his tragic recognition and poignant reaction to the bitter truth are portrayed pathetically, as are his rapid decline into vulgar drunkenness and his desperate attempts at prayer. His simple nature cannot accommodate such extraordinary events; he is ultimately overcome by grief.

The person who first introduces Beltov into the Krutsiferskys' household and who presides over the tragic denouement is the curious figure of Dr. Krupov. He stands outside the class structure of the novel and intervenes in the action to utter prophesies, make predictions, move the plot along, and then cope with the consequences. He appears initially as a cheerful, healthy man of epicurean composure and good nature. As he comments on the action and the characters' motivations, he represents the voice of reason, common sense, and medical science. But we soon learn that as a result of his own bitter experience—primarily his long years as a physician—he has become thoroughly disillusioned with life and love and has retreated into cynicism, unabashed egoism, and complacent materialism.

At the beginning of part II, Dr. Krupov has been incorporated into the Krutsiferskys' happy family circle. He who had warned Dmitry against marrying the "young tigress" Lyubonka now acknowledges his error, modifies his cynical views, and becomes an integral part of their household. All the more ironic, then, that it is Krupov who introduces them to Beltov. By the end of part II, it falls to him to summarize the unhappy consequences of their new friendship with Beltov. Krupov admits that, like Dmitry, he too has come to "love Beltov," even though Beltov has destroyed the Krutsifersky family and made four people miserably unhappy. Reluctantly he banishes the hero, while he himself retreats into gloomy cynicism.

The protagonist, Vladimir Beltov, is Herzen's brilliant portrait of the "lost soul" about whom Chaadaev had written in his *First Letter*. There Chaadaev had defined the essence of that character: "the flightiness of a life totally lacking in experience and foresight . . . which results simply from the ephemeral existence of an individual detached from the species. Such a life holds dear neither the honor nor the progress of any community of ideas or interests, not even a traditional family outlook or that mass of prescriptions and perspectives which compose . . . both public and private life."[16] A wealthy landowner and intellectual of noble birth, Beltov is introduced into the novel late and indirectly—through rumors, gossip, and paradoxes. Even his appearance presents contrasts that tend to heighten the mystery: he is good-natured, but supercilious; a gentleman, but a rake; melancholy, but passionate. Beltov is a figure who arouses both intellectual curiosity and emotional anxiety.

16. Chaadayev, *Philosophical Letters*, 39.

Herzen describes and analyzes the hero's origins, upbringing, and education at great length, obviously in order to explain the formation of his character and world view. His father was a dissolute nobleman, a gambler, and a drunkard, an inveterate womanizer who shamelessly flirted with one of his aunt's serfs (Sofya). An educated girl, Sofya succeeds in buying her freedom in order to escape to Petersburg, where she suffers from economic hardship and psychological humiliation. Finally she writes a scathing letter to the elder Beltov that causes him to repent his sins and to marry her; during their brief married life together she succeeds in discovering the "nobility of his true nature" under the "dross of his surroundings." Beltov dies shortly after his son's birth, but Sofya never fully recovers from the series of traumas that she has endured. She becomes pensive and withdrawn, concentrating her morbid sensibilities on the upbringing of her son. Thus, from an early age, the young Vladimir is separated from his peers, isolated from reality, and reared by an overprotective, *exaltée* mother whose entire existence revolves around her offspring.

In addition to having such an extraordinary mother, Vladimir was educated by an equally extraordinary Swiss tutor named Monsieur Joseph, a forty-year-old "youth," well educated in the works of Rousseau and Romanticism, an "inveterate dreamer," a "child," and a "madman." The environment that he structures for his pupil is compared to a "hothouse;" the education that he provides introduces Vladimir to abstract ideas, noble ideals, and beautiful dreams but seems to be designed to keep him from understanding reality in general, and Russian reality in particular. The author writes with unusually deep conviction: "Education must be climatological: for every age, as for every country, even more so for every class, and perhaps even for every family, there exists a particular kind of education." It was precisely this that Monsieur Joseph never learned and consequently was never able to convey to the young Beltov.

After such an inappropriate early education, his development continues at Moscow University, where, in a close and intimate circle, Beltov discovers the warmth of friendship, his own relative merit, and the value of learning. He graduates full of grand plans and noble goals and then moves to Petersburg, where he enters the civil service and makes his debut in high society. But neither is able to satisfy him: in possession of too great an intelligence, he finds life in the bureaucracy devoid of interest and soon retires. Thus begins a prolonged period of disillusionment. Beltov spends the next ten years "doing everything" but "accomplishing nothing." He tries his hand at medicine, painting, romance, and travel—but the result is always the same: boredom. Beltov, like Negrov, suffers from "spleen." At the end of part I he returns to Russia in order to take part in the local elections in the provincial town of N., hoping to find there some suitable employment for his talents.

However, the events that occasion his greatest crisis are his failure to gain elected office, the news of the death of his beloved Monsieur Joseph, and his acquaintance with the Krutsifersky family. Beltov comes to recognize that he is a useless creature, one who has surrendered to external circumstances; consequently he is without hope, searching for diversion. It is at this moment of spiritual nadir that he wins Lyubonka's love and discovers her strength, intelligence, and sympathy. When Dr. Krupov arrives at Beltov's hotel to upbraid him for destroying so much happiness and to banish him, he discovers that the hero has already composed a farewell letter to his love; however, as in so many previous instances, Beltov had been incapable of carrying through his intentions. The doctor acts as a catalyst yet again; after a poignant final meeting with Lyubonka, Beltov leaves the town of N. to continue his aimless travels—"a wanderer in Europe, a stranger abroad and at home."

Beltov's predicament has been succinctly summarized by Isaiah Berlin in one of his many essays on the life and works of Alexander Herzen: "[The hero is] too idealistic and too honest to accept the squalor and the lies of conventional society, too weak and too civilized to work effectively for their destruction, and consequently displaced from his proper function and doomed to poison his own life and the lives of others."[17] Who (or what) is to blame for Beltov's predicament? Once again, Isaiah Berlin: "Everything is partly the

17. Introduction to Herzen, *From the Other Shore* (London, 1966), ix.

fault of the individual character, partly the fault of circumstance, partly in the nature of life itself."[18] Herzen seems to be affirming the complexity and insolubility of life's fundamental problems and consequently can offer no definitive answer to the question raised by the title of his novel.

Clearly in one sense Beltov's tragedy is indeed a deeply personal one and derives from his "individual character," his own human nature. And in another sense, Beltov's tragedy is a social one, inasmuch as he is the product of his circumstances: his family background and upbringing (especially the influence of his mother Sofya); his early education (especially the teaching of Monsieur Joseph); his later education (Moscow University); his class (landed gentry) and its way of life; and his society, with its fundamental institutions (autocracy, bureaucracy, marriage, "illegitimacy," and serfdom, to name but a few). But in the final sense, Beltov's tragedy is an existential one, which results from the "nature of life" itself—the will of fate, chance, accident. Herzen's question remains unanswered because the author has no answer, at least no simple one. Russian writers and critics would subsequently discover their own answers to Herzen's question; they would even go so far as to pose another, more practical question, one demanding immediate action: what is to be done? Herzen's novel, however, suggests that in spite of its author's own convictions and predilections, in spite of his passionate wish to assign blame and to discover a solution, no solution exists.

The artistic complexity of Herzen's novel has not always been fully appreciated.[19] In addition to the breadth of his characters and the depth of his ideas, he employs a rich assortment of literary techniques with great success: the "biographical" method that gives the novel its structural unity; the omnipresence of the author's voice—introducing, describing, and evaluating his characters—digressing, interrupting, commenting, and apostrophizing to his readers; the striking contrast between the author's empathetic and compassionate attitude toward the victims of the tragedy and his

18. "Alexander Herzen," in Isaiah Berlin, *Russian Thinkers* (New York, 1978), 202.

19. See Gai, *Roman i povest'*, 101–21, for a detailed analysis of Herzen's style.

ironic and satiric treatment of the victimizers; his intelligence—
sharp powers of observation, penetrating insights, and impressive
erudition, evident particularly in the wealth of literary and historical allusions contained in the text; his stylistic range—including
the broad comedy of the scenes describing the Negrovs' family life,
the confessional sincerity of Lyubonka's diaries, the naturalism of
the "physiological sketch" describing Sofya's life in Petersburg,
and the abstract philosophical discourse on Beltov's upbringing and
eduction.

After Herzen's emigration and his involvement with the revolutionary movements in Europe, when his name was banned from the
Russian periodical press, writers and critics were forced to resort to
periphrasis to refer to him. The one most frequently encountered is
"the author of *Who Is to Blame?*." This serves as a clear indication
that the novel was so popular that the author's name had become
synonymous with the title, and as a testimony to the work's importance in the history of Russian literature and thought.[20]

The Critical Reaction

When Belinsky wrote to Herzen shortly after the publication of
Who Is to Blame? and welcomed him into the ranks of Russian
writers, he was in effect initiating the chorus of critical acclaim that
was to surround the novel. Belinsky's review of part I in his "Survey of Russian Literature in 1845" was the first to be published
(1846) and was more an appreciation of the author's literary talent
than an analysis of his novel: "The author of *Who Is to Blame?* was
somehow miraculously able to bring intelligence to poetry, to
transform thought into real characters, the fruits of his observation
into action full of dramatic movement."[21] In other words, Belinsky
praised Herzen's synthesis of art and idea: the author had successfully combined imagination with thought. The critic continued, in
his characteristic declamatory style: "What striking fidelity to real-

---

20. G. G. Elizavetina, *"Kto vinovat?* Gertsena v vospriyatii russkikh chitatelei i
kritiki XIX v." in *Literaturnye proizvedeniya v dvizhenii epokh*, ed. N. V. Os'makov
(Moscow, 1979), 41.

21. *A. I. Gertsen v russkoi kritike*, ed. V. A. Putintsev (Moscow, 1953), 63.

ity, what profound thought, what unity of action, how it's all so much in proportion—nothing superfluous, nothing left unsaid; what originality of words, so much intelligence, humor, wit, soul, feeling!"[22] This was certainly an encouraging review of a young author's first serious attempt at writing fiction.

Belinsky's contemporaries were in general agreement about the worth of part I. Both in their published reviews and in their unpublished letters, there was almost universal recognition of the author's intelligence and the profundity of his philosophical approach to the contemporary scene. Thus the aspiring young writer Dostoevsky wrote to his brother, "There has appeared a whole host of new writers. Some are my rivals. Particularly noteworthy among them is Herzen (Iskander)."[23]

In 1847, after parts I and II were published together, critics acclaimed the novel as a triumph of the "natural school." *Who Is to Blame?* was said to be the first literary work that depicted contemporary life as it really was; therefore it could serve as convincing proof of the maturity of Russian letters. Even one of Herzen's so-called opponents, the Slavophile Ivan Aksakov (1823–86), wrote a moving tribute in a letter to his father: "It is not an artistic work, perhaps—but, aside from a morbid desire to be witty at all times, there are many wonderful things in it. When I read it I felt such a deep sense of oppression and melancholy, all the more so as it is a contemporary work, of the nineteenth century, with whose ills we all sympathize more or less."[24]

Belinsky finally addressed himself to the text of *Who Is to Blame?* in his "Survey of Russian Literature in 1847," published in *Contemporary* in 1848.[25] Here he seems to have retreated somewhat from his main thesis in his earlier review; he insists that it is Herzen's "thought" and "intellect," rather than his "creativity" or "artistry" that merit the attention of Russian readers. He sees the main interest of the novel not in an implied answer to the title question or

22. Ibid.
23. Elizavetina, *"Kto vinovat?"* 42.
24. Ya. El'sberg, *Gertsen* (Moscow, 1956), 163–64.
25. *Belinsky, Chernyshevsky, and Dobrolyubov; Selected Criticism*, ed. R. E. Matlaw (New York, 1962), 35–45.

in the character of the main hero, Beltov, but rather in the spiritual development of the heroine, Lyubonka. He dismisses Beltov as someone whose nature was spoiled by wealth, upbringing, and education and who gradually came to resemble Lermontov's Pechorin. Clearly Belinsky would have preferred more emphasis on the hero's external circumstances in conformity with his own changing attitudes toward the nature and function of literature.

Indeed, the figure of Beltov provoked considerable controversy among critics and writers in the second half of the nineteenth century. To some extent this divergence of opinion was foreshadowed in correspondence between the author and his close friend and fellow publicist, Nikolai Ogarev, in 1847.[26] Ogarev characterized the hero as "artificial," "romantic and pseudo-strong" and described his portrait in the novel as a "psychic study" of a "sick personality." Herzen replied with a more sympathetic reading of his protagonist's predicament, but he himself remained dissatisfied with Beltov's response to the problems of Russian society.

The writings of the radical critics in the late 1850s and early 1860s reflect Belinsky's reservations, Ogarev's criticisms, and Herzen's dissatisfaction. In their attempt to construct a genealogy of the Russian hero, they all assigned to Beltov his legitimate place in the pantheon. In so doing, they defined and redefined him, categorized and recategorized him, in order to fit him into various typologies. N. G. Chernyshevsky (1828–89), in an article entitled "The Verse of N. Ogarev" (1856), explained that "Onegin was replaced by Pechorin, [and] Pechorin by Beltov and Rudin."[27] N. A. Dobrolyubov (1836–61) developed this same theme. In a review ostensibly treating Goncharov's novel *Oblomov*, entitled "What Is Oblomovitis?" (1859), he describes the tradition of the Russian hero as that of "strong natures crushed by unfavorable environments."[28] He compares Pushkin's Onegin, Lermontov's Pechorin, Herzen's Beltov, and Turgenev's Rudin as characters who all manifested

26. See E. N. Dryzhakova, "Problema 'russkogo deyatelya' v tvorchestve Gertsena 40-kh godov," *Russkaya literatura*, 5 (1962) 2, 41–42.

27. Elizavetina, "*Kto vinovat?*" 65.

28. *Belinsky, Chernyshevsky, and Dobrolyubov: Selected Criticism*, 133–75.

early symptoms of the disease. He identifies the common themes uniting these "natures": their writing, reading, civil service, domestic life, attitudes toward women, and tendency toward self-humiliation. He acknowledges that while differences exist among their respective temperaments, they all share astonishing similarities. Most important, Dobrolyubov exonerates each individual from any responsibility for his unfortunate predicament. Under different circumstances, in some other society, these characters would have been entirely different. But in mid-nineteenth-century Russia they all suffer from the same barren striving for activity and from a painful awareness that while they *could* do a great deal, in fact, they will achieve nothing. Herzen's protagonist, although said to be the "most humane among them," belongs nevertheless to this unfortunate group.

On the other hand, in an article devoted to "I. S. Turgenev and His Novel *Nest of the Gentry*" (1859), Apollon Grigoriev (1822–64) distinguishes Beltov from Oblomov and argues that the moral position of Herzen's hero is far superior to that of Goncharov's.[29] Instead, Grigoriev groups Beltov together with Griboedov's Chatsky as a "fighter" and with Turgenev's Lezhnev and Lavretsky as men whose "ideals . . . cannot be reconciled with practice."

It is D. I. Pisarev (1840–68) who finally makes clear the purpose of all these typologies—the dethronement of the liberal aristocratic hero and the coronation of an altogether new character. In an article dealing with Turgenev's *Fathers and Sons*, entitled "Bazarov" (1862), Pisarev establishes a hierarchy of heroes to explain the emergence of Turgenev's young nihilist. The first stage, "will without knowledge," includes Onegin and Pechorin—men who are young, clever, and capable but who suffer from "spiritual hunger, boredom and disenchantment." Beltov and Rudin comprise the second group, "knowledge without will"—gloomy, frustrated idealists who aspire to do good but never achieve anything. Finally there is Bazarov, the representative of "knowledge and will," who unites "thought and deed" into "one solid whole."[30]

29. Elizavetina, "*Kto vinovat?*" 69.
30. In Putintsev, *A. I. Gertsen v russkoi kritike*, 132–38.

One year after Pisarev's review, Chernyshevsky published his revolutionary novel *What Is to Be Done?* (1863). The author intended it to be a direct and complex response in prose fiction to Herzen's *Who Is to Blame?* as well as to Turgenev's *Fathers and Sons.* The title itself dramatizes the move from the mere assigning of responsibility to the question of practical activity, while the subtitle, "Tales about New People," indicates that Chernyshevsky's characters belong to yet another, more radical type of Russian hero—beyond Bazarov's combination of "knowledge and will." A full discussion of the polemical relationship between these novels lies outside the scope of this introduction; suffice it to say that Chernyshevsky's heroes Kirsanov and Lopukhov, his heroine Vera Pavlovna, and his "superhero" Rakhmetov focused the attention of readers and critics alike on the new generation, on the men and women of the sixties, on their aspirations and achievements.

Soviet criticism of *Who Is to Blame?* has, not unexpectedly, tended to concentrate on the assignment of culpability to the conditions of mid-nineteenth-century Russia. As one recent Soviet critic put it, Herzen intended to demonstrate "how the milieu disfigures the consciousness and lives of people at every level of the social hierarchy."[31] Lenin himself led the field in reductive conclusions when he declared that all the issues that Herzen raises in the novel (the nature of family, the institution of marriage, the status of women, the emergence of the intelligentsia, the origins of personality) are subordinate to one main problem: "all social questions are fused in the struggle against serfdom and its remnants."[32]

The purpose of all subsequent Soviet criticism of Herzen was clearly articulated by V. A. Putintsev in his major study, *Herzen: The Writer* (1963): "Reactionary and liberal-bourgeois critics have expended considerable effort to muffle the passionate protest in Herzen's fiction against the autocratic order and against serfdom. The task of Soviet literary criticism is to restore the importance of Herzen's novel as the highest artistic manifestation of Russian democratic thought in the 1840s."[33]

31. V. A. Putintsev, *Gertsen-pisatel'* (Moscow, 1963), 73.
32. Ibid., 70.
33. Ibid.

In fact, "reactionary and liberal-bourgeois" critics have not always done what they are accused of. Martin Malia, in his book entitled *Alexander Herzen and the Birth of Russian Socialism* (1965), comes close to repeating the "party line" on the novel. He argues that no one is to blame, that the question itself is false, and that the answer lies in the defects of Russian society. Thus it is the "alienations imposed by 'cursed Russian reality' that are to 'blame' for this triple failure of human promise."[34]

On the other hand, Nicholas Rzhevsky, in his recent study *Russian Literature and Ideology* (1983), asserts that Herzen does not view his characters as social victims but rather as individual heroic beings and that the "particular moral-fictional stance" that a character assumes is more significant in determining his or her life than class or social position. Rzhevsky concludes therefore, that Beltov and Lyubonka "are at fault much more than the society they inhabit because they allow themselves to be victimized by the social institution of marriage instead of asserting the moral prerogative of their love. The absence of such assertion lies at the heart of their tragic separation and indicates that 'blame' and responsibility, in Herzen's view, must rest finally with the individual, his internal make-up, and his ethical choices."[35] From Lenin's polemic assertion ("serfdom and its remnants") to Rzhevsky's "blaming the victim" ("they allow themselves to be victimized"), all Soviet and some Western critics have conspired to oversimplify the subtle and complex message of Herzen's novel. This new transition of *Who Is to Blame?* is offered in the hope that it may serve as something of a corrective to the excesses of both radical and reactionary zeal and that it may restore Herzen's novel to its rightful and distinguished place in the history of Russian letters.

34. *Alexander Herzen and the Birth of Russian Socialism* (New York, 1965), 270.
35. Nicholas Rzhevsky, *Russian Literature and Ideology: Herzen, Dostoevsky, Leontiev, Tolstoy, Fadeyev* (Urbana, Ill., 1983), 59. Cf. Chances, *Conformity's Children*, 57–60: "It is not society's fault that Beltov cannot put his talents to work. It is not society which is to blame for his not fitting into Russian life."(58)

List of Principal Characters

Négrovs [<*negr* = Negro]

Alekséi Abrámovich (Aléksis)	retired major general and landowner
Glafíra Lvóvna (Glásha, Gláshenka)	his wife
Mikháilo Alekséevich (Mísha, Míshka)	his son
Líza Alekséevna (Lízonka)	his daughter
Lyubóv [<*lyubóv'* = love], Aleksándrovna (Lyubónka, Lyúba)	his illegitimate daughter and ward
Barbásh, Avdótya Emelyánovna (Dúnya)	serf; Lyubonka's natural mother
Elíza Avgústovna ("Madame")	French governess; "sponger"

Krutsiférskys

Dmítry Yákovlevich (Mítya)	tutor to the Negrovs' son
Yákov Ivánovich	physician; Dmitry's father

41

Margaríta Kárlovna — daughter of German pharmacist; Dmitry's mother

Béltovs [surname sounds foreign]

Vladímir [lit. "ruler of the world"] Petróvich (Volódya, Vóldemar) — protagonist

Petr — debauched nobleman; Vladimir's father

Sófya (Sófi) (née Nemchínova) — serf; Vladimir's mother

Monsieur Joseph — Swiss tutor

Kondrátiches

Karp — marshal of the nobility in Dubasov Province

Márya Stepánovna — his wife

Varvára Kárpovna (Váva) — his daughter

Krúpov [<*krup* = croup (med.) and/or *krúpnyi* = large, outstanding]

Dr. Semyón Ivánovich — inspector of the medical board

(Accents have been added here to facilitate pronunciation but will not appear in the text.)

WHO IS TO BLAME?

A Novel in Two Parts

By

ALEXANDER HERZEN

Author's Preface

To Natalya Aleksandrovna Herzen, as a sign of the
author's deep devotion
                                    —Moscow, 1846

Inasmuch as the guilty parties have not been found,
this case is to be consigned to the will of God; the file
can be considered closed and is to be relegated to the
archives.
                                    —Court Record

Who Is to Blame? was my first published novel. I began it during
my exile in Novgorod (in 1841) and finished it much later in
Moscow.

I had made two earlier attempts to write something like a novel,
but one was never actually written, and the other was not really a

---

Epigraphs: *Natalya Aleksandrovna Herzen*. Born in 1817, Natalya Aleksandrovna
Herzen (née Zakharina) was one of several illegitimate children of Aleksandr
Yakovlev, an older brother of Herzen's father. Her mother was a serf. Her father
died when she was eight years old, leaving her to be raised by his older sister. She
married her cousin Alexander Herzen in 1838.

Archives. The original version of the epigraph can be found in Herzen's letter to
A. A. Kraevsky dated October 24, 1845: "This case is to be consigned to the
judgment of God and, having been considered closed, it is to be consigned to the
archives." See E. N. Dryzhakova, "Problema 'russkogo deyatelya' v tvorchestve
Gertsena 40-kh godov," in *Russkaya literatura*, 5 (1962) 2, 49, for an analysis of this
alteration as a reflection of Herzen's changing attitude toward his hero.

novel.[1] Shortly after my transfer from Vyatka to Vladimir,[2] I hoped, by writing a novel, to placate some reproachful memories, come to terms with myself, and drape a certain female image with flowers so as to obscure the tears.[3]

Needless to say, I did not accomplish my task. There remained much that was contrived in my unfinished novel, and perhaps only two or three decent pages. One of my friends later threatened me by saying, "If you don't finish your new article, I'll publish that novel of yours—I still have a copy of it!"[4] Fortunately he never carried out his threat.

At the end of 1840 some excerpts from my *Notes of a Young Man* were published in the journal *Notes of the Fatherland*. One excerpt, "The Town of Malinov and Its Inhabitants," was very well received;[5] the best that can be said for the others is that the influence of Heine's *Reisebilder* was very pronounced.[6] But it was that very excerpt, "Malinov," that almost brought me to grief.

---

1. *Novel.* The former is Herzen's "Elena," part of his unfinished tale entitled "There" (1836–37), based on his involvement in an unhappy love affair with P. P. Medvedeva during his period of exile in Vyatka. The latter refers to his first completed literary work, *Notes of a Young Man*, published in the Petersburg journal *Notes of the Fatherland* (1840–41). Largely autobiographical, it foreshadows both the content and style of Herzen's monumental memoirs, *My Past and Thoughts* (1855).

2. *Vladimir.* Herzen was arrested in 1834 for belonging to a socialist political circle, imprisoned, and subsequently exiled to the Siberian town of Vyatka, where he spent four years working in the local administration. He was transferred to Vladimir, near Moscow, in 1838.

3. *Tears. My Past and Thoughts. Polar Star*, III, 95–98. [Herzen's note]. "Female image" is a reference to P. P. Medvedeva, who served as Herzen's inspiration for Elena. She was the young and attractive wife of the author's cantankerous, invalid neighbor in Vyatka. When her husband died and she was free to remarry, Herzen discovered that his infatuation had cooled. He was plunged into despair and seized with remorse.

4. *One of my friends.* N. Kh. Ketcher (1806–86), poet and translator, was a member of Herzen's Moscow circle. His Siberian origins were in striking contrast to the urban and country estate backgrounds of the rest of the group.

5. *"The Town of Malinov and Its Inhabitants."* Its inhabitants are described as dissipated card players, devoid of all intellectual interests. This section of *Notes of a Young Man* is based on the author's own experience in Vyatka.

6. *Heine's "Reisebilder."* Heinrich Heine (1797–1856), a German poet and journalist, published his *Reisebilder* in 1826. The book is a record of his travels through Germany, written in a style that mixes social satire, lyric verse, and self-analysis.

A certain counselor in Vyatka was about to file a complaint with the minister of internal affairs and to request official support; he argued that since the officials in the town of "Malinov" so closely resembled his own esteemed colleagues, they feared losing the respect of their subordinates. One of my Vyatka acquaintances asked what evidence he had to prove that the inhabitants of "Malinov" were intended to be caricatures of the officials in Vyatka. The counselor replied, "A great deal of proof. For example the *Aukthor* [*sic*] openly states that the wife of the gymnasium[7] director wore a ball dress the color of lingonberries.[8] Doesn't he?" This reached the director's wife, and she became furious, not with me but with the counselor. "Is he color-blind, or has he lost his mind?" she asked. "When has he ever seen me wearing a lingonberry gown? I used to wear a dark dress, but its color was *pensée* [deep violet]." This subtle distinction in hue saved my skin, because the disappointed counselor abandoned the matter. But if the director's wife had really worn a lingonberry gown, and if the counselor had actually filed a complaint, then in those memorable times that lingonberry gown would probably have done me more harm than Madam Larina's lingonberry water could possibly have done Onegin.[9]

The success of "Malinov" caused me to begin writing *Who Is to Blame?*

I brought the first part of the novel with me from Novgorod to Moscow.[10] My Moscow friends did not like it, so I stopped work. Their opinions about it changed a few years later, but by that time

7. *Gymnasium.* A European-style secondary school or academy that prepared students for entrance into university. The first Russian equivalents were founded by Peter the Great in Moscow and Petersburg during the early eighteenth century; during the early nineteenth century they sprang up in many provincial towns.

8. *Lingonberries. Brusnika, (Vaccinium vitis-idaea),* or red bilberry, grows primarily in northern pine forests and in the mountains. Its juice was used in the Russian countryside as a traditional remedy for gastric disorders.

9. *Onegin.* A reference to the hero's observation en route to the Larins', in Pushkin's *Eugene Onegin* (III:4:13–14), "I just hope that [their] lingonberry water / Won't do me any harm." Onegin fears that the rural remedy might upset his delicate city stomach.

10. *Moscow.* Herzen was exiled again in 1841 for his politically "dangerous" correspondence. He served as provincial counselor in Novgorod until his return to Moscow in 1842.

I no longer considered either continuing work on it or publishing it. Then Belinsky happened to get a copy of the manuscript.[11] With his tendency to get carried away, he rated it a hundred times more highly than it was worth. He wrote, "If I did not value you so highly as a person, even more so than as a writer, then I would say to you, as Potemkin said to Fonvizin after seeing a performance of *The Brigadier*, 'You can die now, Herzen.' But Potemkin was mistaken. Fonvizin did not die, but went on to write *The Minor*.[12] I do not wish to be mistaken. I believe that after *Who Is to Blame?* you will write a work that will make everyone say, 'He was not to blame; it has long been time for him to write a novel.' There's a compliment for you, and not a bad pun, either."

The censors made various clips and cuts in my novel. Unfortunately I no longer have these fragments. I managed to recall a few expressions that were censored (they are printed here in italics),[13] and even one whole page (which I added to p. 38 after the proofs had been set).[14] This passage is particularly memorable, since Belinsky became enraged when he learned that it had been eliminated.

8 June 1859

Park House, Fulham[15]   Iskander[16]

11. *Belinsky.* Vissarion Belinsky (1811–48) was the most outstanding Russian literary critic of the early nineteenth century. A prolific essayist and early espouser of radical ideas, he was both a friend and a critic of Herzen's. Here Herzen quotes (inaccurately) from a letter sent him by Belinsky dated February 6, 1846, which contains considerable praise for *Who Is to Blame?*

12. *The Minor.* Prince G. A. Potemkin (1739–91), a favorite of Catherine the Great, was a distinguished statesman, adviser, and noted patron of the arts. Tradition has it that after the first performance of D. I. Fonvizin's (1745–92) comedy *The Brigadier* (1768), Potemkin remarked: "Die, Dennis, for you will never write anything better." *The Minor* (1782), however, was much better.

13. In this edition the passages are enclosed in brackets and identified in footnotes as "author's note." My translations of foreign language phrases in the text are also in brackets.

14. Pp. 78–79 in this edition.

15. *Fulham.* Herzen settled in England in August 1852 and lived there until March 1865. He resided at Park House, Percy Cross, Fulham (near London) from November 24, 1858, to May 25 (?), 1860.

16. *Iskander.* The Turkish form of Herzen's own name, Alexander. This pseudonym soon became synonymous with his radical ideological position.

PART **I**

Chapter 1

The Retired General and the Newly Appointed Tutor

It was getting on toward evening. Aleksei Abramovich was standing on the balcony; he was unable to rouse himself from his two-hour afternoon nap. His eyes kept closing lazily, and he yawned from time to time. A servant boy entered with some kind of report, but Aleksei Abramovich considered it unnecessary to take any notice of him; the servant dared not disturb his master. A few minutes passed before Aleksei Abramovich inquired, "What is it?"

"While Your Excellency was having his rest, the tutor who was engaged by the doctor arrived from Moscow."

"Oh?" (it is unclear whether a question mark [?] or an exclamation point [!] is required here).

"I showed him to the little room where the German tutor used to live, the one you dismissed."

"Oh!"

"He asked to be informed when you had awakened."

"Send him in."

Aleksei Abramovich's face became more pugnacious and majestic. In a few moments the boy announced, "The tutor is here, sir."

Aleksei Abramovich was silent; then he glanced at the boy sternly and remarked, "What's wrong with you, you idiot, is your mouth full of flour, or what? You are mumbling so, I can't make out a thing." Then, without waiting for an answer, he added, "Send in the tutor," and he sat down at once.

A young man, twenty-three or twenty-four years old, thin, pale, with fair hair, wearing a skimpy black tailcoat, entered the room in a timid and embarrassed fashion.

"Greetings, most honored sir!" said the general, smiling graciously but not rising. "The doctor has spoken well of you. I trust that we will be satisfied with each other. Hey, Vaska!" (and he whistled), "Why don't you offer him a chair? You think that just because he's a tutor you don't have to? Will you stop behaving like such a fool and start acting like a human being? Sir, please be seated. My dear sir, I have a son, a good boy, very talented. I would like to prepare him for military school. He speaks French, and although he doesn't really speak German, he understands it. His German tutor was a drunkard and did not attend to him much; in fact, I employed the tutor more for household tasks. He lived in the same room that you will have. I drove him away. I tell you frankly that I don't expect my son to become either a scholar or a philosopher; on the other hand, my dear sir, even though, thank God, I am quite comfortable, I have no intention whatever of spending twenty-five hundred rubles for nothing. You know as well as I do that now all sorts of grammars and arithmetics are required even for military service. Hey, Vaska! Send in Mikhailo Alekseevich!"

All this time the young man had remained silent; he blushed, folded and refolded his handkerchief, and prepared to speak. Blood roared in his ears. Although he did not quite understand all of the general's words, he felt that his entire speech was creating the same sensation as when you rub your hand on a sealskin the wrong way. At the end of the general's harangue, he said: "In accepting the obligation of becoming your son's tutor, I will conduct myself in accordance with my conscience and my sense of honor . . . of course, inasmuch as my abilities; . . . however, I shall make every effort to justify your . . . Your Excellency's trust in me."

Aleksei Abramovich interrupted him: "His Excellency, my dear sir, does not demand anything more than that. The main thing is an ability to arouse your pupil's interest; tell him a few jokes perhaps, if you know what I mean. You have completed your education, have you not?"

"Indeed, I am now a candidate . . ."[1]

"Is that some new rank?"

"It is an academic degree."

"Ah! Are your parents still alive?"

"They are."

"Is your father a clergyman?"

"He is a rural doctor."

"Did you study medicine?"

"Physics and mathematics."

"Do you know Latin?"

"I do."

"It is quite an unnecessary language. Of course, doctors dare not say in the presence of a patient that he is likely to kick the bucket tomorrow, but what good is Latin to us?"

This learned conversation might have gone on longer had it not been interrupted by Mikhailo Alekseevich—Misha, a lad of thirteen, healthy, rosy-cheeked, suntanned, and well fed. He was wearing a jacket that he had managed to outgrow in only a few months and had a look common to all hefty children of wealthy landowners who reside in the country.

"Here's your new tutor," said the father.

Misha clicked his heels.

"Obey him, study hard. I don't begrudge the expense, but it's your job to make good use of the opportunity."

The tutor rose, bowed to Misha politely, took him by the hand, and with a gentle, kind look told him that he would do everything possible to lighten his pupil's burden and make him interested in his studies.

1. *Candidate.* An individual holding the lowest academic degree, roughly equivalent to the bachelor's degree. It is conferred on someone who has earned distinction in a course of study at an institution of higher learning and who has presented a piece of written work on a chosen theme.

"He learned a thing or two from Madame, who is living with us," observed Aleksei Abramovich. "And the priest has taught him as well. Our village priest graduated from a seminary. Be so good as to test Misha's knowledge."

The tutor was embarrassed. He thought for a long time about what to ask. Finally he said, "Tell me, what sort of a subject is grammar?"

Misha looked from side to side, picked his nose, and replied, "Russian grammar?"

"Any grammar, it doesn't matter which."

"We didn't study that."

"What did the priest do with you?" asked the father sternly.

"Papa, we studied Russian grammar up to the gerunds, and the catechism up to the sacraments."

"Well, then, go and show the schoolroom to . . . excuse me, what is your name?"

"Dmitry," answered the tutor, blushing.

"And your patronymic?"

"Yakovlevich."

"Ah, Dmitry Yakovlevich! Would you care for a little refreshment after your journey, perhaps a drink of vodka?"

"I don't drink anything except water."

"He's lying," thought Aleksei Abramovich, feeling extremely tired after such a lengthy learned discourse. He went to join his wife in the sitting room. Glafira Lvovna was dozing on a soft Turkish divan. She was wearing a blouse; it was her favorite attire because anything else was too tight on her. She had profited from fifteen years of genuinely happy married life and had become an *Adansonia baobab* among women.[2] Aleksei's heavy steps awoke her; she raised her sleepy head and for a while was unable to come to her senses. Then, as if she had never before fallen asleep at the wrong time, she exclaimed with astonishment, "Oh, my goodness! I must

---

2. *Adansonia baobab*. A very large tree, native to Africa and India; its wood is used for timber, while its bark and fruit provide food and medicine. The phrase contains a pun on the Russian word *baba*—a peasant woman, frequently of substantial proportions.

have dozed off! Fancy that!" Aleksei Abramovich began to report on his efforts on behalf of Misha's education. Glafira Lvovna was quite satisfied; as she listened to him, she consumed half a pitcher of kvass.[3] She drank some every day just before teatime.

Not all of Dmitry Yakovlevich's difficulties were over after his audience with Aleksei Abramovich. He was sitting in the schoolroom, silent but agitated, when a servant entered and summoned him to tea. Our hero had never frequented the society of ladies. He had an instinctive feeling of respect for women; he considered that they were surrounded by a kind of halo. He would see them walking along the boulevard, all dressed up and inaccessible, or on the stage of a Moscow theater, where all the hideous figurantes appeared to him as fairies or goddesses. And now he was going to be presented to the general's wife! Would she even be alone? Misha had managed to inform him that he had a sister, and that "Madame" and some girl named Lyubonka were also living with them. Dmitry Yakovlevich was extremely eager to learn the age of Misha's sister; he started to ask about this at least three times but didn't dare finish, fearing that he might blush.

"So, shall we go in, sir?" said Misha diplomatically, who, like all spoiled children, was extremely modest and reserved with strangers. When the candidate stood up, he was not sure if his legs would support him; his hands were cold and clammy. Making an enormous effort and feeling somewhat lightheaded, he entered the sitting room. In the doorway he bowed respectfully to the maid who had just brought in the samovar.

"Glasha," said Aleksei Abramovich, "let me present Misha's new mentor."

The candidate bowed.

"Delighted," said Glafira Lvovna, squinting slightly and grimacing in a way that was once quite effective. "Our Misha has long been in need of a good teacher; indeed, we don't know how to thank Dr. Krupov for introducing you to us. Please make yourself quite at home here. Would you care to sit down?"

---

3. *Kvass.* A traditional popular Russian beverage, slightly alcoholic, usually prepared from flour or dark rye bread soaked in water and malt.

"I have been sitting for some time," muttered the candidate, not really aware of what he was saying.

"You certainly couldn't have been standing up in the covered cart!" the general ventured wittily.

This observation was too much for the candidate. He took a chair, placed it at a strange angle, and almost missed it as he sat down. He was afraid to raise his eyes, as if that might yield a greater misfortune. There might have been some other ladies present in the room, and if he saw them, he'd have to bow to them. But how? Surely he couldn't bow from his seat.

"I told you," said the general under his breath, "he's like a bashful young girl!"

"*Le pauvre, il est à plaindre*" ["Poor man, he is to be pitied"], observed Glafira Lvovna, biting her own plump lips.

Glafira Lvovna liked the young man from the moment she cast her eyes on him. There were several reasons for this. In the first place, Dmitry Yakovlevich, with his large blue eyes, was indeed *attractive*. In the second place, besides her husband, servants, coachman, and the old doctor, Glafira Lvovna rarely saw any men at all, not to mention *attractive* young men, and, as we shall subsequently learn, she indulged in Platonic dreams out of old habit. In the third place, women of a certain age look at a young man with the same incomprehensible longing with which men generally look at young women. It is almost a feeling of compassion, a maternal instinct, as if they wanted to protect defenseless, timid, inexperienced creatures—to coddle, caress, and envelop them. This is how it seems to the women, anyway. I don't exactly share their opinion, but consider it unnecessary to speak my mind. . . . Glafira Lvovna personally offered the candidate a cup of tea. He took a big gulp and scalded both his tongue and his palate, but managed to conceal the pain with the courage of a Mucius Scaevola.[4] This circumstance proved to be beneficial; it created a dis-

---

4. *Mucius Scaevola*. Gaius Mucius Scaevola, a legendary Roman hero of the sixth century B.C., who, after being captured by the Etruscans, is supposed to have held his right hand in the fire to demonstrate his strength of will.

traction, and he was able to compose himself somewhat. He even began to raise his eyes, a little at a time.

Glafira Lvovna was sitting on the divan; in front of her stood a table on which towered an enormous samovar, like some Hindu monument. Opposite her she had placed Aleksei Abramovich—either so that she could take advantage of the pleasant *vis-à-vis* [face-to-face view] or so that she could avoid seeing her husband from behind the samovar. He was sprawling on an ancient armchair, strained to the breaking point. Behind his armchair stood a young girl of about ten with an extremely stupid expression. She kept peering out at the tutor from behind her father's chair. It was on account of her that our bold candidate was all atremble! Misha was also seated at the table, on which a bowl of buttermilk and a thick slice of fine-textured bread had been placed. The head of a hunting dog could be seen peering out from underneath a tablecloth on which the town of Yaroslavl was rather neatly depicted, along with its emblem of a bear in each corner. The folds of the tablecloth lent the dog a kind of Egyptian look; her two eyes, encased in fat, were immovably fixed on the candidate. In an armchair over by the window, holding her knitting, sat a diminutive old lady. She had a cheerful, wrinkled countenance with overhanging eyebrows and thin, pale lips. Dmitry Yakovlevich guessed that she was "Madame." At the door stood a young lad who handed Aleksei Abramovich his pipe; next to him a maid in a gingham dress with linen sleeves was waiting in awe for the master and mistress to finish their tea-drinking ritual. There was one more person present in the room, but Dmitry Yakovlevich did not see her face because it was bent over her embroidery. She was a poor young woman who was being brought up by the magnanimous general.

The conversation did not get off to a good start. When it finally did get started, it was fragmented, pointless, and wearisome for the candidate.

This encounter between a poor young man and a wealthy landowner's family was rather strange. These people could easily have lived out their lives without ever meeting, but that is not what happened. The life of this gentle, kind young man, well educated and eager to learn, in some dissonant fashion had become entangled with the overstuffed life of Aleksei Abramovich and his spouse; he became trapped like a bird in a cage. Everything changed, and it was inevitable that such changes could not occur without having an impact on a young man so lacking in knowledge and experience of the real world.

But what sort of people were they, the general and his wife, living in a state of bliss and prospering in their conjugal happiness, and this young man, appointed to mold Misha's mind so that the boy could enroll in a military school?

I do not know how to compose fictional tales; perhaps that is why I feel the need to present the reader with some biographical information obtained from very reliable sources. It goes without saying that I shall begin with. . . .

Chapter 2

The Biography of
Their Excellencies

Aleksei Abramovich Negrov, a retired major general and cavalier,[1] was a tall, corpulent man who, after cutting his baby teeth, was never ill a day in his life. He could serve as a splendid and total refutation of Hufeland's well-known treatise, *On Extending the Human Life Span*.[2] He lived his life in a manner diametrically opposed to every page of Hufeland's book yet was always healthy and ruddy-complexioned. He followed only one rule of hygiene: he never allowed mental exertion to upset his digestion. Perhaps this is what gave him the right to disregard all other rules. He was stern, irascible, harsh in word, and often cruel in deed; yet it could not be said that he was an evil man by nature. Gazing upon his sharply chiseled features, those not yet entirely obscured by layers of flesh, or upon his thick black eyebrows or into his shining eyes, one could conclude that life had destroyed more than one potentiality in him.

At the age of fourteen, having been reared by nature and by a

1. *Cavalier*. A man who has been awarded some kind of decoration.
2. *Hufeland*. Christoph Wilhelm Hufeland (1762–1836) was a well-respected German physician whose patients included Wieland, Herder, Goethe, and Schiller. His most popular treatise, *On Extending the Human Life Span* (1796), was translated into many languages.

French governess who was living at his sister's house, Negrov enlisted in a cavalry regiment. With the large sum of money that he received from his dear mother, he enjoyed a reckless youth. After the campaign of 1812 he was promoted to colonel, but those colonel's epaulettes weighed his shoulders down just as his shoulders were getting tired of wearing a uniform. He was getting bored with military service. After serving a little while longer, he found himself "incapable of continuing for reasons of ill health." He retired with the rank of major general, a mustache that constantly bore reminders of every course eaten at dinner, and a uniform worn only on special occasions. When the retired general settled in Moscow (which had been rebuilt after the fire),[3] there stretched before him an endless succession of days and nights in a monotonous, empty, and very boring life. There was no occupation for which he was suited or to which he was inclined. He went visiting from house to house, played cards, dined at his club, appeared in the first row of the theater stalls or at balls; he acquired two foursomes of fine horses, groomed them, trained his coachman day and night by words and wallops, and taught the mysteries of horseback riding to his own postilion. . . . A year and a half passed in such pursuits; finally, when the coachman learned to sit on the box and hold the reins, and when the postilion learned to sit on a horse and hold the reins, Negrov was quite overcome by boredom; he decided to move to the country and manage his own estate. He convinced himself that such a change was necessary to prevent significant disorders from occurring there.

His theory of estate management was extremely uncomplicated: every day he rebuked both the steward and the village elder, and then he either rode out to shoot hares or went out on foot with his rifle. Never having become accustomed to any kind of activity, he could not imagine what he should be doing; he occupied himself exclusively with details and was very content. The steward and

---

3. *The fire of Moscow.* Napoleon entered Moscow on September 14, 1812, to find only a small fraction of the population still in residence. That night, fires began that quickly spread and raged for five days, destroying about nine-tenths of the city. Although responsibility for the conflagration is still a subject of dispute, it seems likely that the Russians had tried to burn Moscow to the ground.

village elder, for their part, were also content with their master. As for the peasants, I really can't say; they remained silent.

About two months later, a pretty female face appeared at the window of this gentleman's house; at first her lovely blue eyes were red from weeping, but soon they became lovely blue eyes once again.

At about the same time the village elder, who was in no way actually concerned with the management of the village, informed the general that Emelka Barbash's hut was in bad shape. The elder wondered whether Aleksei Abramovich might be so kind as to show Barbash some paternal generosity and provide him with some lumber. Lumber was a sore point for Aleksei Abramovich; he would have had difficulty deciding to cut down a tree to make his own coffin; but . . . he happened to be in a good mood and allowed Barbash to cut down just enough wood for a new hut. He said to the village elder: "You better watch out, you redheaded rogue; I'll remove one of your ribs for every extra log he takes." The elder ran out onto the back porch and reported his smashing success to Avdotya Emelyanovna Barbash, calling her his "little mother and protectress." The poor girl blushed to her ears; but in her own simple way she was glad that her father would have a new hut.

In our sources we find little information about the general's conquest of Avdotya's lovely blue eyes, or even about his first encounter with them. I suppose it's because such conquests happen very simply. However it transpired, Negrov was soon overcome by the boredom of rural life. He assured himself that he had corrected all the defects in the management of his estate, and, even more important, he had provided it with such firm direction that it could now run without him. He planned to return to Moscow once again, though his baggage had increased somewhat: the lovely blue eyes, a wet nurse, and an infant traveled along in a separate carriage.

In Moscow they were placed in a room overlooking the courtyard. Aleksei Abramovich loved the baby, he loved Dunya, and he even loved the wet nurse: this was an erotic stage in his life! Soon the wet nurse's milk soured, and she felt sick all the time. The doctor declared that she was no longer able to nurse. The general felt sorry for her. "What an unusual wet nurse we have. Healthy, hard-working, so eager to please, but her milk has soured . . . what a pity!" He gave her twenty rubles, returned her "married woman's kerchief,"[4] and sent her back to her husband in order to recuperate.

The doctor recommended that the wet nurse be replaced by a nanny goat, and this was done. The goat was very healthy. Aleksei Abramovich loved her very much, fed her black bread from his own hand, and caressed her; even this did not prevent her from providing milk for the child.

Aleksei Abramovich's way of life turned out to be the same as it had been when he first arrived in Moscow. He endured it for almost two years but then could stand it no longer. The complete absence of activity is intolerable for any human being. An animal assumes that all it has to do is survive, but a human being accepts life only as an opportunity to do something. Although from noon to midnight Negrov was never at home, he was still tormented by boredom. This time he didn't even want to return to the country. He was overcome by "spleen."[5] He gave his valet more "paternal lessons" than ever and frequented the room overlooking the court-yard less and less.

One day, upon returning home, the general was in a very un-usual state of mind—preoccupied by something. First he frowned, then he smiled; he paced the room for a while, and suddenly, with a decisive look, he stopped dead. One could see that some matter had been inwardly resolved. Having so resolved it, he whistled; he did this in such a way that the servant boy asleep on a chair in the next room rushed away from the door in such a fright that afterwards he could hardly find the doorknob. "You're always asleep, you scamp," the general said to him—not in his usual voice of thunder, which was often followed by flashes of "paternal" lightning—but in a normal tone. "Go tell Mishka that tomorrow, as soon as it's light,

4. *Married woman's kerchief.* The kerchief (*povoinik*) was the headdress tradi-tionally worn by married peasant women. It consisted of a cloth wrapped around the head on top of a soft cap, usually with a round or oval crown; it had a ribbon band and strings hanging down the back.

5. *Spleen.* The infamous European malady that also afflicted "superfluous men" in nineteenth-century Russian literature. The word (*khandra*) is derived from the Greek (*hypo)chondria* and is usually rendered in English as "spleen" and in French as *ennui.*

he should set off to the German carriage maker and bring him to see me at eight o'clock without fail." It was clear that a weight had been lifted from Aleksei Abramovich's shoulders and that now he could rest peacefully.

The next day, at 8 A.M., the German carriage maker appeared. By 10 A.M. their conference was concluded. During those two hours a carriage large enough to seat four had been ordered, with great attention paid to detail. The body was to be painted *mordoré foncé* [dark bronze], with a golden coat of arms; it was to have crimson upholstery with *blason coquelicot* [a poppy-red coat of arms] and an elaborate coachman's box three cushions wide.

The four-seater meant neither more nor less than that Aleksei Abramovich was intending to marry, and this intention was soon further revealed by unambiguous signs. After seeing the carriage maker, Negrov summoned his valet. In a lengthy and rather incoherent speech (which is very much to his credit, since this incoherence reflected something of the phenomenon that people often refer to as "conscience"), he expressed his gratitude for services rendered and his intention to reward his valet accordingly. The valet could not understand where all of this was leading; he bowed and said more or less politely, "Whom are we to please, if not Your Excellency? You are our father; we are your children." Negrov tired of this comedy and in a few very expressive words announced to his valet that he was "allowing" him to marry Dunya. The valet was a clever man, in possession of a quick mind. Although his master's unexpected kindness startled him considerably, in a few moments he had calculated all the arguments pro and con, and promptly asked to kiss his master's hand in return for his generosity and solicitude. The appointed bridegroom understood exactly what was going on; but, he thought, even if he is marrying her off to me, he is not relegating Avdotya Emelyanovna to total disfavor. I have long been a member of this household, and I know the master's ways. Besides, it wouldn't be a bad thing to have such a pretty wife. In a word, the bridegroom was well satisfied.

Dunya was astonished to learn that she had become a fiancée; she wept and brooded. But after realizing that she could either return to her father's house or become the valet's wife, she resolved on the latter course of action. She could not imagine without shuddering how all her former friends would laugh at her. She recalled how, even at the height of her glory, they still whispered that she was only "half a lady."

They were married within a week. The next morning, when the young couple came bearing sweets to pay their respects, Negrov was very cheerful. He presented them with a hundred rubles and remarked to his cook, who happened to be there, "Learn a lesson, you dolt. I like to punish, but I also like to reward. He has served me well, and consequently he has been rewarded." The cook answered, "Yes, Your Excellency," but his expression said, "Don't try to trick me! After all, I hoodwink you on every purchase! What kind of fool do you take me for?"

That evening the valet staged a feast as a result of which all the servants reeked of vodka for two whole days; nor did he begrudge the expense. There occurred, however, a painfully bitter moment for poor Dunya: the child's little bed, and the child as well, were ordered transferred to the servants' quarters. Dunya loved the child dearly, from the bottom of her simple, artless soul. She was afraid of Aleksei Abramovich. Although she never did anyone any harm, all the other servants were afraid of her. Sentenced to a languorous, haremlike existence, she concentrated all her need for love, all her demands on life, upon her little infant. Her undeveloped and oppressed soul was a beautiful one nonetheless. Humble and timid, she was impervious to all insults. But there was one thing she could not endure: Negrov's cruel treatment of the child when he was annoyed. Then she would raise her voice, trembling not out of fear but out of rage. She despised Negrov at these moments, and he, as if sensing his humiliating position, would shower her with abuse and then slam the door as he stalked out.

When the child's bed was supposed to be transferred, Dunya locked the door and threw herself down on her knees, weeping, before the icon. She grabbed her daughter's hand and made the sign of the cross over her. "Pray," she said, "pray, my treasure; we are going together to lead a wretched life; Holy Mother of God, intercede for this innocent little child. . . . Like a fool I thought that you, my darling, would grow up to ride in a carriage and wear silk dresses. I would have had to watch you through a crack in the door. I would have hidden myself from you, my angel. What good is a peasant mother to you? Now you will grow up without any joy. You will probably become the new mistress's laundress, and the soap will destroy your little hands. . . . Oh, my God! How has this little infant sinned before Thee?" And Dunya threw herself onto the floor weeping; her heart was breaking. The frightened child seized her hand, cried, and looked at her as if she understood everything. . . . Within an hour the little bed stood in the servants' quarters, and Aleksei Abramovich ordered that the child should be instructed to call the valet "Papa."

But who was the master's fortunate bride-to-be? In Moscow there exists a special *varietas* [variety] of the human species. We have in mind those semi-wealthy, aristocratic houses whose inhabitants have left the stage of social life completely and who for generations live modestly in various little lanes. Monotonous orderliness and a certain concealed hostility toward anything new constitute the main characteristics of the inhabitants of these houses. The houses themselves, with their crooked columns and filthy vestibules, stand deep within courtyards. Their inhabitants see themselves as representatives of our national way of life because "they need their kvass like fresh air,"[6] because they ride in sleighs accompanied by two footmen as if they were sitting in carriages, and because all year long they live off supplies transported from their estates in Penza or Simbirsk.

In one such house lived the Countess Mavra Ilinishna. An attractive coquette, she had previously traveled in the whirlwind of aristocratic circles. She had been presented at court and had exchanged pleasantries with Kantemir.[7] He had inscribed a madrigal in syllabic verse in her album, that is, "a eulogy in verse," in which one

6. *"Like fresh air."* A quotation from Pushkin's *Eugene Onegin* (II:35:12), the sympathetic description of the Larins' old-fashioned adherence to Russian customs as part of their traditional way of life.

7. *Kantemir.* Antioch Dmitrievich Kantemir (1708–44)—an outstanding eighteenth-century Russian poet. He held a variety of important diplomatic posts and published nine satires that championed the reforms of Peter the Great. He is also responsible for regularizing Russian syllabic verse, in which structure was determined by the number of syllables in each line.

line ended with the words "Goddess Minerva." This was supposed to rhyme with another line ending in "so much fervor." Still, she was extremely cold-blooded by nature and haughty as a result of her beauty. She refused suitors in expectation of some brilliant match. In the meantime her father died, and her brother, who was managing their entire estate, drank up and gambled away almost all the inheritance within ten years. Life in St. Petersburg became too expensive. They were forced to live more modestly. The countess was already past thirty when she came to understand fully her financial difficulties. In fact, she made two horrible discoveries simultaneously: her estate had been squandered, and her youth had been spent. She made several desperate attempts to marry—all unsuccessful. Then, burying her terrible resentment deep within her breast, she settled in Moscow, explaining that the excitement of high society had become so repulsive to her that she was now seeking only tranquillity.

At first, people made a fuss over her in Moscow. They considered it a special sign of their social status if they could visit a countess. But little by little her spiteful tongue and unbearable arrogance drove almost everyone away. Cast off and abandoned, the old maid became even more disgusted and spiteful. She surrounded herself with various dependent old ladies, half-saints and half-beggars. She collected gossip from all parts of town, was horrified by the depravity of the age, and considered that her own perpetual virginity was a sign of her great virtue. Her brother the count, having irretrievably squandered his entire estate, decided to repair the damage by performing a feat considered heroic at that time. He married a merchant's daughter. Every day, for four years in a row, he reproached her for her lowly origin. He gambled away her dowry to the last kopeck and then drove her away; finally, he drank himself into a stupor and died. His wife followed him a year later, leaving a five-year-old daughter with no means of support whatever.

Mavra Ilinishna undertook to raise the child. It would be difficult to say what prompted this decision: family pride, sympathy for the child, or hatred for her brother. Be that as it may, the little girl's life was not very pleasant. She was deprived of all the joys of childhood, intimidated, frightened, oppressed. The egoism of old maids is appalling: they want to take revenge on those around them for the emptiness of their own frigid hearts. The little countess grew up cheerlessly and monotonously. Unfortunately she did not belong to that group of people whose natures develop as a direct consequence of external oppression. As she became more aware of things, she discovered two strong feelings within herself: an irrepressible desire for external pleasure and a strong hatred of her aunt's way of life. Both feelings were understandable. Mavra Ilinishna not only failed to provide her niece with any diversions but also thoroughly destroyed all the pleasures and innocent enjoyments that the child discovered for herself. She thought that the young girl's life was given meaning only by reading aloud to her until she fell asleep and by looking after her all the rest of the time. The old countess wanted to devour the girl's youth, to suck the life juices out of her soul, all in return for the upbringing that she had not given her but with which she reproached her continuously.

Time passed. The young countess became marriageable—very much so. She was already twenty-three years old. She experienced deeply the oppressive boredom and monotony of her situation. All her awareness revolved around one thought: to escape from the hell of her aunt's house. Even the grave seemed more attractive: she drank vinegar in order to become consumptive, but it didn't help. She wanted to enter a nunnery but lacked sufficient resolve. Soon her thoughts took a different turn. Some aging French novels that she had discovered, I don't know how, in her aunt's wardrobe, made it clear to her that in addition to death and nunneries there existed other important consolations. So she forsook her meditations on Adam's skull[8] and instead began to contemplate live ones—heads with mustaches and curly hair. Thousands of romantic scenes tormented her day and night. She composed entire tales on her own. "He" would carry her off. They would be pursued. "You are forbidden to love." Shots ring out. . . . "You are mine

8. *Adam's skull.* The skull is regarded as a symbol of the transitory nature of life and the vanity of earthly things. There is a legend that Christ's Cross at Golgotha (lit. "place of the skull") was erected over the skull and bones of Adam, suggesting that through Christ's death all men may rise to eternal life.

forever!" he would say, squeezing the trigger, and so on and so forth. All of her fantasies, thoughts, and dreams were based on this same theme in endless variations. Every morning the poor girl awoke in horror to realize that no one had come to carry her off and no one was saying, "You are mine forever!" Her bosom heaved, and tears flowed freely onto her pillow.

With some kind of desperation, she drank whey as her aunt ordered; with even greater desperation she laced herself up in a corset, knowing that there was no one to appreciate her figure. Such a state of mind could not be cured entirely even by drinking whey; it merely led to sentimentality and to a state of exaltation. She eventually began to take a great interest in her maids and to embrace the coachman's grimy children. It was a stage after which a young girl must either get married or begin to take snuff, love pussycats and clipped lapdogs, and belong neither to the male nor the female gender.

Fortunately the countess was fated to enjoy the former alternative. She was not unattractive, and it was precisely at this moment that she had to smite our hero. The appeal of her whole being, her langorous eyes, and her heaving bosom conquered Negrov. As soon as he caught sight of her at the old Church of the Ascension, his fate was sealed. The general recalled his own years as a young cornet[9] in the cavalry and began to seek out every possible opportunity for seeing the young countess. He waited for hours on the church porch. Then, when two footmen dragged the old countess, looking like a crow in a lace cap, out of an antediluvian coach pulled by tall, scraggy nags who had lost even their capacity to die, and prevented the young countess, looking like a cabbage rose, from jumping out of the coach, he became quite embarrassed.

The general had a cousin in Moscow. . . .If a person possesses both rank and fortune, and if the intended isn't already being pursued by a suitor, then he who has such a well-established and wealthy cousin can marry almost anyone he likes. When the gener-

---

9. *Cornet*. The lowest-ranking officer in the cavalry, corresponding to the rank of first lieutenant in the infantry.

al confided his secret to his cousin, she responded with a genuine sisterly concern. For two months or so the poor woman had been languishing in boredom. Then, like a bolt out of the blue, there was a match to be arranged. At once she sent a cab to fetch the wife of a certain titular counselor. She arrived forthwith. All the maids were driven out of the next room so that no one would be able to eavesdrop. In an hour the wife of the titular counselor rushed out of the room with a flushed face. After hurriedly announcing the news in the servants' quarters, she ran out of the house. The next day, around 9 A.M., the Moscow cousin was infuriated by the titular counselor's wife's lack of punctuality; she had promised to come at 11 A.M. and still hadn't arrived! Finally the expected visitor appeared, bringing another person wearing a lace cap. In a word, the whole affair was moving along with unusual speed and in the appropriate sequence.

In the old countess's house, certain important changes began to occur slowly. The dark canvas drapes were taken down from the windows and laundered; the doorknobs were polished with brick dust mixed with kvass (instead of vinegar); and, in the entrance hall, which smelled of leather because four footmen made suspenders there, the winter storm frames were removed. Having been so completely abandoned, Mavra Ilinishna was now ecstatic that not only a general, but a very wealthy one at that, was courting her niece. But to preserve her dignity, she scarcely condescended to grant permission to initiate the matchmaking. One morning the countess ordered her niece to dress more carefully and to expose her neck a bit more. Then she inspected her from head to toe.

"Why on earth, *maman*, are you making me dress up? Are we having guests?"

"It's none of your business, my dear," answered the countess, but in a kind, genial tone of voice.

The niece's muslin dress practically burst into flames as a result of the fire that leapt through her veins. She conjectured, suspected, but dared not either believe or disbelieve. She had to go out for a breath of fresh air, lest she faint. In the entrance hall the maids informed her that they were expecting a visit from a general and that he was coming to court her. Suddenly a carriage drew up.

"Palashka, I shall die, I *am* dying!" whispered the young countess.

"Enough of that, Your Highness! Who ever died from being courted, especially by such a fine suitor? I always said that our young countess would marry a general—ask anyone here."

Whose pen could possibly describe what the poor girl experienced during the *exhibition* and *inspection*? When she had recovered somewhat, the first thing that struck her was Aleksei Abramovich's dress coat: she had clearly expected a uniform with epaulettes. . . . Nevertheless, even without a uniform Negrov could still please any young woman. Although approaching forty, he was in fine physical shape and in good health. While he was not overly garrulous by nature, he possessed that free and easy manner peculiar to officers, especially those in the cavalry. Other defects that a young lady might discover in him were richly compensated for by his splendid mustache, fashionably trimmed for the occasion.

The match was arranged. A week after the inspection had taken place, Mavra Ilinishna's acquaintances began to arrive to offer their congratulations to the countess. Even people long presumed dead crawled out of the woodwork, where they had been struggling stubbornly and unyieldingly against death and had not surrendered, and where, for the last thirty years or so, they had indulged their caprices and hoarded their money; now they were all emaciated, paralyzed, asthmatic, or deaf. The countess told them all the same thing: "I was no less surprised by this news than you. I had not even thought of marrying off my Koko so soon; she is still a child. But such is God's will! He is an honest and respectable man, though old enough to be her father. And she is so inexperienced. The fact that he is a general and rich is of no importance; gold is no guarantee of happiness. Nevertheless, I am now enjoying the fruits of the pious upbringing that I bestowed upon her." (At this she applied a handkerchief to her eyes.) "The girl's upbringing is responsible for everything. Would anyone have predicted that such a child could be the product of a debauched father (may he rest in peace) and a wife from a merchant's family? Who would ever have believed it? Why, she hardly spoke four words to the general. All the while I kept giving her good advice. And she, the darling girl, said not a word against the match. If it pleases you, *maman,* she says, then I will readily agree, she says. . . ." "She is certainly a rare treasure in this dissolute age of ours!" answered Mavra Ilinishna's friends and acquaintances in different variations. Then the gossip started, along with the unconscionable blackening of other peoples' reputations.

Suffice it to say that a very short time elapsed before a team of black horses pulling a four-seater carriage decorated in *mordoré foncé* arrived at a splendidly appointed apartment. Inside the carriage sat General Negrov, dressed in his uniform with a fur-trimmed cape, and his spouse, Glafira Lvovna Negrova, in a heavenly wedding gown adorned with ribbons. The newlyweds were met by a choir, by elegantly attired best men, lights, music, gold, grandeur, and fragrances. All the servants stood in the entrance hall trying to catch a glimpse of the happy couple; even the valet's wife was there. Her own husband, as the highest-ranking servant, was in charge of the study and the bedchamber. The countess had never before seen such wealth firsthand, and now it was all hers, and the general himself was hers too. She was happy from the tip of her smallest toe to the end of the longest strand of hair in her braid. One way or another, all her dreams had come true.

One morning, several weeks after the wedding, Glafira Lvovna, as radiant as a cactus in bloom, wearing a white dressing gown trimmed with wide lace ruffles, was pouring tea. Her husband, wearing a gold-trimmed dressing gown made of fine Oriental silk and holding a huge amber pipe between his teeth, was lying on the sofa and ruminating on what kind of carriage he should order for Easter—a yellow one or a blue one. Yellow would be nice, but then again so would blue. Glafira Lvovna was also preoccupied with something; she forgot all about the teapot and was *pensively* resting her head on her hand. Sometimes her cheeks became flushed; then she displayed definite agitation. Finally, noticing her unusual state, her husband inquired, "Glashenka, is anything wrong? Are you feeling ill?"

"No, I am quite well," she answered and raised her eyes to him with the air of a person begging for help.

"Say what you may, but you do have something on your mind."

Glafira Lvovna stood up, went over to her husband, embraced him, and with the voice of a tragic actress said, "Aleksis, give me your word that you will grant my request."

Aleksis was startled. "We'll see, we'll see," he answered.

"No, Aleksis, swear by your mother's grave that you will grant my request."

He took the pipe out of his mouth and looked at her in amazement. "Glashenka, I dislike such circuitous approaches. I am a soldier: I shall do what I can, but tell me simply what it is."

She buried her face in his chest and wailed through her tears, "I know everything, Aleksis, and I forgive you. I know that you have a daughter, the fruit of forbidden love. . . .I understand inexperience, the passion of youth!" (Lyubonka was only three years old!) "Aleksis, she is your daughter. I have seen her: she has your nose, the shape of your head. . . .Oh, I love her so! Let her be my daughter. Allow me to take her in, to rear her, and give me your word that you will not seek revenge or persecute those from whom I have learned about all this. My dearest, I adore your daughter; please do not deny my request!" And her tears flowed abundantly onto his silk dressing gown.

His Excellency was confused and embarrassed in the highest degree. Even before he could recover his composure, his wife had forced him to grant his permission and to swear by his mother's grave, his father's remains, the happiness of their future offspring, and their own love, that he would neither go back on his word nor would he try to find out how she had discovered the secret.

And so the child who had been demoted to the servants' rank was once again promoted to the gentry. The little bed was carried back to the main house. Lyubonka, who had recently been instructed not to call her father "Papa," now had to learn not to call her mother "Mama." She was to be brought up thinking that Dunya was her wet nurse. Glafira Lvovna purchased some children's clothing in a shop on the Kuznetsky Bridge and dressed Lyubonka up like a doll. Then she pressed her to her bosom and wept.

"Little orphan," she said, "you have no papa and no mama. I will replace them both. Your papa is up there," she said pointing to heaven.

"Papa has wings," babbled the child.

Glafira Lvovna wept twice as hard as before and exclaimed, "Oh, heavenly simplicity!" But the fact of the matter was this: on the ceiling there was an old-fashioned picture of Cupid fluttering his legs and wings and fastening some sort of ribbon around the wrought iron hook from which the chandelier was suspended.

Dunya was as happy as could be. She considered Glafira an angel. Her gratitude contained not the slightest trace of hostility. Nor was she offended that her daughter was being taught that she was not really her daughter. She saw her dressed up in lace and living in the master's house. All she could say was, "How is it that my Lyubonka turned out to be so pretty? It would be impossible for her to wear any other clothing. She will become a real beauty!" Dunya made the rounds of all the convents and in each offered Te Deums for the health of her kind mistress.

Many people will consider the ex-countess a heroine, but I believe that her action was in and of itself extremely thoughtless—at least as thoughtless as her decision to marry a person about whom she knew only that he was both a man and a general. The reason is obvious: romantic ecstasy predisposed her to prefer above all else tragic scenes, self-sacrifice, forced acts of charity. Fairness demands that we add that Glafira Lvovna had no underhanded motives, not even the wish to satisfy her own vanity. She did not know why she wanted to rear Lyubonka: she simply liked the pathetic aspect of the whole affair. Once he had granted his consent, Aleksei Abramovich found the child's strange predicament perfectly normal and spent no time whatever deciding whether in giving his consent he had done a good thing or a bad one. And indeed, was his action good or bad? One could say a great deal both for and against his decision. He who considers development the highest goal of human life, no matter what the cost or consequence, will be on Glafira Lvovna's side. He who considers happiness the highest goal—contentment, no matter in what sphere and at whose expense achieved—will be against her.

If Lyubonka had been left in the servants' quarters and even if she had found out the truth about her birth, her ideas would have been so narrow, her soul in such a deep slumber, that she would never have understood anything at all. Probably, to ease his own conscience, Aleksei Abramovich would have given her freedom and perhaps even a thousand rubles or so as a dowry. With such narrow ideas she would have been extremely happy. She would have married a merchant of the Third Guild,[10] would have worn a silk scarf on her head, would have drunk up to twelve cups of choice tea a day, and would have given birth to a whole brood of merchant's children. On occasion she would have visited the wife of Negrov's valet and noticed with pleasure how her former friends all regarded her with envy. In such a way she might easily have lived to be a hundred and have hoped that a hundred cabs would accompany her bier to the Vagankov cemetery.

But since Lyubonka lived in the master's apartment, it was a completely different matter. However stupidly brought up, she had access to an education. The great distance from the crude ideas of the servants' quarters was a kind of education in itself. At the same time she had to accept the absurd incongruity of her position; insults, tears, and sorrows awaited her in the main house, and all this could foster the further development of her character and, perhaps, the onset of consumption at the same time. And so, decide the matter for yourself: did Madame Negrov do a good thing or a bad one?

The conjugal life of Aleksei Abramovich flowed along smoothly. His handsome carriage drawn by four horses was seen at all the right places, and in it sat the radiantly happy couple. One could doubtless encounter them in Sokolniki Park on the first day of May, in the Palace Garden on Ascension Day, at Presnensky Pond on All Souls' Day, and on Tverskoy Boulevard on almost any other day. During the winter they attended the Nobles' Assembly,[11] gave dinners, and had their own box at the theater. But terrible

---

10. *Third Guild.* A system of merchants' guilds was established by Peter the Great in 1721 and subsequently reorganized by Empress Elizabeth in 1742. Russian merchants were divided into three categories, depending on the amount of capital they possessed. The Third Guild was the lowest.

11. *Nobles' Assembly.* An organization of nobles established in 1766 and subdivided into provincial and district assemblies. It convened to examine and resolve questions that affected the nobility as a class.

monotony can destroy the diversions of Moscow: as it was last year, so it is this year, and so it will be next year. Just as then you met a fat merchant in a magnificent caftan,[12] accompanied by his wife decked out in precious stones and with decaying teeth, so too will you surely meet him again now. Only his caftan will be older, his beard whiter, his wife's teeth blacker. And you will keep on meeting him. Just as then you met a dashing fellow with a devastating mustache in a ridiculous frock coat, so too will you meet him now, but he will be somewhat the worse for wear. Just as then a gouty old man all sprinkled with snuff was taken out for a drive, so too will he be taken out now. As a consequence of this, one might wish to lock oneself up in one's own room.

Aleksei Abramovich was a man with stamina, but human fortitude has its limits. He could endure no more than ten years of this; both he and Glasha were fed up. During this time they produced both a son and a daughter; they started to gain weight, not merely by the day but by the hour; they no longer felt like getting dressed in the morning: they became homebodies. I don't know how or why, I suppose to ensure their absolute peace and quiet, but they decided to retire to the country. This occurred about four years prior to the general's learned conversation with Dmitry Yakovlevich.

12. *Caftan.* A long-sleeved robe tied at the waist with a sash.

Chapter 3

The Biography of Dmitry Yakovlevich

Needless to say, the biography of a poor young man cannot possibly be as entertaining as that of Aleksei Abramovich and his household. We must now move from the world of carriages decorated in *mordoré foncé* to one where people are concerned with providing for tomorrow's meals, move from Moscow to a distant provincial town. Even at that, we will not stop on the one paved street in town on which all the aristocrats live and along which they sometimes ride. Instead we must make our way down one of the unpaved alleys, along which it is almost always impossible either to walk or ride. There we must seek out a blackened, crooked little house with three windows, belonging to the district physician Krutsifersky, a house that stands humbly among its blackened and crooked comrades. All of these houses will soon collapse and be replaced by new ones. No one will remember them. In the meantime, life goes on; in each house passions seethe and one generation replaces another. There is as little known about these creatures as there is about aborigines in Australia, as if they too had gone unrecognized, placed outside the law by mankind.

But look, here is the little house that we are seeking. For the last thirty years or so, a kind, honest old man and his wife have been living here. The man's life has been a continual struggle with every possible hardship and deprivation. True, he has emerged relatively victorious, that is, he has neither perished from hunger, nor has he shot himself in despair; but this victory has been achieved at considerable cost. At the age of fifty he is already grey-haired, thin, and wrinkled, but nature has provided him with an ample supply of strength and health. It was not violent impulses, passions, or traumatic upheavals that so wore down his body and made him appear prematurely decrepit; rather, it was the uninterrupted, severe, petty, humiliating struggle against hardship, a concern for tomorrow, a life spent in deprivation and distress. Among these lower orders of society the soul pines and withers away from constant anxiety, forgetting that it too possesses wings. Restricted to the earth forever, it can never raise its eyes toward the sun.

Dr. Krutsifersky's life was a huge, prolonged heroic struggle in pursuit of an unrecognized career; his reward was his bread for that day and the prospect of not being able to procure the same for tomorrow. He had studied at Moscow University at public expense and graduated as a physician; before accepting an appointment, he married a German woman, the daughter of a pharmacist. Over and above her kind, self-sacrificing soul and the love that in true German fashion she maintained for him as long as she lived, her dowry consisted of a few dresses saturated with the smell of rose oil mixed with rhubarb. He was so passionately in love with her that it never even occurred to him that he had no right to enjoy either love or family happiness, that there exist special requirements for enjoying these rights, similar to the French electoral qualifications.[1] A few days after his wedding he was appointed regimental doctor to the army in the field. He endured eight years of nomadic existence; during the ninth he grew weary of it and requested a permanent post. They offered him one of the first available vacancies. And so

1. *Electoral qualifications.* During the so-called July Monarchy in France (1830–48), voting privileges were restricted to men possessing considerable wealth. The qualifications were so strict that in 1846 only 0.6 percent of the population was eligible to vote.

Krutsifersky moved with his wife and children from one end of Russia to the other and settled in the provincial town of N.[2]

At first he had a modest practice. Although landowners and officials living in provincial towns prefer German doctors, fortunately there were no Germans living in town, except for the watchmaker. This was the happiest period in Krutsifersky's life; it was then that he purchased his small house with three windows. His wife Margarita Karlovna, as a surprise to her husband on his name day, worked all night covering their old sofa and armchairs in chintz; she had saved up the money one kopeck at a time. The chintz was of excellent quality. It depicted Abraham driving Hagar and Ishmael off the sofa and onto the floor three times, while Sarah threatened them. The right side of the armchair showed the feet of Abraham, Hagar, Ishmael, and Sarah; the left side showed their heads.[3]

But this happy time did not go on for long. A certain wealthy landowner whose village was located just outside of town engaged a doctor for his own household who took away Krutsifersky's entire practice. The young doctor was an expert in treating women's ailments, and his patients were all half in love with him. He treated them by applying leeches and by declaring eloquently that not only are all illnesses inflammations but that life itself is nothing more than an inflammation of matter. He referred to Krutsifersky with devasting condescension; in a word, the young doctor became the rage. The whole town embroidered pillow cases and tobacco pouches for him, presented him with souvenirs and surprises, and tried to forget all about the old doctor. True, the merchants and priests remained faithful to Krutsifersky, but the merchants were never ill: they all enjoyed good health, thank the Lord. And if by chance they did get sick, then they would treat themselves by going to the

2. *The town of N.* The standard Russian literary convention for indicating a location anonymously.

3. *Heads.* In Genesis 21:9–14, after Sarah bore Abraham a legitimate son (Isaac), Abraham, acting on God's command and Sarah's urging, banished his Egyptian mistress (Hagar) and their illegitimate son (Ishmael) from the kingdom.

bathhouse, where they would smear and anoint themselves with all sorts of rubbish—turpentine, tar, spirit-of-ants;[4] then they always either recovered or expired within a few days. In either case, there was nothing further for Krutsifersky to do, though he was always blamed if they died. Every time, the young doctor would remark to the ladies, "How strange that Yakov Ivanovich Krutsifersky, who knows medicine so well, did not think to prescribe *trae opii Sydhenhamii* [take Sydenham's opium], ten drops, *solutum in aqua distillata* [dissolved in distilled water] and that he did not think to apply forty-five leeches to the pit of the stomach.[5] That man would still be alive today!" Upon hearing these Latin words, even the governor's wife was convinced that the man would still be alive today.

So Krutsifersky was gradually reduced to living on his salary alone; it consisted, I think, of about four hundred rubles. Since he had five children, his life became more and more difficult. Yakov Ivanovich did not know how to provide for them, but scarlet fever showed him one way. Three children died of it, one after another, leaving only the eldest daughter and the youngest son alive. The boy, it seems, escaped death and illness by virtue of his own extraordinary weakness. He was born prematurely, hardly breathing; he was weak, thin, sickly, and nervous. There were a few occasions when he was less ill, but at no time was he ever really healthy.

The child's misfortunes had begun even before his birth. During Margarita Karlovna's pregnancy an awful catastrophe nearly befell them. The governor developed a strong dislike for Krutsifersky [because he had refused to sign a certificate testifying to the natural death of a coachman who had actually been flogged to death by a certain landowner].[6] Yakov Ivanovich was close to ruin; he awaited the final blow selflessly and silently, with a kind of gentle, heroic

4. *Spirit-of-ants.* Formic acid, a substance found in ants and spiders as well as in nettles, which is irritating to the skin.

5. *Sydhenhamii.* A strong medicinal tonic derived from opium, developed by the English physician Thomas Sydenham (1624–89).

6. *Landowner.* These lines were omitted by the censor [author's note].

sadness—but the blow passed him by. It was during this difficult period of constant tears that Mitya was born—the only one who was ever really punished for the coachman's death. The child became Margarita Karlovna's idol; the more sickly and weak he became, the more stubbornly she resolved to keep him alive. It was as if she shared her own strength with him; her love revived him and snatched him away from the jaws of death. It was as though she felt that he could be their sole support, hope, and consolation.

But what became of his sister? She was seventeen when an infantry regiment was stationed in their town; when it left, the doctor's daughter left too, with a certain lieutenant. A year later she wrote from Kiev, begging her parents' forgiveness and their blessing and informing them that the lieutenant had married her. Another year after that she wrote from Kishinev saying that her husband had left her, that she had a small child, and that she was in great distress. Her father sent her twenty-five rubles. After that nothing more was heard from her.

When Mitya was old enough, they sent him to the gymnasium. He was a good student, always shy, gentle, and quiet. He became the inspector's favorite, even though the inspector considered it incompatible with his own position to be fond of children. After Mitya completed his studies, his father hoped to find him employment in the civil governor's office. The governor's secretary, whose eternally scrofulous children the doctor treated free of charge, had promised to assist him in arranging something. Suddenly Mitya was presented with a different opportunity. A certain philanthropic privy counselor was passing through town en route from his country estate to Moscow. [The director of the gymnasium, who had the uncanny ability to sense the approach of privy counselors, went to him at once and asked him to do them the honor of visiting their "hothouse" and "garden plot" of national education. This Russian Maecenas[7] was not very eager, although he did enjoy warm welcomes, especially deferential ones. The director, dressed in full uniform, holding his hat and his sword,

7. *Maecenas.* Gaius Maecenas (d. 8 B.C.) was a Roman statesman and munificent patron of letters who enjoyed a close association with the emperor Augustus.

explained in great detail to this patron (who was not the least bit interested), why the school vestibule was damp and why the stairs were crooked. All the pupils were assembled in a straight line; the teachers, extremely well groomed, wearing tightly knotted ties, walked around anxiously, casting worried glances at their students and at the night watchman, who preserved more presence of mind than anyone else. The physics teacher asked His Excellency for permission to kill a rabbit under the bell glass of a pneumatic machine, and a pigeon in a Leyden jar. The patron requested that the animals be spared. The director, whose heart was genuinely touched, looked at his teachers and pupils as if to say, "Greatness is always accompanied by magnanimity." (Afterward the pigeon and rabbit resided in the night watchman's locker until graduation, at which time the relentless teacher sacrificed them anyway to the cause of science and education, to the great enjoyment of the assembled crowd of townspeople.) Then one of the pupils stepped forward, and the French teacher asked, "Didn't he have something to say on the occasion of this grand visit to their 'garden of learning'?" At once the pupil began a speech in a strange Franco-ecclesiastical dialect: "*Coman puvonn nu pover anfan remersier lilustre visiter?*" ["How can we poor children show our gratitude to our illustrious visitor?"].

As the patron looked around during this Celto-Slavonic speech, he was somehow attracted][8] by Mitya's sickly and delicate appearance; he called the boy over, spoke to him, and showed him kindness. The director said that Mitya was an excellent student and that he could go far, but that his father was unable to support him in Moscow, etc., etc. This Maecenas, being a philanthropist, told Mitya that in a month or two his steward would come and that if his parents agreed he would take Mitya to Moscow. There Mitya could occupy a small room in the wing of his house where the steward's children lived. The director immediately dispatched his clerk to fetch Yakov Ivanovich. Dr. Krutsifersky arrived to find the patron just climbing into his dormeuse[9] to depart. The old man was

---

8. *Attracted.* This passage was omitted by the censor [author's note].
9. *Dormeuse.* A traveling carriage adapted for sleeping.

genuinely touched. He wept like a child, and in his simple, awkward, abrupt manner he thanked the patron, who pointed to a broad-shouldered man helping to fasten some straps on the carriage and said, "That is my steward. He will come to fetch your son." Having uttered these words, he smiled benevolently and departed.

A month later a covered sledge with bells drove out of Dr. Krutsifersky's gate; inside sat Mitya. He was wrapped in a blanket, fashioned and arranged by his mother. The steward was wearing nothing but a jacket, since he preferred to warm himself from the inside out all along the way.

And so it is that man's fate depends on events such as these. If the patron had never passed through the town of N., Mitya would have gone to work in an office and there would have been no story to relate. In time Mitya would have become senior assistant to the office manager and would have supported his aging parents on his meager earnings, while Yakov Ivanovich and Margarita Karlovna would have enjoyed their retirement. As it was, Mitya's departure marked a turning point in the life of his aging parents. They were left alone; silence and melancholy took possession of their household even more. The patron's steward, not a particularly sentimental man, felt something like a tear in his eye during the parents' parting with their son.

A poor father bids his son farewell quite unlike a wealthy one: he says, "Go forth, my boy, to earn your daily bread. I can do no more for you. Make your own way, but do not forget us!" Whether they would ever see each other again, whether he would even earn his daily bread—all that was hidden by a thick, dark veil. The father wishes to provide his son with a little bit more for the journey, but he simply cannot. Ten times over he calculates how much he might spare from his personal savings of some eighty rubles, and it always seems like too little. The mother sheds so many tears over the meager bundle in which she has wrapped all the necessary items. She understands that it is not enough, yet she knows that there is nothing more that she can do. . . .These scenes, known to no one else, are familiar only in petty bourgeois families; they are carefully hidden away from others, although they are pitiful and heartrending scenes! And a good thing it is that they are hidden!

Four years later the young Krutsifersky received his candiate's degree.[10] He was not endowed with particularly brilliant abilities, nor with extremely quick understanding; but given his deep love for learning and his persistent diligence, his degree was well deserved. Looking at his gentle face, one might conclude that he would develop into one of those pleasant Germanic types—quiet, noble, happy in a somewhat limited but extremely industrious pedagogical activity and in a somewhat limited family circle, one in which the husband would still be in love with his wife twenty years after their marriage and the wife would still blush at any joke containing a double entendre. Such lives as these are still to be found in small, traditional towns in Germany; often they are lived by pastors and seminary teachers—pure, moral beings, unknown outside their own circles. But is such a life even possible here in our country? I am firmly convinced that it is not. That kind of milieu is not well suited to our souls. Our thirst cannot be quenched by drinking such watered-down wine; our life is either much above or far below that one, but in either case it is much broader.

Having received his candidate's degree, Krutsifersky attempted first to procure an appointment at the university; then he tried to support himself by giving private lessons. But all of these attempts were in vain. He had obviously inherited his father's aptitude for success in all endeavors! A few months after the kettledrums and trumpets had heralded the awarding of Krutsifersky's degree, he received a letter from his father informing him that his mother was ill and referring in passing to their strained circumstances. Knowing his father's character well, Krutsifersky realized that only the most terrible need could force him to make such an admission. Krutsifersky had spent all of his money, and only one avenue remained open. He had a patron, a professor in some field of learning or other, who took a sincere interest in him. Krutsifersky wrote him a frank, noble, touching letter and asked him for a loan of one hundred fifty rubles. The professor was moved by the letter, answered in a very polite manner, but did not send any money. In a postscript the learned man reprimanded Krutsifersky in the kindest

10. *Degree.* See chap. 1, n. 1.

possible manner for never coming to have dinner with him. The reply astonished the young man, so little did he know about what people were worth or, more accurately, what money was worth. He was very depressed. He tossed the gracious professor's kind note onto the table and paced back and forth. Then, completely overcome by his sorrows, he threw himself onto his bed; tears flowed quietly down his cheeks. He could imagine so vividly the shabby room in which his mother lay—weak, suffering, perhaps even dying. Next to her sat his father, saddened and crushed by misfortune. The patient would want something, but she would hide it, so as not to increase her husband's misery; but he would guess what it was, and would also hide it, fearing that he would have to refuse her. Dear reader, if you are wealthy or even comfortable, then offer your heartfelt gratitude to heaven. Long live inherited wealth! Long live patrimonial and honestly acquired wealth!

At this awful moment in the candidate's life, the door of his room suddenly opened, and in stepped a strange sort of person, clearly not a resident of the capital. He took off his dark cap with its huge visor, revealing the healthy, ruddy, cheerful face of a middle-aged man. His features reflected an epicurean composure and good nature. He was dressed in a well-worn brown frock coat with an old-fashioned collar and was carrying a bamboo walking stick; as we have already observed, he possessed the appearance of a provincial fellow.

"Are you Mr. Krutsifersky, candidate of Moscow University?"

"I am," said Dmitry Yakovlevich, "at your service."

"First, Mr. Candidate, allow me to be seated; I am older than you are, and I have come on foot."

With these words he was about to sit down on a chair over which Krutsifersky's uniform was draped. But it turned out that this chair could bear only the weight of an empty uniform, not that of a man in a frock coat. Krutsifersky was embarrassed and asked him to sit on the bed, while he himself took the only other chair.

"I am Doctor Krupov," the visitor began with exasperating deliberateness, "inspector of the Medical Board in the town of N. I have come to see you on the following business. . . ."

The inspector was a methodical man. He stopped, took out a

large snuffbox, and placed it beside him. Then he took out a red handkerchief and placed it next to the snuffbox, then a white hand-kerchief to wipe away the perspiration on his face. Taking a pinch of tobacco, he continued, "Yesterday I went to see Anton Ferdi-nandovich. He and I were classmates—no, excuse me, he gradu-ated a year before me; yes, a year before me; that's it precisely. Even so, we were comrades then and have remained good friends to this very day. Well, then, I went to ask him if he could recommend a good tutor for a family in our district. I told him that the terms would be thus and such, the demands thus and such. Anton Ferdi-nandovich gave me your address. I must confess, he recommended you most highly. Therefore, if you wish to leave here and accept the position, you and I can come to an agreement."

Anton Ferdinandovich was none other than Krutsifersky's pro-fessor-patron. He was really very fond of Krutsifersky, although, as we have seen, he was not eager to risk any of his own money. But he was always ready to provide a recommendation.

The ponderous Dr. Krupov appeared to Krutsifersky as a mes-senger from heaven. He explained his predicament frankly and ended by saying that he had no choice but to accept the position. Krupov pulled out of his pocket something halfway between a wallet and a suitcase and took from it a letter that was stashed away among curved scissors, lancets, and probes. He read the following: "Offer the applicant two thousand rubles a year, at the most twen-ty-five hundred, because for three thousand my neighbor hired a French tutor from Switzerland. A room of his own, continental breakfast, servant, laundry, as usual. Dinner with the family."

Krutsifersky made no further demands and blushed when the salary was discussed. He inquired about the lessons and openly confessed that he was scared to death of entering an unfamiliar household and of living among strangers. Krupov was deeply moved and tried to persuade him not to be afraid of the Negrovs. "You are not marrying into their family; you will tutor the young lad and will see his father and mother at dinner. The general will not underpay you, of that I can assure you. His wife is always asleep—so she can do you no harm—except in her dreams. Believe me, the Negrovs' home is no worse and, I must confess, no better

than all other landowners' homes." In a word, the deal was concluded: Krutsifersky rented himself out for twenty-five hundred
rubles a year.

Inspector Krupov had become a lazy man as a result of his
provincial existence, but he remained a human being. He had
learned from a series of bitter experiences that beautiful dreams and
majestic words remain only that—dreams and words. Then he had
settled down in the town of N. forever and gradually learned to
speak slowly and deliberately, to carry two handkerchiefs in his
pocket—one red and one white. Nothing in the world can spoil a
man so much as life in the provinces, but Krupov had not yet
become extinct; sparks still flickered in his eyes. His soul was
profoundly affected by the sight of this pure, noble young man. He
recalled the time when he and Anton Ferdinandovich had dreamt
of effecting a revolution in medicine, of traveling to Göttingen on
foot[11]. . . and he smiled bitterly at those recollections.

When the deal was concluded, he suddenly thought to himself,
"Am I doing right in pushing this young man into the fatuous life
of a landowner half lost in the steppes?" He even considered lend-
ing him some money himself and persuading him not to leave
Moscow. Fifteen years ago he would have done just that, but aging
hands find it terribly hard to undo purse strings. "It is fate!"
thought Krupov, and consoled himself thus. It is a strange thing,
but in this case he behaved exactly as people have from time imme-
morial. Napoleon used to say that fate is a word that has no meaning—which is precisely why it is so consoling.

"And so, it's all settled," said the inspector at last, after a brief
pause. "I am leaving in five days and will be very glad if you would
share my coach."

11. *Göttingen.* Site of a German university founded in 1737 and known officially
as Georg August University of Göttingen. It became the center of German cultural and political life in the early nineteenth century, and many young Russian
noblemen went there to obtain a Western education.

Chapter 4

Daily Humdrum

It has long been accepted that human beings can adapt to any environment—from Lapland to Senegal. Therefore there is nothing surprising about the fact that Krutsifersky gradually became accustomed to the Negrov household. At first he was astonished by the way of life, opinions, and interests of these people; then he became indifferent to them, although he could by no means reconcile himself to their life. While there was nothing striking or unusual about the Negrov household, a fresh young man nevertheless found it difficult to breathe there. Absolute and multifaceted emptiness reigned in the respectable household of Aleksei Abramovich. Why these people got out of bed in the morning, why they moved around, why they lived out their lives—it would be hard to provide answers for these questions. But there really is no need to answer them. These good people lived simply because they had been born into the world; they continued living according to their instinct of self-preservation. Why even talk about purposes and motives? All that is borrowed from German philosophy!

The general arose at 7 A.M. and immediately entered the drawing room, smoking a heavy cherry-wood pipe. Any stranger coming in at that time might have concluded that important projects and ideas were seething inside his head. He looked so serious as he smoked; but the only thing seething was the smoke—and not inside his head, but around it. This deeply thoughtful smoking lasted for about an hour. All the while Aleksei Abramovich paced quietly in the drawing room, often pausing in front of the window and looking out very attentively. Then he screwed up his eyes, wrinkled his forehead, looked extremely dissatisfied, and groaned; but all of this was the same kind of optical illusion as his general air of thoughtfulness. Meanwhile the steward remained standing near the door, next to the servant boy. After he finished smoking, Aleksei Abramovich turned to the steward, received his report, and began abusing him in the worst possible way. Time after time he repeated that he was well aware of the steward's worth, that he knew exactly how to treat crooks, and that as a lesson for all he would demote the steward to looking after the poultry and dispatch his son to the army.[1]

It is difficult to say whether this was another manifestation of the general's regimen of moral hygiene, similar to his daily cold bath, a measure employed to reinforce fear and obedience among his vassals, or whether it was simply a patriarchal habit. In either case his persistence deserved praise. The steward listened to these paternal admonitions with silent humility; he considered that listening was the same kind of necessary obligation connected with his office as stealing wheat, barley, hay, and straw. "You thief, you!" shouted the general. "Hang you three times, and still it wouldn't suffice!" "Just as you wish, Your Excellency," the steward answered with supreme serenity, casting a knavish glance obliquely at the floor.

This conversation lasted until the children arrived to say good morning; Aleksei Abramovich held out his hand to each. They were accompanied by a diminutive French lady who managed to efface herself by drawing into herself and curtseying in the manner

---

1. *Army.* Peter the Great introduced a system of national conscription in 1699 under which a proportion of the male population served for an "unlimited period," i.e., for life. The Empress Anna later fixed the term of service at twenty-five years. Since the gentry and clergy were exempt, conscripts were usually drawn from the peasantry, the selection being made by the landowners. Conditions in the army were extremely harsh.

of Madame Pompadour. She announced that tea was served. Aleksei Abramovich entered the sitting room where Glafira Lvovna was already awaiting him by the samovar. The conversation was usually begun by Glafira Lvovna, who complained about her health and insomnia. She suffered from an inexplicable, pulsating pain in her right temple that moved around to the back of her head, then up to the crown, and prevented her from sleeping. Aleksei Abramovich listened rather indifferently to this bulletin on his wife's health—I don't know whether it was because he was the only one alive who knew for sure that his wife *never* stirred during the night or because he clearly understood that this chronic ailment had a generally beneficial effect on his wife's health. On the other hand, Eliza Avgustovna (the French lady) was horrified by the account; she felt deep sympathy for the sufferer and comforted her by saying that both Princess R., with whom she had previously resided, and Countess M., with whom she could have resided had she wished to, also suffer from a similar sort of pulsating pain, which they refer to as a *tic douloureux* [nervous tic].

During morning tea, the chef came in. The worthy couple set about ordering dinner and reproaching the chef for yesterday's meal, even though only plates licked clean had been cleared from the table. The chef had a certain advantage over the steward, inasmuch as he was abused daily not only by the master (as was the steward) but also by the mistress.

After tea Aleksei Abramovich set off for the fields. Although he had spent several consecutive years living in the country, he had made very little progress in understanding agronomy. He criticized trivial failures; most of all he loved discipline and the appearance of unconditional submission. The most flagrant thievery took place under his very nose, but he rarely noticed it; when he did, he dealt with it so badly that he always wound up looking like a fool. As the genuine head and father of the community, he would often say, "I can pardon a thief and a scoundrel, but I cannot tolerate insolence." This constituted his patriarchal *point d'honneur* [point of honor].

Except for special occasions, Glafira Lvovna never left the house on foot, with the obvious exception of visits to her venerable garden. As a result of benign neglect, this garden, which began right under her balcony, had become quite splendid. She even went out to gather mushrooms in a carriage. This feat was accomplished in the following manner. On the preceding evening the village elder was ordered to assemble a host of village boys and girls with bags, baskets, containers, etc. Glafira Lvovna and the Frenchwoman rode along very slowly, while hosts of barefoot, half-naked, under-fed children, under the direction of the old woman who looked after the poultry, together with the landowner's own son and daughter, searched for mushrooms of all shapes and sizes.[2] Any mushroom that was particularly large or very tiny was carried by the poultry woman to the "general's lady"; after she had admired it, they would drive on. Upon returning home she would infallibly complain of fatigue and would retire before dinner, having first fortified herself with the leftovers of yesterday's supper—milk-fed lamb or veal, turkey raised on walnuts, or something of that sort—a light and tasty snack.

Meanwhile, Aleksei Abramovich had taken a drink of vodka, followed it with a little hors d'oeuvre, repeated this ritual a second time,[3] and then set off for a walk in the garden. It was at precisely such times that he loved to stroll through the garden and busy himself with the greenhouse. He would address all his questions to the gardener's wife, who to her dying day was unable to distinguish between a pear tree and an apple tree, a fact that did not prevent her from having a very pleasant appearance.

It was also at this time, that is, about an hour and a half before dinner, that "Madame" would devote herself to the children's education. What exactly and how she taught them remains a deep, dark secret. Both father and mother were satisfied. Aside from them, who else had the right to meddle in family affairs?

Dinner was served at two o'clock. Each course was sufficient to kill anyone accustomed to European cuisine. Fat, fat, and more fat, scarcely tempered by cabbage, onion, and pickled mushrooms,

2. *Mushrooms.* Herzen specifies five varieties: yellow-brown boletus (*Boletus luteus*), woolly milk cap (*Lactarius terminosus*), russula (*Russula*), saffron milk cap (*Lactarius deliciosus*), and edible boletus (*Boletus edulis*).

3. *Ritual.* Russians traditionally "chase" their vodka with a tasty morsel. (The word *zakuska*—snack, hors d'oeuvre, means literally "the bite after.")

with the assistance of a sufficient quantity of Madeira and port, was incorporated into the resilient body of Aleksei Abramovich, into the abundant flesh of Glafira Lvovna, and into the wrinkled body that barely covered the bones of Eliza Avgustovna. By the way, Eliza Avgustovna did not lag far behind Aleksei Abramovich in her consumption of Madeira. (Witness the advances made in the nineteenth century; during the eighteenth, governesses were not permitted to drink wine at the master's table.) She assured him that in her native Lausanne her family owned a small vineyard, that at home she always drank homemade Madeira instead of kvass, and that she had grown quite accustomed to it.

After dinner the general lay down on the couch in his study for a half-hour's nap that always lasted much longer, while Glafira Lvovna retired to the parlor with the French lady. The governess chatted on endlessly, and Glafira Lvovna would doze off in the middle of her interminable stories. Sometimes, for variety's sake, Glafira Lvovna would summon the wife of the village priest. She was an unsociable, inarticulate woman—always anxious and afraid of something. Glafira Lvovna would spend hours with her and then remark to the French lady, "*Ah, comme elle est bête, insupportable!* ["Ah, how stupid she is, it's intolerable!"]. And as a matter of fact, the priest's wife was unbearably stupid.

Then came teatime, followed by supper around ten o'clock. After supper, yawns would engulf the entire family, and Glafira Lvovna would remark that when living in the country one should do as country folk do—that is, go to bed early. With this announcement the family would disperse. By eleven o'clock the entire household, from the stables to the attic, was snoring loudly.

Occasionally a neighbor would drop by for a visit—someone exactly like Negrov, only with a different last name; or else an old aunt would arrive from the provincial town, possessed by a desire to recruit suitors for her daughters. The order of their life would be temporarily disturbed; but after the guests departed, everything returned to normal.

Needless to say, in spite of all these occupations there still remained plenty of time that no one knew how to use—especially on inclement autumn days and on long winter evenings. All of the

French lady's resources were employed to fill these gaps. It should be noted that she did indeed have many stories to tell. She had arrived in Russia during the last years of Catherine's reign and had worked as a seamstress with a French troupe of actors. Her husband was the second leading man, but unfortunately the Petersburg climate proved fatal to him, especially after he was thrown out of a second-story window by a sergeant of the guard for having defended the honor of a certain actress with more zeal than was appropriate for a married man. No doubt he had failed to take the necessary precautions against the damp night air during his fall. From that moment on he began to cough; he coughed for two months, and then he stopped coughing, for the very simple reason that he also stopped breathing.

Eliza Avgustovna became a widow at precisely the time when a husband becomes most useful, that is, when she was just about thirty years old. She wept for a while and then found a job nursing a man who was suffering from gout. Subsequently she became a governess to the daughter of a very tall widower; then she joined the household of some princess or other, and so on and so forth. The whole story is too long to tell. Suffice it to say that she adapted to the ways of new households very easily. She was taken into their confidence and soon made herself indispensable. She carried out both public and private commissions, managing throughout to retain an aura of deference and subservience. She yielded to her patrons and anticipated their every desire. In a word, she did not find other people's stairs too steep to climb, nor other people's bread too bitter to eat.[4] Always chuckling and forever knitting stockings, she enjoyed a carefree existence, living in clover. She was so involved in all the little affairs that occurred between the maids' quarters and the master's bedroom that she never realized how pitiful her own existence was.

And so Eliza Avgustovna was able to disperse the boredom with her tales, while Aleksei Abramovich played solitaire and Glafira Lvovna sat on the divan doing nothing. Eliza Avgustovna knew

4. *"Too bitter to eat."* A reference to Dante's *Paradiso*, XVII, 58: "You shall come to know how bitter is the taste of another man's bread, how hard the path to descend and mount by another man's stairs."

thousands of stories about the escapades and intrigues of her various "benefactors" (as she referred to those people whose children she had cared for). She related them with significant additions, and in every story she always ascribed to herself the main role— whether it was a good one or a bad one. Aleksei Abramovich listened with even greater interest than his wife to these scandalous chronicles related by the governess of his own children; he roared with laughter and declared that she was not a "French lady" at all but a veritable treasure. In this manner day followed day, time passed, marked sometimes by holidays and fastdays, by the lengthening and shortening of daylight, by name days and birthdays. Glafira Lvovna would say in astonishment, "My goodness, the day after tomorrow will be Christmas, yet it seems as if the first snowfall occurred only yesterday."

Where was Lyubonka's place in all of this, that poor child who was being reared by the kind Negrovs? We have forgotten all about her! She is more to blame than are we; her role in the patriarchal family circle was largely silent. She took almost no part whatever in events and thus introduced a dissonant note into the otherwise harmonious chord struck by other members of the family.

There was much that was strange about Lyubonka. Her face, though full of natural energy, managed to express imperturbable apathy and coldness. She was so indifferent to everything that Glafira Lvovna sometimes found it intolerable and called her a cold-blooded Englishwoman, although there were considerable grounds for questioning the Andalusian nature of the general's wife.[5] Lyubonka's face resembled her father's, except for the pair of dark blue eyes that she had inherited from Dunya. But this resemblance to the general contained such an incomprehensible contradiction that Lavater could have written another whole volume of florid prose about these two faces.[6] Aleksei Abramovich's severe

5. *Andalusian nature.* Presumably the hot-tempered, passionate "Latin" temperament.
6. *Lavater.* Johann Kaspar Lavater (1741–1801) was a Swiss theologian and scientist who wrote a pseudoscientific treatise entitled *Physiognomy* (1789–98), in which he theorized that the shape of a person's face and skull determines his or her mental ability and talents.

features, although imprinted on Lyubonka's face, were somehow compensated for, as it were. Examining her face one could see that Negrov had indeed possessed genuine abilities—ones that had first been suppressed and then destroyed by his life. Her face explained his. Looking at her, one could somehow accept him. But why was she always so pensive? Why did nothing amuse her? Why did she prefer sitting alone in her room? In fact, there were many reasons, both internal and external. Let us begin with the latter.

Her position in the general's house was in no way enviable—not because the Negrovs wanted to turn her out or to make things difficult for her. Rather it was that these people, so filled with prejudices and so lacking in the delicacy that only a cultured upbringing can provide, were unknowingly vulgar. Neither the general nor his wife understood Lyubonka's strange position in their household, and they added to its burden unnecessarily, grating on the most delicate strings of her heart. Negrov's stern and sometimes arrogant nature offended her deeply, often unintentionally. But he also offended her intentionally, though without understanding the impact of his words on anyone with a soul more sensitive than his steward's. Nor was he aware of the need to be more cautious with a defenseless girl—at the same time both his daughter and not his daughter—who was living in his household by right and through his charity. This kind of delicacy was inconceivable in a man like Negrov; it never really occurred to him that the girl might be offended by his words. Indeed, *who was she* to be offended?

Eager to strengthen Lyubonka's love for Glafira Lvovna, Aleksei Abramovich often told the young girl that for the rest of her life it was her duty to pray for his wife's well-being; that she owed all her happiness to his wife alone; that if it were not for her, she would have remained a maid, instead of becoming a lady. He rarely missed a chance to remind her that although she was being given the same upbringing as his own children, nonetheless an enormous abyss separated her from them. When she turned sixteen, Negrov looked at every unmarried man as a possible suitor for her. If an assessor from town came by with a document to be signed, if a rumor began to circulate about some new local petty landowner, Aleksei Abramovich would say in poor Lyubonka's presence: "It would be a fine thing to match up that assessor with our Lyubonka, wouldn't it? It would get her off my hands and be a good match for her. She can't expect to marry a count, can she?"

Lyubonka was less oppressed by Glafira Lvovna. On some occasions Glafira was even nice to Lyubonka in her own way; she would force her to eat even though she was sated, would give her sweets between meals, and so on. Still the poor girl suffered considerably at her hands. Glafira Lvovna thought it necessary, when introducing Lyubonka to one of her new acquaintances, to add: "She is an orphan who is being brought up with my own children." Then she would start whispering. Lyubonka knew what they were discussing and would grow pale and blush with shame, especially when, after hearing the secret explanation, the provincial lady would cast a haughty glance at her, accompanied by an ambiguous little smile.

As of late Glafira Lvovna had changed somewhat in her attitude toward the "orphan"; a thought had occurred to her that might have resulted in terrible consequences for Lyubonka. In spite of all her maternal blindness, Glafira Lvovna had somehow managed to discern that her own daughter, Liza—fat, red-cheeked, bearing a close resemblance to her mother but with the addition of a vacuous expression—would always be eclipsed by Lyubonka's noble appearance. Lyubonka's pensiveness, over and above her beauty, lent a special quality to her face, something that made it impossible not to take notice of her. Once Glafira Lvovna had discerned this, she was in total agreement with Aleksei Abramovich that if a dear little secretary or a nice little assessor turned up, Lyubonka should be married off. The poor girl could not help noticing this.

In addition to all this, Lyubonka was oppressed by her surroundings. Her relations to the servants, including her "wet nurse," were very awkward. The housemaids regarded her as an upstart; faithful to the aristocratic way of thinking, they considered only the nobly born Liza to be a genuine lady. When they realized how extremely meek and mild Lyubonka was, when they observed that she never tattled on them to Glafira Lvovna, they lost all their respect for her. At moments of indignation they would say, nearly audibly, "No matter how you dress 'em up, a lackey's always a lackey. There's nothing ladylike about her looks or her manners." All of these things are mere trifles, unworthy of attention, when considered from the point of view of eternity. But let him who has experienced such a series of demeaning insults and offensive epithets, let him, or rather let her, say whether or not it is so easy to endure them.

To crown Lyubonka's adversities, Aleksei Abramovich's aunt, who lived in the provincial town, would on occasion arrive for a visit, along with her three daughters. The old woman was a wicked, half-crazy bigot. She couldn't stand the sight of the poor girl and treated her with contempt. "For what reason, my dear," she said shaking her head in disapproval, "are you so dressed up? Huh? Answer me, if you please. You might, my dear, be mistaken for my own daughters' equal. Glafira Lvovna, why do you spoil her so? Her aunt Marfushka is my servant and looks after the poultry. So what is all this for, I ask? Aleksei Abramovich, the old sinner, should be ashamed of himself in front of decent folk!" She always concluded these offensive remarks with a prayer that the good Lord forgive her nephew for the terrible sin that had resulted in Lyubonka's birth. This aunt's daughters, three provincial Graces, the eldest of whom had, for the last two or three years, stopped aging in that fatal twenty-ninth year, did not speak with such parental bluntness; still, they always made sure that Lyubonka was well aware of all their condescension. Lyubonka did not openly reveal how deeply these scenes offended her; people around her could not see it or understand it, unless it was pointed out and explained to them. But when Lyubonka retired to her room, she wept bitterly. . . .She could not rise above such insults—I doubt that any girl in her situation could have. Glafira Lvovna felt sorry for Lyubonka, but it never occurred to her to protect the girl or to voice her own disapproval. Instead she usually limited her favors to a double portion of preserves. After bidding farewell to her aunt with a great show of affection and begging that her *chère tante* [dear aunt] not forget them, she would subsequently remark to the French lady that she couldn't stand the old woman; that after every one of her visits she felt an attack of nerves and an indefinable pulsating pain that began in her left temple and threatened to move around to the back of her head.

It is even necessary to mention that Lyubonka's education was in conformity with all the rest? Except for Eliza Avgustovna, no one provided her with lessons of any sort. Eliza tutored the children only in French grammar, in spite of the fact that she herself could not understand the mysteries of French spelling and to her dying day wrote the language with serious errors. She never attempted to teach anything except grammar, although she claimed to have prepared two sons of a certain princess for entrance into university. There were very few books to be found in Negrov's house. Aleksei Abramovich had none himself; on the other hand, Glafira Lvovna was in possession of a small library. A bookcase stood in the drawing room. Its upper shelf was occupied by a festive tea service that was never used. The lower shelf was filled with books, including fifty or so French novels. Some of these had consoled and educated Countess Mavra Ilinishna in days past, while the remainder had been acquired by Glafira Lvovna during the first year of her marriage. That was when she purchased everything imaginable: a hookah for her husband, an album with views of Berlin, a splendid dog collar with a golden clasp. In addition to these unnecessary items she had also acquired some four dozen or so fashionable books, including two or three in English. These were also transported to the country, in spite of the fact that no one in Negrov's household, or, for that matter, within a four-mile radius of his estate, could read a word of English. She had selected them because of their London bindings, which were very fine indeed. Glafira Lvovna gladly allowed Lyubonka to borrow these books; she even encouraged her to do so, insisting that she herself passionately loved to read and regretted very much that her complicated responsibilities of household and children left her with no free time. Lyubonka read willingly and attentively but showed no special partiality for the activity. She had not yet become so accustomed to books that they were essential to her. They always seemed to be so insipid; she found even Sir Walter Scott dreadfully boring at times.

The sterility of the young girl's environment, however, did nothing to hinder her development. On the contrary, the vulgar circumstances in which she found herself only fostered a more powerful development. Why? This is one of the mysteries of the female soul.

A girl either becomes so accustomed to her surroundings that by the age of fourteen she is already flirting, gossiping, making eyes at passing officers, noticing whether or not the maids are stealing tea and sugar, preparing to become a respectable mistress of a household and stern mother, or else she escapes from the muck and mire with unusual alacrity, overcoming external circumstances by her own inner nobility, comprehending the meaning of life through some revelation, and acquiring tact that both protects and counsels her. Men almost never follow this particular path of development. Boys are taught over and over again in gymnasiums, universities, billiard rooms, and other more or less pedagogical institutions; yet it is not until we turn thirty-five and start losing our hair, our power, and our passion that we acquire that same level of development and understanding that comes much earlier to a woman, while she is still young and her feelings are deep and fresh.

Lyubonka was twelve years old when a few unforgivably harsh, vulgar words uttered by Negrov in a moment of paternal irritation educated her in a matter of hours and provided the stimulus after which she never stopped developing. From that time on, her little head, covered with dark curls, began to work. The range of questions aroused in her was rather small and completely personal, but this just made it easier for her to concentrate on them. Nothing in her external surroundings could possibly interest her; she thought and dreamed, dreamed in order to relieve her spirit and thought in order to understand her dreams. Five years passed. In the development of a young girl, five years is an eternity. During this time a pensive, secretly passionate Lyubonka began to feel and understand the sort of thing that many people never learn before they die. Sometimes she feared her own thoughts and rebuked herself for her own development, but she never restricted the activity of her spirit. There was no one to whom she could communicate all that occupied her mind, all that was seething inside her breast. Finally, lacking sufficient strength to contain it all, she arrived at a solution that occurs quite frequently to young girls: she started to record her thoughts and feelings. She began to keep a journal of sorts. So that you may get to know her better, I have transcribed some of her entries:

"Last night I sat by the window for a very long time; the evening was warm, and the garden was lovely. I don't know why, but it made me feel sadder and sadder; it felt as if a dark cloud were emerging from the depths of my soul. I felt so miserable that I wept bitterly. Although I have a father and a mother, still I am an orphan. I am all alone in the world, and I am horrified to realize that *I love no one.* That is awful! Look around at other people: everyone loves somebody. But everyone is a stranger to me. I want to love but cannot. Sometimes it seems that I love Aleksei Abramovich, Glafira Lvovna, Misha, his sister—but I know that I am only deceiving myself. Aleksei Abramovich treats me so harshly; he is even more of a stranger than Glafira Lvovna. Yet he is my own father! Can children pass judgment on their father? Do they need a reason to love him? They love him just for being their father, but I cannot. How many times have I promised myself to listen humbly to his unjust reproaches? But I can't get used to hearing them. As soon as Aleksei Abramovich becomes coarse, my heart starts to pound. If I let myself go, I would answer him back just as coarsely. They have taken away and ruined all my love for my mother. Hardly four years have passed since I found out that she is my mother, but it is too late to get used to that idea. I have always loved her as my wet nurse. I still love her, but I must confess that I feel awkward in her presence. I must conceal a great deal when I talk to her, and this impedes and constrains our relationship. When you love someone you must be able to tell them everything. I don't feel completely at ease with her. Although she is a kind little old woman, she seems more of a child than I am. In addition, she is used to treating me as a lady and addressing me formally. This is almost harder to bear than Aleksei Abramovich's vulgar language. I have prayed for them all and for myself; I have asked God to purge my soul of pride, to make me humble, to send me love. But love has not yet been granted to my heart.

One week later. "Can it really be that everyone is like *them* and that all households are like *theirs?* Although I have lived only in Aleksei Abramovich's house, still it seems that one could lead a better life, even in the country. Sometimes I find it intolerable just to be with them. Have I, perhaps, as a result of my being alone so often, become a wild beast? What a difference when I walk out to the avenue of lime trees, sit down on a bench, and gaze off into the distance! Then I forget all about them, and I feel wonderful. It is a sad feeling rather than a happy one, but it is a nice sort of sadness. There is a village at the bottom of the hill. I like the poor little peasant huts, the stream that flows gently by, and the small grove way off in the distance. For hours I sit looking and listening to a song wafting from afar, to the clatter of flails, the barking of dogs, and the creaking of carts. When the peasant children catch sight of my white dress, they come running toward me, bringing strawberries, chattering about all sorts of nonsense. I listen to them, and I never feel bored. They have such fine faces—honest and noble. If they were to receive the same kind of education as Misha, I think that they would develop into splendid people. Sometimes they come to visit Misha in his father's courtyard, but there I always hide from them. All our servants and even Glafira Lvovna treat them so rudely that it makes my heart bleed for them. Meanwhile the poor children try in every conceivable way to please my little brother; they catch squirrels and birds for him, but still he abuses them. It is a strange thing: Glafira Lvovna is such a sensitive person, weeping when she hears a sad story, but at times I am astounded by her cruelty. She always says, as if ashamed, 'They don't understand at all. You can't treat them like human beings, or else they will forget their place.' I can't believe it! Apparently, my mother's peasant blood still flows in my veins. I always treat peasant women the same way I do other people, all people; and they like me. They bring me baked milk[7] and honeycombs. It's true that they don't bow to me as they do to Glafira Lvovna, but they always greet me with a smile on their cheerful faces. In no way can I fathom why the peasants of our village seem so much nicer than all the neighbors and guests who come to visit us from the provincial town. The peasants are so much smarter too, even though the guests, landowners, and officials have all received a proper education. Still they are all so nasty in spite of it."

7. *Baked milk.* A Russian pudding prepared by baking rich whole milk and repeatedly stirring in the skin until the mixture thickens.

Is it plausible that a seventeen-year-old girl brought up in Negrov's patriarchal household, one who had never traveled, read very little, and seen even less—is it really plausible that she could have felt all this? The conscience of the one who collected these documents must answer for the factual authenticity of the journal; as for their psychological verisimilitude, allow me to speak. You are well aware of Lyubonka's strange position in Negrov's household. Endowed from birth with both energy and strength, she was insulted on all sides: by her ambiguous relationship to the whole family and by her mother's position; by the total lack of delicacy displayed by her father, who considered that the blame for her birth fell on her rather than on him; and finally by all the servants, who, with their aristocratic inclinations, so characteristic of lackeys, viewed Dunya with irony. Lyubonka was rejected all around: what other choice did she have? Had she been a man, she might have run away or joined the army. But as a girl she could only withdraw into herself. For years she endured the grief, insults, idleness, and confusion. Little by little a part of what was seething within her soul began to crystallize. When she found no satisfactory outlet for her insistent, natural need to confide in someone, she took up her pen and began to write, to express what troubled her, so to speak, and thus to relieve her spirit.

Little insight is required to predict that Lyubonka's meeting with Krutsifersky, given the conditions under which they met, would not pass without consequences. Years of strenuous effort spent on upbringing and society life scarcely ever succeed in stunting young people's capacity and readiness to love. Lyubonka and Krutsifersky could not fail to notice each other; they were alone, they were in the middle of the steppe. . . .For a long time the bashful student dared not exchange even two words with Lyubonka, but fate introduced them to each other silently. The first thing that brought the young people together was the paternal bluntness with which Negrov treated his servants. Lyubonka, as she herself confessed, never could get used to Aleksei Abramovich's rude language; needless to say, his outbursts had an even greater effect in the presence of an outsider. Her flaming cheeks and agitation did not prevent her, however, from observing that Negrov's patriarchal manner had exactly the same effect on Krutsifersky; after some time he too, in turn, noticed its effect on her. As a result, a secret understanding developed between them, almost before they had exchanged even two or three sentences. As soon as Aleksei Abramovich began to mock Lyubonka or to lecture some sixty-year-old Spirka or some old gray-haired Matyushka on morals and good sense, Lyubonka, whose eyes were long fixed on the floor, involuntarily turned her look of suffering toward Dmitry Yakovlevich, whose lips trembled and whose face grew mottled. So, too, to relieve his own painful and oppressive feelings, he would steal a glance at Lyubonka's face, to read what was occurring in her soul. At first they did not think about where these sympathetic glances would lead them—especially them, because in all their surroundings there was nothing that could outweigh, restrain, or distract the growing feeling of mutual sympathy; on the contrary, their total isolation from others fostered this development.

I have no intention whatever of telling you word for word the story of my hero's love; the Muses have denied me the ability to describe that emotion: "O wrath, of thee I sing!"[8] Suffice it to say that two months after he established himself in Negrov's household, Krutsifersky, with his tender and exalted nature, was passionately and madly in love with Lyubonka. This love became the focal point of his whole existence. Everything was subordinated to it: love for his parents, for his studies, everything. . . .In a word, he loved as only a sensitive, romantic nature could love; he loved like young Werther,[9] like Vladimir Lensky.[10] For a long time he did not admit this new feeling to himself, a feeling that had taken possession of his whole being. For even longer he did not reveal it

8. "*I sing.*" Herzen's adaptation of the first line of Homer's *Iliad:* "Sing, O goddess, the wrath of Achilles, son of Peleus."

9. *Young Werther.* The hero of Goethe's epistolary novel *Die Leiden des jungen Werthers* (1774). Charlotte, the girl with whom the hero falls in love, has already been promised to another man, whom she eventually marries. The heartbroken young Werther kills himself.

10. *Vladimir Lensky.* Onegin's neighbor and erstwhile friend in Pushkin's *Eugene Onegin.* He is a poet and an idealist who defends his beloved Olga and loses his life in a duel with Onegin.

to Lyubonka, did not dare even to think about it. In fact, one should not think about such things at all; they have a way of happening by themselves.

Once, after dinner, when Negrov was in his study and Glafira Lvovna was in the parlor resting, Lyubonka sat in the drawing room while Krutsifersky read aloud to her some poems by Zhukovsky.[11] How dangerous and harmful it is for a young man to read to a young woman anything but a textbook of pure mathematics! Francesca da Rimini told Dante about this in the other world, as she whirled in the accursed waltz *della bufera infernalé:*[12] reading led to a kiss, the kiss to a tragic outcome. Our young people were unaware of this and had for several days been fanning the flames of their love with the help of Zhukovsky, whose works the candidate had brought with him. So long as they read "The Cranes of Ibycus,"[13] things went well, but after the murderer was revealed they went on to read "Alina and Alsim."[14] Then the following happened: having read the first stanza in a trembling voice, Krutsifersky wiped the perspiration from his face and, gasping for breath, managed to pronounce the following lines:

> When it happens to a life in bloom
> To say with her soul
> To him: You will be mine on earth,—

he suddenly stopped reading and began to weep uncontrollably; the book dropped from his hands, his head fell forward, and he wept

11. *Zhukovsky.* Vasily Andreevich Zhukovsky (1783–1852) was the leading pre-Romantic poet and translator in early nineteenth-century Russian literature. He was both Derzhavin's disciple and Pushkin's mentor.

12. *"Della bufera infernalé."* In the *Inferno*, V, 115–42, Dante relates the tragic affair of Francesca da Rimini and Paolo Malatesta, who fell in love while reading the romance of Launcelot and Guinevere. The lovers were condemned to be swept forever in "the tempest of hell" (*della bufera infernalé*) for their carnal sin.

13. *"The Cranes of Ibycus."* One of Zhukovsky's literary ballads (1813); a romantic transformation of Schiller's classical ballad "Die Kraniche des Ibykus" (1797), depicting the gods' revenge for the murder of an innocent poet.

14. *"Alina and Alsim."* Another of Zhukovsky's ballads (1814); a poetic translation of François Augustin Moncrif's (1687–1770) tragic ballad "Les Constantes Amours d'Alix et d'Alexis" (1751), depicting the extraordinary power of romantic love.

insanely, as only a man who has fallen in love for the first time can weep. "What's the matter?" asked Lyubonka, whose heart was pounding and whose eyes were welling up with tears. "What's the matter?" she repeated, fearing his answer with her whole being. Krutsifersky seized her hand and, possessed by some new, mysterious power, although he dared not raise his eyes, said to her: "Be, oh, be my Alina! I . . . , I . . ." He could say no more. Lyubonka gently drew away her hand; her cheeks were aflame. She burst into tears and left the room. Krutsifersky did nothing to stop her; it is not clear that he even wanted to. "My God!" he thought. "What have I done? . . . But she took away her hand so quietly, so gently. . . ." And he wept again like a child.

That evening Eliza Avgustovna said somewhat playfully to Krutsifersky, "You must be in love! You are so absentminded and melancholy." Krutsifersky blushed to his ears. "See how good I am at guessing! If you like, I'll tell your fortune with my cards." At once Dmitry Yakovlevich experienced everything that the most wicked criminal endures when he doesn't know how much the investigator already knows and what he might be implying. "Well, what do you say?" the importunate Frenchwoman inquired.

"I would be much obliged," replied the young man.

With a demonic smile Eliza Avgustovna began to lay out the cards, saying as she did so, "Ah, here is the queen *de vos pensées* [of your thoughts], . . . and you are very lucky! She has been placed right next to your heart! Congratulations, congratulations. . . . Next to the ace of hearts. She loves you very much. What's this? He does not dare confess it to you. What sort of a cruel lover are you, making her suffer so!" And so on. At every utterance Eliza Avgustovna fixed her penetrating gaze on his face and rejoiced wholeheartedly at the torments that she forced the unhappy young man to endure. "*Pauvre jeune homme* [poor young man], she will not make you suffer so! Where could one possibly find another heart so stony? Have you ever spoken to her about your love? I am sure you haven't!" Krutsifersky paled, blushed, turned blue, then yellow, and finally escaped only by leaving the room.

Having returned to his own room, he seized a piece of paper. His heart was pounding. Ecstatically, rapturously, he poured out his feelings. This was a letter, a poem, a prayer. He wept and felt happy. While writing he experienced a brief moment of absolute bliss. These moments, usually as evanescent as lightning flashes, are the best, most beautiful things in our lives—yet we don't really know how to appreciate them; instead of reveling in them, we rush on, anxiously anticipating something more in the future.

After completing his epistle, Krutsifersky went downstairs. Tea was being served. Lyubonka had complained of a headache and did not leave her room. Glafira Lvovna was particularly charming, but nobody paid her any attention. Aleksei Abramovich was smoking his pipe in profound thoughtfulness (I trust that you have not forgotten that this pensiveness was no more than an optical illusion). Eliza Avgustovna stepped forward to get a cup of tea and managed to communicate to Krutsifersky that she wished to have a word with him. The general conversation did not go well. Misha was teasing the dog and making him bark. Negrov ordered that the dog be taken outside. Finally a maid, wearing a dress with linen sleeves, took the samovar away. Aleksei Abramovich began playing solitaire; Glafira Lvovna complained of a headache. Krutsifersky went into the drawing room. It was just beginning to grow dark. Eliza Avgustovna was waiting for him there. "When it is completely dark, go out onto the balcony; someone will be there waiting for you," she said. Krutsifersky felt more dead than alive. Should he believe her or not? A rendezvous had been arranged. Perhaps she was indignant and wanted to vent her anger; perhaps. . . .He ran out into the garden. It seemed as if far off in the distance he caught sight of a white dress at the end of the avenue of lime trees, but he dared not go there. He didn't even know whether he would go to the balcony, unless, only for one moment, to give her the letter, only that. . . .He was terrified at the very idea of going to the balcony. He looked up: even though it was dark, he could discern a white dress at one corner of the balcony. It was she—pensive, melancholy—and perhaps she loved him too! He placed his foot on the first step of the staircase leading up to the balcony from the garden. I cannot possibly explain how he managed to reach the top.

"Oh, is that you?" whispered *Lyubonka.*

He was silent, gasping for air like a fish out of water.

"What a splendid evening!" she continued.

"Forgive me, for God's sake, forgive me!" answered Krutsifersky and, with a hand as cold as a corpse's, he reached out for her hand. *Lyubonka* did not withdraw hers.

"Read this," he said, "and you will learn what I find so hard to say. . . ."

Once more a stream of tears fell upon his flaming cheeks. *Lyubonka* squeezed his hand; his tears fell onto her hand as he covered it with kisses. She took the letter and hid it in her bosom. His courage grew; I don't know exactly how it happened, but their lips met. Love's first kiss! Woe is he who has never experienced it! An ecstatic *Lyubonka* returned his kiss with a long, passionate, and trembling one. Never had Dmitry Yakovlevich been so happy; he lowered his head and wept. Suddenly, daring to raise his eyes, he cried out, "Oh, my God, what have I done?"

He discovered that the woman whom he had just kissed was not Lyubonka at all, but Glafira Lvovna.

"My dearest, be calm!" she said in a voice quivering with the fullness of life. But Dmitry Yakovlevich had already run down the staircase; he ran through the garden, down the avenue of lime trees, and out of the garden altogether. He walked past the village and there hurled himself down on the road. He was in a state of total collapse, near to having a seizure. Only then did he remember that his letter remained in Glafira Lvovna's possession. What was he to do? He tore his hair and rolled in the grass like an enraged beast.

In order to clarify this strange *quid pro quo* we must now pause and say a few words of explanation. Eliza Avgustovna's little eyes were extremely observant and discriminating in certain situations. Since Krutsifersky's arrival had increased the size of Negrov's household by one, she had noticed that Glafira Lvovna had become somewhat more attentive to her appearance. Her blouse was arranged in a new way; all sorts of new collars and caps appeared; more attention was paid to her coiffure. The maid Palashka's thick braid, which had the misfortune of resembling the color of what was left of Glafira Lvovna's own hair, was once again fastened into place, in spite of the fact that it had become slightly moth-eaten.

On the soft and fleshy face of this respectable materfamilias there now appeared a series of new expressions hitherto concealed in the fullness of her cheeks. First, when she smiled, her eyes became as soft as butter; then, when she sighed, her eyes became as sweet as honey. . . .Eliza Avgustovna noticed all these things. Once, when she just happened to enter Glafira Lvovna's room during her absence and just happened to open the drawer of her dressing table, she discovered an open jar of *rouge végétal* [rouge] that had been lying next to some eyewash in the pantry for the last fifteen years. It was then that she exclaimed to herself, "Now is the time for me to enter this affair!"

That very evening, when she was left alone with Glafira Lvovna, the French lady began describing how a certain princess (it had to be a princess!) had become *interested* in a certain young man; how her own, Eliza Avgustovna's, heart ached, noticing that this angelic princess was pining away and languishing; how finally this princess had fallen on the neck of her one true friend, Eliza Avgustovna, and had vividly recounted all of her anxieties and doubts and asked for her advice; how she then gave her some advice that resolved all her doubts; how afterward the princess stopped suffering and languishing and instead began to grow plump and more cheerful. Glafira Lvovna's soul caught fire as a result of these fabrications. Although it is generally believed that corpulent people are incapable of experiencing passion, this is simply not true. Once they have caught fire, the conflagration often continues for a very long time, since there is so much fatty substance to feed the flames. As you can see, Eliza Avgustovna acted as a bellows and fanned the little erotic sparks that raced all over Glafira Lvovna into a rather large conflagration. She did not, however, drive matters so far that Glafira Lvovna revealed her secret; she even had the grace not to force a confession from her, because it was really quite unnecessary. She wanted to have Glafira Lvovna in her power, and in this she undoubtedly succeeded. In the course of the next two weeks Glafira Lvovna gave her two special presents, a shawl from the famous Kupavna mill and one of her very own silk gowns.

Krutsifersky, chaste in thought and pure in deed, never could discern the meaning of the French lady's extreme graciousness, her

suggestive hints, or of Glafira Lvovna's ambiguous looks. His innocence, shy confusion, and lowered eyes continued to fan the forty-
year-old woman's passions all the more. This strange reversal of
traditional roles was particularly interesting: Glafira Lvovna played
the conquerer and seducer, while Dmitry Yakovlevich played the
innocent maiden, around whom the malevolent spider had begun to
weave its web. The good Aleksei Abramovich didn't notice a thing;
as usual he went off to ask the gardener's wife about the condition
of his fruit trees; peace and tranquillity reigned in Negrov's patriarchal household.

Now, let us return to the balcony.

Glafira Lvovna could in no way comprehend the flight of her
Joseph;[15] after cooling off somewhat in the evening air, she returned to her bedroom. As soon as she was left alone—that is, in
the company of Eliza Avgustovna—she took out his letter. Her
ample bosom heaved; her trembling fingers opened the letter, and
she began to read. Suddenly she screamed, as if a lizard or frog had
been concealed in the envelope and had just jumped down her
bosom. Three maids came running into the room, and Eliza Avgustovna snatched away the letter. Glafira Lvovna called for some eau
de cologne. A frightened maid brought some medicinal ointment
by mistake, and Glafira Lvovna ordered it sprinkled onto her head.
"*Ah, le traitre, le scélérat!* ["Ah, the traitor, the scoundrel!"]. Who
would have expected this from such a modest girl? Our Englishwoman! No, nothing can improve a person born of vulgar parent-
age. Not a spark of gratitude, nothing! I have nurtured a serpent at
my breast." Eliza Avgustovna was in the same position as an official
I once knew: after swindling people all his life, he submitted his
resignation, confident that he was irreplaceable. He did so in order
to be asked to stay on longer, but his resignation was accepted.
Having deceived others for so long, he ended up by deceiving
himself.

The clever Eliza Avgustovna understood what had happened;
she recognized her blunder and realized that both she and Glafira

---

15. *Joseph.* In Genesis 39:1–12 Joseph rejects the amorous advances of Pot-
iphar's wife and flees her house, leaving her holding his robe.

Lvovna were as much in Krutsifersky's power as he was in theirs. She understood that if Glafira Lvovna's jealousy should irritate him, he could expose Eliza Avgustovna. Even if he didn't have conclusive proof, he could still sow seeds of doubt in Aleksei Abramovich's mind. Just as she was reflecting on how best to soothe the abandoned Dido's rage,[16] Aleksei Abramovich entered the bedroom. He yawned and made the sign of the cross over his mouth.[17] Eliza Avgustovna was in despair!

"Aleksis!" exclaimed his indignant spouse. "I would never have predicted it! Just imagine, my dear: that modest tutor of ours is engaged in correspondence with our Lyubonka. And what a correspondence it is—just awful! He has ruined our defenseless orphan. I beg you to make sure that after tomorrow he never sets foot in this house again. Imagine, all this in front of our own daughter! She is only a child, of course; still, it could affect her imagination."

Aleksis was incapable of either considering or comprehending matters very quickly. In addition, he was as astonished by this development as he was when, during their honeymoon, Glafira Lvovna had him swear by his mother's grave and his father's remains that she could adopt the child of his sinful passion. Over and above all this, Negrov was inordinately sleepy; this was an inopportune time to inform him about the intercepted correspondence. A sleepy man can only become angry at the person who is preventing him from going to sleep. His nerves are frazzled, and everything he does is influenced by his state of exhaustion.

"What's that you say? What correspondence with Lyubonka?"

"Yes, yes, Lyubonka's correspondence with that student. . . .Our innocent little angel. . . .I must confess that all of this is entirely predictable, given her origins!"

"Well, what's *in* the correspondence? Are they conspiring together, or what? Just try to stop a seventeen-year-old girl; so that's why she's always sitting alone and complaining about headaches

16. *Dido's rage.* In Virgil's *Aeneid*, Dido, the queen of Carthage, is hopelessly in love with the wandering Aeneas; after he abandons her, she burns herself on a pyre.

17. *Over his mouth.* A superstitious Russian gesture intended to forestall an oral invasion by demons while the mouth is engaged in a yawn.

and the like. Well, I'll make that scoundrel marry her, that's what I'll do! Has he forgotten in whose house he's residing? Where's that letter? Damn it all! The devil take it! What tiny handwriting! This tutor can't even write; he produces little mouse scribbles. You read it, Glasha."

"I refuse to read such scandalous things."

"What nonsense! The woman is forty years old, but she still talks rubbish! Dashka, bring my glasses from the study."

The maid, who certainly knew the way to the study, brought him his glasses. Aleksei Abramovich sat down next to the candle, yawned, and drew up his upper lip, thereby imparting a very dignified expression to his nose. He narrowed his eyes and with great difficulty began to read, with a clumsy, bookish pronunciation: "'Yes, be my Alina![18] I love you madly, passionately, ecstatically, your very name is *Love*. . . .'"[19]

"What nonsense!" remarked the general.

"'I expect nothing. I dare not even dream that you love me. But my heart is full to bursting: I cannot refrain from saying that I love you. Forgive me! I throw myself at your feet and ask your forgiveness. . . .'"

"My God, what rubbish this is! And that's only the beginning of the first page!. . . No, my dear sir, enough! Your obedient servant will not read such nonsense. Wasn't it your job to prevent this from happening? What have you been doing all this time? Why did you allow them to conspire together? Well, it's really not all that terrible. A woman may have lots of hair on her head but very little brains in it. What have we discovered here in this letter? A lot of rubbish. As for . . . the real thing . . . there is nothing at all about it. It's high time for Lyuba to get married, so why not to him? The doctor said that his rank is tenth class.[20] Just let him try to resist

18. *Alina.* See above, n. 14.
19. *Love.* The heroine's first name in Russian is indeed "Love" (*Lyubov'*).
20. *Tenth class.* In 1722 Peter the Great introduced a table of ranks for the civil service, corresponding to military and naval ranks. Promotion was based not on birth or social status but on merit and seniority. The system was intended to ensure performance of the nobility's service obligation, as well as to systematize government administration.

me! But, as they say, 'Mornings are always wiser than evenings': it's time to go to bed. Good night, Eliza Avgustovna. You may have sharp eyes, but you didn't notice this affair. . . .We'll talk about it tomorrow morning."

The general started to get undressed. In a minute or two he was snoring. He dozed off with the comforting thought that Krutsifersky would not escape and that he would marry him off to Lyuba. It would serve both to punish him and to fix her up for life.

What a disastrous day! Glafira Lvovna never expected Negrov to arrive at such a solution. She completely forgot that she herself had been telling him repeatedly that it was high time for Lyuba to be married off. Possessed by the fury of an old woman in love, she threw herself onto her bed and felt like chewing the pillowcase to shreds—perhaps she actually did!

All this time poor Krutsifersky was lying on the grass. He desperately wanted to die; during the female rule of the Parcae, they might well have been unable to endure his sufferings and might indeed have snipped his thread.[21] Distressed by such painful emotions, overcome by despair and anxiety, fear and shame, and utterly exhausted, he ended up exactly as Aleksei Abramovich had begun—that is, he too fell asleep. If he wasn't already suffering from *febris erotica* [erotic fever], as Dr. Krupov had described love, then he surely would have been suffering from *febris catarrhalis* [catarrhal fever]. As it was, the cold dew was good for him: his sleep, though troubled at first, soon became more peaceful.

When he awoke some three hours later, the sun had risen. Heine was absolutely correct in maintaining that it's always the same old story: the sun rises over here and sets over there.[22] Nevertheless,

21. *Parcae.* The Parcae or Fates, goddesses in Greek and Roman mythology, were traditionally depicted as three sisters: one spins the thread of human life, the second assigns to man his lot, and the third cuts the thread.

22. *"And sets over there."* A reference to Heinrich Heine's (1797–1856) poem "Seraphine," x (1834): "The maid looked over the ocean / And sighed with a worried frown; / She sighed with deep emotion / Because the sun went down. // Dear girl, don't let it grieve you, / It's an old trick, you will find; / In front he sinks, to leave you / And come again from behind" (*The Complete Poems of Heinrich Heine*, A Modern English Version by Hal Draper [Cambridge, Mass., 1982], 330). The poet was presumably "correct" in believing that romantic crises are short-lived and that hope eventually prevails.

there is something rather splendid about that same old story. It goes without saying that it must also be true for a man in love. The air was fresh and full of a very special fragrance. The morning mist was rising in heavy, white billows, leaving behind millions of sparkling dewdrops. The purple light and unusual shadows imparted a strange new elegance to the trees and peasant huts, to the entire surroundings. The birds sang their various songs, and the sky was completely clear. When Dmitry Yakovlevich stood up, he felt considerably better. Before him the road wound around and disappeared from sight; he looked at it for a long time and thought about whether he should run away from all these people who had discovered his secret, the sacred secret that he himself had dropped into the muck and mire. How could he possibly return home and face Glafira Lvovna? It would surely be better to run away. But how could he leave *her*? Could he ever find the strength to be parted from her? Slowly he turned back.

Entering the garden, Krutsifersky caught sight of a white dress at the end of the avenue of lime trees. His cheeks blushed at the memory of his terrible blunder and his first kiss. This time it really was Lyubonka. She was sitting on her favorite bench and gazing off into the distance pensively, sadly. Dmitry Yakovlevich leaned against a tree and stared at her with a sort of inspired delight. At this particular moment she looked very lovely; some thought engrossed her. She was sad, and this emotion conveyed a majestic quality to her sharp, energetic, youthfully lovely features. The young man stood there for quite some time, deep in meditation: his gaze expressed his love and devotion. At last he decided to approach her. He felt a desperate need to speak to her, to warn her about the intercepted letter. Upon seeing Krutsifersky, Lyubonka became somewhat embarrassed, but not in an affected or theatrical way. Casting a quick glance at her morning attire (she had never expected to meet anyone) and adjusting it just as quickly, she raised her noble, serene eyes to Dmitry Yakovlevich. He stood before her, arms folded across his chest. She met his imploring gaze—so full of love, suffering, hope, and ecstasy. She held out her hand toward his; with tears in his eyes he took her hand and squeezed it gently. . . .Ah, ladies and gentlemen, how marvelous young people are!

Dmitry's confession of love, which had interrupted his reading of "Alina and Alsim," had affected Lyubonka profoundly. With her feminine perspicacity, already referred to above, she had long felt that he was in love with her. But this was always something implied, never called by name. Now the words had been uttered. That same night she had written in her journal:

"I can hardly put my thoughts in order. Oh, how he wept! My God, my God! I never thought that a man could weep so bitterly. His gaze possesses a power that makes me tremble, but not with fear. It is so tender and as gentle as his voice. I felt so sorry for him. If I had listened to my heart then, I would have told him that I also love him. I would have kissed him and consoled him. He would have been so happy!. . . .Yes, he loves me. I can see that; I love him, too. What a difference between him and all the other men I've met. He is so noble and tender. He told me about his parents—how he still loves them! Why did he say, 'Be my Alina'? I have a name of my own, and it is a nice one. I love him very much, and I think that I can be his yet still remain myself. Am I worthy of his love? I'm not sure that I can love so deeply! Again those black thoughts return to torment me. . . ."

"Farewell," said Lyubonka. "Do not fear that letter. I know them very well, but I am not afraid of anything."

She shook his hand so nicely, in such a friendly fashion, and disappeared among the trees. Krutsifersky remained alone. They had talked for a long time. His present happiness was much greater than yesterday's unhappiness. He recalled every word she had spoken. Daydreams carried him off to God knows where, with one image interwoven throughout: *she* was everywhere. Aleksei Abramovich's servant boy suddenly put an end to his daydreaming; he was being summoned by Negrov. He had never before been summoned at such an early hour.

"What is it?" asked Krutsifersky with the look of a man who has just been doused by a tubful of cold water.

"The master wants to see you," answered the servant boy rather rudely. The story of the intercepted letter had obviously reached the servants' quarters.

"Right away," said Krutsifersky, half dead with fear and shame.

What was he so afraid of? He had no doubt that Lyubonka loved him. What else mattered? Still he felt more dead than alive from embarrassment. He was unable to recognize that Glafira Lvovna's position was no better than his own. He could not even conceive of facing her. Crimes have often been committed to avoid such awkwardness.

"So, my dear fellow," said Negrov with a majestic air appropriate to the important business at hand. "Is that what you learned at the university? To compose sweet love letters?"

Krutsifersky remained silent; he was so upset that Negrov's tone did not even offend him. His despairing and suffering appearance spurred on brave Aleksei Abramovich; looking straight into Dmitry Yakovlevich's eyes, he continued in a very loud voice:

"How is it, good sir, that you dared carry on such intrigues in my house? What precisely is your opinion of my house? And what do you take me for, an idiot? You should be ashamed of yourself, young man. It is immoral to corrupt a poor girl who has no parents, no protectors, no means of support. So this is what the world has come to! And it's all because they teach young men grammar and arithmetic, instead of morality. To defame a young girl, to dishonor her good name. . . ."

"Just a minute," answered Krutsifersky, whose indignation was gradually overcoming his awareness of his uncomfortable position. "What exactly have I done? I love Lyubov Aleksandrovna" (this was her patronymic—probably because her father's name was Aleksei, whereas her mother's husband, the butler, was named Aksyon), "and I have dared to say so. It always seemed more likely to me that I would never breathe a word about my love. I don't even know how it all happened! But what is it that you find so criminal? Why do you think that my intentions are dishonorable?"

"I'll tell you why! If you had honest intentions, then you would not have tried to confuse the girl with your billets-doux, instead you would have come directly to me. You know that I am her real father. You should have come to me and asked for my permission and consent. But you tried to sneak in the back door, and you got caught. Don't reproach me! I do not tolerate such affairs in my house. It's not very hard, is it, to turn a young girl's head? I never expected this from you. You masterfully pretended to be a humble young man. She distinguished herself as well, showing her gratitude for the upbringing and the care we have given her! Glafira Lvovna wept all night."

"The letter is in your possession," observed Krutsifersky. "You can see that it is the first one I wrote."

"Well, 'The first pancake always turns out lumpy,' obviously. In this first letter of yours, did you ask for her hand, or what?"

"I did not even dare to consider it."

"How is it that you are so bold in some things and so timid in others? For what purpose did you cover an entire page of writing paper with little mouse scribbles?"

"Indeed," answered Krutsifersky, struck by Negrov's words, "I did not even dare to consider asking for Lyubov Aleksandrovna's hand. I would be the happiest man alive if I might ever hope. . . ."

"Fine talk—that's what they teach you there, to deceive people with your words! Let me ask you: if I were to allow you to make a proposal, and if I were to allow Lyubov to marry you, then what would you live on?"

Of course Negrov was not an especially clever man, but he was in possession of a good measure of our national trait, that particular practical frame of mind aptly termed "having your wits about you." It was his fondest dream to marry Lyuba off to anyone at all, especially after he and his wife had noticed that their own dear Lizonka was being eclipsed by the girl. Even before this letter it had occurred to Aleksei Abramovich to marry Lyubonka to Krutsifersky and to arrange a position for him in some provincial office. This idea arose from the same source as his saying that if a nice little secretary should turn up, Lyuba should be married off to him.

When he discovered Krutsifersky's love, the first thing that occurred to him was to force him to marry Lyuba. He considered the letter a prank and thought that the young man would not be willing to accept the burdens of married life quite so easily. But from the way Krutsifersky answered, Negrov realized that he was not against the marriage at all. He therefore changed his tactics and began talking about money, fearing that once Krutsifersky had decided upon marriage, he would next ask for a dowry.

Krutsifersky remained silent; the financial question weighed on his chest like an iron weight.

"Make no mistake," Negrov continued, "about her income. She has nothing at all and can expect nothing. Of course, I won't let her out of my house in her skin alone; but except for a few rags, I can't give her a thing. I have a marriageable daughter of my own, you know."

Krutsifersky declared that the question of a dowry was a matter of complete indifference to him. Negrov was very pleased with himself and reflected, "He's a real goat! And he calls himself a scholar!"

"Precisely, my dear fellow! Good people should not begin at the end. Before writing those love letters and mixing everything up, you should have thought ahead. If you really loved her and wanted to ask for her hand, then why didn't you concern yourself with your future?"

"What am I fit to do?" asked Krutsifersky in a voice that would have shaken any man with a soul.

"What are you fit to do? You are a civil servant, I believe, of the tenth rank. Put aside your arithmetic and poetry; request a post in the civil service. You've been loafing long enough; now you should do something useful. Why not a job in the Revenue Office? The vice-governor is a good friend of mine. In time you'll become a counselor. What more could you ask for? It will guarantee you some bread to eat and a respectable position."

Never in his life had Krutsifersky considered a position in the Revenue Office, or in any other office for that matter. He could as easily imagine himself a counselor as he could a bird, a hedgehog, a bumble bee, or . . . I don't know what. Nevertheless, he felt that

Negrov was basically right. He was not shrewd enough to understand this extraordinary patriarchal character, who could maintain
that Lyuba had nothing at all and could expect nothing and, at the
same time, could give her away in marriage as her father.

"I would be better suited to a post as a teacher in a gymnasium,"
said Dmitry Yakovlevich at last.

"Well, that would not be nearly as good. What is a teacher in a
gymnasium? He's not really a civil servant. He's never invited to
the governor's house; only the director, perhaps, is invited there.
And the salary is so poor."

This last speech was uttered in a very ordinary tone of voice.
Negrov was completely satisfied with the negotiations and was
convinced that Krutsifersky would not slip through his fingers.

"Glasha!" Negrov shouted into the other room. "Glasha!"

Krutsifersky was mortified. He assumed that Glafira Lvovna's
"last" kiss of love was just as important and earthshaking to her as
his first was to him, even though it had been delivered to the wrong
person.

"What do you want?" asked Glafira Lvovna.

"Come here."

Glafira Lvovna entered with a proud and majestic air that, needless to say, neither suited her nor concealed her agitation. Unfortunately Krutsifersky was not able to notice this, because he was
afraid to look at her.

"Glasha, Dmitry Yakovlevich has asked for Lyubonka's hand,"
said Negrov. "We have always raised and supported her as if she
were our own daughter, and now we have the right to arrange her
marriage. Nevertheless, it wouldn't hurt to talk it over with her,
and that's a woman's affair."

"My God! Have you arranged a match? What unexpected
news!" said Glafira Lvovna bitterly. "This is like a scene from *La
Novelle Héloïse!*"[23]

23. *Héloïse. Julie, ou la Nouvelle Héloïse* (1756–58), a sentimental novel by Jean
Jacques Rousseau (1712–78), concerns an aristocratic young woman who falls in
love with her impoverished tutor. Whereas the medieval Héloïse had entered a
convent, Julie agrees to marry another man but dies prematurely, still very much
in love with her Saint-Preux.

If I had been in Krutsifersky's place at the time, I would have added, so as not to lag behind Glafira Lvovna's learned allusion, "Perhaps, ma'am, but yesterday's incident on the balcony was more like a scene from *Faublas*."[24] Krutsifersky said nothing at all.

Negrov stood up, as a sign that the conference was over, and announced, "I ask only that you not think of marrying Lyubonka until you receive a position. Above all, sir, I advise you to be very careful. I will be keeping a sharp eye on you. It is somewhat awkward to have you remain in this house. Our Lyubonka has certainly caused us a lot of trouble!"

Krutsifersky left. Glafira Lvovna spoke about him contemptuously and in conclusion declared that such a cold creature as Lyubonka would marry anyone but could bring happiness to no one.

The next morning found Krutsifersky sitting alone in his room, deep in thought. Scarcely had two days passed since the reading of "Alina and Alsim"; yet now they were almost bride and groom, and he was about to enter the civil service. . . .Fate is so strange: it had arranged his life and elevated him to the heights of human happiness. How? He had kissed one woman instead of another and had given her a note intended for someone else. All this was like a miracle or a dream. He recalled over and over again every one of Lyubonka's words and expressions from their conversation under the lime trees; his soul seemed to expand, and he felt exalted.

Suddenly he heard heavy footsteps ascending the steep staircase leading to his room. Krutsifersky shuddered and waited apprehensively for the person possessing such a heavy tread. The door opened, and in walked our old friend Dr. Krupov. His appearance astonished the candidate. Although he visited Negrov once or twice a week, he had never entered Krutsifersky's room. His visit was an indication of something very unusual.

"That confounded staircase," said Krupov, gasping for air and

---

24. *Faublas*. The hero of *Les Amours du Chevalier de Faublas* (1789–90), a novel written by Jean-Baptiste Louvet de Couvray (1760–97). The handsome young Faublas is attracted by three women: one initiates him into the rites of love, the second is capricious and passionate, and the third is pure and naive. He marries the first, but only after satisfying his desires along the way.

wiping the perspiration off his forehead with his *white* handkerchief. "Aleksei Abramovich assigned you quite a room."

"Ah, Semyon Ivanovich!" the candidate replied quickly, blushing for some reason.

"Bah," continued the doctor. "But what a view from your window! Isn't that the Dubasov Church there in the distance, over
there to the right?"

"I think so; yes, it probably is, but I'm not sure," answered
Krutsifersky, staring fixedly toward the left.

"You are still a student, an incurable student! How can you have
lived here for months and still not know the view from your very
own window. Ah, youth! Here now, let me feel your pulse."

"I am quite well, Semyon Ivanovich, thank you kindly."

"'Quite well,' you say," continued the doctor, as he reached for
Krutsifersky's hand. "I knew it: your pulse is rapid and uneven.
Just a moment . . . one, two, three, four . . . yes, feverish and
hyperactive. With a pulse like that a man is capable of making all
sorts of foolish decisions. If your pulse were regular—thump,
thump, thump—then you never would have gone this far. My dear
fellow, they told me downstairs that you want to get married. I
couldn't believe my own ears. I said to myself, 'He's not a stupid
lad. I myself brought him here from Moscow. I don't believe it, so
I'll go and see for myself.' And this is what I find: a rapid and
uneven pulse. With that kind of pulse you might do more than get
married; you might commit the devil knows what kind of foolish
acts. Anyway, who can decide on such an important step in a
feverish state? Think it over. First undergo treatment, restore your
organ of thought—your brain, that is—to its normal condition so
that your blood doesn't interfere with its operation. If you like, I'll
send my assistant over to let some blood, just a teacupful or so."

"Thank you very much, but I see no need for that."

"How do you know what you need and what you don't? You
haven't studied medicine, whereas I have learned it all. Well, if you
don't want any blood let, take some Glauber salts;[25] I have my
medicine bag downstairs, and I will give you some."

25. *Glauber salts.* The crystalline form of sodium sulfate (Na_2SO_4), used in
medicine chiefly as a laxative.

"I am very grateful for your concern, but I must inform you that I feel perfectly well. I am not being frivolous in the least; I really do want to . . . " (here he stammered a bit) "get married, and I do not understand what you have against my happiness."

"A very great deal!" The old man's face became extremely serious. "I like you very much, young man, and therefore I feel sorry for you. Dmitry Yakovlevich, from the vantage point of my declining years I have observed that you remind me of my own youth, my past. I wish you well; therefore, it would be criminal of me to remain silent now. Why get married at your age? Negrov must have pulled the wool over your eyes! Look how upset you are! You don't even want to listen to me. I can see that; but I shall make you hear me out. Age demands its rights. . . ."

"Oh no, Semyon Ivanovich," said the young man, somewhat confused by the old man's words. "I understand that you are sharing your opinion out of love for me and a desire to help. I regret, however, that it is somewhat unnecessary, perhaps even too late."

"Well, if that were all you have against my opinion, it wouldn't matter at all. It's never too late. Marriage is—brr—a very serious business. The trouble is that those who enter into wedlock never stop to consider what it actually means; they think about it later, at their leisure, but by then it's too late. This is no more than *febris erotica*. How can a man decide on such a step, my friend, when his pulse is racing as fast as yours? You are staking your entire fortune on this one card; perhaps you'll succeed and break the bank, but perhaps. . . . What intelligent man would take such a risk? Besides, in a card game, if you make a mistake, then you get punished; a thief gets what he deserves. But in marriage you are sure to ruin another person as well.

"Dmitry Yakovlevich, think it over! I am convinced that you love her and that she loves you, but that doesn't mean a thing! You may be sure that in either case the love will pass. If you leave now, it will pass; if you get married, then it will pass even sooner. I have been in love too, not once, but five times; each time the good Lord spared me. Now, when I return home after a day's work, I can relax in peace and quiet. During the day I belong exclusively to my patients; in the evening I play a game of whist and go to bed without a care in the world. But if you have a wife, then it's all worries, fights, and children. You don't care if the whole world perishes, as long as your family prospers. It's hard to live in one place, but even harder to move to another. Trivial gossip begins to permeate your household; your books are stored away under a bench; you worry about money and provisions.

"Now let's talk about you. If you fall upon hard times, it's no great misfortune—there are good times and bad. I recall how Anton Ferdinandovich (a man not unknown to you) and I would have only a ruble between us. But a man wants both to eat and to smoke. . . .So we would buy a quarter of a pound of tobacco . . . just so, instead of bread, and eat nothing at all. . . .Or else we'd buy a pound of ham and have nothing to smoke. How we would laugh about it, because it never really mattered. But it's different if you have a wife; you'd feel sorry for her, and she would start to wail. . . ."

"Oh no! I'm sure that this young woman will find the strength to endure adversity. You simply don't know her!"

"That, my dear sir, is even worse. If she began to rant and rave, then at least you could spit over your shoulder and leave her. But if she becomes quiet and grows thin, then you say to yourself, 'Poor girl, why on earth did I drag her down with me and force her to subsist on St. Anthony's diet?'[26] And you wrack your brains for some way to make money. Well, brother, you can't get rich by honest means, and you certainly won't become a swindler. So you think and you think. In order to clear your head, you take a little drink. It's not bad at all; I use it myself to aid digestion. And do you know what? You take a second drink and then a third. . . .Do you understand me?

"Well now, let's suppose that you are able to provide your daily bread but nothing more. Even though she is Negrov's daughter and he is very wealthy, I know him well: he won't give you a kopeck. He has put aside five hundred serfs for his own daughter. Even if he were to present Lyubonka with five thousand rubles, what sort

26. *St. Anthony's diet.* Saint Anthony of Egypt (ca. 250–ca. 355) was a hermit and monk who subsisted in a tomb on a meager diet of bread and water for twenty years.

of capital would that be? I feel sorry for you, Dmitry Yakovlevich, I really do. Let those who can't make anything of themselves get married; but you should take care of yourself. I would suggest that you find another position; leave here as soon as possible, and this love will vanish into thin air. A post has opened up in our gymnasium. Don't act like a child! Be a man!"

"I am very grateful indeed, Semyon Ivanovich, for your concern. But everything that you have said is completely beside the point. You want to frighten me as if I were a baby. I would rather part with my own life than renounce this angel. I never dared hope for such happiness; God himself has brought this to pass."

"What a fool!" said the implacable doctor. "And it is I who ruined him! Why did I recommend him for this position! It wasn't God who brought this to pass at all. It was Negrov who pulled the wool over your eyes, and it is the result of your own youthful inexperience. So be it. I can't keep it to myself any longer. My dear Dmitry Yakovlevich, I have lived for a very long time, and while I do not boast about my intelligence, I have acquired considerable experience of life. You must realize that the medical profession does not lead me into people's parlors and drawing rooms but into their studies and bedrooms. I have seen a great many people in my day and have not allowed one to escape without first examining him both inside and out. You can only observe people in their livery and masquerade costumes, while I get behind the scenes. I have had my fill of family dramas. People aren't ashamed in front of me; everything is out in the open, with no formality. Homo sapiens ["human being"]—*sapiens* [wise], my eye! *Ferus* [wild] is more like it! The most ferocious beast is gentle in his own lair, whereas man in his lair becomes much worse than a beast. Why do I say all this? . . . .Let me see. Yes. Well, I have become quite accustomed to discerning people's character. Your fiancée is not a good match for you, whatever you think. Those eyes, that complexion, the quiver that sometimes passes across her face. She is a young tigress, as yet unaware of her own strength. And you! Who are you? You are the fiancée. You, my friend, are as sentimental as a German maiden. And you will become a housewife—is that what you really want?"

Krutsifersky was offended by this last remark and replied in an unusually cold, dry manner: "There are cases in which people who express their concern can help, but not by reciting disquisitions. Perhaps everything that you say is true. I'm not going to argue. The future is unknown to me. I know only one thing for sure: I now have only two choices. Where they lead, it is hard to say, but there are only two: either to drown myself or to become the happiest of men."

"It would be far better to drown yourself and get it over with!" said Krupov, who was also somewhat offended. He took out his *red* handkerchief.

It goes without saying that this conversation did not produce the effect that Dr. Krupov had intended. He may have been a good physician for men's bodies, but his approach was too blunt for their souls. Doubtless he was making judgments about the nature of love on the basis of his own experience. He said that he had been in love several times and consequently had considerable experience, without ever realizing that that was precisely the reason he was unable to judge the kind of love that comes only once in a lifetime.

Krupov departed in anger. Later that evening, during dinner at the vice-governor's house, he held forth on his favorite subject for over an hour and a half: he denounced women and family life, overlooking the fact that the vice-governor was married for the third time and that he had several children left over from each marriage.

Krupov's words had almost no impact on Krutsifersky; I say *almost*, because a vague, indefinable, yet painful impression remained, like that following the ominous cry of a raven or after encountering a funeral procession when one is on the way to take part in a merry feast. Of course one glance from Lyubonka obliterated this impression entirely.

"We must have come to the end of your story," you say with great relief, naturally.

"Sorry, but it has not yet begun," I answer with appropriate respect.

"For pity's sake, all that's left is to summon a priest to marry them."

"Perhaps, but I consider it the end only when a priest is summoned to administer the last rites; sometimes even that is not the end. When a member of the clergy comes to perform a marriage, then that is the beginning of a completely new story in which only the characters remain the same. It will not be long before they appear before you again."

Chapter 5

Vladimir Beltov

In the town of . . . , but there is no need to specify the time and place with chronological and geographical accuracy. Sometime during the nineteenth century, in the provincial town of N., the gentry were holding their local elections.[1] The town came to life. One could hear the ringing of carriage bells and the squeaking of springs. One could see landowners' winter carriages, covered sleds, and conveyances of every conceivable shape and size, loaded with all sorts of things, embellished by hosts of servants all wearing greatcoats or sheepskin jackets fastened with towels as sashes. Upon arriving in town some of these servants would continue along on foot, greeting shopkeepers, smiling to their comrades standing near the gates; the rest of them slept in a variety of positions in which the human body generally finds it most uncomfortable to sleep.

The landowners' horses gradually transported all the leading fig-

---

1. *Local elections.* Under the law on the Administration of the Provinces (1775) and the Charter of the Nobility (1785), the nobles in each province met every three years to elect representatives called marshals to manage their affairs and represent their interests.

ures in the elections to the provincial center. The retired cornet Dryagalov was already present; with his very last ruble he had decorated the windows of the apartment that he had rented with crimson-colored curtains. He regularly traveled to five different provinces for elections and for fairs; he never lost at cards, even though he played from morning till night, and he never became rich, even though he won from morning till night. The retired general Khryashchov was also on hand; he was a wealthy man, well known for his band of musicians, and he was a fine horseman in spite of his age, which was sixty-five. He would arrive at the elections, host four balls, and decline for reasons of ill health the nomiantion as marshal of the nobility that the grateful nobles offered him every time.

Strange frock coats began to appear in drawing rooms; these coats have been lying dormant between leaves of tobacco for the last three years; now their velvet collars were somewhat faded and in desperate shape. In addition to frock coats, there appeared peculiar uniforms of different eras: militia uniforms, single- and double-breasted, with only one epaulette or none at all. Official visits were made from morning till night. Some of these people hadn't seen each other for the last three years. They looked at one another and, with great sorrow, took note of the ravages of time; grey hair or wrinkles, fatness or thinness. The faces were the same as before, but not exactly: the spirit of destruction had left its mark on each. With even greater sorrow, an outsider could have noticed the complete opposite: these three years had passed by just as the previous thirteen or thirty years had.

The whole town was talking about the candidates, dinners, local marshals, balls, and judges. For three days the supervisor of the civil governor's office had been wracking his brains trying to write a speech. He had wasted over two reams of paper composing the opening lines: "Worthy gentlemen, esteemed nobles of N. province!" Then he would stop and consider whether to begin, "Allow me once again, in your midst, to . . . ," or, "I am delighted to be in your midst once again. . . ." Finally he remarked to his senior assistant, "Ah, Kupriyan Vasilevich, it is seven hundred times easier to untangle the most complicated criminal case than it is to write a speech!"

"You should ask Anton Antonovich to lend you his copy of *Model Compositions;*[2] I think it contains some fine speeches."

"A wonderful idea!" said the supervisor, giving his assistant a painful slap on the back. "Hooray for Kupriyan Kupriyanovich!"

The supervisor considered it very witty to call a person first by his real patronymic and then by his own name repeated as a patronymic. That very evening he composed a few lines modeled on Prince Kholmsky's speech in Karamzin's "Martha the Mayoress."[3]

In the midst of all these general, demanding activities, the attention of the townspeople (which was already strained to the breaking point) was suddenly attracted by a completely unexpected and totally unfamiliar figure—one whom no one had ever expected to see—not even Cornet Dryagalov, who expected to see everyone. This was a person about whom no one had thought very much; he was completely superfluous in the patriarchal circle of these heads of society. He seemed to appear like a bolt from the blue, although he actually arrived in a splendid English carriage. This was the retired provincial secretary Vladimir Petrovich Beltov.[4] Whatever he lacked in rank was compensated for rather handsomely by his clear title to an estate of some three thousand serfs. This estate, called White Meadow, was extremely well-known to both the electors and the candidates. But the owner of White Meadow was something of a myth, a mysterious, legendary figure about whom all sorts of strange tales were circulating, like those told about far-off places such as Kamchatka or California, which include very unusual and improbable things. For example, a few years ago it was said that just after he graduated from the university Beltov had

2. *"Model Compositions."* Anthologies published in Petersburg (1816–17) by the Society of Lovers of National Literature which contained original Russian works as well as translations in both prose and verse.

3. *"Martha the Mayoress."* A historical tale (1803) by Nikolai Mikhailovich Karamzin (1766–1826) that treats Ivan the Third's plan to annex the independent republic of Novgorod. In a stirring speech to the people of Novgorod, Prince Kholmsky, the tsar's emissary, advocates autocracy and a united nation.

4. *Provincial secretary.* The next-to-lowest class in the table of civil ranks.

enjoyed the patronage of a certain minister; afterward it was said that he quarreled with that minister and resigned his post to spite his patron. No one believed any of this. There are certain people about whom provincial inhabitants maintain very definite and fixed opinions. It is impossible to quarrel with these people; they can only be accorded the highest esteem. Is it likely that Beltov dared to. . . . ? No. It is unclear whether he aroused his patron's justified wrath, lost at cards, took to drink, or eloped with someone's daughter—not *anyone's* daughter, but *someone's* daughter.

Then it was rumored that he had gone off to France; the shrewder and wiser observers added that he would never return, that he had joined a Masonic Lodge in Paris and that the lodge had appointed him a judicial arbitrator in America.[5] "Very likely indeed!" observed many. "He was left an abandoned child early in life. It seems that his father died the year he was born; his mother—well, you know her background! Besides, she was a foolish woman, very *exaltée* [excitable]. The tutor was totally corrupt and never showed anyone any respect." These rumors were also used to explain why Beltov neglected his own household, although his peasants were renowned for their wealth and were always to be seen wearing boots.[6]

Finally, after three years of not being talked about at all, this strange figure, a judicial arbitrator from a Parisian Masonic Lodge in America, a man who quarreled with those to whom the highest esteem should be accorded, he who had gone off to France forever—this man suddenly appeared in the midst of provincial society in the town of N. like a bolt from the blue. What is more, he arrived there in order to present himself as a candidate in the local elections. There was a great deal about this that was incomprehensive to the inhabitants of N. How could one explain his strange preference for service in the provinces over the capital? Or his strange preference for an elected position? And then: Paris versus the Nobles' Assembly? Three thousand serfs versus the rank of provincial secretary? The people of N. had quite enough to worry about, even before Beltov arrived on the scene.

5. *Judicial arbitrator.* The official who presided over a court of arbitration (established in 1775) that was constituted if both contestants so requested.
6. *Boots.* Russian peasants traditionally wore bast sandals (*lapti*), not boots.

The sharpest mind in town undoubtedly belonged to the president of the Criminal Court. He resolved all questions troubling provincial society once and for all. People came to consult him even about family matters. He was very learned, both as a writer and a philosopher. He had only one rival, Dr. Krupov, inspector of the Medical Board; the president actually became flustered in his presence. But Krupov's authority was not nearly so widespread, especially after one provincial aristocratic lady, who was very sensitive and no less well educated, said in the presence of witnesses, "I respect Semyon Ivanovich, but can he really comprehend a woman's heart, can he possibly understand the soul's tender feelings, when he has to examine corpses and even touch them?" All the ladies agreed with her that he could not; they decided unanimously that the president of the Criminal Court, lacking such shocking habits, was the only one capable of resolving the most delicate issues concerning a woman's heart, not to mention other problems.

It goes without saying that as soon as Beltov appeared, one thought flashed through everyone's mind: what would Anton Antonovich say about him? But Anton Antonovich was not the sort of person to whom one could turn and ask directly, "What do you think of Mr. Beltov?" Far from it! For three days he was neither seen playing whist at the vice-governor's house nor drinking tea at General Khryashchov's house, almost as if it were on purpose (and of course it is possible that it really *was* on purpose). The most curious and enterprising man in town was a certain counselor who wore the Order of St. Anna in his buttonhole.[7] He used this decoration so skillfully that no matter where he was standing or sitting it was always visible from every corner of the room. This holder of the Order of St. Anna in his buttonhole decided on Sunday that on his way home from the governor's house (he always visited the governor on Sundays and holidays) he would stop off at the cathedral and, if the president wasn't there, proceed directly to his house. When he arrived at the cathedral, the counselor asked a

7. *St. Anna in his buttonhole.* In 1797 the Schleswig-Holstein Order of St. Anna was adopted as a Russian decoration. There were four levels of the award; the lowest were worn in the buttonhole or on the hilt of a saber.

police lieutenant if the president's sleigh was anywhere to be seen. "No, sir," answered the policeman, "nor is it likely that His Excellency will come. I just saw his coachman Pafnushka heading into the tavern." The counselor considered this last detail very significant. He deduced from it that Anton Antonovich could not possibly arrive at the cathedral with only one horse, and how could the postilion Nikeshka manage a pair of bays? Without so much as entering the cathedral, he set off immediately for the president's house.

The president was not expecting visitors and was sitting in domestic attire, which consisted of a long knitted jacket, wide trousers, and felt boots. He was a short man with broad shoulders and a huge head (brains require room to breathe). His facial features expressed a particular importance, a certain solemnity, and an awareness of his own power. He usually spoke in a drawl, with frequent emphases, as befits a man entrusted with definitive decisions. If some impudent upstart interrupted him, he would stop, wait a few minutes, then repeat his last word forcefully, continuing his sentence in exactly the same manner as he had begun it. He couldn't tolerate objections and rarely had to hear any, except from Dr. Krupov. It never occurred to other people to argue, although many found themselves in disagreement with him. The governor himself, sensing the superiority of the president's intellect, referred to him as an unusually intelligent man and remarked, "He should occupy a post higher than that of president of the Criminal Court. What knowledge! And listen to his pronouncements: he is a genuine Massillon![8] He has sacrificed a great career in the civil service by devoting so much time to reading and studying."

This very same man, who had sacrificed a great career out of his love for learning, was sitting in a jacket at his writing desk. Having signed some official documents and having inserted in the appropriate place the "number of lashes" to be meted out for bootlegging, vagrancy, etc., he wiped his pen dry, placed it on the table, took a

8. *Massillon.* Jean Baptiste Massillon (1663–1742) was the bishop of Clermont and an eloquent French preacher. He delivered many sermons at the court of Louis XIV in Versailles, declaiming severely on the paucity of the elect yet treating sinners in a very gentle manner.

book bound in morocco from the shelf, opened it, and began to read. Gradually a look of indefinably sweet satisfaction spread across his face. But his reading did not continue for very long. The counselor wearing the Order of St. Anna in his buttonhole arrived on the scene.

"I have been very worried about you, so help me God! I went to the governor's house to offer holiday greetings, but you, Anton Antonovich, were not there. Yesterday you weren't at your game of whist; your sleigh was not at the cathedral. I thought that if worse had come to worst, you might be ill. Anyone can become ill. . . . But words mean nothing! What's the matter? I have been so worried about you, so help me God!"

"I am very grateful to you. Thank the Almighty, I can't complain about my health. Pray be seated, my dear Mr. Counselor."

"Ah, Anton Antonovich! It seems that I have disturbed you. You were reading."

"No matter, my dear sir, no matter. I have enough time both for the Muses and for my good friends."

"I see, Anton Antonovich! You know that I am now in a position to provide you with the latest books. . . ."

"I don't care for the latest books," the president said, interrupting the diplomatic counselor. "I don't care for the latest books at all. Just now I was rereading *Dushenka* for the hundredth time, and I can assure you, it was with new and wonderful delight.[9] What grace, what wit! Alas, Ippolit Fedorovich did not bequeath his talents to any of his successors."

Here the president quoted some lines from the poem:

Malicious envy, everywhere judging harshly, has many eyes and sees hidden things through their veils. Although the princess hid her secret from her sisters and kept up her pretense for one day, two, and three, saying that she was waiting for her husband to appear in person, her sisters presented the cause of his absence in the darkest

9. "*Dushenka.*" A long narrative poem (1783) by the eighteenth-century poet and translator Ippolit Fedorovich Bogdanovich (1743–1803). It is a delightful and polished verse adaptation of La Fontaine's novel *Les Amours de Psyche et de Cupidon* (1669), which, in turn, was a reworking of Apuleius's *Golden Ass*.

possible light. What will perfidious malice not think of? According to their words, he was dreadful and bad-tempered.

"My goodness," said the counselor, interrupting his reading. "That is word for word what is being said about the traveler who has just arrived in town. People do like to engage in idle talk!"

The president looked at him sternly and, as if he had seen and heard nothing, continued:

> According to their words, he was dreadful and bad-tempered, and Dushenka truly was living with a monster. Dushenka then forgot the counsels of modesty. Whether it was the sisters' fault, or destiny or fate or her own flaw of character, she sighed and revealed to her sisters that in her marriage she loved only a shadow. She revealed to them, moreover, how and where the shadow was wont to come and described all the incidents in detail. But the only thing she could not say was who her husband was and what kind of creature he was: a sorcerer or a serpent or a god or a spirit.

"These verses are no mere empty words; they contain both heart and soul. My dear Mr. Counselor, either as a result of my own inadequate abilities or because of an inferior secular education, I can understand none of the latest books, beginning with those written by Vasily Andreevich Zhukovsky."

The counselor had never read a word in his whole life except for the resolutions passed by the provincial administration and of those only the ones pertaining to his own department. He considered himself obligated by his higher sensibilities to sign all other resolutions without ever reading them. He observed, "I agree with you entirely. But I suppose that people from the capital would hold different opinions."

"Why should we care about them?" replied the president. "I know only too well that all the contemporary journals are singing hymns of praise to Pushkin. I have read him too. His verses are smooth, but they contain neither thought nor feeling. And for me, when there is nothing here," (he mistakenly pointed to the right side of his chest), "then it's all merely empty words."

"I myself am extremely fond of reading," said the counselor, still unable to gain control of the conversation, "but I have no time for it. My mornings are spent over those blasted official papers; there is little food for thought or feeling in our administrative affairs. And in the evening there's a bit of whist, a bit of boston."

"Anyone who wishes to read," retorted the president with a restrained smile, "would not sit playing cards every evening."

"Of course not. For example, they say that this Beltov fellow never plays cards; instead, he's always reading."

The president remained silent.

"No doubt you have heard about his arrival?"

"I have heard something of the sort," answered the philosopher-judge casually.

"They say that he is terribly learned; he'd be a good match for you. They say that he can even speak some Italian."

"Who am I to be compared to him?" replied the president with a sense of his own dignity. "Who am I indeed? I have heard about this Mr. Beltov. He has traveled abroad and served in the ministry. Who are we, provincial boors, to be compared to him? But we'll see. I have not yet had the honor of making his acquaintance; he has yet to call on me."

"Nor has he been to see His Excellency the governor; yet I think that he arrived in town five days ago. Yes, at dinner time it will be exactly five days ago today. Maksim Ivanovich and I were having dinner at the chief of police's house; as I recall, it was just as we were eating the *puddin*[10] that we heard some sleigh bells. Maksim Ivanovich, well, you know his weakness; he just couldn't restrain himself. 'Excuse me, dear Vera Vasilevna,' he said and ran to the window. Suddenly he cried out, 'A carriage with six horses, and what a carriage!' I went over to the window too: indeed, a carriage with six horses, and a splendid one at that. It must have been fashioned by Iokhim, so help me God. The chief of police dispatched an officer to make inquiries. He reported back at once. 'A Mr. Beltov from Petersburg.'"

"To tell you the truth," the president began somewhat myste-

---

10. *Puddin.* From English "pudding": in Russia, a baked confection containing kasha (cooked grain or groats), cottage cheese, and fruit.

riously, "I think that there is something suspicious about this man. Either he has squandered his fortune, or he is hand in glove with the police, or he himself is under police surveillance. Just think about it: he owns three thousand serfs, but he travels over nine hundred versts to attend a local election."[11]

"Absolutely, there is no doubt about it whatever. I confess that I would dearly like you to meet him. Then we would get right to the heart of the matter. Yesterday I took a little stroll after dinner, just as Semyon Ivanovich prescribed for my health. I walked past the hotel twice. Suddenly a young man came down into the vestibule; I thought to myself that it must be he. I asked a waiter, who told me that it was his valet. Why, he was dressed like one of us! You couldn't possibly tell that he was only a servant. My goodness, a carriage has just drawn up in front of your house!"

"What's so surprising about that?" remarked the president stoically. "My good friends often come to call on me."

"Yes, but perhaps. . . ."

Just at that moment a fat, ruddy maid in a state of complete dishabille entered the room and announced, "A landowner has arrived in a carriage. I have never seen him before. Will you receive him or not?"

"Give me my dressing gown," said the president, "and ask him to come in."

Something resembling a smile spread across the president's face as he donned his frog-green silk dressing gown. The counselor rose from his chair and was in a state of great agitation.

A man of about thirty, simply and respectably dressed, entered the room and bowed politely to his host. He was slender and well built. His good-natured eyes were strangely combined with supercilious lips, the expression of a respectable gentleman with that of a spoiled child, traces of deeply melancholic reflection with those of unbridled passion. The president, yielding none of his feeling of self-esteem, rose from his armchair and, while standing in one place, managed to indicate that he was actually moving forward to greet his guest.

11. *Verst.* A Russian unit of linear measure equal to about 3500 feet, or about two-thirds of a mile.

"I am Beltov, a local landowner. I have come here to take part in the elections and consider it my duty to make your acquaintance."

"I am very glad to meet you," said the president, "very glad indeed. I ask you, sir, kindly to be seated."

Everyone sat down.

"Have you arrived recently?"

"Five days ago."

"Where from?"

"Petersburg."

"After the bustle of the capital, you are likely to find the quiet life of a small provincial town rather boring."

"I'm not sure, but I don't really think so. I actually found life in large towns to be rather boring."

Let us leave for a few minutes or a few pages both the president and the counselor; the latter, since the day he had received the Order of St. Anna in the buttonhole, had never been in such rapture as he was now. He devoured the visitor with his eyes and ears, his mind and heart. He examined him in great detail: he noticed that the last button of his waistcoat had been left unfastened, that he was missing one tooth in his lower right jaw, and so on and so forth. Let us leave them both and concern ourselves exclusively, like the other inhabitants of the town of N., with this strange guest.

Chapter 6

We are already aware that Beltov's father died soon after his son's birth, that his mother was *exaltée*, and that she was to blame for Beltov's unsatisfactory behavior. Unfortunately we must agree that she was indeed one of the main reasons for the failure of her son's career. The story of this woman's life is remarkable in itself. She was born a peasant and at the age of five was made a domestic servant in the house of a lady who had a husband and two daughters. The husband set up factories, introduced new agricultural methods, and ended up by mortgaging his entire estate to a foundling hospital. Then, after concluding that he had fulfilled his economic mission in life, he died.

His widow was horrified by this state of affairs and wept for some time. Finally, after wiping away her tears, she set about making improvements on her estate with considerable courage. Only a woman's clever mind and a mother's tender heart, intent on providing a dowry for her daughters, could have invented such ingenious means of accomplishing her goal. She dried mushrooms and raspberries and collected reeds for baskets; she underweighed butter, stole firewood from other people's forests, and sold young serfs into the army out of turn. (This was a long time ago—measures taken then are now rarely used).

And, to tell the truth, the landlady of Zasekino village[1] enjoyed the general reputation of being an incomparable mother. Among the various papers of her dear departed agronomist-husband, she discovered a promissory note that had been given to him by the headmistress of a certain boarding school in Moscow. She entered into correspondence with the headmistress, but realizing that it would be difficult to recover the money itself, she persuaded her to accept three or four serfs as pupils in order to make them governesses for her own daughters and for other people's children. A few years later these home-grown governesses returned to their mistress with splendid-looking certificates attesting to their knowledge of divine law, arithmetic, Russian history in full, world history in brief, French, and so on, and with a gilt-edged copy of *Paul et Virginie*[2] that had been presented to each one upon graduation in recognition of her accomplishments.

The mistress had a special room prepared for their homecoming and eagerly awaited the chance of finding them positions. At about that time Beltov's future great-aunt was looking for a governess for her own children. When she learned that her neighbor had some available, she applied to her directly. They haggled over the price, quarreled, raved, separated, and finally, agreed. The mistress allowed the great-aunt to choose any governess she wanted, and she chose the future mother of our hero.

Two or three years after this, Vladimir's father retired to the country. Beltov was a dissolute young man and an inveterate gambler; he loved to drink, shoot, display unnecessary daring, and chase after women under thirty years of age whose faces possessed no significant blemishes. Nevertheless it could not be said that he

1. *Zasekino village*. The peasant village (*selo*) located on Sofya Beltov's estate. Traditionally, a *selo* contained a church, as opposed to the smaller settlement called a *derevnya*. The actual name of this village seems to be derived from the Russian verb *zasech'* (to flog to death), implying the harsh realities of peasant life.

2. *Paul et Virginie*. The novel written in 1787 by Jacques-Henri Bernardin de St. Pierre (1737–1814). A romantic idyll of two young lovers in a tropical Eden, it soon became one of the most popular books of its day.

was altogether a lost soul. Idleness, wealth, lack of culture, and bad company had deposited "seven pounds of silt on him," as a friend of mine used to say; in his favor, however, one must admit that the silt never really settled on him.

Beltov was seldom occupied, and, since the two estates were only about five versts apart, he visited his aunt frequently. Sofya (so the governess was called) quickly caught his eye. She was about twenty years old, tall, brunette, with dark eyes and a thick braid so common among young girls. It seemed foolish to agonize over the matter. Contrary to Vauban's system,[3] he did not dig elaborate trenches; one day when he was left alone with her, he slid his arm around her waist, kissed her profusely, and invited her with great alacrity to meet him in the garden that same evening. She tore herself away and was about to cry out, but stopped from shame and from the fear of being discovered. She rushed off to her own room in great distress; there, for the first time, she began to comprehend the length, breadth, and depth of her ambiguous position.

Beltov was irritated by her refusal and began to pursue her with his love. He presented her with a diamond ring that she refused and promised her a Bréguet watch that he didn't even own.[4] He could not possibly comprehend why this lovely girl was so unreceptive to his advances. He became jealous, in spite of the fact that he couldn't identify any rival. Finally, in exasperation, he resorted to threats and verbal abuse; but even this didn't help.

Then Beltov had a bright idea. He decided to offer his aunt a large sum of money in exchange for Sofi. He was convinced that his aunt's greed would conquer her pretense of virtue. But, like a man who always acts without thinking, he let drop some hints about his intentions in front of the poor girl. Of course, this frightened her

3. *Vauban's system.* Sebastien le Prestre de Vauban (1633–1707) was a leading military engineer in France. In an age when the capture of a fortress was of great strategic importance, he developed different "systems" for laying siege and planning defense.

4. *Bréguet watch.* A fashionable pocket watch invented by the Parisian watchmaker Abraham-Louis Bréguet (1747–1823). It displayed the date and could chime the minute and hour on demand. Pushkin's hero Onegin possesses one (I:15–17).

even more. She threw herself at her mistress's feet, wept profusely, told her everything, and begged for permission to go to Petersburg.

I don't know exactly how it happened, but Sofi took her mistress unawares. The old woman was not acquainted with Talleyrand's rules, "Never follow the first impulse of your heart, because it is always a good one."[5] She was touched by the girl's plight and agreed to grant her freedom for the paltry sum of two thousand rubles. She explained: "I paid that much for you. What about the food and clothing I've supplied since then? Well, until you can pay off the whole amount, you can send me the small sum of one hundred fifty rubles a year, and I will order Platon to issue you a passport. He is a fool, of course, and will probably spoil the sheet of paper, and you know how expensive stamped paper is nowadays."[6]

Sofi agreed to everything, thanked her mistress, wept copiously, and then calmed down. A week later Platoshka issued her a passport, having recorded therein that she was of medium height, had an ordinary face, a normal nose, an average mouth, and possessed no distinguishing characteristics except that she spoke French.

The next month Sofi asked a neighbor, the bailiff's wife, who was traveling to Petersburg in order to pawn some items and to enroll her son in a gymnasium, to take her along. They loaded the covered sleigh with mushrooms, preserves, honey, dried and preserved berries—everything intended as gifts. The bailiff's wife left room only for herself; Sofi had to sit on top of a barrel. In the course of nine hundred versts she was constantly reminded that barrels are not made out of swan's down. The future gymnasium student sat up with the coachman. The student was a lanky lad of about fourteen who smoked Nezhin root[7] and was actually more mature than he appeared at first. He made advances toward Sofi all

---

5. *Talleyrand.* Charles Maurice de Talleyrand-Périgord (1754–1838) was a renowned French statesman and diplomat.

6. *Stamped paper.* During the reign of Peter the Great, Russia adopted a system of stamped paper dispensed by the government and used for all official documents such as contracts, petitions, and passports.

7. *Nezhin root.* A cheap substitute for tobacco, originating in the town of Nezhin, approximately 45 miles northeast of Kiev.

along the way, and if it hadn't been for his mother's sharp eyes (the color of dishwater), he might have outdone even Beltov.

À propos [by the way], Beltov himself had actually attempted to kidnap Sofi as she was making her way from his aunt's house to the bailiff's, and he probably would have succeeded if his coachman hadn't been so drunk that he lost his way. Irritated and sorely displeased by this first taste of sour grapes, Beltov blabbed about his romance, not quite truthfully, to a group of card players. He declared that his aunt, like all old women, was jealous and had forced Sofya, who was madly in love with him, to leave against her own will. In a way he was glad that Sofya had left and taken along certain mementos of his affection.

It is a well-known fact that among European nomadic tribes, gypsies and gamblers never remain in one place for very long. Therefore there is nothing surprising about the fact that within a few days one member of Beltov's audience found himself in Petersburg. He was a very close friend of Mme Joucour, the headmistress of the boarding school. Mme Jourour, who laced up her stays daily until she was forty years old and, out of a sense of modesty, wore dresses with very high necks, was inexorably stern regarding the morality of other people. During one conversation, she told this close friend of hers that a rather strange girl belonging to a wealthy landlady in N. province and speaking excellent French had recently been engaged as a schoolteacher. The nomadic friend burst out laughing. "Bah! An old acquaintance! Splendid! Excellent! Ha, ha, ha! So help me, I've seen her thousands of times with Beltov. She used to arrive at night when everyone else in his aunt's house was fast asleep." Then, manifesting concern for the reputation of his friend's school, he apprised Mme Joucour of Sofi's pregnant condition.

Mme Joucour was frightened out of her wits and exclaimed, *"Quelle démoralisation dans ce pays barbare!"* ["What depravity in this barbarian land!"]. In her indignation she forgot about everything else, including the fact that in a house at the corner of her very own street a certain privileged midwife was raising a set of twins, one of whom closely resembled Mme Joucour, the other her nomadic friend. In her frenzy she wanted first to send for a policeman and then to appeal to the French consul. She soon realized, however, that this was all quite unnecessary and merely turned Sofi out of her house in the rudest possible manner, forgetting in her haste to pay what salary was due her.

Mme Joucour related this horrible tale to three other head-mistresses, and these three told all the others in Petersburg. Wherever the poor girl applied for a job, she was quickly shown the way out. She began to look for private placement, but without acquaintances there was no way she could locate one. She almost secured a reasonably advantageous position outside of town, but before the agreement was sealed the mother went to consult Mme Joucour for a reference; afterwards she gave thanks to providence for sparing her daughter.

Sofi waited another week. She counted up her money; she had thirty-five rubles and no hope of getting any more. The apartment that she was renting cost more than she could afford. After a long search, she finally moved up to the fifth or sixth floor of a large building at the end of Gorokhovaya Street. The building was inhabited by all sorts of riffraff. She had to pass through two muddy courtyards, not unlike the bottom of a lake that had not completely dried up, in order to reach a door so small that it was barely noticeable in a huge wall. A damp, dark, seemingly endless stone staircase with broken steps led up from there; two or three doors opened onto each landing.

At the very top of the staircase, "close to the Finnish sky," as our Petersburg wits like to say, an old German woman occupied a small room. Both of her legs were paralyzed, and for almost four years she had been lying like a corpse next to the stove. On weekdays she knitted stockings, and on weekends she read Luther's translation of the Bible. The room was only three paces wide, but the poor German woman considered two of these an unnecessary luxury. She rented them out together with a window that looked out on the unpainted brick wall of the building next door. Sofi spoke with the German woman and agreed to rent this "boudoir." The space was dirty, damp, dark, and smoky. The door opened onto a cold corridor along which scrambled pitiful, pale, ragged, redheaded children whose eyes were inflamed by scrofula. All the other rooms were inhabited by drunken workmen, except for some seamstresses who lived in the best apartment on the top floor. They never seemed to do any work, at least not during the day, yet their style of life indicated that they were far from poor. The cook who lived with the seamstresses ran out to the tavern five times a day to fill up a pitcher with a broken spout.

All of Sofi's efforts to locate a position were in vain. The kind German woman made inquiries and expended considerable effort to find her a job through her one acquaintance and fellow countrywoman who had been hired to care for some small children. This acquaintance promised to help, but nothing turned up. As a last resort Sofi decided to look for a job as a maid, and she almost found one; a salary was agreed upon, but the *distinguishing characteristic* noted in her passport so astonished her prospective mistress that she replied, "No, my dear, I can't afford a maid who speaks French."

Then Sofi applied to become a seamstress. The head seamstress was very pleased with her stitching and paid her almost as much as had been agreed upon. She invited her to come to tea and then gave her a drink of beer instead. She encouraged the poor girl to move in with them, but some inner repugnance caused Sofi to hesitate, and she ultimately refused. This offended the head seamstress deeply; when Sofi left she slammed the door and proudly declared, "You'll come crawling back to me, you fancy aristocrat, you! We have a German girl here from Riga, and she's just as pretty as you are!"

That evening the head seamstress talked with pungent irony about the poor girl to the police commissar, who occasionally dropped in after his daily labors for an evening's relaxation in pleasant company. He became so interested in Sofi that he immediately dropped in on the old German woman and inquired, "So, Frau-Madame, how are you getting along? Eh? It's about time you stretched out your legs for good, don't you think?"

The German woman hastily put on a cap that she kept next to her for such unforeseen occasions. "Vat can I do?" she replied. "Ze goot Lort so vills it."

"Well, and where is that wench Sofya Nemchinova who belongs to the Telebeevs?"

"Right here," answered Sofi.

"Where on earth did you learn to speak French, huh? You must be a rogue! Well, say something in French."

Sofi was silent.

"I bet you can't. Well, say something."

Sofi was silent and her eyes welled up with tears.

"Frau-Madame, what do you think, can she?"

"Yah, very goot."

"I bet as well as you can do a Russian dance. . . . Why don't you give me a little something to drink? I'm chilled to the bone."

"I haf noting," answered the German woman.

"Too bad. Well, whose apple is that?" (The apple was a gift from the German woman's compatriot; she had been saving it since last Wednesday and planned to eat it next Sunday while she read Luther's translation of the Bible.)

"Mine," said the German woman.

"Why, you won't even be able to bite into it! I bet this French lady will eat it for you. Well, Goodbye," said the commissar, who had done no harm after all! Well satisfied with himself, he returned to the seamstresses' apartment with the apple in his pocket.

The days dragged on interminably. The unfortunate Sofya languished in filth; she was offended and humiliated by everyone and everything. Perhaps if she hadn't been so cultured, she might have managed somehow and not been at such a loss. But her education had disclosed so much tenderness and gentility that her surroundings affected her ten times more than anything else. She experienced moments of such physical exhaustion, such spiritual numbness, that she would likely have fallen very low indeed if she hadn't been protected, as it were, by the sordid, prosaic guise under which vice was revealed to her. There were times when she thought of swallowing poison, she so wanted to escape from her desperate predicament. She was all the closer to despair because she was unable to reproach herself for anything. There were times when malice and hatred completely overwhelmed her; in one such moment she seized a pen and without really understanding what she was doing or why, she wrote a letter to Beltov that was full of solemn wrath. Here it is:

"I do not wish to restrain myself any longer. I am writing to you solely in order to enjoy what may be my last pleasure in life: to express my deepest contempt for you. I will gladly spend my last kopecks on postage for this letter, rather than on bread. I will be sustained by the thought that you will read it. Your behavior toward me in your aunt's house showed you to be an immoral rogue and a callous libertine. Of course in my naiveté I found excuses for you and blamed both your bad upbringing and the narrow circle of friends with whom you are wasting your life. I found excuses for your behavior and blamed my strange position in the household as having occasioned it. But the slander, the vile, mean slander with which you crowned your deed, has shown me the extent of your baseness, not your malevolence, but precisely your *baseness*. Out of revenge, out of petty vanity you decided to ruin a poor, defenseless creature by spreading lies about her. And what for? Did you ever really love me? Search your conscience! Rejoice, for you have succeeded! Your friend has sullied my reputation; I have been driven out by everyone. People regard me with contempt, and I am forced to endure horrible insults. Lastly, I have been left without a crust of bread. Therefore, hear me out: I abhor you because you are a petty, contemptible man. Listen to these words from your aunt's former maid. How pleasant it is for me to imagine your impotent rage and fury while you read these lines. You are thought to be such an honorable man! You would probably put a bullet through a person's head, if these words were said to you by an equal."

Beltov had just lost heavily at a game of cards. Before teatime he was lying on the sofa sorely vexed with himself when his servant, who had just returned from town, brought in some letters, including the one from Sofya. He did not recognize her handwriting; consequently, he was unable to discern from the address who the sender was, and he opened the letter without concern. After reading the first line his hands began to tremble, but he read the letter through calmly to the end. Then he stood up, carefully folded the letter, sat down on a chair, and turned to face the window. He sat in that position for some two hours. His tea had been placed on the table much earlier, but he hadn't taken one sip from the glass. His pipe had long since gone out, but he hadn't summoned the servant boy to refill it. When he finally recovered his wits, it was as if he had suffered a lengthy, severe illness. He was very tired; his legs felt weak, and there was a ringing in his ears. He ran his hand over his head once or twice, as if trying to make sure that it was still attached. He experienced a chill; his face was as pale as a ghost's. He went into the bedroom, sent his servant away, and threw himself down, completely dressed, onto the sofa. An hour or so later he sent for his servant again.

By dawn of the following day a carriage rumbled over the bridge by the mill and was speedily pulled up the hill by four strong horses. The millers came out to look and asked, "Where is our master going?" "To Petersburg, they say," answered one. Six months later the carriage rumbled back over the same bridge. The master was returning home with a new mistress. The village priest who came out to welcome Beltov said to his wife in great astonishment: "Wife, ah, wife! Do you know who the new mistress is? It's that girl who was the governess, the one who was sent by the landlady of Zasekino to Vera Vasilevna. Wondrous are thy works, O Lord!"

"What? I daresay you can't even get near her from all the airs she puts on," answered his wife.

"Yes. But I do not wish to bear false witness," replied the priest. "She is so good-natured and very talkative."

Beltov's aunt, who had been angry with him for two whole days after his initial advances toward the governess, found it impossible to overlook her nephew's unforgivable marriage for the rest of her life; she died without ever setting eyes on him again. She had often repeated that she might have lived to be a hundred had this unfortunate incident not taken away her appetite and deprived her of sleep. Such is the nature of a woman's heart.

Beltov's young wife never recovered from the terrible experiences that she had suffered before her marriage. There are some tender and sensitive constitutions that do not disintegrate under the pressure of grief but seem rather to accommodate it. They do, however, become distorted: they are so deeply affected by their prior experience that they are unable to escape its effect for the rest of their lives. The suffering that they have endured becomes, as it were, a malevolent substance that passes into their blood, into their very life. Sometimes it is invisible; at other times it can suddenly manifest itself with horrible force and can destroy them. Sofya Beltov had precisely that kind of nature. Neither her husband's love nor her obviously beneficial influence on him could expunge all the bitterness from her soul. She feared other people; she was pensive, shy, and withdrawn; she was thin, pale, and distrustful; she was always afraid of something; she liked to weep or to sit on the balcony for hours in silence.

Three years later Beltov caught a cold and died within five days; his body, which had been so worn out by his early life, did not possess sufficient strength to overcome the fever. He expired without regaining consciousness. Earlier, when Sofya brought her two-year-old child in to see him, Beltov had looked at him so ferociously that the frightened child wanted to escape into the next room. Beltov's death dealt Sofya a severe blow. She had loved the man for his passionate repentance. She had recognized the nobility of his nature beneath the filth that had rubbed off on him from his surroundings. She had appreciated the changes in him; she had even come to love his occasional wild outbursts of debauchery and the uncontrollability of his spoiled ways.

After the loss of her husband, Sofya concentrated all her morbid sensibility on her son's upbringing. If he slept badly, she didn't sleep at all. If he seemed slightly indisposed, she became ill. In a word, she lived for him, breathed with him, served as his nurse-maid, wet nurse, cradle, and toy. But even this feverish love for her son was combined with bitterness in her soul. The idea that she might lose the child was constantly woven into her dreams. Often she would look at the sleeping boy in desperation; if he was lying very still, she would timidly bring her trembling hand to his mouth. In spite of her "mother's inner voice," as Sofya referred to these morbid fears, the child survived. While never actually healthy, he was never really sick either.

Sofya never left White Meadow. The boy grew up completely alone, and like any other child in such circumstances, he developed quickly for his age. Actually, even apart from external influences,

there were indisputable signs of strong ability and energetic character in the boy himself. Soon it came time to begin his education.
Sofya set off for Moscow with her son in order to find him a tutor.
Her late husband had an uncle who still lived in Moscow; he was a
great eccentric and was disliked by all his relatives. A willful bachelor, he was very clever, idle, and, in fact, unbearably capricious.

I cannot refrain from saying just a few words about this eccentric
old man. I am always interested in the biographies of everyone that
I meet. On the surface it appears that the lives of ordinary people
are all alike; but that is only the appearance. There is nothing on
earth more individual and more diversified than the biographies of
ordinary people, especially where no two people ever share the
same idea, where each person develops in his own way without
either looking back or worrying about where it will lead. If it were
possible, I would compile a biographical dictionary (in alphabetical
order), starting with people who shave their beards. For brevity's
sake I would exclude all scholars, writers, artists, generals, states-
men—everyone involved in public life. Their lives are all alike and
very boring. Success, talent, persecution, applause, a hermit's existence or a public career, premature death, poverty in old age—
there's nothing individual about that; everything is determined by
the epoch. For this reason I never avoid biographical digressions.[8]
They reveal the full splendor of the universe. The reader who so
wishes may skip over these passages, but in so doing he will miss
the essence of my story. And so, the biography of Beltov's uncle.

His father was a landlord, living in the steppe, who always
feigned poverty. All his life he went about in a raw sheepskin coat
and traveled to the provincial town in order to sell his own rye,
oats, and buckwheat; as can be expected, he cheated in his measur-
ing and was occasionally taught a lesson for it. In spite of his
supposed impoverishment, he sent his son off to join the Guards.
He was accompanied by two teams of four horses each, two chefs, a
valet, a gigantic footman, and four servant boys to boot. Petersburg

---

8. *Biographical digressions.* Compare the author's general observation in *My Past
and Thoughts:* "In no way do I avoid digressions or episodes—so goes any conversation, so goes life itself."

society concluded that this young officer was in possession of a superior upbringing, since he owned eight horses, as many servants, two chefs, and so on.

At first everything went well, but just after the future uncle had become a lieutenant in the Guards, a very significant event occurred in his life. It happened during the seventies. One fine winter's day he decided to go for a drive in his sleigh along Nevsky Prospect. Just as he reached the Anichkov Bridge, a large troika drew even with his sleigh and was about to overtake him. You know the Russian temperament! The lieutenant shouted to his coachman, "Get going!" The tall, stately man in the other sleigh, wrapped up in his bearskin coat, shouted to his coachman in a ferocious voice, "Get going!" The lieutenant overtook him. Choking with rage, the gentleman in the bearskin coat struck out with a whip at the lieutenant's coachman as they rounded a turn and grazed the lieutenant himself on purpose.

"Don't you overtake me, you rogue!" he cried.

"Are you mad, or what?" cried the officer.

"I will teach that fool coachman of yours not to overtake me!"

"I ordered him to do so, my dear sir; you must understand that I respect the uniform of my sovereign too much to permit you to besmirch it."

"Bah, what a rascal you are! And who exactly are you?"

"And who are *you?*" asked the lieutenant, ready to throw himself like a wild beast on the gentleman.

The stately man looked at him with contempt; shaking a fist as large as an elephant's foot, he said, "A fist fight? No, sir, I'll win this race!" Then he shouted to his coachman, "Get going!"

"After him!" shouted the lieutenant to his coachman, adding a few well-chosen words that are so widely known that they cannot be found in any dictionary.

Subsequently, although the young officer discovered where this gentleman lived, he decided not to call on him. Instead he wrote him a letter that he was able to start in a rather satisfactory manner; but, worse luck, he was interrupted. Summoned by the general, he was placed under arrest. Afterward, he was transferred to a garrison at the Orsk Fortress. Although the fortress stands on jasper and other rocks rich in semiprecious minerals, life there was very boring nonetheless. The officer had a set of Crébillon's novels;[9] supplied with such edifying reading, he departed for the fortress located on the border of the Ufa province.

Three years later he was transferred back to the Guards, but according to his friends he was slightly deranged when he returned from Orsk. He retired and returned to the estate that had been willed to him by his impoverished father. Although the latter was always grumbling and walking around in a raw sheepskin coat, he had managed to purchase twenty-five hundred serfs from the surrounding estates, simply in order to round out his own numbers.

Shortly after his arrival, the new landowner quarrelled with all of his relatives and promptly went abroad. He spent three years in English universities and then traveled through most of Europe, omitting both Austria and Spain, two countries he despised. He established contact with all the celebrities of his day; he spent evenings with Bonnet discussing organic matter[10] and nights with Beaumarchais talking over a goblet of wine about the latter's lawsuits.[11] He maintained an amiable correspondence with Schlözer, who had just begun to publish his famous newspaper.[12] He made a special trip to Ermenonville to visit Jean Jacques in his declining years;[13] and he proudly passed by Ferney Castle without calling on Voltaire.[14]

9. *Crébillon.* Claude-Prosper de Crébillon (1707–77) was a popular author whose licentious tales and satiric novels parodied the corruption of the eighteenth-century French aristocracy.

10. *Bonnet.* Charles Bonnet (1720–93) was a Swiss naturalist and philosopher who specialized in the study of small organisms, especially insects. As a result of failing eyesight, he turned his attention to philosophy. His final work of any importance espoused a doctrine of the immortality of all forms of life.

11. *Beaumarchais.* Pierre-Augustin Caron de Beaumarchais (1732–99) was a French dramatist and publicist. He wrote with great wit and eloquence, as is evident from his two most famous plays, *The Barber of Seville* (1775) and *The Marriage of Figaro* (1778). He was constantly involved in lawsuits, ranging from patent fraud to libel, and often defended himself with his pen.

12. *Schlözer.* August Ludwig von Schlözer (1735–1809) was a German journalist and historian known for his newspaper *State News* (1783–93), which publicized his views on various social and political questions. He traveled throughout Europe and Russia and subsequently taught history at Göttingen.

13. *Ermenonville.* Rousseau's country estate near Paris, where the writer spent his last years in peaceful seclusion.

14. *Ferney Castle.* A small Swiss town near the French border, where Voltaire lived from 1758 to 1778.

After ten years he returned from his travels and once again tried living in the capital. But Petersburg was not to his liking, so he settled in Moscow. At first he found everything there rather strange; then everyone there found him rather strange. As a matter of fact, he seemed to have lost his awareness of ordinary things. He began reading only medical books, neglected his appearance, became embittered, capricious, alienated, and totally apathetic.

Just about the time that Sofya was looking for a tutor, a resident of Geneva arrived at the uncle's house. He had been recommended by one of his Swiss friends and hoped to find a position as a teacher. The Genevan was about forty years old, thin, gray-haired, with youthful blue eyes and a sternly pious face. He was an extremely well-educated man; he was fluent in Latin and was also a good botanist. In matters relating to pedagogy he was an inveterate dreamer; with an almost youthful conscientiousness he viewed the fulfillment of his obligations as an awesome responsibility. He studied all kinds of treatises on pedogogy, from *Emile*[15] and Pestalozzi[16] to Basedow[17] and Nicolay.[18] The one thing that he failed to absorb from these books was the single most important purpose of an education: training the young mind to adapt to its surroundings. Education must be climatological: for every age, as for every country, even more so for every class, and perhaps even for every fami-

---

15. *Emile*. *Emile, ou De l'éducation* (1762) was the work in which Rousseau presented his views on education. He argued that the psychology of the individual child corresponds to that of the race and that sensation precedes reflection, which in turn precedes religious faith. Despite the inevitable influence of civilization, Rousseau believed that the child's natural virtues could still be developed.

16. *Pestalozzi*. Johann Heinrich Pestalozzi (1746–1827) was a Swiss educator who pioneered European pedagogical reforms. He abolished the practice of rote memorizing and tried to develop the child's powers of observation and ability to manipulate objects.

17. *Basedow*. Johann Bernhard Basedow (1723?–90) was a German educator who tried to incorporate Rousseau's ideas into a comprehensive program. He founded a school called the Philanthropinum in Dessau, where, in the spirit of the Enlightenment, he stressed the ideas of playful learning, secular education, and a practical orientation to the world.

18. *Nicolay*. Ludwig Heinrich Nicolay (1737–1820) was a German writer and educator who befriended the most prominent figures of the Enlightenment. He arrived in Russia in 1769 and served as tutor to Paul I, as Russian state councilor, and as president of the Russian Academy of Sciences.

ly, there exists a particular kind of education. It was this fact that the Swiss gentleman never learned. He studied the human heart as reflected in Plutarch, and he knew his own historical period through Malte-Brun[19] and the science of statistics. At the age of forty he was still incapable of reading *Don Carlos*[20] without weeping, he believed in total self-sacrifice, he could never forgive Napoleon for failing to free Corsica, and he traveled with a portrait of Paoli.[21] True, he had experienced bitterness in the real world. Poverty and failures sorely oppressed him, but as a result of these, he knew even less about reality. He strolled sadly along the beautiful shores of his lake, indignant at his own fate, indignant at Europe. Suddenly his imagination pointed him northward, to a new land, which, like Australia in the physical realm, presented in the moral one something of enormous dimensions—new, different, emerging. The Swiss gentleman acquired Lévesque's history[22] and read Voltaire's *Peter the Great*;[23] a week later he set out on foot for Petersburg. Armed with a naive world view, he possessed an unshakeable solidity, even a kind of coldness. A cold dreamer is absolutely incurable: he will remain a child until the day he dies.

Sofya made his acquaintance at the uncle's house. She had hardly hoped to find the tutor of her dreams, but this Swiss gentleman

19. *Malte-Brun.* Conrad Malte-Brun (1775–1826) was a leading Danish geographer who viewed his subject as intimately related to the history and customs of mankind.

20. *Don Carlos.* Schiller's (1759–1805) first play in blank verse which was published in 1787. It concerned the sensitive heir to the Spanish throne who was deeply in love with his father's second wife. This rivalry resulted in the hero's being committed to a monastery by his father.

21. *Paoli.* Pasquale Paoli (1725–1807) was a leader in the Corsican fight for independence from Genoa and later from France. Successful in his first struggle against the Genoese, he headed the Corsican government from 1747 to 1768. Later the French subjugated Corsica, but Paoli returned from exile to become governor after the French Revolution.

22. *Lévesque's history.* Pierre-Charles Lévesque (1736–1812) was a French historian and classicist. At Diderot's urging, Catherine the Great appointed him professor of the Imperial Corps of Nobles. As a result of his Russian experience, Lévesque wrote his *Histoire de Russie* in 1782.

23. *Voltaire's "Peter the Great": L'Histoire de Russie sous Pierre le Grand* (1759–63) was one in a series of historical works in which Voltaire traced mankind's slow evolution from barbarism to civilization.

came very close to that indeed. She offered him four thousand rubles a year (a large sum in those days). He said that he needed only twelve hundred and agreed to accept the position. Sofya expressed her astonishment. He explained calmly that he would take no more or less than he needed; he had drawn up a budget consisting of eight hundred rubles for expenses, with another four hundred for unforeseen circumstances. He added, "I do not wish to become accustomed to luxury, and consider the acquisition of capital to be dishonorable." It was to this madman that Sofya entrusted the education of the future landlord of White Meadow, with its rich fields and its wastelands.

Only the old uncle, who was dissatisfied with everything, was dissatisfied with their arrangement. While Sofya was beside herself with joy, the uncle (the only one of her husband's relatives ever to accept her) said, "Oh, Sofya, Sofya! You are doing a foolish thing. The Swiss should stay here, content to be my reader. What sort of a tutor will he make? He himself is still in need of a nursemaid! And what will he make out of your Volodya? Another Swiss! I think it would be better to take your son off to Vevey or Lausanne."

Sofya interpreted the old man's words as evidence of his selfishness: he cared so much for his Swiss gentleman! Not wishing to offend him, she said nothing at all, but two weeks later she left for her estate with Volodya *and* the forty-year-old youth.

It was springtime. The Genevan began to foster a passion for botany in Volodya. Early in the morning they would set off to collect herbs; boring lessons were replaced by lively conversations. Every object that came into view became a subject for discussion; Volodya listened to his tutor's explanations with rapt attention. After dinner they would sit out on the balcony overlooking the garden. The tutor would narrate biographies of great men or accounts of distant voyages; sometimes, as a reward, he would allow Volodya to read Plutarch.

Time passed, two elections were held,[24] and the time came to send Volodya off to a university. His mother didn't really want to part with him. During the last few years she had come closer to

24. *Two elections.* Six years had passed.

experiencing humble happiness than at any other time in her life. She felt so at ease in her serene, harmonious life that she feared any change whatever. She had become so used to it all: She liked to wait on her beloved balcony for Volodya's return after his long walks. She so enjoyed it when, after wiping the perspiration from his flushed, happy face, he would throw his arms around her neck. She would look at him with such pride and pleasure that she often felt like crying.

Indeed, there was something very touching about Volodya's appearance. He was so noble; there was something so direct, open, and trusting about him, that anyone looking at him would feel glad for himself, but sorry for the boy. Clearly life had not yet imposed its burdens on this handsome, lithe youth who still had such bright sparks in his eyes. He had never experienced fear; his mouth had never uttered a lie; he had no idea about what to expect from life. The Swiss tutor had become almost as attached to his pupil as Sofya was. Sometimes, after gazing at him for a long time, he would lower his tear-filled eyes and think to himself, "My life has not passed in vain; it is enough for me to know that I have furthered the development of such a young man. My conscience cannot reproach me!"

How strange and confusing everything can be! Clearly neither the boy's mother nor his tutor ever considered the trials and tribulations that might result from his hermitlike upbringing. They did everything they could to ensure that he would never come to understand reality. They deliberately concealed from him everything that was happening in the real world; instead of providing him with an initiation into life's bitterness, they implanted in him a set of gleaming ideals; instead of taking him into the marketplace and showing him the greedy, disorderly, money-grubbing mob, they took him to see splendid ballets, assuring him that this graceful combination of music and movement constituted ordinary life. They were preparing him to be their own moral version of Kaspar Hauser. . . .[25]

25. *Kaspar Hauser.* Kaspar Hauser (1812?–33) was a young boy discovered in Nürnberg in 1828 who had apparently spent his youth in complete seclusion. His case attracted considerable attention because it was related to the most controversial issues of the time: nature versus nurture, the development of personality, and

This is precisely what the Swiss tutor was like! But what a tremendous difference there was between him and young Volodya. He was a poor scholar, ready to wander the earth with a small bundle of possessions, a portrait of Paoli, his precious dreams, an ability to be satisfied with very little, a contempt for luxury, and an eagerness to work. What on earth did he have in common with Volodya's destiny, with his social position?

However much Sofya grew to like her hermetic life and however painful it was to tear herself away from the serenity of White Meadow, she finally decided to go to Moscow. Shortly after their arrival she took Volodya to see his great-uncle. The old man was very feeble; she found him half reclining in a Voltaire armchair. His legs were wrapped up in a goatskin shawl; thin strands of gray hair were hanging down onto his dressing gown; a green visor protected his eyes.

"Well, well, and what have you been doing, Vladimir Petrovich?" asked the old man.

"I have been preparing to enter the university, sir," answered the youth.

"Which one?"

"Moscow University."

"And what will you do there? I was personally acquainted with both Matei[26] and Heim,[27] but I still think you would fare better at Oxford. What do you think, Sofya? It is better there, you know. What field are you interested in?"

"The law, sir."

The old man's face showed contempt.

"What for? You will learn *le droit naturel, le droit des gens, le code de Justinien* [natural law, international law, Justinian's *Code*]—and then what?"

---

the origin of language. The boy was adopted by a German lawyer and turned over to a gymnasium teacher to receive an education. He was murdered in 1833, perhaps by the person who had locked him away as a child.

26. *Matei*. Christian Friedrich Matei (1744–1811), a professor of classics at Moscow University.

27. *Heim*. Ivan Andreevich Heim (1758–1821), a professor at Moscow University who taught history, statistics, and German.

"Then," answered Sofya with a smile, "he will enter the civil service in Petersburg."

"Ha, ha, ha! And is it really necessary to know the *Pandects*[28] and all those *Glosses?*[29] Perhaps, Vladimir Petrovich, you intend to become a legal counselor, ha, ha, ha, or even a lawyer? Do as you wish! I think you should study medicine. I will leave you my large library; I have kept it in good order and have subscribed to all the latest books. Medical science is much better than other contemporary sciences. You could serve your fellow man: you would be ashamed to charge money for your services, so you would cure people for nothing, and your conscience would always be clear."

Knowing the old man's stubbornness, neither Volodya nor his mother voiced any objections. The Swiss tutor, however, could not endure this and said, "Of course, a career as a doctor would be splendid. But I don't know why Vladimir Petrovich shouldn't study the law when great efforts are being made to attract educated young men into the civil service."

"He is trying to instruct me as well as you! Well, I visited Geneva when you were still crawling around on all fours," answered the stubborn old man, "my dear *citoyen de Genève!* [citizen of Geneva]." "And do you know," he added in a milder tone, "that in one of the translations we have of Jean Jacques I found the inscription, 'By the Genevan commoner Rousseau'?" The old man laughed so hard that he started coughing.

Although he had told this story of the translation at least a thousand times before, he always assumed that his listeners had never heard it.

"Volodya," he continued in a better mood, "do you write poetry?"

"I've tried to, sir," answered Vladimir blushing.

28. *Pandects.* A five-volume collection (*Digesta Corpus Juris Civilis*) of the decisions, writings, and opinions of classical Roman jurists, compiled in A.D. 533 under Emperor Justinian.

29. *Glosses.* Commentaries on the *Pandects*, compiled at the University of Bologna by Irnerius and his successors between the eleventh and the thirteenth centuries; they served to establish the study of Roman law as a separate academic discipline.

"Please desist, my dear boy; only stupid people write poems. It's mere *futilité* [futility]. You should do something more useful."

Vladimir accepted only this last piece of advice and actually did stop writing poetry. He did not, however, enroll at Oxford but at Moscow University, and not in the medical faculty but in ethics and politics.

The university completed Beltov's education. Before that he had been entirely alone; now he joined up with a boisterous group of young fellows. He learned his own relative worth and encountered warm affection from his peers. Once he encountered genuine beauty, he began to pursue his studies with dedication. The dean became quite fond of him and considered that all Volodya had to do to become an excellent student was to cut his hair shorter and to behave with greater respect.

At last his course of studies came to an end. During graduation the young men received their "travel documents" for life. Sofya decided to move to Petersburg. She wanted to send her son on ahead; then, after settling her affairs, she planned to join him there.

Before these university friends dispersed across the face of the earth, they gathered at Beltov's house on the eve of his departure. They were still filled with hope: the future opened its arms to them enticingly, a bit like Cleopatra reserving the right to punish in return for an experience of ecstasy.[30] The young people sketched out their splendid plans. No one suspected that among them one would end his career as head of some department, squandering his entire fortune in a game of cards. Provincial life would cause another to stagnate, and he would feel ill unless he drank three glasses of herb-flavored vodka before dinner and slept for three hours after. A third would occupy an important post and complain that the younger generation was just not the same as the older one, that their manners and morals were much worse than even his administrator's, and that they were nothing more than idle dreamers.

---

30. *Ecstasy.* Pushkin treats this exotic motif in several works: a lyric poem entitled "Cleopatra" (1828), an unfinished story "*Egyptian Nights*" (1835), and in the curious fragment that begins, "We spent the evening at Princess D.'s dacha" (1835).

Beltov could still hear the vows of friendship, the pledges of loyalty to their ideals, and the sounds of clinking glasses when the Swiss tutor, already dressed in his traveling clothes, came to wake him.

Our dreamer set out for Petersburg with great enthusiasm. Activity! An active life! There his hopes would be fulfilled and his plans realized; there, at the very center of Russia's new life, he would learn about reality. Moscow, he thought to himself, has fulfilled its goal; like a warm, pulsating heart, it has brought together all the veins of government; but Petersburg in Russia's brain, sitting up above, encased in a skull of ice and granite; it represents the mature concept of empire. A series of similar ideas and images drifted effortlessly through his mind with a sort of sacred sincerity.

Meanwhile the coach progressed from station to station. In addition to our two dreamers, it was carrying a retired cavalry colonel with a gray mustache, a civil servant from Arkhangelsk who had brought along some hard, dry fish and some camomile for indigestion, a lackey dressed in a mangy sheepskin coat, and a fair-haired cadet whose cheeks were darker than his hair and who was proud of his impact on the conductor. Vladimir considered all these people interesting and colorful. He laughed good-naturedly when the man from Arkhangelsk offered him some fossilized fish; he smiled at his prolonged rummaging in his purse for money to pay for his portion of cabbage soup and at the impatient colonel who paid instead. He marveled both at the way the native of Arkhangelsk addressed the colonel as "Your Excellency" and at the way that same colonel was totally incapable of uttering even one sentence without beginning and ending it with words far less respectful. He was even amused by the clumsy old lackey wrapped up in *cuir russe* [*yukt* or Russian leather], despite the cold, who served the traveler from Arkhangelsk, or rather who managed to stay alive in spite of his master. The youth took it all in good-naturedly.

Both his arrival in Petersburg and his initial appearance in society were extremely successful. He had a letter of introduction to an influential spinster. After setting eyes on the splendid young man, she decided that he was very well educated and that he spoke several languages fluently. Her brother was the head of a certain department in the civil service. She introduced Vladimir to him. He spoke to the lad for a few minutes and was astounded by his direct manner, his comprehensive education, and his lively, passionate mind. He offered him a post in his own office and recommended that the director pay special attention to him. Vladimir applied himself zealously to his new work. He liked the bureaucracy, as he perceived in through the prism of his youth—a busy, bustling establishment with numbers and registrations, men with anxious looks and piles of papers under their arms. He saw the office as a mill wheel that put into motion masses of people scattered across half the globe. He poeticized everything.

At last Sofya arrived in Petersburg too. The Swiss tutor was still residing with them. Lately he had made several attempts to leave the Beltovs, but he was unable to follow through. He had become such an integral part of their family, he had given so much of himself to Vladimir, he had come to have such a deep respect for Sofya that it was very difficult for him to part with them. He became glum and inwardly torn. As we have said before, he was a cold dreamer, consequently an incurable one.

One evening, soon after Beltov had received his civil service appointment, this small family was gathered around the fireplace. Young Beltov, whose self-esteem and awareness of his own strength and preparedness were well developed, was dreaming about the future. Various hopes, plans, and expectations were seething within him. He dreamt of great civil activities and of devoting his whole life to service. In the midst of these plans for the future, the ardent youth suddenly threw his arms around his tutor: "How indebted I am to you, my good, true friend," he said, "that I have become a man. I am indebted to you and mother for everything. You have meant more to me than my own father!" The Swiss tutor covered his eyes; then he looked at Sofya and at her son and wanted to speak. But he could say nothing. He stood up and left the room.

When he reached his own small room the tutor locked the door, took his dusty old suitcase out from under the divan, wiped it off and began to pack up his treasured possessions, examining each one lovingly. These possessions revealed the man's infinite tenderness. He had preserved a carefully wrapped, crookedly fastened portfolio that had been assembled for him secretly by the twelve-year-old Volodya as a New Year's present. On the front was pasted a portrait of George Washington that had been torn out of a book. The tutor had also saved a watercolor portrait of Volodya at age fourteen. He was depicted with an open collar and a suntanned face; his eyes reflected his cleverness and contained the same look of hope and expectation that had remained with him for the next five years or so. This look still shone forth like the Petersburg sun at special moments; it was a glimpse from his past that did not quite fit together with the rest of his features. The tutor still had the silver mathematical instruments presented to him by the boy's old uncle, as well as a huge tortoiseshell snuffbox imprinted with a scene of Federalization Day.[31] This box had belonged to the old man and never left his side; the tutor had purchased it from the uncle's valet after the old man's death.

When he had packed away these and other treasures, he selected fifteen books and put the rest aside. Early the next morning he quietly slipped out of the house into Morskaya Street. He called a carter. With his servant's help, he carried out his suitcase and books; he told the servant to say that he had gone off to the country for a few days. He put on his long frock coat, picked up his walking stick and umbrella, shook hands with his servant, and set off walking alongside the cart. Large tears were streaming down his cheeks onto his frock coat.

Sofya was extremely surprised at the tutor's departure and fully expected his return. Two days later she received the following letter:

"Dear Madame, Last evening I received the full reward for all my labors. You can rest assured that the moment will remain in my memory forever; it will be with me to the end of my days as a form of consolation and self-justification. At the same time, however, it has solemnly concluded my work once and for all. It demonstrated

31. *Federalization Day.* Swiss Independence Day, or the Anniversary of the Founding of the Swiss Confederation, celebrated on August 1, in commemoration of the unification of the cantons of Uri, Schwyz, and Unterwalden, which joined in a perpetual league for their mutual defense in 1291.

that the time has now come for the teacher to leave his pupil to his own resources; that his influence is now more likely to hinder his pupil's individual development than to promote it. A man must continue to educate himself throughout his life, but there comes a time when his teacher must stop educating him. What more could I possibly do for your son? He has left me far behind.

"For some time I have intended to leave your house, but my weakness and my affection for your son prevented me from doing so. If I were not running away now, I would never be able to fulfill the obligation imposed upon me by my own sense of honor. You know my principles very well. Furthermore, I would not be able to remain with you any longer, since I consider it humiliating to eat another person's bread without earning it. So you see, it follows that I must leave your home now. We shall always be friends but must never speak about this subject again.

"When you receive this letter I shall be on my way to Finland; from there I shall go to Sweden and travel for as long as my funds allow; then I shall find work again, since I still have my strength.

"I have not accepted any salary from you lately. Do not try to send it to me; give one half of it to my servant and divide the rest among the remaining servants. Please convey my warmest regards to all of them. I know that at times I caused those poor people a great deal of trouble. Present to Voldemar the books that I left behind. I shall write to him separately.

"Farewell, farewell, most noble and esteemed lady! May your house be blessed. Indeed, if one has such a son, what more could one wish for? I can hope for only one thing: that you and he live long lives. I kiss your hand."

His letter to Vladimir began as follows:

"My last words to you, Voldemar, are those of a friend rather than of a teacher. You know that I have no living relatives and there is no one closer to me than you are, in spite of the incalculable difference in our ages. My hopes and expectations rest with you. Voldemar, I have earned the right to give you some friendly advice in parting. Proceed along the path that fate has indicated. It is a splendid one! Do not be afraid of failure or misfortune: your great strength will prevail. Fear success and good fortune: you will find yourself on a slippery road. Serve your work, but beware that the opposite does not occur: your work should not serve you. Voldemar, do not confuse the means with the ends. Love of your fellow man and goodness must be the ends. If love should dry up within your soul, then you will never accomplish anything; you will merely be deceiving yourself. Only love can create that which is vital and lasting; pride is futile because it requires nothing outside of itself. . . ."

I cannot possibly copy the whole letter: it is at least three pages long.

Thus did this good, kind figure disappear from Vladimir's life. "I wonder where our Monsieur Joseph is now?" Sofya or her son would frequently say aloud. Then they would both become pensive and in their mind's eye would see his gentle, serene, monastic figure in a long travel frock coat disappearing behind the proud and independent mountains of Norway.

Chapter 7

Azaïs has demonstrated (in an exeedingly boring manner) that there is compensation for everything in the world.[1] Of course in order to accept this conclusion, one cannot be too strict or quibble over details. On this basis we ask your permission to introduce Osip Evseich, as a way of compensating for the loss of Monsieur Joseph. Osip Evseich was a thin, grey-haired man with reddish cheeks, about sixty years old, who wore a shabby civil service uniform and a satisfied expression. For thirty years or so he had been the supervisor of the Fourth Section in the office to which Beltov had been assigned. For fifteen years before that he had been a clerk in that same section; the other fifteen years of his life had been spent in the courtyard of the same office building where he used to occupy the exalted post of doorman's son; this lent him aristocratic significance in the eyes of the watchman's children.

More than anyone else, this man serves as living proof that a person is not educated only as a result of extensive travel, univer-

---

1. *Azaïs*. Pierre-Hyacinthe Azaïs was a French philosopher (1766–1845) who, in a series of short treatises published from 1806 onward, propounded a theory of compensation: in life, happiness and misery always balance out.

sity lectures, or a wide range of activities. Osip Evseich was extremely experienced in the affairs of the civil service and in the knowledge of other people; in addition, he was such a diplomat that he would not have lagged far behind Ostermann[2] and Talleyrand.[3] Clever by nature, he had had the time and opportunity to develop and educate his practical intelligence by sitting in an office since the age of fifteen. Nothing interfered with this process—neither scholarship, nor reading, nor eloquence, nor abstract theories derived from books that can corrupt the imagination, nor the glitter of social life, nor poetic fantasy. All the while he copied documents onto fresh white sheets of paper he came to see people in darker and darker colors. Every day he acquired a deeper knowledge of reality, a truer understanding of his environment, and a mode of behavior that steered him calmly through the troubled waters of office life, which, unprepossessing at best, are often murky and extremely dangerous.

Ministers and directors were replaced, department heads came and went, but the supervisor of the Fourth Section remained the same. Everyone liked him, both because he was so indispensable and because he himself carefully concealed that fact. Everyone singled him out and paid him his due, precisely because he tried to efface himself so completely. He knew absolutely everything and remembered every detail about the affairs of the office. People came to him with inquiries as if he were an archive, yet he never thrust himself forward.

The director offered him a post as head of another department, but he remained loyal to the Fourth Section. They wanted to nominate him for the Order of the Cross, but he postponed the nomination for two years; he requested that he receive a year's salary instead, simply because he thought that the supervisor of the Third Section might envy him. He was that way about everything. No

2. *Ostermann.* Count Andrei Ostermann (1686–1747) was a German-born Russian diplomat during the reigns of Peter the Great and his wife Catherine I. He belonged to the faction that supported the Empress Anna but was exiled to Siberia when Elizabeth gained control of the throne.

3. *Talleyrand.* See Chap. 6, n. 5.

outsider could ever accuse him of taking bribes; no colleague could ever suspect him of being unselfish.

You can well imagine how many matters passed through his hands during the course of his forty-five years of service; never did one of these documents anger or disgust Osip Evseich or so much as spoil his good mood. Not once in his life did his mind wander from the matters described in the documents to the real people and circumstances behind the words. He regarded these matters abstractly, like a large pile of memoranda, communications, reports, and inquiries arranged in a particular order according to specific rules. It goes without saying that for him "acting on matters within his own section" or "setting them in motion," as our romantically inclined supervisors put it, always consisted in clearing his desk of all documents. He would dispense with these as expediently as possible: he sent an inquiry to Krasnoyarsk that could not possibly be returned in less than two years; he prepared a definitive decision on some matter; or, best of all, he transferred the document to another office where another supervisor would terminate this grand game of solitaire according to its rules. He was so objective that he never considered, for example, that people might be reduced to poverty before the answer was ever received from Krasnoyarsk. Themis is supposed to be blind. . . .[4]

It was this most esteemed colleague of Beltov's who, three months after the latter's arrival, completed a thorough examination of some freshly copied documents. Having provided new sustenance for the pens of four clerks, he took out his silver snuffbox, inlaid with black enamel, and offered it to his assistant, saying, "Try some, Vasily Vasilevich; it's Voroshatin tobacco. A friend brought me some from the town of Vladimir."

"Excellent tobacco!" answered the assistant after a brief moment spent hovering somewhere between life and death. He had inhaled a large pinch of the dry, bright-green powder.

---

4. *Themis*. In classical mythology, Themis is the goddess of divine justice, the source of law; her predictions reveal the truth. She is represented as a majestic woman, blindfolded, attesting to her impartiality. She holds the sword of justice in her right hand and the scales in her left.

"Well? It stings a bit, doesn't it?" said the supervisor, rather pleased that he had seared his assistant's nasal membranes.

"Osip Evseich," replied the assistant, gradually recovering from the paralysis caused by the Voroshatin tobacco and wiping his eyes, nose, forehead, and even his chin with a blue handkerchief, "I have not yet asked you how you like the young man newly arrived from Moscow?"

"He seems to be a lively lad; they say that he was appointed by His Excellency himself."

"Yes, indeed, he's a clever fellow, there's no denying that. Yesterday I heard him arguing with Pavel Pavlovich. You know how little he appreciates being contradicted! But this Beltov fellow has a quick tongue. Pavel Pavlovich started to get angry. 'I tell you,' he says, '*this* is how it must be done.' But Beltov replies, 'I beg your pardon, but *that* is how it must be done.' For my part, I rather enjoyed the whole thing. After Beltov left, Pavel Pavlovich said to his friend. 'Just try to maintain order in an office when they assign you that sort of person. Why, I myself am as good as any university. I'll teach him to have a mind of his own! I don't care who appointed him.'"

"So that's how it is," said the supervisor, upon whom, apparently, the story had also produced a cheering effect. "So he doesn't care who appointed him? Three cheers for Pavel Pavlovich! Did he say that to Beltov's face?"

"No. At the end he just added something in French. I must confess, as I watched that exchange, here's what I thought: you and I, Osip Evseich, will still be sitting here opposite each other in the Fourth Section, and *he'll* be sitting over there," and he pointed to the director's office.

"What a mind you have, Vasily Vasilevich!" retorted the supervisor. "There isn't anyone cleverer than you in all three other sections, but I'm afraid you don't know what you're talking about! My friend, in my time I have seen the raw material that produces real men of affairs and heads of offices. This pipsqueak lacks what it takes! Sure, he's clever and zealous, but will that cleverness and zeal take him very far? If you like, I'll bet you a bottle of absinthe vodka that he'll never even become a supervisor."

"I don't want to bet on it, but yesterday I was reading some documents he prepared. He writes very well, so help me God. The only other place I've encountered a similar style is in the *Son of the Fatherland*."[5]

"I've read those documents too; my eyes may be old it's true, but they can still see. He isn't aware of the appropriate forms. If it were because he is stupid or inexperienced, it wouldn't be so bad. He could learn them. But it is because he's so intelligent. He makes romance out of business matters, and the main point slips through his fingers. He doesn't care who submitted the communication, or what the proper procedure is, or to whom it should be forwarded. He merely 'skims the surface,' that's what. Yet, if you ask him a question, then for sure he will try to educate us old-timers.

"No, my friend, I can recognize a promising young man right away; when I first saw him I thought, 'He seems to be a clever fellow; perhaps he'll have a career here. He's not yet accustomed to the civil service; but he'll manage—he'll get accustomed to it.' But now, three months later, he is still fussing about every trifle and losing his temper as if, God forbid, he were trying to save his own father from being murdered. Where will that get him? We've seen that kind of young whippersnapper before: he's not the first, and he won't be the last. They all use words to great advantage: 'I will eradicate these evil practices'; but they don't even know which *practices* or why they are *evil*. They may scream and shout, but they will remain civil servants *without distinction* for their whole lives, all the while foolishly mocking others. They refer to us as office drudges; but it is the drudges who do all the work. When they have to submit a petition to the Civil Bureau regarding one of their own business matters, they don't even know how. They come right to the drudges. The drones!" concluded the supervisor eloquently.

As a matter of fact, the supervisor's opinions were well founded; it was as if events, as though by design, hastened to confirm them. Soon Beltov lost interest in the affairs of the office; he became

5. *Son of the Fatherland*. A Russian historical, political, and literary journal published in Petersburg from 1812 to 1852 under various editors, including N. I. Grech and later F. V. Bulgarin.

irritable and careless. The office supervisor summoned him and talked to him like a tender mother—but it didn't help. The minister summoned him and talked to him like a tender father, in such a touching and generous way that even the administrator who happened to be present shed a few tears, in spite of the fact that, as his subordinates could readily testify, he was by no means a kindhearted man. But that didn't help, either. Beltov began to get so far out of hand that he was offended by these personal interventions of interested parties, by these maternal and paternal attempts to assist him.

In a word, three months after the eloquent conversation between the supervisor and his assistant, Osip Evseich got angry with one of his clerks for failing to understand something and said to him, "When are you ever going to learn? How many times have you already written this kind of document? Why do I have to compose a model for you each time? It's all because you're not concentrating on your work, thinking about gallivanting in your frock coat down the Admiralty Boulevard chasing after 'mamzelles.' I've seen you at it more than once. So, now write down: 'This passport, containing the necessary signatures and official stamp, is hereby issued to retired Provincial Secretary Beltov and entitles him to free residence in any part of the Russian Empire.' Finished? Let's see it!" And then he muttered: "'from his estate . . . serfs . . . district . . . course . . . state . . . September 18 . . . Orthodox'. . . . Good!" And Osip Evseich wrote something on the edge of the paper in very small script.

"Here, now take it over and hand it in; after it's been signed, take it to the Registry Office; the stamp should be placed right here on this side; you see where it says, 'of this passport.' He will come to collect it tomorrow."

"Well, Vasily Vasilevich, you didn't want to bet that bottle of absinthe vodka, and now you see that I would have won it. What can I say? It all happened very quickly!"

"And he was only fourteen and a half years away from earning his first badge," observed the assistant wittily. The supervisor and other officials burst out laughing.

This outburst of Olympian laughter marked the end of our good friend Vladimir Petrovich Beltov's career in the civil service. It was precisely ten years before that momentous day when, just as the *puddin*[6] was being served at Vera Vasilevna's dinner table, the sound of sleigh bells was heard and Maksim Ivanovich could not refrain from running over to the window. What had Beltov been doing during the course of those ten years?

Everything, or almost everything.

What had he accomplished?

Nothing, or almost nothing.

Who is not aware of the popular old belief that children who seem all too promising rarely live up to their promise as adults? Why is this? Can it be that a person's life-forces are distributed in such limited quantity that if they are expended in youth nothing remains for maturity? It is such a complicated question. I cannot answer it, nor do I even want to try. But I think that one should seek the answer in the atmosphere, environment, influences, and contacts of a particular person rather than in some kind of incongruous personal psychological makeup.

Whether true or not, this old belief was further validated by Beltov's example. With youthful vehemence and a dreamer's irresponsibility, he grew angry at circumstances. With inward horror he arrived at almost the same conclusion that had been expressed so eloquently by Osip Evseich: "Only the drudges do any work." And Beltov realized that they do it only because the badgers and mongooses simply can't accomplish anything. All they can contribute to humanity is their strivings and aspirations—often noble, but almost always futile. . . .

One morning—not a fine one, but a typical Petersburg morning, combining the discomforts of all four seasons—wet snow was beating against the windowpanes. It was still dark outside at 11 A.M.; in fact, it seemed to be getting even darker. Sofya was sitting in front of the same fireplace where the last conversation with the Swiss tutor had taken place. Vladimir was reclining on a sofa holding a book from which he was both reading and not reading; finally he stopped reading altogether and put the book down on the table.

6. *"Puddin."* See Chap. 5, n. 11.

After spending some time in a state of lethargic pensiveness, he said, "Mother, do you know what has just occurred to me? That old uncle of ours was right when he advised me to study medicine. What do you think, shall I take it up?"

"As you wish, my dear," answered Sofya with her usual meekness. "The awful thing, Volodya, is that you may have to visit your sick patients, and some illnesses are contagious."

"Mother," said Vladimir smiling and taking her hand affectionately, "Your love makes you so selfish. Of course, it would be safer just to lead an idle life; but I think that one must have a calling to live in idleness, just as one must to lead an active life. Not everyone who wishes can do nothing at all."

"Well, try medicine then," replied his mother.

The next morning Vladimir entered the anatomy theater to commence his study of medicine, as enthusiastically as he had begun his career in the civil service. But he did not carry with him into the theater that same pure love of learning that had earlier accompanied him at Moscow University. Try as he might to deceive himself, medicine served only as an escape. He had chosen it as a result of his failure and boredom, having nothing else to do. A huge abyss separated the once cheerful university student from the retired civil servant, now dilettante in medicine.

Beltov's fine mind soon confronted those questions concerning which medicine is so learnedly silent yet on which everything else depends. He was ready to attack those questions, armed only with the desperate boldness of his thought. He paid no attention whatever to the fact that the answers that he sought can come only as a result of long, persistent, and inexhaustible labor. He was incapable of such labor, and his enthusiasm for medicine, especially for other doctors, waned. He recognized his colleagues from the office all over again. He wished that doctors would dedicate their lives to answering the questions that troubled *him*. He wished that they would approach the beds of their patients as if they were performing sacred rites. But all they wanted to do was to play cards in the evening, to build up large practices, and to enjoy their leisure time.

"No," thought Vladimir, "I don't want to become a doctor! How could I, in good conscience, dare to treat a patient in the face of such disagreement on all physiological matters? Let me put aside all practical pursuits! Indeed, what sort of an official or scientist would I make? I . . . dare I confess it, I am really an artist!" It was in the middle of sketching a human skull that Beltov reached this conclusion. No sooner said than done. He draped the lower windows of his study with impenetrable curtains. A small Venus was placed next to his two anatomical skulls. Everywhere there appeared plaster of paris heads bearing expressions of fear, shame, jealousy, valor, etc., just as experienced sculptors depict these emotions, that is, *not* as they actually appear in nature.

Vladimir stopped cutting his hair and went about all morning wearing a smock, a proletarian garment made expressly for him by an expensive tailor on Nevsky Prospect. He began to visit the Hermitage every week and worked zealously at his easel. . . . His mother sometimes entered his study on tiptoe, afraid to distract this future Titian from his work. He began to talk about making a trip to Italy and about undertaking a work on a historical theme in a forceful, contemporary style. He was hoping to depict the meeting between Biron[7] returning from Siberia and Minikh[8] on his way there. They would be surrounded by a winter landscape—snow, covered sleds, the Volga River. . . .

It goes without saying that painting did not completely satisfy Beltov. Inwardly he did not find it a fulfilling occupation. Outwardly he lacked the proper environment, the lively interaction and exchange that support an artist. Nothing could inspire his work! It was completely unnecessary and depended exclusively on his personal whim. But more than anything, he was troubled by his for-

7. *Biron*. Ernst Johann Biron (1690–1772), a favorite of Empress Anna, was appointed grand chamberlain and count of the Empire. He exercised considerable power upon her ascent to the throne in 1730. Although he was blamed for many of Russia's problems, he nevertheless assumed the regency upon her death in 1740. He was soon banished to Siberia by Minikh (see n. 8, below) but was later permitted to return to the capital by Peter III.

8. *Minikh*. Burkhardt Christoph, Graf von Minikh (1683–1767), a field marshal in the Russian Army who led the palace revolt in 1740 that ousted Biron. Soon afterward, however, Minikh was also sent to Siberia as a result of a power struggle from which the Empress Elizabeth emerged as the ruler of Russia.

mer dreams of a career in the civil service or in government. Nothing in the world is so enticing to an ardent nature as a role in current affairs, history-in-the-making. Anyone who has once harbored such dreams within his breast has spoiled himself for all other activities. In whatever career he may pursue, he will always feel like an interloper. His true calling remains elsewhere. So he introduces political themes into his art, painting his idea if he's an artist, singing it if he's a musician. If he moves into a different career, he will deceive himself just as a person who has left his homeland always tries to convince himself that it really doesn't matter where he lives, that his homeland is any place where he is most useful. He tries—but inside him a persistent voice calls him to another place, reminds him of other songs, a different landscape. Somberly but lucidly these thoughts haunted Beltov. He would look enviously at some German who lived only for his piano, who was content to play Beethoven and study contemporary life *ex fontibus* [according to the original sources], that is from the ancients.

In addition there were those long Petersburg evenings when it was impossible ·to paint. . . . Vladimir often spent them at the home of a young widow, a passionate patroness of the arts. The widow was young and pretty; she possessed all the attractions that luxury and higher education can provide. It was there that Vladimir timidly uttered his first words of love and boldly signed his first promissory note for a huge sum of money that he lost at cards that same happy evening, when, absentminded and enraptured, he was paying no attention whatever to the game. What did he care about cards? *She* sat across from him: what love and caring he could see reflected in her eyes!

This is not the time to relate the entire life story of my hero; its events are most ordinary, but somehow they did not affect his soul in an ordinary way. Suffice it to say that after the experience of love, which consumed a large amount of his energy, and after several promissory notes, which consumed no small part of his fortune, he departed for foreign lands to seek distractions, impressions, pursuits, and so on. His mother, weak and prematurely aged, went to White Meadow to repair the breaches created by his promissory notes, to pay with her yearlong efforts for the momentary diversions of her son, and to amass new funds so that Volodya would lack for nothing during his travels. None of this came easily to Madame Beltov; although she loved her son dearly, she did not make a good landlady for Zasekino Village. She was always prepared to be lenient and allowed herself to be deceived, not out of carelessness or slow-wittedness but as a result of tender delicateness, which kept her from letting on that she knew the truth. The peasants of White Meadow prayed to God for their mistress and paid their quitrent very well indeed.[9]

Beltov wrote often to his mother. And here you might discern that there exists another kind of love, on that is neither so proud nor so demanding as to lay exclusive claim to this term, but a love that is cooled neither by years nor by illness, one that even in old age would open a letter with trembling hands and with aged eyes would shed copious tears onto the dear lines. For Beltova, her son's letters were the source of life itself; they strengthened and comforted her. She leafed through the pages of each letter a hundred times over. His letters were glum, though full of love, and he concealed much from his mother's weak heart.

It was apparent that ennui was consuming him; the role of spectator, to which any traveler condemns himself, had already begun to bore him. He had seen enough of Europe, and there was nothing left for him to do. Everyone around him was busy, as people usually are at home. He saw himself as a guest: a chair was offered, he was showered with courtesies, but he was not let in on the family secrets; and soon the time came for him to go home. But when he recalled his Petersburg experiences, Beltov was overcome by an attack of "spleen," and, without knowing why, he would move from Paris to London.[10] Several months before his return, his mother received a letter from Montpelier. He informed her that he was on his way to Switzerland, that he had caught a mild cold in the Pyrenees, and that therefore he would remain in Montpelier for

9. *Quitrent.* The cultivation of estates in feudal Russia was carried on under the system of either quitrent (*obrok*) or corvée (*barshchina*). Under the former, serfs farmed the land of an estate and paid the landowner an annual sum known as the quitrent. It was customary to supplement it with payment in kind.

10. *Spleen.* Chap. 2, no. 5.

another five days or so. He promised to write soon after his departure; there was not a word about his returning to Russia.

"A mild cold": his mother immediately began to worry and waited for a letter written en route. Two weeks passed, and no letter arrived; almost a month went by, and still no letter. The poor woman was deprived of even the last comfort in separation: the opportunity of writing with the assurance that her own letters would be received. Not knowing if they would, but just to relieve her mind, she sent off two letters to Paris *confiées aux soins de l'ambassade russe* [in care of the Russian ambassador]. Each night she would tell Dunya to dispatch the coachman on horseback bright and early the next morning to the district seat to inquire whether there was a letter from him, although she knew very well that the mail arrived only once a week.

The postmaster was a good-natured old man, completely devoted to Sofya. Every day he told the coachman to report back to her that there were no letters and that as soon as one arrived he would deliver it himself or send it by courier. With what dull grief did the mother listen to this answer, after several hours of anxious waiting! She considered going abroad herself and was just about to summon her neighbor, a retired artillery captain, to whom she always turned for important legal advice (for example, how to compose a polite inquiry as to why there was no store for provisions in their area, etc.). She wanted to ask him where to apply for a passport—to the Records Office or the district court house. Her days of waiting were made even more tedious by the fact that it was autumn. The lime trees had long since turned yellow; dry leaves crunched underfoot. Rain had been falling for days—unwillingly, but constantly. One evening Sofya's maid asked if she could be allowed to attend vespers.

"Yes, of course you may go. Is tomorrow a holiday?"

"Have you forgotten that tomorrow is September 17, your name day—the day of our blessed St. Sofya, and of her three daughters Faith, Hope, and Charity?"

"You may go, Dunya, and don't forget to pray for Volodya," answered Sofya, her eyes welling up with tears.

If a person lives to be a hundred, he still remains a child; if he were to live to be five hundred, a part of him would still be child-like. It would be a pity if that part of him were ever lost—it is so poetic.

What exactly is a name day? Why should we feel joy and sorrow more poignantly on that particular day than on the day before or the day after? I don't know why, but still it is so. Not only a name day but any sort of anniversary produces a great impression on one's spirit. "Today, it seems, is the third of March," says one person, afraid to miss the deadline for selling his estate at public auction. "The third of March, yes, the third of March," replies another, and his thoughts carry him back eight years or so into the past. He recalls a reunion after a long separation;[11] remembering every detail, he adds with a feeling of solemnity, "Yes, exactly eight years ago!" He is afraid to profane the day. He feels that it is a holiday; it never occurs to him that on the thirteenth of March it will be exactly eight years and ten days since that reunion or that every day is some kind of anniversary.

So it was with Sofya. The thought of separation and the absence of communication became harder to bear, almost intolerable, when she realized that Volodya would not be there to congratulate her on her name day, that he might even have forgotten all about it. She sank into a pensive reverie. She recalled how on her name day fifteen years earlier the entire tearoom had been decorated with flowers; how Volodya had deceived her and kept her from entering the room; how she had guessed but had not let on; how eagerly Monsieur Joseph had helped Volodya weave the garlands.

Then she imagined that Volodya was lying ill in Montpelier, at the mercy of some greedy innkeeper. She was afraid to grant her imagination license to go any further, and she consoled herself with the thought that perhaps Monsieur Joseph had met up with him and was staying on to nurse him. He was so affectionate and kind; he so loved Volodya; surely he would look after him, following the

11. *Separation.* An autobiographical reference to March 3, 1838, when Herzen traveled secretly from Vladimir to Moscow in order to meet his fiancée, Natalya Zakharina. It was a dangerous and impulsive act that allowed him to see her only long enough to exchange a few words.

doctor's orders strictly and watching over him as he slept. But why on earth should Joseph be in Montpelier? Well? . . . Perhaps Volodya sent for him as a friend. . . . But then. . . . Once again she became unbearably despondent; a series of gloomy scenes, interwoven with happy reminiscences, haunted her throughout the night.

The next day Sofya was occupied with various chores; this distracted her as much as possible. From early morning the entrance hall was filled with the "peasant aristocracy" of White Meadow. The village elder, wearing a blue caftan, was holding a huge platter with an enormous Easter cake that had been fetched from the district town by the local policeman. The cake gave off a strong odor of hempseed oil that was sufficient to discourage anyone from attempting to violate its integrity. Oranges and eggs were arranged around the edge of the platter.

Among these handsome and imposing bearded peasants, only the clerk was distinguished by his clothes and appearance. He was not merely clean shaven; his face was nicked in several places because his hand (I don't know whether it was as a result of all the letters he had written or because he never greeted the splendid country morning without first consuming at public expense a mug of raw brandy in the local tavern) had the very strange habit of shaking, a fact that seriously impaired his ability to shave, as well as to take snuff. He was wearing a long blue frock coat and velveteen trousers tucked into his boots: he resembled the well-known Australian duckbilled platypus, a distressing combination of animal, bird, and amphibian.

Outside, a six-week-old milk-fed calf mooed plaintively from time to time; it was a hecatomb that the peasants had prepared for their mistress on the occasion of her "nemday."[12]

Sofya was incapable of appearing before her peasants with an appropriately imposing manner. She knew this fact very well herself and always became flustered on such occasions. After the presentation came the liturgy; a public prayer service was held. The artillery captain arrived at that very moment, not in his capacity as

12. *"Nemday."* The peasants' version of the standard form (name day).

legal adviser but rather in his former military guise. As everyone was leaving the church and heading toward home, Sofya was terrified by some loud noise. A neighbor had brought along a small falconet in his carriage and had it fired in honor of the celebration. Sofya's pointer, who happened to be there at the time, stupid hound that she was, failed to understand that a shot could be fired without a target; she got very tired searching for the rabbit or grouse.

Everyone returned home. Refreshments were served. Suddenly the sound of bells was heard, and a handsome post chaise flew across the bridge, dipped behind the hill, and disappeared, only to reappear two minutes later. The driver headed straight toward the manor house, approached it boldly, and halted the horses masterfully right at the bottom of the front steps. It was the old postmaster. He climbed out of the carriage and could not refrain from remarking to his coachman, "Hey, Bogdashka, you're a fine dog, you are! I really must hand it to you!"

Bogdashka, of course, was delighted with the postmaster's compliment. He screwed up his right eye, adjusted his cap, and replied, "It would be a poor show if I didn't try my best to please Your Excellency."

With a solemn and mysterious mien, oozing satisfaction from every pore, the postmaster entered the living room and set about initiating the hand-kissing ritual.

"I have the honor, my dear Sofya Alekseevna, to congratulate you on the great occasion of your name day and to wish you good health. Greetings, Spiridon Vasilevich!" (This remark was directed toward the artillery captain.)

"My compliments to you, Vasily Loginovich," replied the captain.

Vasily Loginovich continued, "I have been so bold as to bring you a little present in honor of your name day. Please forgive me—it's the best I can do. What I have I'm glad to give. It's not an expensive gift—one ruble and fifteen kopecks for shipping and insurance, eighty kopecks for postage. Here, Madame: two letters from Vladimir Petrovich. Judging by the postmarks, one is from Montrachet, the other from Geneva. Forgive me, Madame, I am a sinful man. The first letter arrived two weeks ago, the other one, only five days ago, but I saved them both for today. I kept thinking, what a nice surprise it would be on Sofya Alekseevna's name day, what a nice surprise!"

Sofya Alekseevna treated the postmaster in exactly the same way as the famous French actor Aufresne[13] dealt with Théramène's tale:[14] she didn't hear a thing from the moment she saw the two letters. She seized the packet with a convulsive gesture. She was about to read them right then and there, but suddenly stood up and left the room.

The postmaster was delighted that he had nearly destroyed Sofya first with grief, then with joy. He rubbed his hands together so good-naturedly, savoring the success of his surprise, that not one cruel soul present could find the strength to reproach him for his little joke or to resist inviting him to partake of the refreshments. Sofya's neighbor made the offer, "Well, Vasily Loginovich, you certainly did surprise her with those letters, yes you did! Perhaps, while Sofya Alekseevna is perusing them, it would do no harm if we partook of her generosity. I get up awfully early in the morning!"

So they partook.

One letter had been written en route, the other from Geneva. The second concluded with the following lines: "This meeting, dear *maman*, and this conversation were so overwhelming, that, as I have already indicated above, I have decided to return home to take part in the local elections. I shall leave here tomorrow; I will spend one month on the the banks of the Rhine and go from there directly to Tauroggen without delay. I am sick and tired of Germany. I shall meet briefly with some friends in Petersburg and Moscow and then will come straight home to you, dear mother, to White Meadow."

---

13. *Aufresne.* Jean Rival Aufresne (1729–1806) was an actor well known for his success at *La Comédie Française.* After 1785 he lived in Petersburg and soon became a favorite actor of Catherine the Great.

14. *Théramène's tale.* A reference to Théramène's speech in Racine's tragedy *Phèdre* (1677), based on *Hippolytus* by Euripides, in which she learns of her beloved Hippolyte's death.

"Dunya, Dunya, fetch me a calendar at once! Oh, my goodness, what are you doing? You foolish girl! It's right over there!"

Sofya ran for the calendar herself; she began counting and figuring the days, converting dates from new style to old, from old style to new,[15] all the while thinking about how to rearrange her son's room. . . . She didn't forget anything—except her guests! Fortunately, they were taking good care of themselves and were "partaking" yet a second time.

"It is a very strange thing," continued the president. "I would think that life in the capital would have provided so many amusing diversions that a young man, especially one of independent means, would never be bored."

"Well, what can you do!" replied Beltov with a smile and stood up to take his leave.

"Still, spend some time here with us. Even if you don't find the same sort of dazzling brilliance and education, you will surely encounter some good, simple people who will receive you hospitably into their peaceful family circles."

"That is certainly true," unceremoniously added the counselor who was wearing the order of St. Anna in his buttonhole. "Whatever our little town lacks, it is not hospitality. Moscow has nothing on us!"

"I don't doubt it," said Beltov as he took his leave.

15. *New style to old*. Russians traditionally calculated the year not from Christ's birth but from what they believed to be the moment of creation. In December 1699, Peter the Great decreed that henceforth the Russian calendar would be brought into conformity with Western practice.

PART **II**

Chapter 1

You have already witnessed the sensational and lasting impression that Beltov produced on the respectable inhabitants of the town of N. Now, with your permission, I will report on the impression that the town of N. produced on the respectable Mr. Beltov.

He stopped at the Keresberg Inn, which bore its name not to distinguish it from other hotels, since it was the only one in town; more likely it was named in honor of some nonexistent German town.

This inn was both the hope and the despair of all the petty civil servants in the town of N. It was their source of consolation in time of trouble and of merriment in time of joy. To the right of the entrance the imperturbable proprietor was always standing in the same place behind a large reception desk. In front stood his clerk, wearing a white shirt; he had a thick beard and wore his hair parted rakishly above his left eye. During the first days of each month this desk became the repository of more than half the salary received by each department head, their assistants, and the assistants to these assistants. (Secretaries rarely frequented the Keresberg, least of all at their own expense. The rank of secretary generates a love of acquiring money, along with a love of keeping it; in a word, they become very "conservative.")

The proprietor stood clicking the beads of his abacus with grave dignity. The accursed desk opened its hinged lid to swallow up paper notes and silver coins and returned only ten-, five-, and one-kopeck pieces in change. Then its key clicked, and the money was safely buried.

On only two occasions did the desk feign mortal illness: when Yakov Potapych, the district police officer, appeared before it. No doubt he had come by to pay off his own debts. . . .

Sometimes counselors would drop in for a game of billiards or a glass of punch; they would open one bottle and then another—indulging in bachelor sprees behind their wives' backs. (An unmarried counselor is as inconceivable as a married abbot!) For two weeks afterward they would brag to absolutely all and sundry about their binges.

When such dignitaries did appear at the Keresberg, all the low-ranking officials hid their pipes behind their backs (in such a way that this gesture would surely be noticed, since the idea was not to hide the pipe but to display the appropriate deference). They would bow respectfully. Feigning great embarrassment, they would retire to another room without even completing their game of billiards. It was at the billiard table that Cornet Dryagalov would spend his spare hours (that is, those hours when he wasn't playing cards), astonishing onlookers with his strikingly daring shots and his improbable, perpendicular strokes.

The proprietor, a peasant from a nearby village who had managed to accumulate considerable wealth, knew precisely who Beltov was and what sort of estate he owned. Consequently he had resolved to give him one of the best rooms in the Keresberg Inn. This room was usually reserved for special persons—generals, tax farmers,[1] and the like. *Therefore*, he showed Beltov all of his filthy,

---

1. *Tax farmers*. Individuals hired by the state to collect taxes. The revenues that they brought in from taxes on liquor constituted more than 40 percent of the income generated from all taxes in the state budget. Tax farmers frequently managed to increase their personal wealth during the performance of their official duties.

sordid rooms first, so that when he finally led him to the one that he had already chosen and observed, "Now if this room did not lead directly into the billiard room, I would be delighted to let you have it," Beltov began to insist vehemently that he be given none other than that very room. The proprietor, touched by his eloquence, agreed and demanded a very handsome rate in return. The proprietor's civility toward Beltov was further emphasized by his rudeness toward his other guests.

Beltov's room really did lead into the billiard room. In order to make it private, the proprietor locked the connecting door and cut off the main access to the billiard room from the hallway. Those who wished to play would have to enter through the kitchen. A majority of the guests accepted this inconvenience without protest, just as they had previously accepted all the other trials and tribulations meted out to them by fate. There were those, however, who cried out openly against the proprietor's rude and prejudicial behavior. One assessor, who ten years earlier had served in the military, threatened to break a billiard cue over the proprietor's back. He was so offended that in addition to a series of colorful expressions he added such coherent protestations as, "I am a nobleman myself! Devil take it! If he'd rented the room to a general, I could see it. But to that milksop who's just come from Paris? Pray tell me, in what way is he better than I am? I am a nobleman myself, the oldest in my line and I was awarded a medal in 1812. . . ." "Enough of that, you hothead," replied Cornet Dryagalov, who had his own opinions concerning Beltov. In any case, the proprietor had his way, albeit quietly, trying to joke his way out of it, with the firm indifference and compliant inflexibility of a genuine Russian merchant.

The room that Beltov received (causing injury to the delicate *point d'honneur* [point of honor] of so many others) could have satisfied him only after the sly proprietor had shown him the horrors of four other rooms. It was dirty and uncomfortable and from time to time was filled with the odor of burning fat. This smell, combined with the permanent stench of stale tobacco, produced a foul odor that could have nauseated an Eskimo raised on rotten fish.

The initial bustle caused by Beltov's arrival soon passed. Travel cases, bags, and boxes were delivered to his room. These were followed, finally, by the arrival of Grigory Ermolaevich, Beltov's valet, who brought in the leftovers of their travel provisions—a tobacco pouch, a half-empty bottle of Bordeaux, and the remains of a stuffed turkey. When all these items were distributed on various tables and chairs, the valet went off to the buffet for a drink of vodka, assuring the attendant that in Paris he had acquired the habit of drinking a large *petit verre* [small glass] at the conclusion of every undertaking (whereas in Russia every undertaking is *begun* in a similar way). A crowd of officials wanting to learn all about the newcomer from such a reliable source gathered around. It must be said, however, that the valet did not respond very warmly; he snubbed them all. He had lived abroad for several years and was proudly aware of his status.

Meanwhile Beltov had been left alone. He sat down for a while on the sofa and then went over to the window, which afforded a view of half the town. The lovely scene that greeted him was typical of a provincial locale. The first thing he noticed was a badly painted fire tower with a soldier keeping watch from the upper platform. Then he saw an ancient cathedral standing behind a long building housing public offices, erected in the usual style and painted the inevitable yellow. There were two or three parish churches, each revealing two or three different architectural styles: ancient Byzantine walls adorned with either Greek portals or Gothic windows, or both. There was the governor's mansion, decorated with a gendarme and two or three petitioners of the kind who wear beards.[2] Finally there were the ordinary houses, exactly like those in any other town. Each had consumptive-looking columns attached directly to the facade, or an attic uninhabitable during the winter because of an Italian louvered window extending its entire length, or a smoke-blackened wing to house the servants, and a stable for the horses. As a rule, these houses are purchased by

2. *Beards.* During Peter the Great's campaign to westernize Russia, beards were permitted only upon payment of an annual graduated tax: a few kopecks for peasants, considerable sums for wealthy merchants. These petitioners fall into the latter category.

gallant gentlemen in their wives' names. An arcade of shops extended along the street in a crooked line. They were all painted white, but inside they were dark, always damp, and very cold. In them one could find all sorts of things to buy—calico, muslin, quilting—everything except what one really needed.

Beltov was somewhat touched by the scene that met his gaze. He lit a cigar and sat down next to the window. A thaw had set in, and that always harbingered springtime. Water was dripping from the roof, and streams of melted snow were flowing along the streets. It was as if nature were about to reawaken and emerge from under the ice and snow. But only a newcomer could feel this way—someone who vainly hoped to find spring in the town of N. at the beginning of February. The streets themselves, knowing that there would be more frosts and blizzards and knowing that no leaves would begin to appear until the middle of May, did not rejoice. A sleepy torpor prevailed. Two or three dirty peasant women were sitting outside the arcade of shops, selling crab apples and pears. Taking advantage of the thaw, they were knitting stockings, keeping careful count of their stitches, exchanging a few words occasionally, picking their teeth with their knitting needles, sighing, yawning, and making the sign of the cross over their mouths after every yawn.[3] Not far from them a merchant about seventy years old, with a white beard and a high sable hat, was sleeping very soundly on a folding chair. From time to time the shopkeepers would run out of one shop and into another; a few of them began to close up. No one seemed to be buying anything. Hardly anyone was walking along the street except for a police inspector all wrapped up in a greatcoat with a fur collar. He strode along at a brisk, businesslike pace, with a concerned look on his face and a scroll of paper in his hand. The shopkeepers doffed their hats respectfully, but the policeman paid them no attention.

Then a rather strange-looking carriage passed by. It resembled a pumpkin from which one quarter had been sliced off. This pumpkin was being drawn by four mangy horses. The footman and the gray-haired, wizened old coachman were dressed in coarse, undyed

3. *Yawn.* See pt. I, chap. 4, n. 17.

caftans; behind, a lackey, dressed in a greatcoat adorned with dark green braid, was bouncing up and down. Inside the pumpkin sat another pumpkin—a plump, good-natured landowner and pater-familias with a special sort of map traced in purple veins across his nose and cheeks. Beside him sat his inseparable life companion, who did not resemble a pumpkin in the least but looked more like a dried pepper pod hidden beneath a taffeta tent instead of a hat. Sitting opposite was a pleasant little bouquet consisting of three rural graces—the objects of their mama's and papa's fondest hope but one that burdened their loving hearts with concern. When this mobile vegetable garden had passed through town, silence prevailed once again.

Suddenly a bold Russian song burst forth from a little lane. A moment later three barge haulers appeared with their arms intertwined. They had athletic builds, a familiar swaggering expression on their faces, and wore short red blouses and decorated hats. One of them was holding a balalaika, not so much to provide musical accompaniment but more to lend the group a particular flavor. The barge hauler with the balalaika could hardly refrain from breaking into a dance. The movement of his shoulders indicated that he desperately wanted to crouch down and start kicking his legs. Why didn't he? Here's why. Either from under the ground or from under one arch in the arcade there appeared a patrolman or a police officer with a truncheon in his hands. The song, which had momentarily roused the town from its tedious slumber, was immediately cut off, stopped dead. The balalaika player shook his finger at the patrolman. The venerable guardian of tranquillity proudly withdrew to his arch like a spider retreating to his dark corner after partaking of a fly's brains.

Now the silence was even more firmly established than before. It grew dark. Beltov sat watching and began to feel oppressed, as if an iron weight were bearing down upon him and preventing him from inhaling sufficient air. Perhaps it was the combination of stale tobacco and burnt fat coming up from the floor below. He reached for his hat and coat, locked the door behind him, and went outside.

The town was not very large; one could cross it in no time at all. The same emptiness prevailed throughout. Of course he did encounter a few people here and there. A worn-out servant girl was carrying a yoke with two buckets of water over her shoulder; barefoot and exhausted, she was toiling up a slippery hillside, panting and pausing to rest. A fat and amiable priest in his domestic cassock was sitting in front of his house, watching the servant girl. Beltov also encountered a few lean clerks and a fat counselor. Everyone was so filthy, so badly dressed—not out of poverty but rather from slovenliness—and everyone went about with such pretensions! Titular counselors behaved as if they were Roman senators; collegiate registrars as if they were titular counselors. The chief of police went galloping past in his sleigh, bowing with utmost gracefulness to the counselors, pointing anxiously to the paper that was stuffed inside his jacket. This indicated that he was hurrying to an *afternoon* appointment with His Excellency. . . .

Finally, two fat merchants' wives passed by on their way home from the public bathhouse. They were followed by a cook who was carrying their birch besoms[4] and a bundle of clothes. Their red cheeks indicated that the besoms had served their purpose well. Beltov met no one else on his walk.

"What is the meaning of this silence?" he wondered. "Does it indicate profound thought or the profound absence of thought? Melancholy or mere indolence? I can't tell. And why do I find this silence so oppressive that I want to leave here at once? Why does it weigh upon me so? I am fond of silence. Silence at the seaside, in a village, or just out in a field—on a flat, endless field—inspires me with a poetic feeling of piety or a state of gentle torpor. But not here! There vast spaces are filled with silence, but everything here is oppressive, stifling, petty. Pitiful buildings, not even ruins, all painted and whitewashed. Where are all the inhabitants? Was the town attacked and taken by siege only yesterday? Was it the plague, perhaps? Nothing of the sort! The inhabitants are all at home resting. But when did they ever do any work?"

Beltov's imagination drifted to other towns where noisy streets were bustling with people—towns less patriarchal but more in-

---

4. *Besoms.* A bundle of twigs (usually birch) traditionally used in the Russian bathhouse, where bathers beat themselves and each other to stimulate the flow of blood to the skin and hence to increase perspiration.

volved in worldly pursuits. He began to feel the discomfort that usually attends a wrong decision, especially when we first start to realize our error. Sadly he turned back toward the Keresberg Inn. As he approached it, he heard the deep, drawn-out sound of a bell from the monastery at the edge of town. This sound reminded him of something deep in his past. Vladimir set off in the direction of the bell but suddenly smiled, shook his head, and hastened back to the Keresberg. Poor victim of an age of doubt! You will find no peace in the town of N.!

Beltov spent the next few days engaged in serious reading, studying the rules and regulations governing elections among the nobility. Then he chose his clothes with a certain care and set off to pay the obligatory visits. Three hours later, visibly distressed and exhausted, he returned to the Keresberg with a bad headache. He asked for some mint water and dampened his forehead with some eau de cologne. The mint water and cologne restored some order to his confused mind. Lying there alone on the sofa, he frowned and then almost laughed as he recalled all the events of that day. First there was the governor's waiting room, where he spent a few pleasant minutes with a gendarme, two merchants of the First Guild,[5] and two lackeys who greeted and bade farewell to all those entering and leaving with a very odd salutation: "Best wishes for the holiday just gone by!"[6] Then, like proud Britons, they extended their hands, those same hands that enjoyed the daily privilege of helping the governor into his carriage. Finally there was the drawing room of the marshal of the nobility, where the venerable representative of outstanding nobles in the town of N. assured him that the best preparation for a career in the civil service was the military, because it would provide a person with the "most important thing." Of course, if a person had acquired that most important thing, then nothing else mattered. Then he admitted to Beltov that he was a true patriot; that he was building a stone church for his village; that

5. *Guild*. See pt. I, chap. 2, n. 9.
6. *"Gone by."* Russians traditionally greet each other, "[Best wishes] For the approaching holiday!" The two lackeys alter that formula to produce a very strange salutation.

he couldn't bear nobles who played cards or who went to Paris and had French mistresses, instead of serving in the cavalry and managing their own estates. All of these remarks were intended as some sort of barb aimed at Beltov.

Beltov kept seeing in his mind's eye the faces of all these people. First he pictured the provincial prosecutor, who, in the course of a three-minute conversation, had managed to repeat six times: "You are an educated man. You can understand how little I have in common with the governor. I write directly to the minister of justice, who is also the prosecutor general. The governor is a good man. I have done everything for His Excellency that I possibly can—'I've read and read and read'—but I can do no more. He sees things differently, and I accord him the respect due his high office. But nothing more. And no one can make me. I am not a counselor in the provincial administration." Each time he said this he took a pinch of strong tobacco from a silver snuffbox decorated with a circular pattern. The tobacco was strikingly similar to the French variety, distinguished from it only by a foul odor.

Then, another time, it was the president of the Civil Court—a tall, thin, emaciated man, miserly and unkempt, whose slovenliness bore witness to his incorruptibility.

Then there was General Khryashchov, surrounded by two police superintendents who had been dismissed from their posts and by impoverished landowners, hunting dogs, hunters, servants, three nieces, and two sisters. Beltov recalled how the general had shouted as if he were in his own study, how he'd whistled for Mitka to come in from the entranceway, and how he'd treated his hunting dog with a great show of human affection.

Then there was our friend Anton Antonovich, the president of the Criminal Court, wearing a dressing gown the color of a frog's back and in the company of the counselor with the Order of St. Anna in his buttonhole.

Little by little this distinguished assembly of faces receded in Beltov's mind and merged into the fantastic face of one enormous official: he was frowning, taciturn, and evasive, but he could stand up for himself. Beltov realized that he was no match for this Goliath—not only would a small stone from a slingshot leave him unharmed but even the granite pedestal under the monument to Peter the Great would have little effect on him.

It was a strange thing: ever since he had departed for foreign lands, Beltov had experienced a great deal in both thought and feeling, a stimulation of both intellect and emotion. Life does not just pass by for people in the throes of a powerful idea. Everything seems normal, today goes by like yesterday and everything is ordinary, but suddenly you turn around and notice with astonishment that the distance traversed is enormous; an infinite amount has been experienced and assimilated. So it was with Beltov. He had gone through all of this, but he had not yet achieved a settled state.

For the second time Beltov had encountered reality under the same circumstances as in the office—and once again he shrank from it in fear. He lacked that practical sense that teaches a person to decipher the cursive script of real life; he was too detached from the world around him. The reason for Beltov's detachment was understandable: Joseph had made him the kind of man he was, as Rousseau had Emile.[7] The university continued this general development. A circle of five or six young friends, full of hopes and dreams as vast as their ignorance of life beyond the classroom walls, served to hold Beltov ever more firmly within a sphere of ideas alien and inappropriate to the environment in which it was his lot to live. And after the school doors were closed, his circle of friends, eternal and true unto the grave, paled, paled, and remained only in his memory, or was resurrected in random and needless encounters, and even then only with the help of a glass of wine.

Other doors had opened, not without some creaking. Beltov went through them and wound up in a realm completely unfamiliar to him, so alien that he was unable to adjust to anything. Not one single aspect of the life that seethed around him seemed congenial. He lacked the ability to be a good landowner, an excellent officer, or a diligent official. Therefore there remained in fact only the role of good-for-nothing idlers—gamblers and the general set of merrymakers. In all fairness to our hero, we must acknowledge that he had greater sympathy for the latter group than for the former, but

7. *Emile*. See pt. I, chap. 6, no. 15.

even here he was unable to let himself go. He was too sensitive, and the debauchery of these gentlemen was too sordid and crude. He struggled first with medicine and then with painting. He went on a few binges, gambled a bit—and then left for foreign parts. Needless to say, there too he found no meaningful activity. He worked aimlessly, engaging in every pursuit on earth. He astonished the Germans with the versatility of his Russian mind, and the French with the profundity of his thought. But while the Germans and French accomplished a great deal, he accomplished nothing. He wasted time firing his pistol on a shooting range, sitting in restaurants until late at night, and yielding up body, soul, and wallet to some grisette.

Eventually such a life could not but lead to an agonized need for some serious activity. Despite the fact that in the midst of his apparent idleness Beltov experienced a great deal both in thought and feeling, he had retained from his youth a lack of any practical sense in matters relating to his life. This is why, driven by a longing for activity, he conceived the excellent and praiseworthy plan of becoming a candidate in the election in the first place. And, in the second place, he was so astounded by people he was supposed to have known since birth or about whom he should have been informed (inasmuch as he was entering into such close relations with them), and he was so stunned by their language, manners, and cast of mind that with no effort or struggle he was willing to drop the intention that had occupied him for several months. Fortunate is the man who continues something already begun, who inherits a task. He can accustom himself to it early, without wasting half his life on the choice. He can concentrate, limit himself in order not to spread himself too thin—and he gets things done. But we are more apt to begin anew. From our fathers we inherit only personal property and real estate, and even these assets we preserve badly. As a result, we really don't want to do anything, or if we do, then we venture out into a boundless steppe—where, no matter where you go or what you do, you get nowhere. Such is our multifaceted inactivity, our active sloth.

Beltov belonged entirely to this category of people. In spite of the maturity of his thought, he was not really an adult. In a word, now, more than thirty years since his birth, he was *just getting ready* to begin his life, like a sixteen-year-old boy, without noticing that the door that had been gradually opening was not the one through which gladiators enter but the one through which their bodies are carried out. "Of course, Beltov himself is to blame for much of this." I am in complete agreement with you, while others think that there are people whose faults are better than any virtues. Everything in life is upside down!

Less than a month had passed since Beltov had settled in the town of N., and he had already succeeded in earning the hatred of the provincial landowners. This fact did not prevent the local officials from coming to despise him as well. Among them were some people whom he had never even met; others had met him but had not had any relations with him whatever. Theirs was a pure, disinterested hatred. But even the most disinterested emotions have some cause or other. It is not at all difficult to guess the reason for this attitude toward Beltov. Both landowners and officials existed in their own more or less exclusive circles, close-knit and intimate. They shared their own interests, quarrels, parties, social opinions and customs—all of them, by the way, common to landowners in any province and to officials throughout the Empire. If a counselor from the town of R. were to arrive in the town of N., within a week he would be an active and respected colleague and member of the community. If our dearly respected friend Pavel Ivanovich Chichikov were to arrive to town, the chief of police would surely arrange a drinking party in his honor, and others would flock to him and begin to address him as "chum."[8] Obviously they would recognize their kinship with Gogol's hero.

But Beltov was a man who had retired from the civil service with "fourteen years and six months left to serve until he received his first badge," as the assistant to the department head had put it. He cared deeply for everything that these gentlemen despised. While they spent their time at useful games of cards, he spent his reading harmful books. A wanderer in Europe, a stranger abroad as well as

---

8. *Chichikov.* The hero of Gogol's novel *Dead Souls* devises a scheme to purchase dead serfs ("souls") and to "settle" them on an estate, which he then plans to mortgage. His scheme is eventually thwarted, but not until he has traveled throughout provincial Russia encountering a colorful assortment of landowners.

at home, Beltov was an aristocrat by the elegance of his manners and a man of the nineteenth century by the strength of his convictions. How on earth would provincial society accept him? He could not come to share their interests nor they his. They conceived a hatred for him, realizing intuitively that Beltov constituted a "protest," an indictment of their way of life, a rejection of their entire order. In addition to all of this, there were also a great many "relevant circumstances." Beltov paid very few official visits; those he made were too late. He wore a frock coat at all his morning calls. He addressed the governor too infrequently as "Your Excellency" and never said it at all to the marshal of the nobility, a retired commander of a dragoon regiment, in spite of the fact that his office made him temporarily "Excellent." He treated his own valet so politely that his guests felt offended, and addressed women as if they were human beings, too. In general, he was much too "familiar" in his manner of speaking.

Add to this the fact that he forfeited the good will of the lower levels of the bureaucracy on the day that he arrived at the Keresberg Inn, when access to the billiard room was closed off.

It goes without saying that this hatred of Beltov was so very polite that it was expressed only behind his back. To his face this strong antipathy lavished such crude and stupid attention on its victim that one might have mistaken it for simple, unaffected love. Everyone tried to attract Beltov home to be able to boast subsequently of having made his acquaintance and to win the right to insert into any conversation, "Well, when Beltov was at our house, . . . and I said to him. . . ." Then he would conclude with some innocent slander.

All possible measures were taken by the good citizens of the town of N. to *blackball* Beltov at the local elections or at least to elect him to a post that no one would ever accept voluntarily. At first he was unaware of their hatred toward him and of their parliamentary machinations. Later he began to guess what was going on, but altruistically decided to see it through to the end. . . . Reader, have no fear! For reasons that are well known to me but that I wish to conceal as an authorial ruse, I shall spare you all further details and description of these elections. For the moment, events of a personal rather than a public nature claim our attention.

Chapter 2

No doubt you have long since forgotten about the existence of two young people relegated to the background during the narration of this long episode: Lyubonka and dear, modest Krutsifersky. During all this time many events have occurred in their lives. When we left them, they were almost engaged. Now we meet them as husband and wife. And, as if this were not enough, they are leading by the hand a three-year-old bambino named Yasha.

There is little to report about the last four years. They were happy years that passed in peace and quiet. The happiness of love, especially of love fulfilled and lacking the anxiety of anticipation, is a total mystery shared by two people alone. A third person is superfluous, an unnecessary witness. In this exclusive dedication of two people to each other lies the special charm and ineffability of mutual love. Of course, I could narrate the story of their external lives, but it would not be worth the effort. Their daily cares, lack of money, quarrels with the cook, acquisition of furniture—all this external dust settled on them as it does on everyone else. Matters such as these they found mildly annoying per se, but a minute later this dust was wiped away without a trace and completely forgotten. Through Dr. Krupov's good graces, Krutsifersky procured a post as senior teacher in the gymnasium. He also gave private lessons and even managed occasionally to find parents who paid him in full for his work. Thus they could afford to live modestly in the town of N. They aspired to nothing more.

Aleksei Abramovich refused to provide more than ten thousand rubles for Lyubonka's dowry, in spite of Dr. Krupov's intervention. On the other hand, Negrov resolutely took it upon himself to furnish the young couple's house. He solved this difficult problem rather successfully by transporting to their home everything from his house and storeroom that he no longer needed, probably assuming that it was precisely what they needed. In this way the carriage of sacred memory—the very one upon which Aleksei Abramovich was ruminating while Glafira Lvovna was thinking about his unfortunate daughter of an illegitimate love—the carriage that was now antiquated, lopsided, tarnished, with a broken spring and a sizable dent on one side, was delivered with considerable difficulty to the Krutsiferskys' small courtyard. Since they had no carriage house, the carriage itself served for a long time as a refuge for some tame hens.

Aleksei Abramovich also dispatched a horse to go with the carriage, but she suddenly died along the way, something that she had never done before during her twenty years of impeccable service in the general's stable. Whether her time had come or whether she was mortally offended when the peasant driver made his own horse the trace horse and her the shaft horse as soon as they got out of sight of the master's house—all the same, she died.[1] The peasant was so astounded that for six months or so he kept out of the master's sight.

One of the nicest gifts of all was presented on the morning of the young couple's departure. Aleksei Abramovich summoned Nikolashka, a consumptive young man about twenty-five years old, and Palashka, a very pockmarked young woman. When they entered the room, Negrov assumed a serious, almost stern mien, and said, "Bow down to the ground and kiss the hands of Lyubov Alek-

---

1. *Carriage.* The carriage in question is actually a troika, a vehicle drawn by three horses running abreast. The direction is determined by the center or shaft horse; the outside or trace horses run with their heads pointed toward the sides.

sandrovna and Dmitry Yakovlevich." The second command was not too easily executed. The embarrassed young couple blushed, hid their hands, kissed each other, and didn't know what to say or do next. But the head of the household continued, "Here are your new master and mistress," he said in a loud voice appropriate to such a grave announcement. "Serve them well, and all will go well for you." (You might observe that here he was repeating himself!) "And you," he said, turning to the young couple, "be kind and merciful to them if they behave themselves properly. If they don't, then send them back to me. I have a special 'school' for servants who misbehave, and when they return to you they'll be as soft as silk. Don't spoil them either. This is my generous gift to you at parting. I am well aware that you are unaccustomed to managing a household. You would have a hard time dealing with freed servants, since they are all scoundrels. If they feel like it, they can pick up their passports and go off just like a lord of the manor to seek a job elsewhere. Well, now bow down again and get out of here!" concluded the general eloquently. Nikolashka and Palashka bowed once again and went out. Thus ends the story of their transfer to new ownership. That same day our young couple moved into town accompanied by Nikolashka with a cough and Palashka with a bas-relief complexion.

The Krutsifersky family got off to a good start. They made so few demands on the external world and were so pleased with themselves, so filled with mutual affection, that it was difficult not to think of them as foreigners in the town of N. In no way did they resemble anything around them.

It is remarkable that there are folks who consider Russians in general, and provincial Russians in particular, as patriarchal people, primarily devoted to family life. The truth is that we are unable to drag the Russian family across the threshold of education. What is even more remarkable, perhaps, is that when we lose our enthusiasm for family life, we do not move on to anything else. Neither our personalities nor our mutual interests develop any further. The family merely withers away.

We adopt a particular kind of official formality in our family life. As in a stage setting, everything is arranged for external effect. If husbands didn't abuse their wives and if parents didn't oppress their children, then it would be quite impossible to understand what these people had in common, why they continued to live together and annoy each other. He who wishes to rejoice in our family life must seek the reason in the drawing room but must not set foot in the bedroom. We are not like the Germans, who can inhabit all rooms of their houses for thirty years in a row and be conscientiously happy.

Our young couple was one of the few exceptions to this general rule. They set up their household simply and modestly, not worrying about how others lived. They stayed cautiously within their means, without trying to keep up with others or throwing away their last meager earnings to create a pretense of wealth. They did not seek to cultivate twenty or thirty unnecessary acquaintances. In a word, the home of our modest gymnasium teacher remained unaffected by a large part of those artificial restraints, those "mutual persecutions," of the Lancastrian system called "communal life."[2] Although we all laugh about it, no one has yet had the audacity to rise above it. Here it must be added that even Dr. Krupov, observing his "dear children," became more reconciled to the idea of family life.

A few days after the occasion on which Beltov, dissatisfied and tormented by vague forebodings and by the complete absence of life in the town, had wandered the streets wearing a glum face, with hands thrust deep in his pockets, he might have been able, in spite of his bitterness and indignation, to witness in one of the houses he passed one of those splendid, consoling family scenes that provide proof in all respects of the possibility of happiness on this earth. There was something about this family scene that suggested a summer evening in the garden, when the wind has abated and the pond resembles a shiny mirror gilded by the sun. A small

---

2. *Lancastrian system.* An English system of education devised by Joseph Lancaster (1778–1838) in which each teacher, aided by monitors, was responsible for as many as five hundred pupils. The system was successful in educating large numbers with minimal staff and materials. Although Lancaster was a Quaker, he devised a set of punishments to ensure discipline: shackles, cages suspended from the roof, and bondage to pillars.

village can be seen way off in the distance among the trees; the mist is rising; the herd is making its way home accompanied by a mixed chorus of cries, moos, and the stamping of hooves. One is ready to swear that there could be nothing more desirable in the whole world. And what a good thing it is that the evening passes within an hour, to be replaced by night just in time, so that it never loses its reputation; it forces us to regret its loss before we have time to tire of its beauty.

Semyon Ivanovich Krupov, the single and highly honored guest, was seated on the sofa in a small, tidy drawing room. A young woman was smiling as she filled his pipe. Her husband, sitting in an armchair, glanced with calm serenity and love first at his wife, then at the doctor. Presently a three-year-old child came into the room, waddling from side to side; he made his way directly (that is, going between the legs of the table as though through a tunnel, rather than going around it) toward Dr. Krupov, whom he loved for his pocket watch with a chiming mechanism and two cornelian seals hanging down from his waistcoat.

"Hello, Yasha," said the doctor, reaching down to his little friend, who had come out from under the table. He picked him up and sat him on his lap.

Yasha reached for one of the seals and pulled out the watch.

"Now you won't be able to drink your tea or smoke your pipe. Let me take him," said the mother, who was firmly convinced that Yasha could never be a nuisance to anyone.

"Please leave him here. When he becomes a nuisance, I'll send him on his way." Dr. Krupov took out his watch and made it strike. Yasha listened to the sound rapturously, then put the watch up to Dr. Krupov's ear, finally to his mother's ear; after taking careful notice of their astonished looks, he proceeded to bring the watch up to his mouth.

"Children are one of life's greatest joys," said the doctor. "It's especially pleasant for an old man like me to stroke their curly hair and to gaze into their bright eyes. The sight of such young seedlings keeps one from becoming coarse and self-centered. But I shall tell you quite frankly that I don't regret not having children of my own. What would I do with them? Now, God has given me a little grandson. When I get too old to work, I'll become his nanny."

"There nanny," said Yasha, pointing to the door with a look of great satisfaction.

"Let me be your nanny," said the doctor.

Yasha was about to object to this offer by emitting a loud howl, but his mother prevented him from doing so by directing his attention to a gold button on Dr. Krupov's coat.

"I am very fond of children," he continued, "In general I like people. When I was younger, I was especially fond of a pretty face. In fact I was in love five times, but family life is repulsive to me. A man can live a free and peaceful life only when he lives alone. Family life seems to be organized precisely so that people living together under the same roof tire of one another. They are forced to go their separate ways. If you don't live together, then you can preserve a friendship as long as you like; but if you live together, it becomes oppressive."

"Enough of that, Semyon Ivanovich," protested Krutsifersky. "What are you talking about? You really have no conception of that whole side of life, the best side, replete with joy and rapture. What is it that you see about that freedom of yours? It consists in the absence of all feeling, in pure egoism."

"There you go! How many times have I told you, Dmitry Yakovlevich, that you can't frighten me by using the word 'egoism'? What excessive pride you have! 'The absence of all feeling'— as if the only important feeling on earth was the idolatrous worship of a husband for his wife or a wife for her husband, and their jealous desire to swallow each other up completely, leaving nothing for anyone else, to weep only over their own sorrows, to rejoice in their own joys. No, sir. I know only too well your self-sacrificing love. I don't want to boast, but since we have started on this topic. . . . As I go to visit a patient I feel my heart sinking. When I last left him, he was in a bad way. Now I approach his bed with trepidation. But wait, yes, his pulse is stronger now! He looks up at me with his weak eyes and gives my hand a little squeeze. That, my dear sir, is also 'feeling.' 'Egoism?' Except for the insane, who is not an egoist? Some people are outright egoists, while others are. . . . Well, you know the proverb: 'It's still only a pike, even if it's covered with horseradish sauce.' The fact of the matter is that there is nothing more exclusive than 'family egoism.'"

"I don't know what it is, Semyon Ivanovich, that so terrifies you about family life. I have been married for four years now, and I enjoy complete freedom. I am not aware of any sacrifices or burdens either in my life or in my husband's," said Lyubonka.

"Those who have broken the bank have nothing but praise for the card game. Miracles happen. You are an exception, and I am very happy for you. But that doesn't prove a thing. Two years ago our tailor's child. . . . You know them, the tailor Pankratov on Moskovsky Street . . . well, his child fell out of a second-story window onto the pavement. And what do you think? Was it hurt? Not at all! Sure, a few scratches and bruises, but nothing more. Now, shall we try it with another child to see what happens? Unfortunately, something even worse has happened to the Pankratovs. The child is ailing."

"Is this some evil omen for our family?" asked Lyubonka, amiably placing her hand on Semyon Ivanovich's shoulder. "I'm not afraid of your prophecies since you warned my husband of the dire consequences of our marriage."

"You have been holding a grudge all this time! Aren't you ashamed of yourself? And that blabbermouth husband of yours told you everything? A fine man he is! Well, thank God, thank God, that I have been proven wrong. Please forget everything I said. 'He who remembers an old wrong must pay for it with an eye,' even if the eyes are as lovely as yours," he said, pointing to Lyubonka.

"I see that Semyon Ivanovich is still paying compliments."

"I'll pay you an even bigger and better compliment. Observing you, I have become more reconciled to the idea of family life. But don't forget that in all my sixty years your home is the first place I have encountered an example of family happiness outside of fiction or poetry. Examples are not all that common."

"How do you know that?" replied Lyubonka. "Perhaps other couples have passed by you completely unrecognized. Genuine love is not very eager to reveal itself in public. Have you ever searched for it, and if so, how? In the end it is mere chance that you have met so few examples of family happiness. It may be, Semyon Ivanovich," she added with that mocking malice and even indelicacy that characterize all happy people, "that you now feel you must stand firm. If you were to confess that you had made a mistake, then you would be judging your entire life and would have to recognize that there is no way at all to change it."

"Oh, no," retorted the old doctor vehemently. "Don't worry about that! I never regret the past—in the first place, because it is stupid to grieve over something that cannot be returned and in the second place because I am an old bachelor and will live out my life in peace and quiet, while you are just splendidly beginning to live yours."

"I have no idea," said Krutsifersky, "why you just said what you did, but it has affected me deeply. It has revived one of those persistent, melancholy thoughts that reside deep within the soul and that can poison any moment of the most perfect rapture. At times my own happiness terrifies me. Like the owner of enormous riches, I tremble in fear before what the future may hold. It's as if. . . ."

"As if you'd have to pay for it later. Ha! What dreamers you are! Who was it who measured out your happiness? Whom will you have to pay? What a childish attitude! You yourself and Chance combined to create your happiness; therefore, it is yours. It would be ridiculous to punish you for it. Of course, that same irrational, irresistible Chance can destroy your happiness. Anything can happen! Perhaps the beams holding up this ceiling are rotten; perhaps it will cave in. So let's get out of here! But how can we? We might be attacked by a mad dog in the courtyard or knocked down in the street by a runaway horse. . . . If one submits to fear of all possible evil, then it would be better to swallow a large dose of opium and fall asleep forever."

"I have always been surprised, Semyon Ivanovich, at the ease with which you accept life. It is your good fortune, your great good fortune, but such good fortune has not been granted to everyone. You say the word 'Chance' with complete composure. I cannot do that. Things would not be any easier if I called 'Chance' that incomprehensible, but still palpable element that joins all the events of my life. Everything in life has its purpose; everything has its lofty meaning. It was not without good reason that you came upon me that day in my attic room. There was no shortage of tutors in Moscow. Why did you choose me? Was it not because I could serve as the instrument for liberating this pure, noble creature and because that which I was afraid to think and dream about would suddenly happen and my happiness would be immeasurable? And where is there justice if this continues for the rest of my life? I submit to happiness as others submit to unhappiness, but still I cannot rid myself of a fear of the future."

"That is, of what does not exist. For my part I can say that all my life I have never understood and never will understand the kind of morbid imagination that takes pleasure in torturing itself with fantasies, thinking up terrible misfortunes and grieving in advance. To possess such a character is itself a kind of misfortune. If a catastrophe occurs and grief overtakes you, then of course you will hang your head and weep. But to think that tomorrow fate will offer you a glass of sour kvass while today you should be drinking a goblet of fine wine, that is a kind of madness. The inability to live in the present, to value the future and to trust in it—that is one of the most widespread moral epidemics of our time. We are all still like the Jews who refrain from eating and drinking in order to save a few kopecks for a rainy day. And no matter how rainy the day, we still won't open the trunk. What kind of life is that?"

"I agree with you completely, Semyon Ivanovich," said Lyubonka vehemently. "I have often spoken with Dmitry about this. If things are going well, why worry about the future? It's as if it didn't even exist. He frequently agrees with me, but a secret sorrow is so deeply implanted within him that he cannot overcome it. Besides, why should he?" she added, smiling cheerfully and sweetly at her husband. "I love even this sorrow of his; it is so profound. I think that you and I don't really understand, or at least we don't sympathize with his sorrow, because we possess more superficial and accommodating characters. We can be distracted and amused by external things."

"You began with a wedding march but ended with a funeral dirge. When you started talking, I wanted to kiss your hand and say to your husband, 'That shows a genuine human understanding of life.' But you finished by calling his fantasies 'profound.' What sort of profundity is it to torture himself when he should be rejoicing, to grieve over things that may never come to pass?"

"Semyon Ivanovich, why are you being so exclusive? There are tender natures who cannot enjoy complete happiness on earth, who are prepared to sacrifice everything except the note of sadness that lies at the bottom of their hearts. That note is always ready to emerge. . . . In order to be happier, one must be coarser. This thought has often occurred to me. For example, look at how imperturbably happy birds and beasts are, because they understand so much less than we do."

"But it is rather unpleasant," said the relentless Dr. Krupov, "to be a creature endowed with a lofty nature and still be obliged to live no higher and no lower than on earth. I confess that I consider such 'loftiness' a physical disorder or an attack of nerves. Take cold sponge baths and get more exercise, and half of your starry-eyed fantasies will disappear. Dmitry Yakovlevich, you have had a weak constitution since birth. Often in weaker physical specimens intellectual capabilities are extremely well developed; but almost always they are skewed in an abstract, fantastic, or mystical direction. That's why the ancients argued *mens sana in corpore sano* [a sound mind in a sound body]. Just look at the pale, blond Germans. Why are they such dreamers? Why do they hold their heads to one side and weep so often? Because of scrofula and their climate! As a result they are prepared to spend their whole lives debating mystical controversies, and they never get anything accomplished."

"It is said, not without good reason," Semyon Ivanovich, "that a medical education fosters a dry, materialistic outlook on life. You have become so well acquainted with man's physical side that you have forgotten all about his other side, the part that has escaped your scalpel and that alone can give meaning to coarse matter."

"These idealists will be the end of me," said Semyon Ivanovich who was beginning to get noticeably angry. "They always blurt out some nonsense or other! Whoever told them that all medicine consists only of anatomy? They thought it up themselves and were thus consoled. What kind of 'coarse matter'? I know neither coarse nor refined matter, only living matter.[3] You are clever, you modern

---

3. *Living matter*. Krupov is here crudely restating Hegel's idea of nature. See A. I. Volodin, "Gertsen i Gegel'," in *Problemy izucheniya Gertsena*, ed. Yu. G. Oksman (Moscow, 1963), 98.

scholars, but you are swimming in very shallow water! This is an old argument. It will never be resolved, so better leave it alone."

"Look, we've put Yasha to sleep with our silly debate. Sleep, little one! Your papa has not yet taught you how to despise the earth and all matter, nor has he convinced you yet that these sweet little hands and feet are nothing but clumps of mud fastened on to you. Lyubov Aleksandrovna, please refrain from instilling such ridiculous ideas in him. You can make allowances for them in your husband. Good luck to him! But at least don't corrupt an innocent young child with that nonsense. What will you make of him? A dreamer! He will spend all his time searching for the firebird;[4] meanwhile, real life will pass through his fingers. Would that be a good thing? Here, take him."

The old doctor handed Yasha to his mother and picked up his cap. Slowly buttoning his coat, he said, "Oh, by the way, I forgot to tell you. A few days ago I made the acquaintance of a most interesting gentleman."

"Could that be Mr. Beltov?" asked Lyubonka. "His arrival has created such a commotion that even I heard about it from the director's wife."

"Yes, indeed it could. The commotion is all because he is wealthy; but the fact is that he is really an extraordinary man. He knows everything, has seen everything, and is really very clever. He's a little spoiled, perhaps—you know, his mother's beloved child. He was not brought up with any adversity, as we were. Thus far he has been living without a care in the world. But now he's here and dying of boredom; he's suffering from spleen.[5] You can well imagine what it's like to be here after Paris."

"Beltov. Wait a minute," said Dmitry Yakovlevich, "the name is familiar. Wasn't he at Moscow University at about the same time I was? Beltov was finishing up his course of study just as I was beginning mine. Even then he was reputed to be very clever. They said that he had been reared by a Swiss tutor."

4. *Firebird*. An image from Slavic folklore of a bird whose brightly colored wings "shine like fire." It must be captured by the hero of a number of Russian folktales. Many try, but only the youngest (and supposedly "foolish") son ever succeeds.

5. *Spleen*. See pt. I, chap. 2, n. 5.

"That's him, the very one."

"I do remember him. We were slightly acquainted."

"I'm sure that he would be very glad to see you. Coming across an educated man in these remote parts is like discovering a rare treasure. And, as I have already observed, Beltov is totally incapable of being alone. He needs to talk and wants to exchange ideas. He is pining away from loneliness."

"If you don't object, perhaps I'll call on him."

"A fine idea. Let's go together. . . . No, wait a minute. Although I am getting on in years, I'm still too impulsive. His wealth makes it awkward for you to call on him first. I'll tell him about you tomorrow. If he wants to, he can come along with me to visit you. Good-bye, my dear debater. Good-bye."

"Oh, do bring your Beltov here tomorrow," said Lyubov Aleksandrovna. "We've heard so much about him that I can hardly wait to meet him."

"He is worth meeting, indeed he is," said the old doctor as he stepped into the hall.

Every time he came to visit, Krupov argued with Krutsifersky; he always got angry and said that they were growing farther and farther apart. This did not prevent them in the least from growing closer and closer together every day. For Dr. Krupov, Krutsifersky's family was his own family. He went there in order to give his heart free rein (for it was still a warm heart) and to rest, as he enjoyed their happiness. For the Krutsiferskys, Dr. Krupov represented the senior member of their family—a father or an uncle—the sort to whom love ties, rather than kinship, conveyed the right to scold them or be rude. Both Lyubonka and Dmitry forgave him from the bottom of their hearts and were sad if they didn't see him for two days in a row.

The next evening after dinner, at about seven o'clock, Semyon Ivanovich brought Beltov to the Krutsiferskys in his wide sledge covered with a yellow rug and drawn by a pair of small roan horses. Needless to say, Beltov was absolutely delighted to make the acquaintance of such a decent fellow. It never even occurred to him that he was paying a "first visit." His host and hostess were a little embarrassed. Semyon Ivanovich's lavish praise, rumors about his life abroad, even his great wealth—all of this was recollected vaguely as he entered the room, and it made the occasion seem rather awkward. But this feeling quickly passed. Beltov's manner and speech were so open and unaffected, and he displayed such tact, a characteristic common to people with refined and sensitive souls, that before half an hour had passed their conversation assumed a very friendly tone. Even Lyubonka, unaccustomed to meeting strangers, was involuntarily drawn into the discussion. Beltov and Dmitry reminisced about their university days, retold a number of old stories, recalled hopes and dreams of years gone by. It had been a long time since Beltov had felt so happy. During the drive back to the Keresberg Inn he thanked the doctor profusely for introducing him to the Krutsiferskys.

"Well, what do you think?" Semyon Ivanovich asked the Krutsiferskys afterwards. "How do you like your new acquaintance?"

"Need you ask?" answered Krutsifersky.

"I liked him very much," said Lyubov Aleksandrovna.

Semyon Ivanovich, extremely satisfied that he had afforded them so much pleasure, playfully shook his finger at her. Lyubov Aleksandrovna blushed.

Family scenes are fascinating. Now, having finished this one, I cannot refrain from beginning another. Let me assure you that the close connection between them will soon become apparent.

Chapter 3

Karp Kondratich, marshal of the nobility of the Dubasov district,[1] had a daughter named Varvara. Under normal circumstances this would have been no great misfortune either for the venerable Karp Kondratich or for his dear daughter Varvara Karpovna. But in addition to having a daughter, Karp Kondratich also had a wife. And, in addition to having a father, Vava (as she was called at home) also had a dear mommy named Marya Stepanovna. This fact radically altered the entire situation.

Karp Kondratich was the perfect model of meekness in family matters. It was amazing to observe the change in him as he passed from the stable into the dining room or from the barn into the bedroom or parlor. If we were not in possession of reliable documents from eminent travelers testifying to the fact that one and the same Englishman could be both an excellent estate manager and a loving father, then we too would have doubts about the possibility of

---

1. *Marshal of the nobility.* A representative of the nobles of a certain province or district, elected for three years to manage their affairs and to represent their interests in local government. Each elected official had to be confirmed by the government.

such a dual personality. However, if we consider the matter on yet a deeper level, we can observe that this is precisely as it should be. Outside the house, that is, in the stable or the barn, Karp Kondratich was waging a war. He was a military commander who rained down blows upon his enemies. His enemies, of course, were those rebellious conspirators—indolence, inadequate devotion to the master's best interests, insufficient attention to his four fine bay horses, and other similar crimes. On the other hand, in his own drawing room, Karp Kondratich enjoyed the soft embraces of his loyal, pudgy spouse, and he implanted tender kisses on his daughter's upturned face. He removed the heavy armor of his manorial duties and became, if not a good-natured man, then a good-natured Karp Kondratich.

His wife's situation was altogether different. For the last twenty years she had been carrying on limited guerrilla warfare within the four walls of her house, occasionally venturing out on small sorties to obtain eggs and yarn from the peasants. Energetic skirmishes with maids, the cook, and kitchen assistant kept her in a state of constant irritation. But in all fairness to her it must be said that her soul did not find these trivial and belligerent occupations altogether fulfilling. When her daughter Vava finished her studies either at an institute or a boarding school and was brought home from Moscow by a great-aunt, Marya Stepanovna embraced the seventeen-year-old girl warmly and tearfully. It was clear that this was not merely the cook or one of the maids—but her own daughter. The same blood flowed through their veins. Marya Stepanovna recognized her sacred duty. At first Vava was allowed to rest and to run in the garden, especially on clear, moonlit nights.

For a young girl who had been reared within four walls, all of this was quite new, "charming and enchanting." She looked at the moon and, remembering one of her beloved friends, was convinced that her friend was thinking about her at that very same moment. She carved their initials on trees. . . .

Vava was at a stage that cold-hearted people find very amusing. But in us this stage produces a smile—not one of scorn but the same kind of smile with which we watch children at play. We ourselves can no longer play, but let them enjoy it. It is altogether unjust to accuse young girls who have just left boarding school of "affectation and exaltation," as is usually done. A sacred sincerity pervades all their dreams and self-sacrifices of this period, with its readiness to love, its absence of egoism, its devotion and self-denial. Life has reached a turning point; the curtain has not yet been raised on the future. Behind it are terrible but enticing mysteries. The heart yearns in earnest for something unknown, the body is in a process of maturation, the nervous system is in a state of irritation, and tears are ready to flow unceasingly. Five or six years later, everything will be different. If the girl marries, then that's the end of it. If she doesn't, and, if she possesses only a spark of healthy nature, she will not wait until someone comes to raise that mysterious curtain. She will raise it herself and look at life altogether differently. It is ridiculous for a twenty-five-year old woman to look at the world through the eyes of a young girl who has just left school. It is sad for a young girl who has just left school to look at things as if she were a twenty-five-year old woman.

Vavara Karpovna was no beauty, but she did possess that splendid substitute for beauty, *a special something, ce quelque chose*, which, like the bouquet of a fine wine, is appreciated only by the discriminating. And this *special something*—as yet undeveloped, prophetic, clairvoyant, in combination with youth (which colors and adorns everything)—conferred upon her a particular delicate, subtle charm inaccessible to most. Catching sight of her rather thin face and dark complexion, her clumsy figure, her thoughtful eyes with their long lashes, one could not help wondering when these traits would be transformed, how they would take shape, when these thoughts and feelings and those eyes would receive their proper definition, meaning, explanation, and how lucky the man upon whose shoulder this head would come to rest!

Marya Stepanovna, however, was extremely dissatisfied with her daughter's appearance. She referred to her as a "plain Jane" and ordered her to wash her face every morning and evening with cucumber lotion to which she added some special powder that was supposed to cure the swarthiness of her daughter's complexion, which she referred to as her "suntan." Vava's behavior in the presence of guests forced Marya Stepanovna to devote special attention to her. Vava was shy; she didn't try to attract men or make eyes at them. Instead, she went out to the garden to read. First the main culprit, the book, had to go. Then came endless maternal admonitions. Marya Stepanovna felt that Vava obeyed her with insufficient cheerfulness, that she knitted her brows and sometimes even dared to *answer back*. You yourself will doubtless agree that it was high time to implement decisive measures against such behavior. For the time being Marya Stepanovna suppressed all maternal love and affection for her daughter and began to persecute her and oppress her at every turn. She did not permit Vava to go out for a stroll when she wanted to, and sent her out for one when she wanted to sit at home. She forced her to eat against her will and reproached her daily for not gaining more weight. Her mother's persecutions made Vava withdraw even more. She became more unsociable and thinner than ever. Karp Kondratich occasionally thought that his wife was persecuting the poor girl for nothing. He even tried speaking to her about it in a roundabout way. But as soon as the conversation began to move toward greater clarity, he felt the onset of insurmountable terror and left for the barn at once. There he compensated for his one brief moment of terror by subjecting his vassals to prolonged terror. The battlefield was abandoned to Marya Stepanovna. With great zeal she acquired hand-woven tablecloths, napkins, and linen for Vava's future dowry. She was almost the cause of blindness in seven maids who were set making lace and three who were forced to embroider unnecessary sundries for Vava. At the same time she incessantly persecuted and oppressed her daughter as if she were her personal enemy.

When the Kondratich family arrived in the town of N. for the provincial elections, Karp had to struggle to fit into his nobleman's uniform, since in the last three years the marshal had expanded considerably, while the uniform, on the other hand, had shrunk slightly. First he went to pay a call on the head of the province, then on the marshal of the provincial nobility, whom he distinguished from the governor by using the witty title of "*Our* His Excellency." Marya Stepanovna occupied herself with arranging their living quarters and unloading all sorts of rubbish transported from the country on four carts. She was assisted in this work by three lackeys whose hair had never once been combed since birth. They were wearing short grayish tailcoats made from a material that was not quite flannel and not quite wool. Things were proceeding full speed ahead when suddenly the mistress, struck by a sudden thought, stopped and shouted in her sonorous voice, "Vava, Vava, where are you hiding yourself, eh?"

The poor girl, sensing the ominous tone, entered the room timidly. "Here I am, *maman.*"

"Just look at you! Are you ill or what? To tell you the truth, someone might think that you lead a difficult life in your parents' house. Those boarding schools! And she comes in with such a face when called." Here Marya Stepanovna mocked the girl's doleful expression. "I was a daughter once, too, you know. When my mother summoned me, I would go to her with a cheerful look." Then Marya Stepanovna demonstrated her own cheerful, smiling look. "But you, you can only scowl. . . . Hey, you idiot, you'll break it! And what's so funny about that? . . . He's dragging it, the peasant! You can never teach them a thing. Well, my dear, joking aside, I'm telling you for the last time that your behavior distresses me. While we were still living in the country I could remain silent, but here I simply cannot tolerate it. I didn't drag myself all this way so that people would say that my daughter is a foolish little savage. I will simply not allow you to sit in a corner here. How is it that you don't know how to attract the attention of even one admirer? When I was only fifteen years old I had so many suitors that I could hardly escape from them! It's high time for you to settle down once and for all, do you understand? . . . Oh, you scoundrel, you! I said you would break it. Come here. Over here! I'm talking to you. Show it to me! See? You fool! How did you manage to break it in two? You'll pay for this! Wait until the master returns! I would pull your hair out myself, but it's disgusting to get that close to you. You put so much oil on it. I know. It's that kitchen boy Mitka who steals oil from the master. Just you wait, I'll get my hands on him, too! . . . Yes, my dear Varvara Karpovna, do me a favor and find yourself a husband during these elections. I will provide the suitors. I will not stand for any more of your nonsense. Who do you think you are, a great beauty or what, that men will come in search of you? Neither your face nor your body would attract anyone. And yet you don't want to do a thing to improve yourself! You don't know what to wear or how to talk, even though you studied in Moscow. No, my fine lady. Put your books aside. You have read more than enough. It's time, my dear, to set to work. I shall drive you out of my sight if you don't mend your ways."

Vava stood like someone who has just been condemned to death. Her mother's last words came as a small consolation.

"How is it that you can't find a suitor? Three hundred and fifty serfs! And each one of our serfs is worth two of our neighbors'! And what a dowry! What? What's that? You're starting to cry! Yes, cry. Go on, make your eyes red! That's how you reward my maternal efforts on your behalf."

Marya Stepanovna moved very close to her daughter. Vava's hair was so soft and dry: it is not at all clear how this episode would have ended, had the bearlike servant wearing the short frock coat not dropped a dessert plate at that very moment. Marya Stepanovna transferred all her rage to him.

"Who broke that plate?" she shouted in a hoarse voice.

"It broke all by itself," answered the servant, obviously exasperated.

"What? All by itself! You dare tell me that it broke all by itself?" She said the rest with her hands, doubtless believing that actions speak louder than words.

The tormented girl could bear no more. Suddenly she burst into tears and threw herself down on the sofa in a terrible fit of hysterics. Marya Stepanovna became frightened and called for help: "Somebody! Water! Smelling salts! Send for a doctor, at once!" The fit was a prolonged one; the doctor did not arrive immediately. A second messenger was sent to fetch him but he returned with the same answer, "He told me to say that you will have to wait a little while. He's helping a woman through a difficult labor."

"Bah! Curse him! Who is it who couldn't wait to have her baby?"

"The prosecutor's cook," answered the messenger.

That was all that was needed to complete Marya Stepanovna's tragic predicament: she turned bright red. Her face, which was never very attractive, became positively repulsive.

"A cook? A cook!" She couldn't utter another word.

Karp Kondratich entered with a happy and contented look on his face. The governor had amicably shaken him by the hand, and His Excellency's wife had taken him in to the living room to see the new rug sent from St. Petersburg. After seeing the rug, he said with an expression full of patriarchal simplicity (behind which we know so well how to conceal both flattery and servility), "My dear Anna Dmitrievna, who should own such fine rugs if not Your Excellencies?"

Karp Kondratich was very pleased by all of this, particularly by his own appropriate response. But suddenly a family scene came crashing down on his head. His daughter was having hysterics, his wife was in a rage, and a broken plate lay on the floor. Marya Stepanovna's face was indescribable, and her right hand was bright red, almost as red as Tereshka's left cheek.

"What's going on? What's happened to Vava?"

"Obviously it's the result of our journey here. She's only a young girl," replied the tender mother. "How can she possibly endure a trip of 120 versts? I told you to postpone it until Wednesday, but you said no. Now *you* revive her."

"But on Wednesday it would still have been the same number of versts!"

"You always know best! And never allow that murderer Krupov to set foot in our house again. He's a Freemason[2] and a scoundrel! I sent for him twice. Surely I'm not the least important person in town! . . . And why is it? It's because you don't know how to act. You behave worse than a mere juryman. I sent for him, but he chose to make fun of me. The prosecutor's cook, he says, is in labor. My daughter is dying, and he's attending to the prosecutor's cook. He's a Jacobin,[3] that's what!"

2. *Freemason.* A member of a religious and ethical movement that arose in England during the early eighteenth century and then spread throughout Europe and the world. The first lodges in Russia were established during the 1730s and became forums for the expression of opinion opposed to the autocracy. The movement was persecuted by Catherine and banned in 1792. Alexander I tolerated the lodges and tried to use them for his own purposes but failed. The Masons subsequently became associated with the Decembrists.

3. *Jacobin.* A member of the group that spearheaded the French Revolution of 1789. At first they supported a constitutional monarchy; later they helped to overthrow the regime and advocated a democratic republic; finally they carried out terrorist policies under Robespierre.

"A rogue and a scoundrel," confirmed the marshal.

Marya Stepanovna's boiling torrent of words had still not abated when the door to the hall opened and old Dr. Krupov entered, walking stick in hand, with his somewhat pedantic expression. He looked more pleased with himself than usual. Even his eyes were lit up with a smile. Without taking any notice of the fact that he got no greeting from either Karp Kondratich or Marya Stepanovna, he asked, "Who is in need of my assistance?"

"My daughter," replied Marya Stepanovna.

"Ah, so it's Vera Mikhailovna, is it? What's the matter with her?"

"My daughter's name is Varvara, and mine is Karp," observed the marshal, not without a sense of self-importance.

"Excuse me. So what is the matter with Varvara Kirillovna?"

"First of all, my good man," interrupted Marya Stepanovna in a voice trembling with rage, "be so kind as to relieve our anxiety. Did the prosecutor's cook give birth?"

"Yes, indeed, and all is well," Krupov replied with enthusiasm. "It was the first time in my life that I've seen a case such as hers. I really thought that both mother and child were done for. The midwife was incredibly clumsy. My hands are aging, and I don't see very well any more. Just imagine, an umbilical cord as long as. . . ."

"Oh, good heavens, the man is insane! I can't bear to hear such abominations. Why did you bring that up? In our village about fifty peasant women give birth every year, and I don't need to hear all the sordid details." Having said this, she spat in disgust.

Krupov had some difficulty taking in the whole situation. He had spent the entire night in a stuffy kitchen attending the poor woman in labor. Since he was still under the influence of the happy outcome, he did not catch Marya Stepanovna's tone at first.

She continued, "And does the prosecutor pay you so much money that you couldn't possibly leave his cook even for one minute, while my daughter is hovering at death's door?"

"Not even for one minute, madame, not for one minute could I leave, neither for your daugher nor for anyone else. Clearly she is not all that ill, since you are in no rush for me to see her. I knew that it would be so."

This last observation confounded Vava's tender parents. But Marya Stepanovna quickly recovered and declared, "She is a little better now. I don't intend to let you see her. Why you haven't even washed your hands."

"I must confess, my dear doctor," added the marshal, "that I would never have expected such impertinent behavior and impertinent explanations from an old and experienced doctor such as you. If it were not for my respect for that cross that adorns your chest, I would no longer be able to restrain myself. Since I have been marshal these last six years or so, no one has dared to insult me as you have."

"For pity's sake," said Dr. Krupov. "Even if you lack a single spark of humanity, then at least you must realize that as the local inspector for the Medical Board I must observe all the rules and regulations of medical practice. Am I to forsake a woman who may die in labor for a healthy girl who has a migraine headache, a fit of hysterics, or something similar—as the result of some domestic scene? That would be against all laws! So why get so angry about it?"

Karp Kondratich, in addition to everything else, was a very great coward. He was afraid that the doctor might now be accusing him of seditious freethinking. He suddenly felt dizzy and hastened to reply, "I didn't know, I swear I didn't. I stand in silence before the power of the law. Look, here comes Vava herself."

Krupov went over to examine her. He checked her pulse, shook his head and asked two or three questions. Then, knowing that he couldn't possibly get away without it, he wrote out an innocuous prescription. "The most important thing is peace and quiet, or else she could get worse," he said upon leaving.

Alarmed by her daughter's hysterics, Marya Stepanovna became slightly less tyrannical. But as soon as she heard the rumors of Beltov's arrival in town, her heart began pounding with such force that her little lapdog, which had been resting peacefully on her lap for the last six years or so along with a handkerchief and a small snuffbox, suddenly began growling and sniffing around in order to discover the source of the pounding. Beltov—now there was a suitor! Beltov—just the man!

Naturally, Beltov paid a visit to Karp Kondratich. The following day Marya Stepanovna made her husband pay his respects to Beltov. A week later Beltov received a greasy note smelling strongly of the coachman's sheepskin coat in which it had been tucked away. The note read as follows: "The marshal of the nobility of Dubasov district and his wife respectfully request the honor of Vladimir Petrovich Beltov's company at dinner on such and such a day at 3 P.M." Beltov read the invitation with dismay. He tossed it down on the table and thought, "Why on earth have they invited me? It will cost them a fair amount, and they're as miserly as old Koschei.[4] It will be very boring. . . . But there is nothing I can do about it. I'll have to go, or they'll be offended."

Vava's preparation and rehearsals began two days before the actual event. Marya Stepanovna dressed and undressed her from morning to night. She even wanted to make Vava appear in some sort of red velvet dress, because she thought it would suit her complexion best. But she yielded to the advice of one of her cousins who was a frequent visitor to the governor's mansion. The cousin claimed to be familiar with all the latest fashions, since the governor's wife had promised to take her along to spend the next summer in Karlsbad.[5] The evening before the dinner Marya Stepanovna ordered the almond skins that were left from the preparation of the next day's blancmange brought in. As she showed Vava how to rub her face, neck, and shoulders with these skins, she declared in a solemn tone, obviously refraining from a desire to indulge in foul language, "Vava, if God helps me marry you off to Beltov, all my prayers will have been heard, and I will value you more than ever. Comfort your poor mother! You are not an unfeeling girl with a heart of stone. Can't you do this one thing for me? How could you fail to please a handsome young man? Are there so many eligible maidens around here? No, only two or three, that's all. The chairman's daughters, reputedly so beautiful, are hideous if you ask me, and it's said that they flirt with mere secretaries. And what sort of

4. *Koschei.* Koschei (the Deathless)—an evil figure in Russian folklore—is a wicked, covetous old man in possession of various treasures.

5. *Karlsbad.* A fashionable spa, famous for its hot springs. It is located in northwestern Bohemia, formerly in the Austro-Hungarian Empire, now in Czechloslovakia and called Karlovy Vary.

family do they come from? Their father rose up through the ranks of civil servants in the State Chamber. If you had even a shred of ambition, you could make a laughing stock of them. . . . Those shameless hussies ride past Beltov's room in an open carriage. But they don't have a chance! So here I am going to great lengths, but just look at her. She stands there staring at me as if she were a doorpost! The good Lord has sent me a wooden puppet instead of a daughter, as punishment for my sins."

"Mama, mama," murmured Vava, her face revealing desperation. "What can I do? I can't behave differently! You be the judge. I don't know the man at all; he may not pay any attention to me. I can't throw myself at him!"

"What a boor you are! Who is telling you to throw yourself at him? Is that how you want to fulfill your mother's request? I've never seen the likes of this. Do you think that your mother is a fool or a drunkard, incapable of choosing a suitor for you? Are you some sort of princess, or what?"

She stopped, not wanting to reduce her to tears, which would only make her eyes red for tomorrow's dinner.

Finally, the day of the ordeal arrived. From twelve noon Vava was combed, oiled, and perfumed. Then Marya Stepanovna laced up her daughter's corset, transforming an already skinny Vava into something resembling a wasp. On the other hand, with wise foresight, she made extraordinary use of cotton to pad out other vital areas. Still, Marya Stepanovna was not entirely satisfied with the results of her labors. First, Vava's collar seemed too high, then one shoulder appeared lower than the other. Throughout these proceedings Marya Stepanovna remained angry; she lost her temper, bestowed encouraging shoves on the maids, ran into the dining room to check on the preparations, instructed her daughter on how to make eyes at a man, and the kitchen attendant on how to set the table, and so on. This was a difficult day for Marya Stepanovna, but maternal love is all-powerful.

It is altogether understandable that these measures are both appropriate and necessary in family life. Whatever one's fantasy, it is essential to concern oneself with a daughter's fate and well-being. What a pity that these preparatory behind-the-scenes measures deprive a young girl of the splendid experience of her first, spontaneous, and unexpected encounter with a man. They reveal secrets to her that should not have been revealed, and they show her too early that success is not a result of mutual affection or happiness but rather of how the cards are marked. These preparations vulgarize relationships that can only be sacred and sincere if they lack all vulgarity. Stern moralists may add that all such measures do more to corrupt the heart of a young girl than any so-called "fall." We shall not venture quite that far. Besides, whatever you say, a daughter must still be married off. That is all they are born for. I think that all moralists will agree with that.

At three o'clock a beautifully attired Vava was sitting in the living room, where, since half past two, several guests had gathered. The tray in front of the sofa had already been stripped of half its caviar and smoked sturgeon, when suddenly a footman entered and delivered a note to Karp Kondratich. He took his eyeglasses out of a pocket, smeared the lenses with his dirty handkerchief, and, judging by the time it took him to read through the two-line note, must have had to sound out each syllable. He then announced in a voice far from tranquil, "Masha dear, Vladimir Petrovich Beltov asks your forgiveness. He is ill. He has caught a cold and deeply regrets that he will be unable to attend." He turned to the footman, "Tell his servant that we are . . . uh, very sorry."

The expression on Marya Stepanovna's face changed at once, and she cast a glance at her daughter that seemed to accuse her of infecting Beltov with the cold. Vava was triumphant. Marya Stepanovna had never seemed so ridiculous. In fact, she seemed so ridiculous that Vava felt sorry for her. Marya Stepanovna instantly conceived a deep hatred for Beltov with all her heart and soul. "This is positively an insult," she mumbled to herself.

"Dinner is served," said the footman.

The marshal of the nobility escorted his wife into the dining room.

Two weeks after this episode Marya Stepanovna was having a cup of tea. Either alone or with close friends, she loved to linger over her tea, drinking it from a saucer through lumps of sugar held between her teeth. She appreciated this custom all the more as it saved her considerable sugar. In front of her sat a tall, thin figure of the female gender wearing a lace cap. A slight head tremor kept the ruffles on the cap in constant motion. She was knitting a woolen scarf on two huge needles, regarding her work through thick lenses, set, it must be said, into a silver frame resembling a cannon mount rather than an object to be placed on anyone's nose. A dark, well-worn dressing gown and a huge handbag filled with all sorts of knitting needles indicated that this woman was both a close friend and not very well off. This last fact was particularly evident in Marya Stepanovna's tone of voice. The old woman's name was Anna Yakimovna. She was descended from fine nobility and had been a widow for some time. Her estate consisted of four serfs, representing one-fourteenth of an inheritance granted her by some relatives. These very wealthy relatives had shown their appreciation of her position as a needy widow by generously slicing off for her and her four peasants a piece of swampy land that was rich in grouse and pheasants but totally unsuited for any normal agricultural use. Try as she might, Anna Yakimovna was unable to collect a substantial quitrent from her estate. Nor was the inheritance that she had received from her deceased husband very substantial. It consisted of his rank as a lieutenant colonel, one son, and a collection of prescriptions for curing horses from stringhalt, strangles, and so on. Each prescription included an indication of its own astounding rate of success. When her son reached the age of nineteen, he was dispatched to some regiment, but he returned home shortly thereafter, discharged from the service for drunkenness and unruly conduct. Ever since then he had been living in a wing of Anna Yakimovna's house, drinking homemade vodka flavored with lemon rinds and constantly quarreling either with the servants or with his friends. His mother was terrified of him and hid all her money and possessions, swearing to him that she didn't have a kopeck, especially after he smashed the lid of her store chest with an axe and stole seventy-two rubles and a turquoise ring that she had been treasuring for some fifty-four years in memory of one of her dear departed husband's true friends.

In addition to her serfs and prescriptions, Anna Yakimovna had three young maids, one elderly maid, and three footmen. She never supplied the young maids with clothes, yet they always seemed to be very well-dressed. Anna Yakimovna was delighted that they managed to earn some extra money on the side for their clothes, even though she kept them busy with her own work from morning to night. But she wisely refrained from commenting whenever she noticed certain irregularities. The footmen, who were old and ugly, lived exclusively on wine and were in close partnership with the maids. In addition, they made foul-smelling shoes out of goatskin for half the town. It goes without saying that Yakim Osipovich, the old lady's son, also took advantage of human frailty; he didn't miss an opportunity for settling his accounts.

The respected head of this patriarchal phalanstery was in the process of drinking her fourth cup of tea in Marya Stepanovna's living room. She had managed to repeat for the hundredth time the story of how a Georgian prince, who died with the rank of commanding general, had once wooed her, and how in 1809 she had gone to visit some relatives in Petersburg where all the top brass gathered every evening, and how the only reason she chose not to remain there was because she couldn't bear the taste of Petersburg water, which didn't agree with her digestion. Having finished these aristocratic reminiscences and her fourth cup of tea, and having ostentatiously turned her teacup upside down, placing the tiny remains of her sugar lump on top (a disingenuous indication that she would drink no more), she suddenly began, "Yes, my dear, Marya Stepanovna, if only the Good Lord would allow me to live to see your daughter Varvara Karpovna settled in life. I feel as you do; I can't wish for anything more. My heart rejoices at the sight of your family. Your household is brimming over with riches and enjoys such respect. Settle that one matter, and you can put your mind at ease."

"Why have you turned over your cup? Have some more tea."

"Thank you, but I've had enough. I usually drink only three cups, but today I've already had four. Thank you so much. Your tea is always excellent."

"Yes, I always say, even if it costs as much as a ruble a pound, it's worth it in order to enjoy my tea. Have another cup." Anna Yakimovna accepted a fifth.

"Of course everything is within God's power, Anna Yakimovna, but Vava is still so young. Why should I hurry to marry her off? And to tell the truth, these days suitors are apt to ruin a young girl. And when I think of having to part with her, I can't endure it, I simply can't."

"May God be with you, my dear. Who hasn't had to marry off a daughter? A daughter is not the sort of commodity one should keep around for too long. She's likely to get stale. No, I do think that if the Holy Virgin Mary grants you her blessing, it would be desirable to arrange an advantageous match. Sofya Alekseevna Beltov's son has just arrived in town. He's a distant relative of ours. But nowadays people don't care much about distant relatives, especially if they're impoverished. He must be very wealthy, though—two thousand serfs and an excellent estate."

"But what sort of a person is he? You are obsessed with his money, but wealth is more a burden than a boon. Trouble and anxiety! From a distance it all seems fine: one hand dipped in honey, the other in treacle. But look closer; wealth merely saps one's health. I know Sofya Alekseevna's son. He tried to make Karp Kondratich's acquaintance. Needless to say, we received him cordially. Why should we be the ones to instruct him? But it's written clearly all over his face: he is completely corrupted. What bad manners he has! In a nobleman's house he behaves exactly as if he were in a restaurant. Have you seen him?"

"Yes, on the street, from a great distance. He frequently drives by or goes out for a stroll."

"Where on earth is he going that he should pass your house?"

"I don't know, my dear. At my age and in my condition" (she sighed deeply) "it's no business of mine who goes where. I have my own troubles. . . . I don't want to keep any secrets from my Creator or from you: my son Yakisha has gone on another drinking spree. He will drive me into the grave. . . ." After saying this she began to weep.

"Why not consult with the elder of our church? He knows a miraculous cure. He takes some home brew, says a few words over the mug, gives it to the patient to taste, drinks the rest down himself, and that's that. When the devils of drink begin their fiendish machinations, the poor patient never touches a drop again!"

"No doubt he asks a huge fee. And you know our situation,"

"No, he cured our cook for only five rubles."

"Did it work?"

"It certainly did. He was just about to indulge again when Karp Kondratich gave him a dose of a different kind of medicine. 'So,' he says to him, 'You don't appreciate a boyar's generosity, eh?[6] I paid five rubles to have you cured, and you're still no better? You scoundrel!' And he gave it to him, you know. . . the Russian way. . . . Since then he hasn't taken a drop. I'll send the church elder to you. You know, I wouldn't have been able to endure the mystery. If I were you, I would have found out where that young Beltov is off to!"

"Well, I did ask my Vasiliska. She's such a frisky lass. I had nothing better to do, you see, so I asked her where she thought that young man was going when he passed our house. Well, the very next day she told me. 'Yesterday you asked me where that Beltov gentleman goes. He goes off with the old doctor to visit the fellow who used to tutor Negrov's son.'"

"With Dr. Krupov? To the Negrovs' former tutor?" asked Marya Stepanovna, hardly concealing a pleasant sense of agitation, which she herself could not have explained.

"Yes, my dear, and now he's teaching here in the gymnasium."

"Aha, so that's where he's off to! I knew from the first that he was completely corrupted. So what's so surprising about that? From childhood Beltov's tutor initiated him into the Masonic order. What other choice did he have? As a young boy he lived in the French capital without any supervision, and you can well imagine what sort of morality prevails in Paris! And now he's showing an interest in the Negrovs' ward, is he? Fine thing, that! What an age we live in!"

"What a pity, Marya Stepanovna, what a great pity for her poor

6. *Boyar*. A member of the old Russian nobility, next in rank to the ruling princes. Peter the Great abolished many of their privileges and made the rank dependent on state service.

husband. They say he's a respectable man. But she! Well, you
know her background! As I always say, lackey blood will eventually show itself."

"Well, and isn't our Dr. Krupov playing a fine role! Splendid.
The old sinner. He has no fear of God. He's probably a Mason too.
Birds of a feather flock together. And I wonder how much money
he's getting paid for his services? And for what? In order to ruin a
young woman. And why on earth, tell me, Anna Yakimovna, why
on earth does this old miser need the money? He lives all alone, has
neither friends nor relatives, and won't donate a kopeck to charity.
Accursed greed! A Judas Iscariot! And for what? He'll die like a
dog, and his money will go to the state."

This conversation continued for another quarter of an hour or so
in the same spirit and direction. During the heat of the debate,
Anna Yakimovna managed to consume three more cups of tea.
Then she began to take her leave. She removed her eyeglasses,
placed them in a case, and sent a servant out to the hall to inquire
whether Maksyutka had arrived to escort her home. Having been
informed that Maksyutka was ready and waiting, she stood up. It
had been quite a while since Marya Stepanovna had received her so
affectionately. Her hostess accompanied her into the hall where
Maksyutka, a comical old man of about sixty, unshaven, dirty, and
reeking of cheap wine, dressed in a coarse frieze greatcoat with a
black collar, stood holding Anna Yakimovna's rabbit fur cloak in
one hand, while shoving a snuffbox back into his pocket with the
other. Maksyutka was in a very bad mood. He had been playing a
game of checkers and was just about to block a king. He had placed
his dirty finger on top of his man to move it forward, when his
mistress suddenly opened the door. "Damned old crow," he muttered rudely, as he placed the cloak over the widow Anna Yakimovna's frail shoulders.

"What a fool you are," observed his mistress. "You still don't
know how to help me on with my cloak."

"It's time to drive us all out of your house and find yourself some
smarter servants," muttered Maksyutka.

"You see, my dear, what it means to be a widow. You see what I
must endure, even from the lowest of creatures. What can I do? It

is a woman's lot. If only my dear husband were still alive, then I would be able to deal with this wretch myself. He'd mend his ways. Mine is a bitter fate. May God spare you from it!"

This speech had no effect whatever on Maksyutka. As he helped his mistress down the stairs, he managed to turn to the assembled crowd and, pointing to Anna Yakimovna, he winked. This gesture provided genuine and prolonged satisfaction to all the servants of the venerable marshal of the nobility in Dubasov district.

I leave it to the reader to imagine the joy and satisfaction that the good Marya Stepanovna experienced upon hearing such news and upon being granted an opportunity to spread such a scandalous tale involving not only Mr. Beltov but Dr. Krupov as well. Of course, in the process it might prove necessary to destroy the reputation of a certain young woman. That would be a pity, but what could be done about it? There are certain matters of sufficient importance to require the sacrifice of innocent persons in the name of great ideals!

Chapter 4

At the same time that the respected widow Anna Yakimovna was having tea with the no less respected Marya Stepanovna and the two were discussing Mr. Beltov's affairs with that tender solicitude so characteristic of the female heart, Beltov himself, feeling extremely melancholy, was sitting in his room oppressed by gloomy thoughts. Had he possessed the gift of clairvoyance, he would have been easily consoled, for he would have heard the voices of these two women. Only one large dirty street and one small dirty lane away, they were expressing their most intimate involvement in his affairs. One woman listened to the other's tale with devastating interest. But Beltov did not possess the gift of clairvoyance. If his Russian soul had not been so corrupted by Western innovations, he might at least have begun to hiccup; that would have indicated that somewhere or other he was being talked about. But in our age of doubt even hiccups have lost their mystical character and have become a mere gastric disorder.

Beltov's spleen, however, had no connection whatever to the aforementioned conversation over a sixth cup of tea. He had awakened late that morning suffering from a bad headache. On the previous evening he had read until very late, inattentively and half asleep. Lately he had been feeling *not himself;* it was some indefinable sensation, one predisposing him to fits of depression. It seemed as if something was missing; he couldn't concentrate on anything. At about one o'clock he finished his cigar and coffee and considered at length how best to begin his day—by reading or by taking a stroll. He decided on the latter. He took off his slippers but suddenly remembered that he had promised himself to spend his mornings reading the most recent works in the field of political economy. So he put his slippers back on, lit up another cigar, and settled down to devote himself to that subject. Unfortunately, lying next to his box of cigars was a copy of Byron. Beltov stretched out on the sofa and read *Don Juan* until five that evening.[1] Having finished his reading, he looked at the clock and was astonished to see how late it was. He summoned his valet and instructed him to lay out his clothes as soon as possible. Both Beltov's astonishment and his instructions were more the result of instinct than anything else. He had nowhere to go, and it made no difference to him whether it was 6 A.M. or 12 P.M. Having dressed with the care and attention to which we become accustomed after living abroad for a certain time but that we soon forget upon retiring to live in the provinces, he lay down again on the sofa with the firm intention of devoting himself to political economy. He opened an English pamphlet on Adam Smith.[2]

Meanwhile Beltov's valet pulled out a small table and began to set it for dinner. Fate smiled upon the valet more graciously than upon his master. Grigory was going about the business of setting the table without a care in the world. He placed a pitcher of water and a bottle of Burgundy on it and put a decanter of absinthe and some cheese on a sideboard. Then he serenely inspected his work. When he was sure that everything was in order, he went out for the soup. A minute later he returned, not with the soup but with a letter.

---

1. *Don Juan.* Byron's (1788–1824) great satiric poem (1819–24), which narrates a series of romantic adventures in the life of its legendary, wandering young hero.

2. *Adam Smith.* A Scottish political economist (1723–90) whose treatise *The Wealth of Nations* (1776) exerted considerable influence on subsequent political and economic theory.

"From whom?" asked Beltov without lifting his eyes from the pamphlet on Adam Smith.

"It must be from foreign parts. It's not our stamps. And here's a notice that a parcel has arrived."

"Let me see," said Beltov putting the pamphlet aside. "I wonder who it could be from? Geneva? Really? No, surely not. . . ."

Of course it would have been much easier to tear open the envelope and to read the signature at the end of the fourth page than it was to guess who might have sent it. No doubt about it! Why is it that people always try to guess who letters are from? This is a mystery of the human heart, founded, by the way, on man's vainglorious desire to prove himself both shrewd and perspicacious.

Finally Beltov opened the envelope and began to read the letter. With every line his face paled and tears welled up in his eyes.

The letter was written by a nephew of Monsieur Joseph and informed Beltov of the old man's death. The life of that simple, noble creature had ended as peacefully and beautifully as it had been lived. For many years he had served as head teacher in a village school not far from Geneva. He had been taken sick and was ailing for two days; by the third day he seemed to recover. With difficulty he made his way back to his classroom. There he collapsed and was carried home. Some blood was let, and he recovered consciousness. In complete control of his powers, he bade farewell to the frightened and distraught children who stood silently around his bed. He urged them to come and play on his grave. Then he asked for Voldemar's portrait. For a long time he gazed at it lovingly; then he said to his nephew, "What a man he could have become. . . . I guess his old uncle was right after all. . . . When I'm gone, send this portrait back to Voldemar. . . . His address is in my briefcase, the old one—with Washington's picture on it. . . . I feel sorry for Voldemar . . . very sorry. . . ."

"At this point," wrote the nephew, "the sick man became delirious. His face assumed a pensive expression that accompanies the last moments of a person's life. He asked to be lifted up. Opening his bright eyes, he wanted to say something more to the children, but his tongue would not obey. He smiled at them, and then his white head dropped to his breast. We buried him in our village cemetery between the organist and the sacristan."

Beltov finished the letter, put it down on the table, wiped away a tear, paced back and forth in his room, stood for a while by the window, picked up the letter again, and read it through once more from start to finish. "An amazing man," he muttered, "simply amazing. The happiest of men. He knew how to find contentment. He knew how to work, how to be useful wherever he found himself. . . . Now I have no one left in the whole world except for my mother. No one. Although I didn't hear from him very often, I was always relieved to learn that he was alive and well. And now he is no more! Ah, how painful it is! Surely, if the rules of the game were announced in advance, few would be foolish enough to take life on."

"The soup is getting cold, Vladimir Petrovich," announced the valet, noting with concern that the letter had brought bad news.

"Grigory," said Beltov, "do you remember the tutor who used to live with us?"

"Of course I remember the Swiss gentleman, sir."

"He has passed away," said Beltov turning away from Grigory to hide his agitation.

"May he rest in peace," said Grigory. "He was a kind man and always treated me well. Not long ago I was talking about you to Maksim Fedorovich, one of your mother's servants. To tell the truth, Maksim Fedorovich still can't get over you. Thanks to you, I've seen all sorts of people and different ways of life. But he's lived his whole life in the provinces, and so he's astounded by you. 'Of course,' he says, 'he was born with a good heart—his mother's. But he also learned a thing or two from that tutor of his. I recall how when the village boys would bow to Vladimir Petrovich, the tutor would tell him to take off his cap. After all, he would say, they are made in God's image, too.'"

Beltov remained silent and gloomily set about eating his soup.

News of Joseph's death naturally caused Beltov to remember his past youth and then to consider the direction of his entire life. He recalled Joseph's precepts that he had listened to so fervently and believed in so passionately. His life had turned out to be quite different from what Joseph had hoped for. Strange to say, everything that Joseph had said was so beautiful and true (inside and out) was so absolutely false for Beltov. He compared himself now to what he was then: the two had nothing in common except for the thread of memories that connects two different people. As a young man he was full of hope, believing in self-sacrifice, eager to undertake difficult exploits and unrecompensed labors; now, having surrendered to external circumstances, he was without hope, searching for some kind of diversion.

When Grigory brought the parcel from the post office, Beltov hastily unwrapped it and eagerly removed the portrait. Gazing at the features that were once his own, his expression changed markedly, and he almost averted his eyes. He saw the representation of everything that had been going through his mind. The young lad's face was so fresh and bright; his shirt was open at the neck, his collar folded back onto his shoulders, and some indescribable expression of pensiveness hovered around his eyes and mouth—that indefinable pensiveness that prophesied the power of future thought. "This boy will achieve great things," any abstractly thoughtful person would have said, glancing at the portrait. So Monsieur Joseph had said. But Beltov had become no more than an idle tourist. He clung to the idea of winning a post in the provincial elections in the town of N. as if it were his very last chance. "Then," thought Beltov as he looked reproachfully at the portrait, "then, I was only fourteen. Now I'm over thirty. What lies ahead? Nothing but a vast gray mist, a dull, monotonous continuation of the present. It is too late to begin a new life, but it is no longer possible to continue the old one. How many beginnings have I made! How many people have I met! Yet everything has resulted in idleness and loneliness. . . ."

This bitter train of thought was temporarily interrupted by Dr. Krupov, but soon it became the subject of their dialogue too.

"How do you feel, Vladimir Petrovich?"

"Ah, hello, Semyon Ivanovich. I'm very glad to see you. I feel so bored and miserable, I can hardly bear it. I think that I am ill. I have a slight fever, and it keeps me in a state of constant agitation."

"You are leading the wrong kind of life," replied the doctor, rolling up the long sleeve of Beltov's frock coat in order to check his pulse. "Your pulse is not good at all. You lead your life at a pace twice as fast as it need be; you are burning the candle at both ends. You won't get far like this."

"I feel as if I'm fast approaching a physical and spiritual breakdown."

"It's a little too early for that. The current generation lives its life at too fast a pace. You really should be more concerned about your health and take some precautions."

"What kind?"

"Quite a few. Go to bed earlier, get up earlier, read less, think less, take more walks, banish gloomy thoughts, consume less wine, give up strong coffee."

"Do you think that any of that would be easy, especially banishing gloomy thoughts? And how long would I have to keep to such a regime?"

"For the rest of your life."

"Most esteemed sir, that would be boring, repulsive, and serve no purpose whatever."

"What do you mean, no purpose? It seems to me that it is worth making some sacrifice so that one can live longer and reach old age."

"Well, and why should I want to live longer?"

"A strange question, that! I can't say that I know why. It's simply better to live than it is to die. Every creature has a love of life."

"And what if a creature turns up who has no such love?" observed Beltov with a bitter smile. "Byron was right when he said that no decent man has the right to live past the age of thirty-five. What good is long life? It must be very tedious."

"You've absorbed these sophisms from reading too many of those accursed German philosophers."

"In this case, allow me to defend the Germans. Since I am a Russian, life has taught me how to think, instead of thought teaching me how to live. It's a good thing that you and I have broached this subject. Tell me now, honestly, thoughtfully, what difference does it make if I live another fifty years instead of only ten? Who needs my life, besides my mother, whose condition is itself precarious these days? Whether because of some inherent weakness or because of a flaw in my character, I still remain a useless person. Once convinced of this, I assume that I have control over my own life. I have not yet come to despise life enough to shoot myself, nor to love it enough to adhere to the regimen that you propose, to tread lightly, to avoid strong emotions and tasty cuisine in order to prolong the life of an ailing patient for an indefinite period."

"You prefer a slow suicide," replied Krupov, beginning to get angry. "I can well understand that you are sick and tired of your idle life. Since you have nothing to do, you must be bored. Like all wealthy people, you have never become accustomed to hard work. If fate had granted you a genuine occupation and had taken away your estate of White Meadow, then you might have had to work to earn your daily bread, and your work would also have been of use to other people. That's the way the rest of the world runs."

"Semyon Ivanovich, do you really believe that aside from hunger there is no other strong motive to work? The simple desire to express oneself, to fulfill oneself, can force a person to work. As for me, I would never go to work just to earn my daily bread—to work my whole life so as not to die of starvation, and not to die of starvation just in order to work. What a clever and useful way to spend one's time!"

"And how much have you accomplished, with your satiety and desire for self-expression?" asked the doctor, who was now quite irritated.

"There's the rub! Of course I didn't choose this idle and tedious life by my own free will. I was born neither a scientist nor a musician. And it seems that no other profession has been conceived for me."

"That is to say, you console yourself that way. The earth is too small for you; you have no place on it. The fact of the matter is, you have no willpower, persistence. *Gutta cavat. . . .*"

"*Lapidem*," supplied Beltov.[3] "You are such a pragmatic character. How can you talk about willpower?"

"Fine words, indeed," observed Krupov. "Still, it seems to me that a good worker would never find himself without work."

"Well, what do you think about the workers of Lyons, then?[4] Why do you think they're dying of starvation? They're eager to work, but there is no work available. Do you think it's because they're incompetent or they're playing games? Oh, Semyon Ivanovich! Don't rush to make judgments and to prescribe spiritual serenity and a diet of sorrel. The former is impossible, and the latter is useless. There are few ailments worse then the recognition of one's own impotence. What good will a regimen do? Remember Napoleon's answer to Dr. Antommarchi, 'It is not cancer that devours me, but Waterloo.' Everyone has his own *Waterloo rentré*.[5] Semyon Ivanovich, let's go to the Krutsiferskys. There I have managed several times to find some relief from my spleen. Such treatment does me more good than any decoction."[6]

"That's the gratitude and appreciation I get! And who was it who first prescribed a visit to their home?"

"I apologize. I had quite forgotten. O, thou mighty son of Hip-

3. "*Gutta cavat lapidem.*" "Drops of water hollow out a stone." From Ovid, *Epistulae ex Ponto*, IV:10:5:

> Can you compare any flint, Albinovanus,
> any iron to my endurance? Drops of water
> hollow out a stone, a ring is worn thin by
> use, the hooked plough is rubbed away by
> the soil's pressure. So devouring time
> destroys all things but me: even death
> keeps aloof, defeated by my endurance.

4. *Workers of Lyons.* The difficult conditions of French workers in Lyons led to two uprisings (1831 and 1834). Their struggles gained the attention and sympathies of liberals throughout Europe.

5. *Waterloo rentré.* "Internal waterloo." Waterloo, a village in Belgium just south of Brussels, was the scene of Napoleon's final defeat (June 18, 1815). Francesco Antommarchi (1780?–1838) was a Corsican physician who attended Napoleon during his last years on the island of St. Helena (1815–21).

6. *Decoction.* From *decoctum* (Lat.), a medicine in liquid form made from certain medicinal plants.

pocrates!"[7] replied Beltov, filling his cigar case and smiling graciously at the doctor.

So now let us finally ask, along with Marya Stepanovna, what was it that attracted Beltov to that teacher's modest little house? Had he found a friend, a sympathetic soul, or was he really in love with the teacher's wife? Granting Beltov's own desire to tell the truth, even he would have had considerable difficulty answering these questions. Many things drew him to that house. The elections were over, as were all the dinners and balls associated with them. Needless to say, Beltov was not elected to any office. He remained in town only to hear the end of some lawsuit that was being tried in the Civil Court. I leave it to you to imagine the endless tedium of his life in the town of N. had it not been for his acquaintance with the Krutsiferskys. Their quiet, tranquil life represented something altogether new and attractive for him. He had spent his whole life on general problems, on science and theory, living in foreign cities where it was difficult to gain access to domestic life or in Petersburg where there is very little of it. He had always considered domestic fulfillment to be a mere invention of the property of vulgar and petty people. But the Krutsiferskys were different.

It is very hard to define Dmitry's character. He possessed a gentle nature, loving in the highest degree, feminine and submissive. He was so simple-hearted and pure that it was impossible not to love him, even though his purity was a result of his inexperience and constantly reminded one of a child's innocence. It would be difficult to find a person who knew less about the practical side of life. Everything he knew came from books; as a result, his knowledge was unreliable, romantic, and rhetorical. He believed absolutely in the reality of the world as described by the lyric poet Zhukovsky[8] and in a set of ideals soaring high above the earth. From the cloistered seclusion of student life, during the course of which he had ventured into the world of passion and conflict only from the top row of a Moscow theater, he entered into "real life" very quietly, on one gray autumn day. He was confronted by an

7. *Hippocrates.* A Greek physician (b. 460 B.C.) traditionally regarded as the "father of medicine."

8. *Zhukovsky.* See pt. I, chap. 4, n. 11.

existence of oppressive necessity. Everything seemed so hostile and alien. More and more the young candidate learned to discover joy and consolation in the world of dreams in which he took refuge from people and circumstances. It was this same external necessity that had driven him into the Negrovs' household. That confrontation with reality had made him even more withdrawn than before. Gentle by nature, he had no intention whatever of entering into any struggle against reality. He retreated, asking only that he be left in peace. But then came love. It took on the form appropriate to his constitution. His was not a furious or insane love but one to last forever, with such complete surrender that no part of him was left untouched. Nervous excitement kept him in a constant state of melancholy ecstasy. He was always brooding and often on the verge of tears. On peaceful evenings he loved to stare endlessly at the heavens; who knows what visions appeared to him in that stillness. He frequently gave his wife's hand an affectionate little squeeze and gazed into her face with inexpressible ecstasy. But Dmitry's joy was tinged with such deep sorrow that Lyubov Aleksandrovna herself was frequently unable to refrain from weeping. All of his actions manifested the same gentleness that was expressed in his face, the same tranquillity, sincerity, and shy pensiveness. Is it even necessary to ask how such a man would love his wife? His love grew constantly, especially since nothing distracted him from it. He was incapable of spending two hours alone without seeing his wife's dark blue eyes. He began to tremble if she left the house and hadn't returned at the expected time. In a word, it was absolutely clear that his very existence was rooted in Lyuba. The world in which he found himself contributed considerably to this state of affairs.

As used to happen in our schools in days of old, the teachers at the gymnasium in the town of N. were, by and large, indolent types who had grown coarse as a result of their provincial life, who had succumbed to vulgar habits and materialistic values, and who had lost all real desire for any kind of knowledge. It is unlikely that Krutsifersky ever had the ability to make a significant contribution to knowledge, to devote himself exclusively to the problems of science, and to make them his own vital problems. Nevertheless he felt some interest in scholarly pursuits, and many of them were open to him in all ways but one—material means. He couldn't even afford to think about ordering books for himself. The gymnasium acquired some, but not those that could sustain a young scholar's interests. In general, provincial life is disastrous for those who want to preserve more than their real estate and for those who do not want their bodies to become as immovable as their property. In this realm of spiritual lethargy, devoid of all theoretical interests, who would not fall into a very prolonged, if not downright enjoyable, sleep? A man needs external stimuli. He needs newspapers to bring him into daily contact with the whole world. He needs journals to acquaint him with every current in contemporary thought. He needs conversation, theater. Needless to say, one can get unaccustomed to these things. Sometimes it can even seem as if all of these things are actually unnecessary. Then one day these things really become unnecessary, because the person himself has become entirely unnecessary.

Krutsifersky certainly did not belong to that group of strong and persistent people who create for themselves that which is lacking in their environment. The absence of any genuine human interest in his surroundings had a negative rather than a positive impact on him, especially as it occurred during the best period of his life, that is, just after his marriage. Subsequently he grew accustomed to it all. He was left with his dreams, a few bold, though out-of-date ideas, a general love of learning, and some theoretical problems that had long since been resolved by others. He sought fulfillment for the more pressing needs of his soul in love. In the strong character of his wife he discovered complete satisfaction. The arguments with Dr. Krupov, which had been going on for some four years, suffered from the same kind of stagnation so characteristic of provincial life in general: they rehashed the same issues day in and day out. Krutsifersky rose to the defense of spirituality, while the old doctor flailed away at him rudely and indignantly with his medical materialism.

The lives of these good people were flowing along a quiet course, when all of a sudden they were interrupted by a person with a completely different temperament. Beltov possessed an encyclopedic and highly active mind, capable of bold and decisive thought and open to all contemporary issues. Krutsifersky involuntarily submitted to the energetic nature of his new friend. Beltov, on the other hand, by no means remained immune to the influence of Krutsifersky's wife. It is almost impossible, even for a strong man occupied by nothing in particular, to resist the influence of an energetic woman. He would have had to be narrow-minded, very egotistical, or completely characterless in order to preserve his own dull independence in the face of such moral force appearing in the guise of a beautiful young woman. Beltov, it must be said, was passionate by nature and unused to exercising any form of self-restraint. Consequently he was an easy conquest for a coquette, or any pretty face for that matter. Several times he had fallen madly in love with some prima donna, a dancer or a mysterious beauty taking the waters alone at a spa; a red-cheeked, flaxen-haired *Fraulein* with a penchant for dreaminess, always ready to love *à la* Schiller,[9] and, accompanied by nightingales, to vow eternal love both in this world and in the next; a fiery Frenchwoman, true to her passions and indulging her desires wholeheartedly. . . . But this was the first time that Beltov had encountered an influence such as Lyuba's.

At the beginning of their acquaintance Beltov thought that he would flirt with her a bit. He had acquired considerable experience in this field and was no longer frightened off by an aristocratic setting or by false modesty. He was confident, as a result of his success with some not very reluctant beauties. Possessing a skillful and dangerously bold tongue, he felt eminently capable of numbing the conscience of any provincial maiden. But the perspicacious Beltov abandoned any idea of a vulgar flirtation once he realized that his trap was too weak to catch this kind of prey. The woman who presented herself to him in this provincial backwater was so simple and natural, so strong and intelligent, that Beltov soon lost all desire to intrigue her. It was difficult to launch an assault on her, because she did not defend herself in any way; she was never *en garde* [on guard]. An entirely different relationship, a much more human one, quickly brought Beltov and Lyuba together. She understood his melancholy, the ferment in his soul that so tormented

9. *Schiller.* A reference to Schiller's poem "Der Pilgrim" (1803) and its line *"Und das Dort ist niemals hier!"* ("That which is Beyond doesn't happen here!"). Schiller conceived of love as enduring beyond the grave.

him; she understood these things a thousand times more broadly and deeply than Dr. Krupov did, for example. Once she understood, she could no longer look at him without sympathy and concern. Regarding him in such a way, she came to know him better and better. Every day she observed new aspects of this man fated to destroy within himself such awesome strength of character and such staggering breadth of intellect. Beltov quickly came to value the difference between Krupov's conscientious, moralistic concern, Dmitry's romantic, tearfully sentimental sympathy, and Lyuba's genuine discretion. Many times, when all four of them were sitting together, Beltov would happen to express his innermost convictions. As a result of his old habits, he would always try to conceal his views by disguising them with sarcasm or by referring to them briefly, in passing. His audience rarely responded, but when he cast his longing glances at Lyuba's face, he smiled gently, seeing that *she* understood him. It is vexing to make the comparison, but I have no choice. Beltov and Lyuba unwittingly found themselves in the same situation as Lyuba and Dmitry once had in the Negrov household, where they realized they understood each other even before they had managed to exchange a single word. This kind of affinity can neither be nurtured nor suppressed. It merely demonstrates a fact of parallel development in two individuals, whenever and wherever they meet. If they come to recognize each other, to understand their kinship, then each of them will sacrifice a less important relationship for this higher one, if circumstances so dictate.

"Can you guess who this is?" asked Beltov, handing the portrait to Lyubov Aleksandrovna.

"Why it's you!" she cried, blushing. "Your eyes, your forehead. . . . What a handsome youth you were! What a bold and carefree face. . . ."

"It required great courage for me to decide to bring this portrait painted over fifteen years ago to a woman for comparison. But I desperately wanted to show it to you, so that you could see for yourself 'What I was like when I was in bloom. . . .'[10]

10. *"In bloom."* A quotation from "Onegin's Journey" (19:5), a series of fragments omitted from the final version of Pushkin's *Eugene Onegin.* Here the narrator is reminiscing about his own youth, wondering whether it had been as tumultuous and romantic as the hero's.

"I must admit that I am surprised that you can still recognize me; not a single trait is left."

"Of course, I recognized you," answered Lyuba without taking her eyes off the portrait. "Why didn't you show it to me before?"

"I just received it today. My beloved tutor Joseph passed away about a month ago. His nephew sent me this portrait with a letter."

"Poor Joseph! Because of your accounts, I consider him to have been one of my own close friends."

"The old man died in the midst of his gentle pursuits. You, who never set eyes on him, the crowd of children he taught, my mother, and I will remember him with love and will grieve at his passing. His death will come as a great blow to many people. In this respect I am more fortunate than he: after my mother's death I am sure that my own demise will cause nobody a moment's grief, because I mean nothing to anyone."

Although he said this sincerely, Beltov was also flirting a bit. He hoped to provoke Lyubov Aleksandrovna to a heartfelt protest.

"You do not really think that," she answered, gazing straight at him. He dropped his eyes.

"Well, after my death I really won't care who laughs or cries," observed Krupov.

"I don't agree," chimed in Krutsifersky. "I can well understand this fear of death, when you consider that there won't be a loved one standing near your bedside or anywhere in the whole wide world, and that some unknown hand will indifferently toss a shovelful of dirt into your grave, put down the shovel, pick up a hat, and then go home. When I die, Lyuba, please visit my grave frequently; I will enjoy it. . . ."

"Yes, no doubt you will," said the doctor with considerable irritation. "But you won't even be able to weigh your enjoyment on the apothecary scales. . . ."

"You talk as if you had no friends except for Joseph," said Lyuba. "How can that be?"

"Previously I had many warm and devoted friends. What didn't I have then? I had a face like the one in that portrait. But now nothing is the same. Besides, I don't need friends. Friendship is a pleasant disease of youth. Woe to him who is not able to be self-sufficient."

"But as far as I know, Joseph remained close to you until the end of his life."

"Because we lived so far from one another. We were friends because we saw each other only once in fifteen years. At that fleeting encounter I could summon up old memories to disguise the great gulf that existed between us."

"So you did see him after his departure for Sweden?"

"Once."

"Where?"

"In the town where he died."

"Was it long ago?"

"About a year."

"Well, instead of sharing such gloomy thoughts, why don't you tell us about your last meeting with the old man."

"With pleasure. I would like to think about him, and it would be nice to talk about him. Here's what happened.

"At the beginning of last year I arrived in Geneva from the south of France. Why? It's hard to say. I didn't feel like going on to Paris because I could never manage to do anything there but always suffered from envy. Everyone around me was so busy—bustling about either with important business or trivial nonsense, while I sat reading in cafés or wandered about, a well-meaning but alien onlooker. I had never been to Geneva before. It's a quiet town, somewhat isolated, so I chose to spend the winter there. I planned to study political economy and spend my spare time thinking about where I would go and what I would do next summer. Needless to say, by my second or third day in town I was making inquiries of moneylenders, bankers, and others, trying to discover some information as to the whereabouts of Monsieur Joseph. No one had any clues, except for one old watchmaker who said that he knew Joseph. He had been at school with him but hadn't seen him since he left for Petersburg.

"I was disappointed and abandoned my search. My studies were not going well. It was early spring, and the weather was clear and cool. My life of wandering had inculcated a passionate wanderlust. I decided to make a few short excursions on foot into the surroundings of Geneva. The open road exerts an enormous influence over me; I come alive, especially when traveling by foot or on horseback.

The noise of a carriage is distracting, and the presence of a coachman destroys my solitude. But alone, on horseback or with a walking stick, one can go on and on. The road winds away like a ribbon before one's eyes, disappearing into the distance; there is nobody around—only trees, streams, and startled birds who take flight and then settle down again. How splendid!

"Once, several miles outside of Geneva, I had been walking alone for quite some time. . . . Suddenly, from a side road, some twenty peasants emerged onto the main road. They were having a very heated conversation, which was accompanied by energetic gestures. They were walking so close to me, but paying so little attention to any strangers, that I could easily overhear their conversation. It was about some elections in the canton.[11] The peasants were divided into two parties and were supposed to cast their votes the next day. Apparently the question before them was totally engrossing: they waved their arms wildly and tossed their caps in the air. I sat down under a tree; the band of voters went by, and for a long time afterward I caught snatches of their demagogic speeches and conservative rejoinders. I am always filled with envy when I see people so absorbed in something, so engrossed in serious business. . . . Therefore I was in a rather bad mood when another traveler appeared on the road. He was a well-built young man, wearing a heavy blouse and a gray hat with a huge brim, carrying a knapsack over his shoulder and holding a pipe in his mouth. He sat down in the shade of the same tree. As he did so, he touched the brim of his hat. When I returned his greeting, he took off his hat and began wiping the perspiration from his face and his handsome brown hair. I smiled, having understood the lad's cautiousness. He hadn't removed his hat before, because he didn't want me to think that he was doing so for me. After sitting there for a while, the young man turned to me and asked, 'And where might you be heading?'

"'That's more difficult for me to answer than you think. I am simply following my nose.'

"'You are a foreigner, no doubt?'

11. *Canton.* One of the twenty-two states of the Swiss Confederation.

" 'Yes. I'm Russian.'

" 'Oh, from so far away! It must be very cold there now.'

"It goes without saying that not a single foreigner can talk about Russia without mentioning cold winters or swift troika rides, in spite of the fact that it is high time they knew that winters aren't really all that cold and troika rides aren't really so fantastic.

" 'Yes, it is winter in Petersburg now.'

" 'And how do you like our climate?' asked the Swiss lad proudly.

" 'Very much,' I answered. 'Are you from around here?'

" 'Yes, I was born not far from here, and now I am headed home to take part in our local election. I still don't have the right to vote, but I intend to voice my opinion. Even though it won't be counted in the tally, it may influence other voters. If you have nothing better to do, come along with me. My mother's house is at your disposal; you can have some wine and cheese. Tomorrow you can see how our side will trounce the old men.'

" 'Oho! So, he's a young radical!' I thought, glancing over at my companion once again.

" 'I will come along with you,' I said to him, extending my hand to shake his. 'I have nothing better to do.'

" 'You may find it interesting to observe our elections. You don't have elections in Russia, do you?'

" 'Who told you that?' I replied. 'You probably had some stupid geography teacher in school. We have quite a few different elections: nobles, merchants, craftsmen, and townspeople. Even in villages belonging to landowners an elder is still elected.'

The young man blushed.

" 'I studied geography a very long time ago,' he said, 'and not for very long. But I must say, with all due respect, that our teacher was excellent. He himself had spent some time in Russia. If you like, I'll introduce you to him. He is such a philosopher. He could have become whatever he wanted to, but all he wants to do is to be our teacher.'

" 'I am most grateful,' I said, without any desire whatever to meet some sort of rural pedant.

" 'He really did live in your country.'

" 'Where?'

" 'In Petersburg and in Moscow.'

" 'What's his name?'

" 'We call him père [father] Joseph.'

" 'Père Joseph!' I repeated. I couldn't believe my ears.

" 'Well, what's so surprising about that?' asked my companion.

"Suffice it to say that after two or three more questions I was completely convinced that this lad's père Joseph was none other than my Joseph. We doubled our pace. The young man was positively delighted to have provided me with such a pleasant surprise, and even more delighted to do the same for Joseph, whom he loved and respected immensely. I inquired about the old man's life and concluded from the lad's answers that Joseph had remained the same simple, noble, exalted, youthful man. From what I was told I realized that I had overtaken Joseph in years and that now I was actually older than he was. Five years had passed since he had assumed the post as senior teacher and headmaster of the local school. He did three times as much work as his job required; he possessed a small library that was available to the whole village; he had a garden in which he spent all his spare time digging with his pupils.

"When we stopped in front of the schoolteacher's neat little cottage, brightly illuminated by the rays of the setting sun, intensified by the reflection from the surrounding mountains, I sent my companion on ahead, so as not to shock the old man by my unexpected arrival. I told him to say that a Russian gentleman wished to see him.

"Père Joseph was sitting on a bench in his garden, leaning on a spade. He was roused by the word 'Russian' and rushed out to meet me. I threw my arms around him. The first thing that struck me was the appalling destructive force exercised by time. Not quite ten years had passed since I had last seen him—but what a transformation! He had lost almost all of his hair, his face had grown thin, his walk unsteady, and his back was hunched over. Only his eyes were as youthful as ever. I can't begin to describe the joy with which he greeted me. The old man wept, laughed, asked me countless questions all at once. He wanted to know whether my Newfoundland dog was still alive. He recalled my childish pranks. Talking all the while, he led me over to a gazebo, sat down to rest, and sent Charles (my young companion) to fetch a jug of his best wine from the cellar. I must admit that never have I savored even the finest champagne with the same enjoyment as that with which I swallowed glass after glass of Joseph's slightly sour wine. I felt animated, youthful, and happy. But the old man quickly destroyed my splendid mood with a single question. 'What have you been doing all this time, Voldemar?' he asked.

"I told him the story of my failures, concluding, of course, that my life might have turned out better but that I had no regrets. While I had lost my youthful beliefs, I had nevertheless acquired a sober view of life—perhaps a joyless, gloomy one, but at least a truthful one.

"'Voldemar,' the old man replied, 'beware of embracing too sober a view of life. It can chill your heart and destroy all the love within it. I did not foresee many of the events in your life. You have had a hard fight, but you mustn't lay down your arms just yet. The value of human life lies in the struggle. One must earn one's rewards through suffering.'

"By that time I had come to regard such vital issues more simply, but the old man's words made a deep impression on me.

"'Père Joseph, I would rather hear about you. How have you spent these last few years? My life has not been a success. Away with it! I am just like the heroes of those folktales that I used to translate for you. They went around shouting at every crossroads, "Is there a man left alive on this battlefield?" But no one ever answered. That is my misfortune. And, as they say, "One man left on a battlefield does not a warrior make." So I have forsaken the field and come to see you.'

"'You have surrendered much too soon,' said the old man, shaking his head. 'What can I tell you about myself? My life goes on peacefully. After I departed from your house I lived a while in Sweden; then I left for London with an Englishman and spent two years as tutor to his children. But my way of thinking so diverged from his honorable lordship's that I soon left his employ. I wanted to return home and left England for Geneva. But I found no one in

the city except for my sister's young son. For some time I thought
about how to spend my last years. Then a teaching post opened up
in a local school. I accepted it and have been extremely satisfied
with my work. It is neither possible nor desirable for each and
every man to thrust himself to the fore. Let each one contribute
what he can within his own circle. Work is always to be found;
after completing it, one can fall asleep peacefully when the time
comes for one's final rest. Our desire for a prominent social position
only reveals our immaturity and, in part, our lack of self-respect,
which in turn leads to dependence on external circumstances. Believe me, Voldemar, I speak the truth.'

"Our conversation continued in this same vein for an hour or so.

"I was deeply touched by this meeting with Joseph and consequently was very responsive and in an extremely good mood. All
the half-forgotten dreams of my youth returned. I gazed into
Joseph's serene, tranquil face, and my heart felt heavy. I was oppressed by my own maturity. How splendid he was! Old age possesses its own form of beauty, manifesting itself not in passionate
outbursts but rather in soothing calm. The remaining strands of his
white hair waved in the evening breeze; his eyes, enlivened by our
meeting, shone with a gentle, youthful happiness. I looked at him
and recalled the Catholic monks of the first centuries A.D. as they
were depicted by the masters of the Italian school. They always
appeared to be youthful, in spite of their gray hair. I thought to
myself, he is still young, while I have grown old. Why have I come
to know so much that he has remained unaware of?

"Joseph took me by the arm and stood up to return to his cottage.
With deep love he repeated, 'Voldemar, it is time for you to return
home!' I spent the evening in his house. All night long I was
tormented by a myriad of plans and projects. Joseph's example was
too powerful for me. Here was an old man without means who had
created his own life's work and was content with it; whereas I, *par
dépit* [out of spite], had forsaken my homeland, and, like a useless
alien, was wandering across the face of the earth without anything
to do.

"The next morning I told the old man that I had decided to
return to Russia, to the town of N., to take part in the provincial

elections. Joseph burst into tears. He placed his hand on my head and said, 'Go, my friend, go. You will see—a person who pursues his business honestly and nobly can accomplish a great deal.' Then he added, in a trembling voice, 'May your soul find peace.' We parted. I set off for the town of N., and he for the great beyond. That's all there is to it. That was the last enthusiasm of my youth. Since that time I have completed my own upbringing."

Lyubov Aleksandrovna looked at Beltov with deep sympathy. His eyes and the expression on his face reflected his profound sadness. His grief particularly affected her because it did not seem to fit his character as it did Krutsifersky's. An attentive observer would have understood that external circumstances had long been weighing on his luminous nature and had forcibly introduced into it gloomy, disparate elements that were slowly devouring it.

"Why did you come here?" Lyuba asked quietly.

"Thank you. I am deeply grateful for that question," replied Beltov.

"It is strange, of course," observed Dmitry Yakovlevich. "It is simply incomprehensible why people should be endowed with strength and aspirations that they can never utilize. Every animal is cleverly adapted by nature to a particular kind of life. But man? Perhaps there's been some kind of mistake. It is simply repugnant to one's heart and soul to have to agree with the proposition that man has been endowed with splendid strength and aspirations merely so that he will be devoured by them. How can this be?"

"You are perfectly correct," replied Beltov excitedly. "And with that point of view you will never extricate yourself from the problem. The fact is that these forces are constantly developing and preparing themselves, but the need for them is determined by history. Surely you are aware that every morning in Moscow a crowd of workers, day laborers, and hired hands sets out in search of employment. Some find work, while others, after a long wait, make their way home, their heads drooping; even more often, they head straight for a tavern. It's precisely the same in any field of human endeavor; there are plenty of candidates available. If history has need of them, they are called. If not, it's their own affair how they fritter away their lives. Consequently it is very amusing to consider public figures in this light. France needed military leaders—there appeared Dumouriez,[12] Hoche,[13] Napoleon and his marshals—no end to them. When the wars were over, there was no more talk of military capabilities."

"But what happens to the others?" asked Lyubov mournfully.

"Come what may. Some of them fade away and become part of the crowd, others go off to populate distant lands, or to the galleys, or to provide practice for executioners. Certainly not all at once. First they become celebrities at taverns or else gamblers; later, depending on their calling, they become travelers along the big highways or the little byways. Sometimes they receive a summons along the way, and the scene changes. Instead of a brigand, you get a Yermak, conquerer of Siberia.[14] Least of all do they settle down and become good, quiet folk; sitting at the hearth, they are troubled by bitter thoughts. In fact, the strangest thoughts occur to a man when he has no outlet for his energy, when the desire for activity invades his heart and soul like a dreadful disease, and when all he can do is sit around twiddling his thumbs. His muscles are strong, and good red blood flows through his veins. Only one thing can save such a person and absorb him totally . . . and that is an encounter . . . an encounter with. . . ."

He did not complete his sentence.

Lyubov Aleksandrovna shuddered.

"What a deranged mind!" observed Krupov. "What nonsense he spouts! Chaos, pure chaos! Well, what can I say? Fine candidate for assessor or provincial judge!"

Everyone laughed.

---

12. *Dumouriez.* Charles-François du Périer Dumouriez (1739–1823), a general and statesman who served as minister of foreign affairs, minister of war, and commander-in-chief of the army during the French Revolution. Outlawed by the Convention and deserted by his troops, he joined the Austrian army in 1793.

13. *Hoche.* Louis-Lazare Hoche (1768–97), son of a royal stableman, became a general under Napoleon. He drove out the Austro-Prussian armies from France (1793), suppressed a counterrevolution (1794–96), and helped expel the royalist government.

14. *Yermak.* Yermak Timofeevich (?–1584) was a Cossack chieftain. He and his men, armed by the Stroganovs, a family of wealthy merchants, advanced into western Siberia in 1581 and conquered the territory.

Chapter 5

Among the interesting sights in the town of N., the public park deserves particular attention. The rich natural beauty of the central region of our country renders parks entirely superfluous; as a result, no one ever visits them, that is, on weekdays. But on Sundays and holidays you can encounter the entire population of any town in its park between six and nine in the evening. However, at that particular time people gather not to enjoy nature but to meet each other. If the governor has maintained cordial relations with the commander of the local regiment, then on these special occasions you can hear a brass band or a fife and drum corps, depending on what kind of regiment has been assigned to the province. Operatic overtures from *Lodoiska* and *The Caliph of Bagdad*,[1] as well as French quadrilles recalling the unforgettable period of Greek emancipation[2] and the *Moscow Telegraph*,[3] will gladden the ears of

1. *"Lodoiska" and "The Caliph of Bagdad."* Two French operas performed in Russia at the beginning of the nineteenth century. *Lodoiska*, by Rodolphe Kreutzer (1766–1831), had its premiere in Paris in 1791; *The Caliph of Bagdad*, by François Adrien Boieldieu (1775–1834), was first performed in 1800.

2. *Greek emancipation.* A reference to the nationalist uprisings in Greece during the 1820s. The fierce struggle against the Ottoman Empire was supported (financially and morally) by liberal Europeans who espoused the cause of freedom for all nations.

3. *Moscow Telegraph.* A Russian literary and scientific journal published by N. A. Polevoi in Moscow from 1825 to 1834. Progressive in its political inclination, it

many a merchant attired in his summer wardrobe (satin and velvet) and of those provincial ladies whose hands in marriage no one is seeking (and who are rarely under forty years of age).

On weekdays, as has been said, the park is deserted, except perhaps for some unfortunate traveler, desperate because there are no horses to enable him to continue his journey and because *this* town is just like all others. He sets off for the park in the hope of finding a modicum of adequate scenery. It has long been observed by poets that nature is disgustingly indifferent to the activities of people who scramble around on her back, as it were. Nature neither weeps over poetry nor laughs over prose; it merely goes about its own business in an extremely logical manner. Nature in the town of N. behaved itself in precisely this way. It paid no attention whatever to the fact that few people came to stroll around the park, and that if they did they paid no attention to the trees but rather admired a splendid little pavilion built in a "Chinese-Grecian" style. The pavilion was indeed charming in its own way. The governor's wife had chosen an appropriate name for it: *Mon Repos* [my retreat]. Its most soothing feature was a little gingerbread-style horse cut out of tin, which, like a dragon guarding the entrance, stood on a tall post and constantly revolved in the breeze, emitting a pitiful wail that was both conducive to daydreaming and also confirmed the fact that the wind (having just carried off your hat to the left) was indeed blowing from the right. Above this "dragon" and between the columns were positioned ferocious, shaggy lion heads carved out of alabaster. These heads had been cracked and worn down by the rain and were always willing to drop an ear or a nose onto the head of some innocent passerby. In spite of the "dragon's" wail and lions as ferocious as those in Daniel's den, indifferent nature had grown abundantly, especially along the side paths. And

---

promoted the development of trade and industry and opposed the feudal system. The journal's literary department was controlled by progressive critics and advocated romanticism over classicism. It published works by well-known authors, including Pushkin, Zhukovsky, Baratynsky, and A. I. Turgenev. The journal was shut down by Nicholas I when it printed an unfavorable review of N. V. Kukolnik's patriotic play *The Hand of the Almighty Has Saved the Fatherland.*

this it did not out of modesty but because the previous governor had pruned the splendid old lime trees that grew along the main path, since he found such willful growth excessive and incompatible with strict adherence to duty. These lime trees, once deprived of their tops, sprouted new branches and came to resemble convicts whose heads have been half-shaved to identify them in case they attempted to escape. Like Titans, these trees seemed to be repeating Ozerov's verse, "There are gods in heaven, but the earth has been handed over to evildoers."[4]

Along the little side paths, however, the trees were free to grow as they pleased or as their sap allowed. On one of these paths, on a warm day in April probably meant to allow the inhabitants of the town of N. to appreciate the true significance of the cold spell yet to come in May, a lady in a white cape was strolling beside a gentleman in a black coat. The park was set on a hill on top of which stood two benches decorated anonymously with bold inscriptions. Despite his best efforts, the police sergeant was unable to apprehend the culprit; before every holiday he generously dispatched a member of the fire brigade (a man used to destruction of all kinds) to erase the various works of art periodically etched into the benches.

The lady and gentleman sat down on one bench. The view from the hill was rather pleasing. A large, muddy road encircled the park and led directly to the river. The water was high, and on both banks there stood all sorts of carts, wagons, carriages, unhitched horses, peasant women with large bundles, soldiers, and tradesmen. Two large flat-bottomed boats were constantly ferrying people back and forth. Loaded with people, horses, and carriages, these boats were slowly rowed across the river and resembled some ancient, recently excavated sea monsters, regularly raising and lowering their numerous appendages.

4. *"Evildoers."* A quotation from *Oedipus in Athens* (1804) by the Russian playwright V. A. Ozerov (1769–1816). The play was based on *Oedipe à Colonne* (1797) by the French tragedian J. F. Ducis (1733–1816), which in turn was based on Sophocles' *Oedipus at Colonus.* Ozerov reworked the story of a man in exile whose death brings good fortune to the country in which he dies; he also added a happy ending in which the gods strike down the "evildoers."

A multitude of sounds was carried up to the ears of the lady and gentleman seated on the bench: the squeaking of carts, the tinkling of bells, the shouting of oarsmen, and the barely audible replies from the other side of the river; the cursing of impatient passengers, the stamping of horses' hooves on the deck of the ferryboat, the mooing of cows whose horns were tied to the carts, and the boisterous conversation of peasants gathered around the campfire on the opposite bank.

The lady and gentleman interrupted their conversation; they contemplated the scene quietly and listened to the medley of sounds. Why is it that such distant sights and sounds have such an impact on us? I don't know. But I wish that Viardot[5] and Rubini[6] could be listened to with the same kind of heart-throbbing attention with which I too have often listened to the long-drawn-out song of the boatman keeping watch over his barge at night—a mournful song, accompanied by the sounds of waves lapping on the riverbanks and wind rustling in the leaves of willow trees. Listening to the mournful, monotonous noises, all sorts of thoughts have occurred to me. At times it even seemed that the poor boatman was attempting to escape from this stifling world into another one by means of his song, that he was unknowingly giving voice to some deep personal grief, that his soul was singing because of its oppressive sorrow, and so on and so forth. All of this happened during my youth!

"How lovely it is here," said the lady in the white cape at long last. "You must admit that our northern scenery is also splendid."

"As it is everywhere. Wherever a person looks and whenever he

5. *Viardot.* Pauline Garcia Viardot (1821–1910) was one of the most famous French singers of her day. She met the writer Ivan Sergeevich Turgenev (1818–83) while on tour in Moscow in 1843; this meeting soon resulted in an extraordinary ménage à trois. For the next forty years Turgenev spent long periods of time living near the singer and her husband.

6. *Rubini.* Giovanni Battista Rubini (1795–1854) was an Italian tenor who achieved great fame in Europe and Russia. In 1843, after a successful tour of European capitals, Rubini arrived in Petersburg, where he attracted the interest of Tsar Nicholas I. Rubini was retained as "Director of Song" in Russia, but he soon departed the country, convinced that the severe climate would damage his voice.

contemplates either nature or life openly, directly, unselfishly, he will always receive a rich reward."

"That is true. One can admire absolutely everything, if only one has the desire. A strange question often occurs to me: why is it that a person can enjoy everything and find beauty in everything, except in people?"

"One can understand why, but that doesn't make it any easier. We always have ulterior motives in our dealings with other people; this immediately pollutes poetic relationships with the most trivial prose. A person always regards someone else as an enemy with whom he must struggle, use deceit, and hasten to define his conditions for a truce. Where is the enjoyment? This is the way we were reared, and it is almost impossible to free ourselves from our upbringing. In each of us there is some philistine self-love that forces us to look around very cautiously. People neither fear nature nor compete with it. That's why we feel so free and easy in solitude. We can give ourselves over completely to impressions. If you invite even your best friend to accompany you, then it's no longer the same."

"I rarely meet any new people now, let alone any I can feel close to. But I think that there is, or at least there could be, an affinity between two people such that all external barriers to understanding would disappear and nothing would ever come between them."

"I have my doubts about the permanence of such a complete affinity. All that is mere words. Fully compatible people have yet to broach those subjects on which they will disagree. Sooner or later it will happen."

"Still, until it happens they can share a moment of complete sympathy when they do prevent each other from enjoying nature and one another."

"It is only in such moments that I believe. They are sacred instants of spiritual extravagance, when a person does not behave like a miser; instead, he gives unselfishly and is astonished at the richness and fullness of his own love. But these moments are very rare indeed. And for the most part, we are incapable of appreciating or cherishing them at the time; most often we allow them to slip through our fingers or sully them with all sorts of nonsense. They pass from a person's life and leave behind both painful heartache and a vague recollection of something that might have been, but wasn't. I must admit that people organize their lives very stupidly. They waste nine-tenths of it on trivial matters and don't know how to make good use of the remaining tenth."

"Why should a person lose such moments if he knows their worth? You see and understand all of this so well," observed Lyubonka with a smile. "You have a double responsibility."

"I cherish every pleasure, not only those moments. But it is quite easy to say, 'Don't lose them.' One false note, and the whole piece is ruined. How can you surrender completely when you can see all sorts of apparitions that threaten and berate you?"

"What apparitions? Aren't they merely our own caprices?" observed Lyubonka.

"What apparitions?" repeated Beltov, whose voice was slowly modulating as a result of his inner agitation. "It is difficult for me to explain it to you, although it is really all very clear to me. People have become so repressed that they dare not express their true feelings. All right, listen, I'll give you an example. It's something I really shouldn't say, but I will anyway. Now that I've started, I really can't stop myself. I have loved you from the very first day of our acquaintanceship. I don't know whether it's friendship, or love, or simply an affinity. But I know that you and your presence have become indispensable to me. I know that I spend my mornings in childlike impatience, in eager anticipation of the evening. When evening finally arrives, I run to your house, breathless with the thought that I will get to see you. Deprived of all else, surrounded by cold indifference, I have come to regard you as my last consolation. Believe me, these are by no means empty phrases. I cross the threshold of your house with great trepidation; I enter your presence feigning indifference; I speak about extraneous matters—many hours have passed by thus. What is the purpose of this stupid comedy? I will say more! You have not remained indifferent to me. Surely there are evenings when you wait for me. I have seen the joy in your eyes when I finally appear. At those times the loud pounding of my heart takes away my breath. And yet you greet me with feigned composure, you sit as far away from me as possible, and we pretend to be strangers. What on earth for? Could it be that there is something hidden deep within my soul or within yours that we should be ashamed of, that we should conceal from others? No, indeed! From others? And what's more amusing, we hide our intimacy from each other. This is the first time we are even talking about it. Even now we still seem to be hiding half the truth. The most joyous feeling can become painful, irritating, saddening—not to use an even stronger word—if we fear it or conceal it. We will begin to believe that it is criminal, and then it will actually become so. In fact, to enjoy something the way a thief does his booty— behind closed doors, aware of even the slightest sound—degrades both the object of enjoyment and the person who is enjoying it."

"You are being unfair," answered Lyubonka in a trembling voice. "I have never hidden my feeling of friendship for you; I have had no need to do so."

"Then tell me why," replied Beltov, seizing her hand and squeezing it firmly, "why is it that I am so tormented, in possession of a soul that is brimming over with a desire to reveal itself and confess its love? Why have I not found the strength to come directly to that woman, to take her by the hand, to look into her eyes, to speak freely, and to lay my weary head upon her breast? Why is she unable to greet me with those very same words that I can read on her lips but that never, ever cross them?"

"Because," replied Lyubonka with a desperate surge of energy, "because that woman belongs to another man and she loves him— yes, she loves him with all her heart."

Beltov let her hand drop.

"Just imagine. That was the one answer that I did not expect, yet now it seems as if none other was possible. But tell me this. Must you absolutely reject one attachment for another, as if you had only a limited quantity of love to dispense?"

"Perhaps, but I don't understand how a woman can possibly love two men. In addition to everything else, my husband has earned an enormous, sacred right to my love by virtue of his own boundless love for me."

"Why do you begin to defend your husband's right? No one is

attacking it. Besides, you don't defend it very well. If your husband's love has given him a right to yours, then why does the sincere, profound love of another man have no rights at all? That seems strange. Listen to me, Lyubov Aleksandrovna. Let us be frank, completely frank, at least once in our lives, and then I will never broach the subject again. I will even go away from here if you wish. You say that you can't understand how you could love both your husband and another man. But don't you really understand? Look deep into your heart and see what it is feeling at this very moment. Well, have the courage to admit that I am right. At least tell me that you too have experienced this and have thought about it. I know you have. I have read these same thoughts on your face and in your eyes."

"Ah, Beltov, Beltov, why are you saying all this, why?" uttered Lyubonka in a voice filled with somber sorrow. "We were such good friends; now it will be different, you'll see."

"Because we have finally called things by their right names? What childishness!" Beltov shook his head sadly and narrowed his eyes. His face, which a moment ago had looked so inspired and had expressed such infinite tenderness, now assumed its usual ironic mien.

The frightened woman regarded him anxiously, with tears in her eyes. Lyubonka was strikingly beautiful at that moment. She had taken off her hat, and her dark hair was being ruffled and uncurled by the damp evening breeze. Every feature of her face was animated and expressive. Love streamed forth from her lovely blue eyes. Her trembling hand first squeezed her handkerchief, then pulled and tore the ribbon off her hat. At times her breast rose up high, but it seemed as if she could not draw sufficient breath into her lungs. What did this proud man want from her? He wanted her to utter one word, he wanted to triumph over her—as if that word were even necessary! If he had been younger in spirit, if his mind had not been besieged for so long by strange, proud thoughts, then he would not have demanded that word from her.

"You are a horrible man," muttered poor Lyubonka at last, and raised her timid eyes.

He withstood her stare and asked, "Where on earth did Semyon

Ivanovich go? He wanted to join us here. I wonder if he's looking for us along another path. Let's go meet him before it gets too dark."

Offended by the tone of his last words, she didn't stir. After a brief silence, she once again raised her eyes to look at Beltov, and said in a quiet, imploring voice, "I have fallen in your estimation. You forget that I am a simple, weak woman." Tears streamed down her cheeks.

As always, the woman's warmth and love conquered the man's demanding pride. Beltov was deeply touched; he took her hand and pressed it to his chest. She heard the pounding of his heart and felt his warm tears dropping onto her hand. He was so handsome, so irresistible in his proud passion. Her blood was racing so fast, she felt so confused but so wonderful, her heart was overflowing with such emotion that on an uncontrollable impulse she threw herself into his arms, and her tears rained down onto Vladimir Petrovich's colorful Parisian vest. Almost at the same instant Dr. Krupov's voice rang out. "Where are you?" he shouted. "Are you here?"

"Over here," replied Beltov, offering Lyubonka his arm.

Beltov was intoxicated with his own happiness. His slumbering soul had suddenly been revived in all its earlier powers. Love, which had been suppressed up to now, burst forth within him. A feeling of inexpressible bliss filled his entire being. It was as if only yesterday or the day before he still hadn't known whether he loved and was loved in return. After escorting Lyubonka home, he returned to the park alone and threw himself down onto the same bench. He felt so full of emotion; tears streamed down his cheeks. He was surprised to have discovered so much youthful vigor in himself. True, a certain feeling of awkwardness soon intruded upon his joyful mood, a feeling that caused him to frown. But upon returning home, he ordered Grigory to serve him a bottle of champagne with his supper. The awkwardness was drowned in champagne, while the joyfulness became more manifest.

Lyubonka, pale as death, said farewell to Beltov at her house, to which Dr. Krupov had accompanied them. She did not dare recall or try to understand what had happened. But there was one thing that she could not keep from remembering, that she felt with every fiber of her being: the prolonged, burning, passionate kiss on her lips. She wanted to forget all about it, but it was so wonderful that she could not part with its memory for anything on earth. Semyon Ivanovich tried to leave, but Lyubonka was frightened and asked him to come in, because she was much too afraid to cross the threshold alone.

They entered together. Dmitry Yakovlevich was sitting at the table, deeply engrossed in a journal. His face seemed to be more tranquil and composed than usual. He smiled affectionately at Lyuba and at Dr. Krupov, closed his journal, and held out his hand to his wife. "Where on earth have you been? I have been waiting for you so long that I have become quite depressed."

His wife's hand was cold and clammy, like the hand of a sick person who is lying at death's door.

"We were strolling in the park," answered Krupov for her.

"Is anything the matter with you?" Dmitry asked his wife. "Your hand feels so strange! And you look awful, my dear."

"I feel slightly dizzy. Don't worry about it, Dmitry. I shall have a drink of water and a little rest, and I'm sure it will pass."

"Wait a minute. Where are you off to? Let me have a look. Have you forgotten that I am a doctor? What's this? No, she really isn't well. Dmitry Yakovlevich, let's sit her down on the sofa. There, take her under the arm . . . the arm . . . yes, that's it. On the way home I noticed that she didn't look at all well. The spring air, her thin blood, the evaporation of melting ice, all sorts of nasty things thawing out. . . . If only I had some English mustard handy to make small compresses, about the size of your palm, and some black bread and vinegar, too. Is your cook at home? Send her over to my house. Karp knows what to do. Ask him for some mustard. Yes. We will apply compresses to her calves. If that doesn't help, then we'll put a few more below her shoulders, on the fleshy part."

"I am not ill, really I'm not," Lyubov Aleksandrovna kept repeating in a weak voice after she had revived a bit. Trembling all over she said, "Dmitry, come here, close to me. Dmitry, I am not ill. Give me your hand."

"What is it? What's the matter, my angel?" asked her husband, who had also begun to feel faint and had started to cry.

She cast a strange, sorrowful glance at him but was unable to say why she had summoned him. He asked again what was wrong. "Give me a drink of water, and let me have a little rest. I'm sure that I'll be all right."

Two or three hours later Lyubov Aleksandrovna lay on her bed in a deep, comatose sleep or in a half-conscious state, punished both inwardly by pangs of conscience and outwardly by mustard plasters, for Beltov's passionate kiss. The shock was too great, and her organism could not withstand it.

In the drawing room on a sofa lay Dr. Krupov, still fully clothed. He had remained there as much for the patient's sake as for Dmitry's—who was frightened and distraught. At first Krupov had become furious with the sofa springs. Instead of making the piece of furniture soft and comfortable, they imparted to it all the characteristics of the wooden barrel in which the Carthaginians had rolled Regulus.[7] But fifteen minutes later Krupov was fast asleep, snoring away like a person burdened neither with pangs of conscience nor by indigestion.

Next to the patient's sickbed stood a small night lamp that threw a bright circle of light on the ceiling. The circle was constantly changing in size, wavering, and reflecting all the movements of the little flame in the oil lamp. Next to this table sat Krutsifersky, pale and distraught. Anyone who has spent a night at the side of someone seriously ill—a friend, a brother, or a loved one—especially one of our genuine winter nights, will understand what the nervous Krutsifersky was experiencing. A dull, stupid feeling of helplessness, fear of the future, and the feverish strain of sleepless exhaustion—all combined to put Dmitry into a stare of nervous anxiety. He got up frequently to gaze at his wife; he put his hand on her forehead, found that her fever had eased, and began to worry whether that might bode ill, indicating that the disease had penetrated her interior. He stood up, rearranged the night lamp

---

7. *Regulus.* According to legend, the inhabitants of Carthage captured the Roman military leader Marcus Atilus Regulus in the third century B.C. He traveled to Rome on parole to negotiate; when he returned to Carthage voluntarily, legend has it that he was stuffed into a barrel with spikes and rolled down a hill (Horace, *Odes*, III, 5).

and vials of medicine, took out his watch, brought it up to his ear to see if it was still ticking, and put it away again without even noting the time. Then he sat down on his chair and began to stare at the wavering circle of light on the ceiling; he started thinking and dreaming; his inflamed imagination was on the verge of delirium.

"No," he thought. "This can't happen. It's not possible, simply impossible. How can this be? She is all I have on earth, and she is still so young. Surely God will recognize my love for her and will have mercy upon us. It's nothing at all, pure nonsense. It will pass. Yes, it's just the cold, damp wind, her thin blood, the evaporating ice. . . . But spring colds are so fierce, often leading to nervous fever and consumption. . . . Why is there still no cure for consumption? What a terrible illness! But it is most dangerous for those under eighteen years of age. Still, our French teacher's wife was thirty years old when she died of consumption. Yes, died! Well, what if. . . ." Then he vividly imagined a coffin standing in their drawing room. It was covered with a shroud, and funeral rites were mournfully being read. A sorrowful Semyon Ivanovich stood nearby, and Yasha was being held by his nurse, who wore a white kerchief on her head. Then he saw an even more terrifying scene. There was no longer a coffin. The room had been cleaned up, the floors washed . . . only the odor of incense remained. . . .

Dmitry was about to faint. He stood up and went over to his wife's bed. Her cheeks were aflame; she was having trouble breathing and lay deep in a feverish sleep. Krutsifersky folded his arms on his chest and wept bitterly. . . . Yes, indeed! This man was capable of loving. One need only look at him to see that. He sank to his knees, took his wife's burning hand, and raised it to his lips.

"No," he said aloud. "No, He will not take her. She will not leave me. What would become of me without her?" He lifted his eyes toward heaven and started to pray.

Just then Dr. Krupov entered the room, looking very sleepy. His left eye refused to open, try as he did to move the muscle intended for just that purpose.

"What is it? Is she delirious?"

"No, she is sleeping soundly."

"I heard it myself. Or was I dreaming?"

'You must have been dreaming, Semyon Ivanovich," replied Dmitry Yakovlevich, with the look of a schoolboy caught in the act.

Dr. Krupov went over to the patient's bed.

"Still a bit of fever, but on the other hand . . . not too bad. . . . You should lie down, Dmitry Yakovlevich. What's the use of torturing yourself?"

"No, sir. I will not lie down," answered Dmitry.

"Do as you wish," said Krupov. He yawned and headed back to the lumpy sofa, where he slept peacefully until seven thirty, the hour at which he usually woke up, regardless of whether he went to bed at 10 P.M. or 7 A.M.

After examining the patient, Semyon Ivanovich decided that Lyubonka had a slight fever due to a cold, as he put it; he added that there was "a lot of it about," especially at that time of year.

Let Lyubov Aleksandrovna herself tell us what happened after that "slight fever." Here are some excerpts from her diary.

"*May 18.* How long has it been since I wrote in this book? Over a month, one month! Sometimes it is as if years have passed since I fell ill. Now, it would seem, my sickness has passed, and my life will once again proceed in peace and quiet. Yesterday I left the house for the first time. How delighted I was to breathe the fresh air. The weather was splendid! But I've become very weak during my illness. After taking a brief stroll around the garden, I felt so tired that I suddenly got dizzy. Dmitry became frightened, but the spell passed quickly. Good Lord, how he loves me! Nice, kind Dmitry, how he looks after me! I had but to stir or open my eyes at night, and he was by my side asking what I wanted and offering me a drink of water. Poor Dmitry, he has lost so much weight, as if he too had been ill. What a capacity for loving! A person would have to possess a heart of stone not to love such a man. Oh, I do love him! I cannot help loving him. That incident in the park doesn't mean a thing. My illness must have been starting, and I was in a very susceptible condition. My nerves were irritated. Yesterday I encountered *him* for the first time since I fell ill. I heard his voice as if in a dream, but I hardly saw him. He was very agitated, although he was trying to conceal it. His voice trembled when he said, 'At last, you feel better at last.' He said little else. Something was distracting him. He passed his hand over his forehead a few times, as if to wipe away some idea, but in vain. Not the slightest allusion to what had passed between us! No doubt he too understands that it was only morbid intoxication. Why haven't I told Dmitry about it? That evening when he offered me his arm so tenderly, I wanted to throw myself into his embrace and tell him everything. But I didn't have the strength, and I felt faint. Besides, Dmitry is so sensitive that it would distress him sorely. I shall tell him later, for sure."

"*May 20*. Yesterday Dmitry and I were in the public park. He wanted to sit down on that very same bench, but I said that I was afraid of a draft from the river. That bench has become so frightening. It would seem an insult to Dmitry if we sat on it. Is it really true that one can love two men at the same time? I don't understand. Perhaps one can love not only two but several people at the same time. But isn't this merely a play on words? One can love only one person with real love, and that is the way I love my husband. I also love Dr. Krupov. I'm not afraid to admit that I love Beltov, too. He is such a forceful man that I cannot help loving him. He is an extraordinary person, destined for greatness. Signs of genius shine forth in his eyes. That sort of man has no need of a woman's love. What would she mean to him? She would disappear in the profundity of his soul. He requires a different sort of love. He suffers so deeply, and the tender friendship of a woman could help relieve his suffering. He will always have such a friend in me. But he interprets this friendship in too passionate a manner. He interprets everything too passionately. In addition, he is unaccustomed to any attention or sympathy. He was always so lonely. His soul, embittered and distressed, was instantly revived by the voice of a sympathetic listener. It is only natural.

"*May 23*. Sometimes there occur strange moments when one is troubled by a desire to lead a fuller sort of life. I don't know whether this is a lack of gratitude for one's own fate or simply human nature. But I have been experiencing this desire frequently of late. It is very hard to put into words. I love Dmitry dearly, but sometimes my soul needs something more, something that I don't find in him. He is so gentle and affectionate that I can share with him every dream and childish thought that occurs in my soul. He appreciates each one; he neither laughs sarcastically nor offends me by a cold response or some learned observation. But that's not enough. There still exist other needs; the soul yearns for strong, bold thoughts. Why does Dmitry lack this need to search for truth, to be tormented by an idea? Whenever I turn to him with a burdensome question or with some doubt, he always comforts and consoles me. He wants to soothe me as if I were a little child. But that's not what I want at all. He may soothe himself with those childish beliefs, but I cannot.

"*May 24.* Yasha is ill. For two days he lay in a feverish state, and today he broke out in a rash. Dr. Krupov is deceiving me. It is ten times better to tell the truth, better to shock one's imagination than to grant it free rein. It will invent things much worse than reality. I can't look Yasha straight in the eye. My heart bleeds; the suffering of a little child is terrible. He has grown so thin, the poor dear, and very pale! Even so, the minute he feels a little better, he smiles and asks for his ball. It is terrible to contemplate the fragility of everything we hold so dear! The whirlwind can come and carry off anything, good and bad alike; people get caught in it, and this wind hurtles them up to the heights of bliss and then casts them down again. A person imagines that he has control over his fate; but he is no more than a little splinter of wood floating on a river, twisted around, carried away by the waves—perhaps to the riverbank, or out to sea, or caught in the mire. How dreary and distressing!

"*May 26.* Yasha has scarlet fever. Three of Dmitry's brothers died from it. Semyon Ivanovich is gloomy, irritable, rude, and never leaves Yasha's bedside. My God, my God! What is happening to us? Dmitry can hardly stand on his own two feet! Is this the kind of happiness that I have brought him?

"*May 27.* Time is dragging on, nothing has changed. How will it end—with a death sentence or with God's mercy? If only it would come soon! How monstrously healthy I am . . . how can I endure all of this? Semyon Ivanovich keeps repeating, 'Have patience, patience. . . . Farewell, Yasha, my angel, farewell, little one!'

"*May 29.* He has been resting calmly for the last day and a half. The crisis has passed. Now we must be exceedingly careful. All the while I have been under considerable strain. Now I am beginning to feel a deep spiritual exhaustion. I long to pour out my heart to someone. How wonderful it is to talk when there is someone who can understand and sympathize completely.

"*June 1.* All goes well. It seems that this time the cloud has passed us by. Yasha played with me for about two hours today while I was sitting near his bed. He has become so weak; he can't even stand on his own two feet. Dear, kind Semyon Ivanovich. What a remarkable man!

"*June 6.* The crisis is over. Yasha is much better, but I know that I am very ill. At times I sit at his bedside, and instead of feeling joy, a strange kind of grief rises from the depths of my soul and overpowers me; it grows and suddenly becomes such a dull, cruel pain that I long to die. During the bustle over Yasha's sickness I have had no time to myself. What with my illness and then Yasha's scarlet fever, all my cares and worries have left me not a moment to think about myself. As soon as things became a little calmer, a mournful, tormenting voice summoned me to look inside my heart, and I did not even recognize myself. Yesterday afternoon I felt so faint. I sat down next to Yasha's bed, put my head on his pillow, and fell fast asleep. I don't know how long I slept, but suddenly I felt overburdened. I opened my eyes. Beltov was standing there before me. No one else was in the room. Dmitry had gone off to teach his lessons. Beltov was gazing at me, his eyes filled with tears. He said nothing, only reached out and gave my hand a firm, painful squeeze—and then left. Why didn't he say anything? I wanted to stop him, but I couldn't speak.

"*June 9.* He spent the entire evening with us and was extremely cheerful. He spouted witticisms and caustic remarks; he laughed and joked, but I saw that it was all artificial. It even occurred to me that he had consumed a great deal of wine to sustain his mood. He is having a hard time. He is deceiving himself but is really very unhappy. Could it be that instead of providing him relief I have occasioned some new grief in his soul?

"*June 15.* The weather today was stifling. I was exhausted by the heat. During dinner there was a thunderstorm, and the pouring rain refreshed me more than it did the grass and trees. We went out to the public park. It was unusually lovely. The damp trees emitted a fresh fragrance that was very bracing. I felt much better. For the first time I was able to recall the events of *that day* and see them in a different light. There was so much that was beautiful about it. Is it possible that something so full of loveliness, tranquillity, and happiness can really be a criminal act? We strolled along the same path. Someone was sitting on that bench. We went up to it. It was *he*. I almost cried out for joy. He looked very sad; his words were gloomy, bitter and caustic. He is right: people invent torments for themselves. Well, what if he were my brother? Wouldn't I be able to love him openly, telling Dmitry and everyone else all about it? It wouldn't seem at all strange to anyone. And he is my brother; I can feel it. How splendidly we would organize our lives and our little circle of four. We share mutual trust, love, and friendship—yet we make compromises, sacrifices, and hesitate to speak our minds. It was late as we walked home. The moon had risen. Beltov walked alongside me. What strange, magnetic power in that man's look! Dmitry's is as quiet and peaceful as a clear blue sky, but his is so disturbing; I become agitated for a little while, and then it passes.

"We spoke very little . . ., only at our parting he said, 'I have been thinking a great deal about you all during this time. . . . I would very much like to have a talk with you—I have so much to say.' 'I have thought about you, too. Good night, Voldemar.' I don't know why that particular word escaped my lips. I had never used the name before, but somehow it seemed that I could use no other. He shuddered when he heard it. He bent toward me with that characteristic tenderness that he shows at certain times and said, 'You are the third person ever to use that name. It soothes me as if I were a little child. Now I shall be happy for the next few days.' 'Good night, Voldemar, good night,' I repeated. He wanted to say something, reconsidered, squeezed my hand gently, looked into my eyes, and left.

"*June 20.* Since my meeting with Voldemar I have changed a great deal and have grown much stronger. His ardent, active nature, constantly occupied, has touched my innermost fibers and has affected every aspect of my life. How many new questions have emerged within my soul! He has made me reflect on so many simple, everyday things that I never looked at before. Many things that I scarcely dared contemplate have now become clear. Of course, in the process I have had to sacrifice some cherished dreams that I had nourished and harbored. Sometimes the moment of parting with a particular dream seems very bitter; but that passes, and then I feel much freer. It would be extremely painful for me if he left. I did not look for him; it was fate's doing. But now that we have met, our lives can never be completely separate again. He has opened up a new world inside me. Isn't it strange that this man who was unable to discover either work or peace for himself, who has roamed the world all alone, should here, in a little town, with a woman of little education, limited means, from a very different social background, suddenly discover genuine sympathy? Perhaps he loves me too much. But are such things subject to willpower? Besides, he has endured so much coldness and indifference that he is ready to return any warm feeling a hundred times over. I could never leave him to his solitude, nor could I ever isolate myself from him. It would be a crime to do so. . . . Yes. He is right: his love does possess certain rights.

"Lately Dmitry has not been in a very good mood. He is always so pensive, more absent-minded than usual. This has always been a part of his nature, but now it seems to be increasing. His sadness troubles me; sometimes I am driven to a very unfair explanation for it. . . .

"*June 22.* It seems that I was not mistaken. Yesterday Dmitry was so depressed that I could bear it no longer. I asked him what was wrong. 'I have a headache,' he replied, 'I must get some fresh air.' He picked up his hat. 'Let's go together,' I said. 'No, my dear, not now. I walk very fast, and you will get tired.' He left with tears in his eyes. I could not endure it and wept bitterly all the time he was out.

"He found me sitting in the same place, next to the window. He saw that I had been crying, sadly gave my hand a tender squeeze, and sat down. We remained silent. Then after a few minutes he said, 'Lyubonka, do you know what I am thinking? How splendid it would be on such a warm, summer night to put my head down on your lap and to fall asleep forever in some peaceful grove.' 'Good heavens, Dmitry,' I replied, 'what a gloomy thought. Wouldn't you regret leaving anyone behind?' 'Yes, I would,' he answered. 'I would feel very sorry for you and for Yasha. But Semyon Ivanovich says that I can only harm Yasha's upbringing; I myself agree that you can bring him up better than I can. Besides, my dear, there, in the afterlife, just as here, in this life, my prayers will always be for you. I know that these prayers, so full of faith and hope, will be heard. You will feel sorry for me, my dearest! You are so kind. But I know that you will find the strength to withstand the blow; admit it, yourself.'

"It was unbearably painful for me to listen to him. As a result of his words, I saw and heard something ominous and wept copiously. What is happening? It is beginning to seem as if I have brought down only misfortune upon us. But my conscience is still clear. Could I have reduced him to such a state because my love was incomplete? . . . I can see that he no longer has any faith in me. Is it possible that his noble soul can be harboring an emotion I choose not to call by name? Could he possibly suspect that I have fallen out of love with him and that I am in love with someone else? Good Lord! How can I explain it to him? It's not that I love someone else; I love him *and* I love Voldemar. My affection for Voldemar is completely different, though. It is strange, but it seemed as if our life had calmed down and that it would now flow along in a broad, rich stream. Suddenly a yawning abyss opened up right before us. We must keep hold of the edge. It is hard to bear. If I were able to play the piano well, very well indeed, then I would express in soulful sounds what I cannot possibly convey in words. Dmitry would understand me; he would realize that my soul is pure. Poor Dmitry! You are suffering because of your boundless love for me. I love you, my dear Dmitry. If I had been frank with you from the very beginning, then none of this would have happened. What dark power kept me from doing so? As soon as he calms down, I will have a talk with him and tell him everything, absolutely everything.

"*June 23.* It seems that Dr. Krupov has also changed his attitude toward me. But what have I done? I don't understand anything, either what I have done or what has been done. Dmitry is calmer today. We had a long talk, but I did not tell him everything. There were moments when it seemed to me that he understood, but a minute later I could see that he and I regard life very differently. I am beginning to think that Dmitry never really understood me, never sympathized with me. What a terrible thought!

"*June 24. Late in the evening.* Life! Oh, life! In the midst of darkness and sorrow, morbid forebodings and genuine pain, the sun suddenly bursts forth, and everything becomes bright and cheerful again. Voldemar has just left. We talked for a long time. He is also gloomy and suffering a great deal. How I understand his every word! Why do people and circumstances misinterpret our mutual affinity and try so hard to spoil it? Why?

"*June 25.* Yesterday was St. John's Day.[8] Dmitry attended a name day party for one of the teachers. He returned home late and inebriated. I had never before seen him in such a state. His face was pale, his hair disheveled, his walk unsteady as he staggered around the bedroom. 'Are you ill, my dear?' I asked. 'Would you like a drink of water?' 'Yes,' he replied, gasping for breath in an agitated manner so completely out of character. 'If you would bring me enough water to drown myself, I would be most grateful to you.' I looked him straight in the eye, and he became embarrassed. 'Don't pay any attention to me, for God's sake, I am raving,' he said, undoubtedly frightened by my look. 'I myself don't know why I drank that extra glass of wine. That's why I feel so hot. That's why I'm raving. . . . Good night, my dear, I will have a little rest here, and he threw himself completely dressed onto the sofa and immediately fell into a deep sleep. I couldn't sleep all night. While he rested, his face expressed profound suffering. At times he smiled, but it was not even his own smile. . . . No, Dmitry, you cannot deceive me! It was not by chance that you drank that extra glass of wine, and you were not raving when you said those words; it was the wine that released a kind of cruelty that is not usually present in

---

8. *St. John's Day.* St. John the Baptist's Day, or Midsummer Day (24 June, O.S.).

your heart. Oh, merciful God, what on earth is happening to us? It is more than human strength can endure. Poor Dmitry, it must be so difficult for you! And I must be a witness to his suffering, knowing that I am the cause of it!

"*Three hours later.* I still can't put things in order. My soul is as troubled as the waves after a storm at sea. Blood is pounding through my temples; my heart is beating so fast that I have to keep pressing my hand to my chest. Dmitry! Are you not ashamed to interpret my feelings so pettily? And, you poor thing, how you are suffering for it. Grant him relief, blessed relief. Ah, how my head spins and burns! Has my fever returned? I spoke with Dmitry. I demanded an explanation for his depression, his actions, his words. Yes, he has lost faith in me! He will never understand what is happening to me. This is terrifying, because I cannot change anything. A dark cloud is settling upon us; I feel trepidation and pain. Oh, why did I ever meet Voldemar?

"*June 26.* How strange and confusing are peoples' conceptions! Sometimes, if you think about it, you don't know whether to laugh or cry. Today it occurred to me that self-sacrificing love is nothing more than an extreme form of egoism, and that great humility and meekness are merely a terrible form of pride or disguised harshness. I am frightened of such thoughts, just as, when I was a young girl, I used to consider myself a monster or a criminal for not being able to love Glafira Lvovna and Aleksei Abramovich. What can I do? How can I protect myself from such thoughts? Why should I? I am not a child any longer. Dmitry does not blame me, reproach me, or make demands on me. He has become even more affectionate. *Even more.* It is that *even more* that indicates that it is artificial, not at all what it seems to be. It shows the depth of his pride, my humiliation, and a lack of any true understanding. He is suffering greatly, but what about the woman who is giving him back only venom in return for his love? The good Lord knows that I did not ask for this! I have spoken with him more openly than any other woman would have. Apparently he starts to relent, but then some new feeling builds up inside of him, and he is unable to cope with it.

"*June 27.* His grief is taking the form of hopeless despair. In days past, following our gloomy conversations, he would experience some brighter moments. But not any more! I don't know what to do. I am exhausted. A great deal was necessary to drive this gentle man to despair. And I am the one who did it! I was unable to sustain our love. He no longer believes in my words of love and is perishing. If only I could die now, right now, this very moment.

"I am beginning to despise myself. Yes. Worse than anything else, and least comprehensible, is that my conscience is still at peace. I have dealt a terrible blow to a man whose whole life was devoted to me, whom I love, and all I feel is unhappiness. It seems that it would be easier if I considered myself a culprit. Oh, then I could throw myself at his feet, embrace him, and make amends with my repentance. Repentance erases all stains from the soul. He is so loving; he could not possibly resist. He would forgive me, and we would suffer together and be happier for it. But what is the nature of this accursed pride that refuses to allow repentance even to enter my heart? I would like to be alone now, somewhere far away. I would take only Yasha with me. I would wander among strangers and would recover my strength. Dmitry, you will not find peace within your soul. My dear, I would give away even my last drop of blood if only you could understand me, if only you wanted to understand me. How much better it would be for you! You are falling victim to your own lofty incomprehension. I shall follow you into this abyss because I love you and because diabolical forces have chosen me to be the cause of your downfall. Sometimes it seems that two or three words from Voldemar could bring me some relief, but I am afraid to seek an opportunity to talk with him. That's what all the innuendos have done. They have managed to make me afraid and to besmirch a bright and noble feeling. May God forgive them all. Dr. Krupov gave me a little sermon indirectly. Oh, dear Semyon Ivanovich. I feel so sorry for him. He doesn't understand a thing, yet he talks about the sacred obligations of motherhood. Does it ever occur to him that I sometimes think about it, too? Sympathy from other people can be more offensive than their indifference. Why is it that friendship is thought to convey the right to drag someone to the pillory? And then make him heed your advice, however repugnant it might be? Oh, how pretty it all is! Ugh, it's as stuffy as being shut up in a little room where all the windows are closed and flies keep buzzing around."

If Beltov had never come to the town of N., the Krutsifersky family would have enjoyed many years of happiness and serenity. But this fact offers no consolation. Sometimes, when passing a burned-out house, one blackened by smoke, windowless, with only the chimneys left standing, it occurs to me that *if* only a spark had not landed there and had not been fanned into flames, then the house would have stood for many more years. People would have feasted there and made merry. But now it is no more than a heap of stones.

Strictly speaking, our story is ended. We could stop it here and allow the reader to decide, "*Who is to blame?*" But there are still a few more details that seem rather interesting. Allow me to share them with you. Let us turn first to poor Krutsifersky.

Soon after his wife's illness, he noticed that she was preoccupied by something. She was always pensive and restless. Her face expressed more pride and strength than ever before. Strange and unlikely explanations began to occur to Krutsifersky. He laughed at them inwardly and tried to dismiss these ideas, but they kept returning.

Once Lyuba was sitting with Yasha. Suddenly there came a knock at the front door, and someone inquired, "Are you home?" "It's Beltov," said Krutsifersky, raising his eyes. He observed his wife's slight blush and animated expression; the latter, it seemed, was not intended for him. He shuddered but said nothing. He knew, of course, that his wife had a very close relationship with Beltov, so in no way did this surprise him. But that expression of hers, that blush? "Could it be?" he wondered, and he looked again at what was happening. Beltov was playing with Yasha, but what tenderness and passion were relfected in his gaze directed at the child's mother! A person would have to be blind not to recognize that this gaze was full of love, ardent love, and what is more, requited love. Lyuba stood with lowered eyes. Her hands were trembling slightly, and she seemed very happy. Dmitry Yakovlevich said a few words and left the room.

"Could it be true?" he asked himself, suddenly feeling very frightened. The confusion in his head and the roaring in his ears were so great that he had to sit down on the bed. After five minutes or so, during which he thought about nothing at all but rather experienced intense anguish, he returned to the room. They were chatting away so amiably and harmoniously that it occurred to him that his own presence was totally superfluous. He began to pace the room, recalling trifles that had seemed so insignificant at the time but that now appeared as positive proof, confirmation of his suspicions.

When Beltov rose to leave, she accompanied him to the door. She smiled at him, and what a smile! "Yes, she is in love with him." Having once recognized it, he was horrified. He began to push the thought away, but it was so insistent, it kept on returning. He was overcome by dark, insane despair. "So, here it is, my premonition come true! What am I to do? And you, Lyuba! You no longer love me!" He tore his hair, bit his lips, and suddenly, in his soft, tender heart there emerged the terrible possibility of hatred, malice, envy, and a need for revenge. In addition, he found the strength to conceal all of this.

Night fell. He wanted to cry, but no tears would come. For brief moments sleep closed his eyes, but he awoke immediately, drenched in a cold sweat. He dreamed of Beltov leading Lyubov Aleksandrovna by the hand, gazing at her lovingly. She was going away with him, and he realized that it was forever. Then he dreamed of Beltov again. Lyuba was smiling at him. Everything was so terrifying that he got out of bed. The day was dawning. His wife was still asleep. Her face was serene. The face of a sleeping person often possesses a particularly poignant loveliness. This was true of Lyuba's face at that very moment. Suddenly she smiled. "She is dreaming of him," thought Krutsifersky, and he looked at her with such hatred and ferocity that had he not subscribed to the peace-loving customs of our age, he would have smothered her in bed just as the Venetian Moor did Desdemona.[9] But our modern tragedies do not end so drastically.

9. *Desdemona.* Othello strangles his innocent wife Desdemona in the awesome concluding scene of Shakespeare's tragedy.

"So this is how she repays my boundless love? Oh, my God, my God! For such love!" he kept repeating, as if wishing to break free of himself and such terrible temptation. He went up to Yasha's bed. The child was sleeping soundly, his limbs sprawled about, one hand under his cheek. "Soon you will be left an orphan," Dmitry thought, standing before him. "Poor Yasha! I am no longer your father. I cannot and will not endure this. Poor child! I entrust you to the protector of all orphans. And he looks so much like Lyuba!" Dmitry began to cry. His tears, his prayer, and the sight of the child sleeping so peacefully brought some relief to the sufferer. His mind was flooded by a host of other, more generous thoughts. "Am I right to accuse her? Did she really want to fall in love with him? What's more, he. . . . I am nearly in love with him myself. . . ." Our ecstatic dreamer, having become an insanely jealous and punitive husband, suddenly and self-sacrificingly resolved to remain silent. "Let her be happy. Let her recognize my altruistic love. So long as I can see her and know that she exists. I will become a brother to her, a friend!" And he wept from a feeling of tenderness and experienced great relief, once having decided on such an enormous act of total self-sacrifice. He consoled himself with the thought that she would be deeply touched by his altruism. But these feelings were merely the result of his spiritual tension. In less than two weeks he became exhausted from the burden of such a sacrifice.

We shall not blame him. Such unnatural acts of righteousness and intentional self-abnegation are not at all in keeping with human nature; they belong more to the realm of imagination than to reality. He persevered for a few days. But the first thought that undermined his heroism was cold and narrow: "She thinks that I don't see a thing. She is scheming and pretending." About whom did he think this? About the woman he had loved and respected, the woman he was supposed to know but didn't. Then the internal torment, which had been eating away at him, began to burst forth into words, primarily because words have a way of relieving sadness. This led to arguments and explanations that he didn't know how to stop and that Lyuba didn't want to stop. After these conversations with her, things became even harder for him. He tried to avoid being alone with her, but given their hermetic existence they almost always found themselves alone together. He tried to spend more time at his work, but the material would not penetrate. He couldn't force himself to read. While his eyes followed the lines, his imagination returned to recollections of his happy past. Often his copious tears flowed onto the pages of some scholarly treatise. An emptiness developed in his soul, expanding, as it were, with every passing hour. It was becoming impossible for him to live with this feeling. He began to seek distraction. We have already seen from Lyuba's journal how he returned from his learned friend Meduzin's name day party.

Incidentally, for some relief from these pathetic pages, let us drop in on the erudite discussion at Meduzin's. In order to do so, we must begin by making his acquaintance. This will prove to be so delightful that we shall devote a new chapter to it.

Chapter 6

Ivan Afanasevich Meduzin, Latin teacher and proprietor of a private school, was a splendid man who was not at all like Medusa[1]—neither externally, since he was bald, nor internally, since he was filled not with malice but with vodka liqueur.[2] He received the nickname Meduzin when he was attending seminary, first because he had to have a nickname and second because in those days the hair of this future scholar stuck out in all directions and was remarkable for its texture (one might easily have mistaken it for wire). But the destructive power of time had "scattered it to the four winds." From seminary Ivan Afanasevich received not only his pleasant mythological nickname but also a solid education, one that usually accompanies seminary students to the grave and stamps them with such a unique seal that they can immediately be recognized at any time or place. Aristocratic manners, however, were not among Meduzin's distinguishing characteristics. He could nev-

1. *Medusa.* One of three frightful maidens in Greek mythology called Gorgons, who had wings, claws, and enormous teeth, and whose heads were covered with serpents instead of hair; her gaze could turn men to stone.
2. *Vodka liqueur.* An alcoholic beverage consisting of vodka flavored with berries, fruit, or herbs.

er learn to use polite, formal address when speaking to his students and always added certain words to his conversation that are rarely uttered in high society. Ivan Afanasevich was about fifty years old. He had begun his career as a private tutor in various people's houses; he soon decided to establish his own school. One day a colleague of his named Kafernaumsky, also a former seminary student, who was distinguished by the fact that he had been perspiring since the day he was born (when it was 20 degrees below he was constantly mopping his brow, and when it was 90 degrees above sweat dripped from every pore of his face), having met Ivan Afanasevich in class one day, said to him in a voice loud enough for everyone to hear, "Well now, Ivan Afanasevich, if I am not mistaken, your name day is approaching. We shall of course be celebrating it this year according to your own delightful custom?"

"We shall see, my good sir, we shall see," answered Ivan Afanasevich with a chuckle. For some reason or other he had already decided to celebrate this year's name day with even greater splendor than usual.

Ivan Afanasevich's household was not very well "established." Although he had lived in town for the last fifteen years without ever leaving, still one might conclude that he had just arrived here yesterday and hadn't yet had time to settle in. This was true less from any stinginess on his part than from his total ignorance of what a person needs to live in civil society. Now, in preparing to give a party, he examined his household carefully. It turned out that he possessed only six teacups, two of which had been transformed into tumblers as a result of having lost their handles; three saucers, a samovar, a few plates that wobbled when set on the table, because the cook had acquired them in a sale of defective merchandise; two pieces of stemmed glassware that he modestly referred to as his "vodka goblets"; and three cracked pipes coated inside with grime, probably to prevent drafts. That was it! Yet he had invited all his colleagues from school. He thought about the matter for quite some time. Finally, he summoned his cook Pelageya. (Note that he never called her Palageya, but Pelageya, just as it should be; in like manner, he did not replace the old-fashioned names for the days of the week with the newer, effete words "Thursday" and "Friday.")[3]

Pelageya was the wife of a very brave warrior who had gone off to join the militia one week after their wedding day and who, since then, hadn't found the time either to return home or to communicate the news of his own death. As a result Pelageya was left in the unpleasant position of being a widow with a strong suspicion that her husband was still alive. I have a great many reasons for suspecting that this tall, fat woman, her head wrapped in a kerchief, her face adorned with warts and very dark eyebrows, was the mistress not only of Meduzin's kitchen but also of his heart. But I will not reveal my reasons to you, since I consider that the secrets of a person's private life should remain sacrosanct. Pelageya appeared. Meduzin explained his predicament to her.

"My goodness! The devil is certainly making a fool out of you, isn't he?" replied Pelageya. "And you are supposed to be so clever! God forgive me, but you are as stupid as a little baby. You've invited a horde of people here, when I can't even squeeze ten kopecks out of you to do the laundry. Well, what are we going to do now? We'll be so ashamed in front of them! It's as if we lived in a burnt-out house."

"Pelageya," replied Meduzin in a loud voice. "Do not try my patience. I want to celebrate my name day with some friends, and I will do just as I like. I will not tolerate any objections from some old woman." Cicero's influence on this speech was clearly apparent to anyone listening, but Pelageya was so upset by the news of the imminent celebration that she couldn't even think about Cicero.[4]

"Of course, I won't say a word. It's your own business if you want to throw your money out of the window, if it gives you some *plaiseer* [pleasure]. Give me fifty rubles, and I will buy everything you need, except for the drinks."

Pelageya knew very well that Meduzin would not be pleased at

3. *Thursday and Friday.* Meduzin employs the archaic forms inherited from Old Russian, in contrast to the contemporary, standard literary forms.

4. *Cicero.* A sarcastic reference to the first line of Cicero's speech "*In Catilinam*": "How long, Catiline, are you going to abuse our patience?"

all by her answer; therefore it was with a profound sense of her own self-worth that she rested her right elbow on top of her left hand, her chin on top of her right, and awaited the effect of her words.

"Fifty rubles on that lot of good-for-nothings! Have you gone completely mad, or what? Fifty rubles, and without the drinks! What nonsense! Stupid old woman! Is that the kind of advice you give? Go to Father Ioanniki at once. Invite him to come on the twenty-fourth, and ask him if we can borrow his dishes for that evening."

"A fine thing to go around begging dishes!"

"Pelageya! Are you acquainted with that particular object over there?" asked Meduzin, pointing to a gnarled stick standing in the corner.

Pelageya, seeing that old acquaintance, went quietly into the kitchen, put on her cloak and silk kerchief; then, with considerable grumbling, set off for Father Ioanniki's house. Meanwhile, Meduzin sat at his desk in deep thought for an hour or so. Then, suddenly, "he resorted to his hand as an instrument": he seized a piece of paper and began writing. If you think that he was preparing a commentary to *The Aeneid* or to Eutropius's *Brief History*,[5] then you are quite mistaken. Here's what he wrote:

1. Russian grammar and logic—partakes a lot.
2. History and geography—partakes plenty.
3. Pure mathematics—poor.
4. French language—wine, a lot.
5. German language—beer, a great deal.
6. Drawing and penmanship—only liqueur.
7. Greek language[6]—partakes of everything.

After making these anthropological observations, Ivan Afanasevich wrote the following plan:

5. *Brief History.* Eutropius was a fourth-century Roman historian who wrote *A Brief History of Rome* in ten volumes, covering the period from the founding of the city to the accession of the Emperor Valens (364), to whom the work was dedicated.

6. *Greek language.* I had written "Reverend Teacher of Religion. . . ." The censor changed this to teacher of the "Greek language." [Herzen's note]

20 pts. of sauterne	16 rubles	
10 pts. of liqueur	8 rubles	
10 pts. of beer	4 rubles	
2 bottles of mead		50 kopecks
10 bottles of Crimean wine	10 rubles	
3 bottles of Jamaican rum	4 rubles	
1 liter of sweetened vodka	2 rubles	50 kopecks
Total	45 rubles	

Meduzin was very pleased with his tally: not too expensive, but plenty to drink. In addition, he allocated a considerable sum for the purchase of fish to make pies, for ham, pressed caviar, lemons, herring, tobacco, and mint spice cakes (the last, clearly a luxury rather than a necessity).

The guests arrived at about 6 P.M. By 9 P.M. perspiration was dripping from Kafernaumsky's face like rain. At 10 P.M. the geography master, who had been talking to the French teacher about the death of his (the latter's) wife, suddenly burst out laughing, although he himself didn't understand what should be so funny about the demise of this venerable lady. But what was even more amazing was that the French teacher, an inconsolable widower, looked at the geography teacher and couldn't refrain from laughing either, in spite of the fact that he had been drinking nothing stronger than wine.

Meduzin set a good example for his guests. He drank continuously, whatever Pelageya offered him: punch, beer, vodka, and sauterne. He even managed to consume a glass of mead, although there were only two bottles of it. Encouraged by this splendid paragon, the guests did not lag far behind their host. Only Krutsifersky, who had been invited to grace the occasion (since he belonged to the most respected group of scholars in town), took no part in the merry festivities. He sat alone in a corner smoking his pipe. At last his host's sharp eye lit upon him.

"Dmitry Yakovlevich, won't you have a little punch and lemon? Come now, you are sitting there alone, looking so forlorn, not drinking anything, spoiling everyone's fun."

"You know that I never drink, Ivan Afanasevich."

"My dear sir, I know no such silly thing! Whether you drink or not, when you are with friends you have to drink and engage in friendly conversation. . . . Yes, indeed. Pelageya, give him a glass of punch, and make sure it's good and strong."

This last remark by the host was clearly the result of the fact that Krutsifersky had no desire even for a weak drink.

Pelageya brought him a glass of vodka punch in which a piece of lemon lay in a drunken stupor and into which a few teaspoonfuls of boiling water had disappeared without a trace. Krutsifersky took the glass in order to escape his host and in the hope that he would soon find the opportunity of spilling most of it out the window. This proved to be difficult, since Meduzin had found a substitute for himself at the card table and proceeded to sit down next to Krutsifersky.

"Well, now, Dmitry Yakovlevich, I shall tell you sincerely that I am now very grateful to you, yes, very, very grateful. Otherwise a young man like you would be sitting home under lock and key. Yes, of course you have a young wife. But still, you really must get out sometimes. Here now, Dmitry Yakovlevich, let me give you a little kiss for joining us." Without waiting for permission, and in spite of the fact that he smelled very much like a tavern, he implanted his rather thick lips on Krutsifersky's cheek. The next moment, without a word, Kafernaumsky, dripping with perspiration, also embraced Dmitry Yakovlevich. The latter, eager to wipe his face without obvious insult to a fellow enlightener of young people, retired to a corner and took out his handkerchief. There, with his back toward Dmitry, stood the French teacher (the inconsolable widower) and the German teacher, Gustav Ivanovich, filled with beer to the very tips of his fingernails and smoking a pipe with a quill mouthpiece. Neither one noticed Krutsifersky, and they continued their conversation in a whisper. Needless to say, Krutsifersky had no intention of eavesdropping, but the mention of Beltov's name, uttered rather loudly and in combination with his own, made him shudder. Instinctively he pricked up his ears.

"It's the same old story," said the Frenchman, somehow running all his Russian sounds together. "And if Adam didn't wear horns, then it was simply because he was the only man in Eden."

"Ja," answered Gustav Ivanovich. "Ja! That 'Peltov' is a regular 'Don Schuan,'" and one minute later he burst out laughing. That one minute, according to German custom, was spent in profound reflection on the French teacher's words about Adam. Having understood them at last, Gustav Ivanovich burst into loud guffaws. Removing the quill mouthpiece from his pipe (which had now been completely chewed up by his German teeth), he added with great satisfaction, *"Ich habe die Pointe, sehr gut"* ["I get the point, very good"].

This story produced the greatest impact of all not on Gustav Ivanovich but on a person who had scarcely heard it, that is, on Krutsifersky. What could this mean, the combination of these two names, his own and Beltov's? Was it possible that the horrible secret that he himself hardly suspected, that he dared not even admit, had become common gossip? Had they really said what he thought they had? Of course they did! There they were, still standing on the same spot, and Gustav Ivanovich was still laughing. Krutsifersky felt as if something had torn inside of him, that his chest was filling up with warm blood, and that the stream was rising higher and higher in his throat and would soon come gushing out of his mouth. His head was reeling, and flames were dancing before his eyes; he was afraid to encounter anyone's glance and feared that he would fall down on the floor. He leaned up against the wall. Suddenly someone's heavy hand took him by the arm. He shuddered, "What will happen next?" he wondered.

"Oh, no, my dear Dmitry Yakovlevich," said Meduzin, holding Dmitry's sleeve with one hand and a glass of punch in the other. "Decent folk do not behave like this. No, my friend, don't think that you have escaped me by hiding away in a corner. I have a house rule: take a glass or not, it's your own choice. But once you've taken one, you must drink it."

For a while Krutsifersky stood looking at him and listening to him, just as Gustav Ivanovich had when considering the French teacher's witticism. At last he understood vaguely what was being said. He took up his glass, drank it down in one gulp, and burst out laughing.

"That's what I like to see! There's an honest fellow for you!

What do you think? And you say you don't drink, you scoundrel! Well, Dmitry Yakovlevich, Mitya, my friend, have another small glass. Pelageya," said Meduzin, solicitously fishing the piece of lemon out of Krutsifersky's glass with his finger, "another glass of punch—and make it stronger! Will you drink it?"

"I will indeed."

"Bravo, bravo!"

The only reason Meduzin refrained from kissing Krutsifersky again was that his mouth was full of lemon, which he had devoured, rind, seeds and all, adding by way of explanation, "Once the foundation is laid, it's a good idea to have something sour."

The punch was brought in, and Krutsifersky drank it down as if it were a glass of water. No one noticed that he was as white as a sheet and that his blue-tinted lips were trembling, perhaps because to the assembled guests it already seemed as if the whole world were trembling.

Meanwhile, as things were getting into full swing, the indefatigable Pelageya carried in a tray with a decanter and some wine glasses and placed them on a small table. Then she brought in a plate with herrings sprinkled with scallions. Although the fish had been cut up, the backbone and ribs had not been removed, and this gave the herring a particular, very pleasant pungency. The card game ended with minor losses but with major arguments among those who had played a round of boston. Meduzin had won; consequently, he was in a very good mood.

"Enough, enough!" he cried. "Let's forget all about it and move on, with God's blessing, to taste the 'cantafresco' [cool song]." (Ivan Afanasevich always insisted on referring to liqueur as "cantafresco." I have no idea why, but I suppose that he had sufficient and reliable Latin sources.)

The guests headed off toward the table.

"Dmitry Yakovlevich. Surely you will not refuse to try the cantafresco?"

"Of course not," replied Krutsifersky, and he downed a huge goblet of foamy liqueur, spoiled by the addition of various herbs, all of which taste horrible but are supposed to be good for the digestion; at least that's what gullible people think.

The guests' delight was indescribable. Then Pelageya brought in a fish pie of legendary proportions. I shall assume that we are all rather well acquainted by now with the kind of Belshazzar's feast that Meduzin had organized in celebration of his name day;[7] therefore, I shall consider it unnecessary to describe it in greater detail. I can assure the reader that it went on in exactly the same way as it had begun.

On the following day Krutsifersky had a very long talk with Lyubov Aleksandrovna. Once again she rose in his estimation, rose to unattainable heights. He was able to understand her and appreciate her. But something had come between them, and Dmitry was plagued by the terrible thought that "people were talking about it." He did not, however, breathe a word of this to her. He found it difficult to talk to her and hastened off to the gymnasium. He arrived there a little before the beginning of class and stood looking out the window of the recreation hall. It hadn't been very long since he had stood there last, looking serenely out that same window, experiencing the height of human happiness, eager to hurry home to his wife. Suddenly, everything was different! Now, he wanted to run away from home. At the same time he felt overwhelmed by Lyuba's strength and majesty. He realized that she was suffering no less than he and that she was concealing her suffering out of love for him. "Out of love for me! But does she really love me? Can one possibly love a log lying across one's path to happiness? Why wasn't I able to hide what I know? If only I had been more careful, she would not be suffering so. And I could have done everything to make her happy. What should I do now? Run away, escape? But where to?"

He was interrupted by Anempodist Kafernaumsky. Obviously he had not yet recovered from the revels of the previous evening. His eyes were red and encircled by puffy rings, like the moon or

7. *Belshazzar's feast.* The raucous celebration organized by the Babylonian king Belshazzar, son of Nebuchadnezzar, and described in Daniel 5: 1–4, at which an enormous quantity of wine was consumed by the king, his princes, wives, and concubines.

cold winter nights. Bluish blotches had appeared on his nose and cheeks.

"So, my dear fellow," said Kafernaumsky, wiping the perspiration from his face, "do you have a splitting headache?"

Krutsifersky remained silent.

"I am barely alive. 'Have you seen the wreck of the ship? / You have, but what of it? This is my life'. . . .[8] What do you think of our Meduzin? That old dog, he really let himself go! What about you, Dmitry Yakovlevich, have you treated what ails you? You know the proverb, 'a hair of the dog that bit you'. . . ."

"What do you mean, 'treated what ails me'?"

"I'll show you what I mean. I can see that you're still a novice! Come along with me. I live right next door. . . 'For a taste of rum and arrack, / Come and pay me a little visit.'"[9]

Krutsifersky set off for Kafernaumsky's house. Why? He didn't know why himself. Instead of rum and arrack, Kafernaumsky offered him a goblet of home brew with a few pickles. Krutsifersky drank it down and, to his own great astonishment, realized that he did indeed feel somewhat better afterward. Needless to say, such a discovery could not have come at a more appropriate time, since he was being devoured by grief and despair.

Around ten in the morning Semyon Ivanovich Krupov turned up in the small vestibule of the Keresberg Inn and began pacing back and forth with a worried and angry look. About five minutes later the door to Beltov's room opened, and Grigory came out carrying a brush in his hand and his master's coat over his arm.

"Well, I suppose he's still asleep," said Krupov.

"He just woke up," replied Grigory.

"Tell him that I am here and have something important to discuss with him."

8. ". . . my life." From Ozerov's *Oedipus in Athens*. See pt. II, chap. 5, n. 4.

9. ". . . a little visit." From a poem entitled "To Burtsov," by the nineteenth-century poet Denis Davydov (1784–1839). In the original, the line reads, "For the sake of God"; this phrase was labeled "blasphemous" by the censor, and the word "God" was replaced by "rum." Arrack is a strong alcoholic beverage made from either rice or molasses.

"Semyon Ivanovich!" called Beltov. "Semyon Ivanovich! Come in," he said, appearing at the door.

"Might you have half an hour or so to spare?" asked Krupov.

"You may have the whole day, if you wish," replied Beltov.

"I'm not disturbing you? You usually spend the morning studying political economy or something like that?" The old doctor did not attempt to conceal the sarcasm in his question.

"You must have awakened very early this morning and gotten out of the wrong side of the bed," observed Beltov, taking the cranky old man's remark as gently as possible.

"Actually I got up on precisely the side that I wanted to."

"I see," said Beltov, gesturing towards the door. "Do come in."

"Vladimir Petrovich," began the doctor. Try as he did to appear cool and calm, he was not very successful. "I have not come to see you on the spur of the moment; I have thought long and hard about what I am doing. It is very painful to have to tell you the bitter truth. Nor did I find it easy when I first understood the situation. I have been made a fool of in my old age. I made the sort of mistake about a fellow human being that would make a sixteen-year-old boy blush."

Beltov looked at the old man in amazement.

"Since I have begun to speak, I will go on, like a Macedonian soldier, and will call things by their right names.[10] What comes of it is none of my business. I am old, but no one can call me a coward. Nor will I, out of cowardice, call an ignoble deed a noble one."

"One moment please, Semyon Ivanovich. I am certainly convinced that you are not a coward and even more convinced that you don't consider me one. However, I would consider it extremely unpleasant if I felt the need to convince you of this fact—you, whom I deeply respect. I can see that you are very irritated; therefore, let us both agree to avoid offensive language, no matter what. It always has a strange effect on me. It forces me to forget all the good qualities of the person who resorts to such verbal abuse. Bad

10. *Right names.* An allusion to the unhappy fate of messengers who deliver bad news.

language does not solve anything. Therefore, let us come right to the point. Forgive me this *aviso*" [warning].

"Very well. I will be civil, my dear sir, extremely civil. Allow me, Vladimir Petrovich, to be so bold as to ask whether or not you are aware that you have destroyed the happiness of a certain family that for four years has afforded me great joy and that I have come to regard as my own family. You have poisoned their happiness and in the process have made four people miserably unhappy. I introduced you into this family because I felt sympathy for you in your loneliness. They accepted you as if you were their own kin; they offered you warmth. And how did you repay them? You will be pleased to learn that one of these days the husband will either hang himself or drown himself—in water or in wine, I still don't know which. The wife will develop consumption, take my word for it. The child will become an orphan and be raised by strangers. To top it all off, the whole town is trumpeting your 'victory.' Allow me to add my congratulations!" The noble old man was trembling with rage as he pronounced these last words. "But perhaps it's all the same to you—from your superior point of view," he added after a few moments.

Beltov stood up and began to pace. Suddenly he stopped in front of the old doctor.

"Now, permit me to inquire who gave you the right to meddle in the most sacred secrets of my life in such a rude and vulgar fashion? How do you know that I am not twice as miserable as everyone else? I will overlook your tone of voice. All right, I shall respond. What is it that you wish to know? Whether I love that woman? Yes, I love her. Yes, yes indeed. I will repeat it a thousand times over: I love that woman with all my heart and soul. I love her. Do you hear me?"

"Then why are you destroying her? If you had a soul, you would have stopped at the very first step. You would never have allowed your love to be discovered. Why didn't you leave their house? Why didn't you?"

"Why not simply ask me how I go on living? I really don't know the answer! Perhaps in order to destroy that family, to ruin the finest woman that I have ever met. It's easy enough for you to ask and to condemn. Obviously your heart has been quiet since your youth, or else something similar would have remained alive in your own recollections. Let me answer your questions. Yes, I now feel the need not to justify myself but to speak out. I accept no one as judge of my actions except myself. Besides, you have nothing more to say to me. I have understood you completely. You will only try to repeat your thoughts in more offensive words. Ultimately that will be exasperating for both of us. I have no desire whatever to challenge you to a duel, if for no other reason than that she needs you so desperately."

"Go on, speak. I will listen to you."

"I came here at one of the most difficult times of my life. I had recently parted company with my friends abroad. There was not a single person who was close to me. I was in contact with some acquaintances in Moscow, but we had nothing in common. That further strengthened my intention to come to this town. You know what awaited me here, and you saw what a splendid life I was leading. Then suddenly I met that woman. You love and respect her, but you don't really know her at all, just as you don't really know me. You value highly her family happiness, her love for her husband and child—but that's all. Don't be angry. There come certain moments when it behooves one to hear something other than the pleasant truth. Don't think that it is only physical proximity or similarity in age that allows someone to unburden his soul to another person. Not at all. Very often people who have lived together for twenty years or more go to the grave as total strangers. Sometimes they can even love each other, yet not really know each other. On the other hand, a feeling of sympathetic intimacy can reveal ten times as much in one quick moment. Besides, your tendency to moralize led you to look down on her from above, in a didactic sort of way, whereas I was astonsihed by her extraordinary strength and idolized her. She is an amazing creature! How has it happened that conclusions that I sacrificed half my life trying to reach, that I worked toward and suffered for, that seemed so novel that I came to value them as something I had really worked out— these same conclusions are simple, self-evident truths that seem perfectly ordinary to her. I just don't know. I have met a great many people in my time. Sooner or later I have reached the limits of each, the gulf over which he or she is unable to leap. I have yet to reach that limit in her. What moments of pure bliss I have experienced during our long evenings spent talking together! I have managed to recover from all the coldness suffered throughout my life. For the first time a man discovers what love is and what happiness is—and you want to know why he doesn't stop! Your question is comical. I don't possess such firm powers of reason. Later, reason was unnecessary. When I finally realized what was happening and understood its significance, it was already too late."

"Well, tell me once and for all what your purpose is. What happens next?"

"I really haven't thought about it. Therefore, I can't say anything."

"Well, the results of your thoughtlessness are now right before your very eyes."

"Do you suppose that I can regard these results with complete indifference, that I have been sitting here waiting for you to come and tell me all about it? Well before you I realized that my happiness had faded, that the period of poetry and rapture had passed, that this poor woman will be torn to shreds . . . primarily because she stands so high above everyone else. Dmitry Yakovlevich is a good man, and he is madly in love with her, but his love is pure mania. He will destroy himself as a result of it. Nothing can be done to stop it. And worst of all, he will destroy her, too."

"And so you think that he should sit back in total indifference to the fact that his wife is in love with another man?"

"That's not what I'm saying. Probably he did just what he should have. Each person's nature is true to itself, especially in moments of crisis. But do you know what he should *not* have done? Joined his life with that of a woman who possesses such strength of character."

"Unfortunately, I said the very same thing to him just before his marriage. But you will agree that it is a little late to be talking like that now. Also, before your arrival here she was happy."

"That happiness would not have lasted forever, Semyon Ivanovich. That kind of 'misunderstanding' always comes to the surface sooner or later. . . . Why are you being so inconsistent?"

"Yes indeed, it's all quite complicated. That's precisely why I have always maintained that family life is an extremely perilous venture. But my sermons have fallen on deaf ears, like John the Baptist's voice crying out in the wilderness. Nobody ever listened to me. But now, if only you could show some compassion and. . . ."

"Honestly, I have no idea what you want from me. After her illness I began to notice both her melancholy and his silent, incurable despair. I almost stopped going to visit them, you know that. But only I can appreciate how dearly that decision cost me. I sat down to write her at least twenty times, but fearing that it would aggravate her condition I decided not to. When I went to see them, I sat in silence. What are you reproaching me for? What do you want from me? I hope that you did not come here for the sole purpose of hurling a few insults at me."

"Well, Vladimir Petrovich, you can prove that you are a man of strong character. I know that it will be difficult for you; nevertheless, you must make a sacrifice, a very great sacrifice. As for us, perhaps we can still save this woman. Vladimir Petrovich, go away from here at once!" And a kind of tenderness replaced the old doctor's cruel tone. Krupov's voice quivered. He loved Beltov.

Beltov opened his portfolio, searched through his papers, and pulled out an unfinished letter. "Here, read this," he said. The letter was addressed to his mother. He was informing her of his intention to go abroad again in the very near future.

"You see, I *am* going away. But do you really think that this will save her, my dear, dear Semyon Ivanovich?" he asked sadly, shaking his head.

"What else is there to do?" asked Dr. Krupov with a sort of despair.

"I don't know," replied Beltov. "Semyon Ivanovich, I will write her a letter and bring it to you. Give me your word of honor that you will deliver it."

"I will," answered Krupov.

Beltov escorted the saddened and troubled doctor to the door. Then he threw himself down on the sofa in a state of complete exhaustion. It was clear that this conversation with Dr. Krupov had come as a terrible blow. He was as yet incapable of overcoming its impact, of understanding it, of coping with it. For two hours he lay there with a burnt-out cigar between his lips. Then he seized a piece of paper and began to write. After finishing his letter, he folded it, got dressed, picked it up, and set off for Dr. Krupov's house.

"Here is the letter," announced Beltov. "Semyon Ivanovich, could you possibly arrange for me to see her for a few minutes in your presence?"

"What on earth for?"

"What difference does it make to you? It cannot make things any worse. If you ever felt even the slightest affection for me, then you will do this one thing."

"When are you going away?"

"Tomorrow morning."

"Be in the park at eight this evening."

Beltov shook his hand.

"Today I saw *him* in the most pitiful condition."

"Stop it. Not another word, Semyon Ivanovich, I implore you."

Pale, emaciated, with eyes red from weeping, the unhappy Lyubov Aleksandrovna walked along, holding on to Dr. Krupov's arm. She was feverish, and the look in her eyes was terrifying. She knew where she was going and why. They approached the cherished bench and sat down. She was weeping; the letter was in her hand. Semyon Ivanovich was unable to supply any edifying observations and kept having to wipe away his own tears.

Beltov came up to them. All the brightness had disappeared from his face. Unbearable suffering was evident in all of his features. He took her hand. His entire appearance resembled that of a corpse.

"Farewell," he said to her in a voice scarcely audible. "Once again I shall resume my wandering. But know that our friendship and your image will always be a part of me. It will console me even in the last moments of my life."

"Forever?"

He said nothing.

"Oh, my God!" she said and fell silent. "Farewell, Voldemar," she added in a whisper. Then it seemed as if her strength had suddenly increased tenfold; she stood up, squeezed his hand, and said in a loud, clear voice, "Voldemar, remember that you are loved beyond measure, beyond all measure, Voldemar." She started to walk away; he did not try to restrain her. She found the strength to leave with a firmer step than when she had arrived.

He watched as they withdrew, catching brief glimpses of her white cape among the birch trees until it finally disappeared. She had not found the strength to look back. Voldemar remained alone. "Is it really possible that I must leave her, and forever?" he wondered. He rested his head on his hands, closed his eyes, and for a half hour sat there—oppressed by grief, feeling utterly destroyed. Suddenly someone called his name. He raised his head and hardly recognized the counselorlike face of the counselor. Beltov nodded to him stiffly.

"It seems, Vladimir Petrovich, that you come here to indulge in daydreams and reflections."

"Yes, and for that reason I prefer to be alone."

"Yes, indeed. I concur that for an educated man there is nothing more agreeable than solitude," observed the counselor as he sat down on the bench. "On the other hand, sometimes company can be just as enjoyable as solitude. I have just met Semyon Ivanovich Krupov. You should have seen the little lady he's found for himself."

Beltov had stood up just as the counselor had sat down; he wanted to leave, but these last words deterred him. The counselor's sarcastic expression clearly indicated his intention in speaking these words. Most likely he had come to the park to carry out a secret mission for Marya Stepanovna or some other person.

"I am well acquainted with the lady who was being escorted by Dr. Krupov," said Beltov, breathless with rage.

"Yes, I'm sure you are," replied the counselor, rudely chuckling to himself. "You young men are well acquainted with all the pretty girls around here."

"You are either mad or a fool! In either case, farewell," said Beltov, and set off down the pathway.

"How dare you insult me?" cried the counselor, turning as red as a peony and jumping up from the bench.

Beltov stopped dead.

"What do you desire of me?" he asked the counselor. "To fight a duel? Very well. Repulsive though it may be, I accept your challenge. If that is not what you want, then please excuse me, but I have the nasty habit of using my cane to drive away people who prevent me from enjoying my stroll."

"What! Your cane?" asked the counselor. "Who do you think you are? How dare you threaten me with your cane?"

At any other time Beltov would have burst out laughing at the antics of this silly counselor. But at this particular moment, when he was already so irritated and hardly knew what he was doing, he gave the counselor a little demonstration of exactly what he meant. The counselor was astonished. Beltov strode off.

The next morning, while Grigory was packing up and bustling about, Beltov was pacing the floor. He felt a strange emptiness in his head and his chest, as if half his life, half his being had suddenly disappeared without a trace. It was a terrible, painful feeling. He was trembling all over, afraid that he might start crying at any moment. A dozen times or more Grigory turned to him with some question, and each time he answered, "It doesn't matter." In fact, at that particular moment not only didn't it matter what coat he wore for the journey, it didn't even matter where he was headed, to Paris or to Tobolsk. Semyon Ivanovich arrived in a completely different mood from yesterday's. There were traces of tears in his eyes. He entered quietly, wiped his hat with his sleeve, stood for a while next to the window, and then remarked to Grigory that the splinter bar in Beltov's dormeuse was not properly fastened.[11] In short, he was not quite himself.

"And are you satisfied with me, Semyon Ivanovich?" asked Beltov with a little laugh and some tears.

"I offended you yesterday. Well, what can I say? Forgive me. If you leave like this. . . ." The old man's voice died away.

"Enough of that, Semyon Ivanovich, enough." Beltov held out his arms.

"Here is a little something. Accept it as a memento from me. I

11. *Dormeuse.* See pt. I, chap. 3, n. 8.

truly loved you, and I want to. . . ." He held out a large morocco briefcase. "I want to give you something that is very dear to me."

Beltov opened the briefcase, glanced up at the old doctor, and threw his arms around him. The old man started to weep and muttered, "I can't help laughing at myself. I must be losing my mind. What nonsense! I've become a crybaby in my old age."

Beltov sat down and placed the briefcase on his lap. Inside was a watercolor portrait of Lyubov Aleksandrovna.

Dr. Krupov stood in front of Beltov. To convince him that he had regained his composure, he pronounced the following little speech while secretly wiping away his tears: "Two years ago an English painter was passing through. He was a fine artist. He painted large oil portraits. He did a picture of the governor's wife that hangs in His Excellency's office. I persuaded Lyubov Aleksandrovna to sit for him, too. Only three sittings! Little did she know then that. . . ."

Beltov was not listening at all. Thus it made little difference to him when Krupov's commentary was interrupted by the innkeeper, who burst in breathlessly to announce the arrival of the chief of police.

"What does he want?" asked Beltov.

"He has some business with your worship," answered the innkeeper.

"Tell him to come in."

The chief of police entered with his sword clanking loudly. In the doorway stood a thin policeman and a waiter who was respectfully holding the chief's greatcoat.

Beltov stood up. His whole figure expressed a question. Words were unnecessary. Naturally, his question was, "What the devil are you doing here?"

"I deeply regret, Vladimir Petrovich, that I must detain you for a few moments. It seems that you intend to depart from our town?"

"Yes, I do."

"The general has asked that you come to see him. The counselor Firs Petrovich Elkanevich has submitted a formal complaint through a private letter to His Excellency, alleging that you besmirched his honor. I am ashamed to have to do this, but as you yourself will agree, it's my duty. You know that it is my job to carry out such commissions in an incorruptible manner."

"This comes at a very awkward moment. Permit me to inquire how long it will detain me?"

"That will depend on you. Mr. Elkanevich is a true gentleman. I think that he will not drag it out if you offer an appropriate explanation for your action."

"What sort of explanation?"

"My dear Vladimir Petrovich," said Dr. Krupov. "What am I to do with you? You don't understand a thing! Well, if you wish, I will accompany the chief of police as your deputy and will dispense with this business in a quarter of an hour."

"I would be much obliged to you, very much obliged."

"You may rest assured," said the chief of police, "that it is my sacred and pleasant obligation to settle such matters by peaceful means and to ensure everyone's satisfaction."

And so it was done.

Two weeks later Beltov's dormeuse was traveling along the same road on which some time ago a carriage drawn by four lively horses had galloped past the mill on its way from White Meadow, heading toward the town of N. Grigory was sitting up on the box smoking his pipe; the driver was urging the horses to pull together. In order to guarantee that they would understand him, he uttered only vowels: o . . . o . . . o . . . u . . u . . u . . . a . . . a . . . a . . , and so on. On the other side of the river there stood an elderly lady in a white cap and a dressing gown. She was leaning on her maid's arm waving a handkerchief drenched with tears to a gentleman who was leaning out of the dormeuse and waving his handkerchief back to her. The road veered off to the right. When the carriage turned, only its back remained visible; soon it too was concealed by a cloud of dust. When the dust settled, nothing was visible except the road. The elderly woman still stood there, rising up on her tiptoes, trying to catch yet another glimpse of the carriage.

After that, the elderly lady's life at White Meadow became boring and empty. Previously Voldemar would come home to see her once a week or so. She had gotten so accustomed to hearing the approaching sound of his carriage bells; she would run out to meet him on that same balcony where many years before she had awaited the return of her suntanned young son with his cheerful face.

She also felt drawn to the town of N. It was there that a young woman lived who was much beloved by her son and who had fallen an unfortunate victim to her own love for him. In fact, the elderly woman decided to move into town for the winter. She found Lyubov Aleksandrovna in a desperate state, declining rapidly. Dr. Krupov had become twice as gloomy as before and now only shook his head sadly when asked about Lyuba. Dmitry Yakovlevich was overcome with grief; he prayed to God[12] and drank a great deal. Sofya Alekseevna asked permission to look after the patient and spent long days sitting at her bedside. There was something sublimely poetic in this juxtaposition of declining beauty and splendid old age, of this dying young woman with her sunken cheeks, enormous sparkling eyes, and hair tumbling down onto her shoulders—especially when she rested her head on her frail hands and, with parted lips and tearful eyes, listened to the old woman's endless tales about her beloved son—about their Voldemar who was now so very far away from them both.

12. *God.* Another phrase omitted by the censor.

Selected Bibliography

Other English Translations of *Who Is to Blame?*

Who Is to Blame? A Novel by A. Herzen. Trans. and ed. R. Busch and T. Yedlin. Edmonton, Alberta: Central & East European Studies Society, 1982.

Who Is to Blame? A Novel in Two Parts. Trans. Margaret Wettlin. Preface by Ya. Elsberg. Moscow: Progress Publishers, 1978.

English Translations of Other Works by Herzen

"From the Other Shore" and "The Russian People and Socialism, An Open Letter to Jules Michelet." Introduction by Isaiah Berlin. Cleveland: World, 1963.

My Past and Thoughts: The Memoirs of Alexander Herzen. Trans. Constance Garnett, translation revised by Humphrey Higgins. New York: Knopf, 1968. 4 volumes.

My Past and Thoughts: The Memoirs of Alexander Herzen. Trans. Constance Garnett, translation revised by Humphrey Higgins, abridged by Dwight MacDonald. New York: Knopf, 1973.

Selected Philosophical Works. Trans. L. Navrozov. Moscow: Foreign Language Publishers, 1956.

Nineteenth-Century Criticism in English

Annenkov, P. V. *The Extraordinary Decade: Literary Memoirs.* Trans. I. R. Titunik, ed. A. P. Mendel. Ann Arbor: University of Michigan Press, 1968.

Belinsky, Chernyshevsky, and Dobrolyubov: Selected Criticism. Ed. R. E. Matlaw. New York: Dutton, 1962.

Lenin, Vladimir Ilich. *In Memory of Herzen.* Moscow: Progress Publishers, 1966.

Contemporary Criticism in English

Berlin, Isaiah. "Alexander Herzen" (in "A Remarkable Decade"). In Berlin, *Russian Thinkers.* New York: Viking Press, 1978, 186–209.

Chances, Ellen. *Conformity's Children: An Approach to the Superfluous Man in Russian Literature.* Columbus, O.: Slavica Publishers, 1978, 50–63.

Malia, Martin. *Alexander Herzen and the Birth of Russian Socialism.* New York: Grosset & Dunlop, 1965, 268–77.

Partridge, Monica. "Herzen's Changing Concept of Reality and Its Reflection in His Literary Works." *Slavonic and East European Review,* 46 (1968), 397–421.

Rzhevsky, Nicholas. *Russian Literature and Ideology: Herzen, Dostoevsky, Leontiev, Tolstoy, Fadeyev.* Urbana: University of Illinois Press, 1983, 29–65.

Stites, Richard. *The Women's Liberation Movement in Russia: Feminism, Nihilism, and Bolshevism, 1860–1930.* Princeton: Princeton University Press, 1977, 11–25.

Winter, R. J. "Narrative Devices in the Fiction of Alexander Herzen." Ph. D. diss., Columbia University, 1971.

Contemporary Criticism in Russian

Dryzhakova, E. N. "Problema 'russkogo deyatelya' v tvorchestve Gertsena 40-kh godov (ot *Kto vinovat?* k "Dolg prezhde vsego')" (The problem of the "Russian hero" in Herzen's work of the 1840s [from *Who Is to Blame?* to "Duty above all]). *Russkaya literatura,* 2 (1962), 39–51.

Elizavetina, G. G. "*Kto vinovat?* Gertsena v vospriyatii russkikh chitatelei i kritiki XIX v." (*Who Is to Blame?* in the perception of Russian readers and critics of the nineteenth century). In *Literaturnye proizvedeniya v dvizhenii epokh* (Literary works in the movement of epochs). Ed. N. V. Os'makov. Moscow: Nauka, 1979.

El'sberg, Ya. *Gertsen: Zhizn' i tvorchestvo* (Herzen: life and works). Moscow: Gosudarstvennoe izd. khudozhestvennoi literatury, 1956.

Gai, G. N. *Roman i povest' A. I. Gertsena 30-40-kh godov* (The novel and tales of A. I. Herzen of the 1830s-'40s). Kiev: Izd. Kievskogo universiteta, 1959.

Oksman, Yu. G., ed. *Problemy izucheniya Gertsena* (Problems in the study of Herzen). Moscow: Academy of Sciences, 1963.

Putintsev, V. A., ed. *A. I. Gertsen v russkoi kritike* (A. I. Herzen in Russian criticism). Moscow: Goslitizdat, 1953.

Putintsev, V. A. *Gertsen—pisatel'* (Herzen—the writer). Moscow: Academy of Sciences, 1963.

Rozin, A. G. *Gersten i russkaya literatura 30-40-kh godov XIX veka* (Herzen and Russian literature of the 1830s and '40s). Krasnodar: Knizhnoe izd., 1976.

Library of Congress Cataloging in Publication Data

Herzen, Aleksandr, 1812–1870.
    Who is to blame?

    Translation of: Kto vinovat?
    Includes bibliography.
    I. Katz, Michael R.   II. Title.
PG3337.H4K813   1984   891.73'3   84-7666
ISBN 0-8014-1460-1